MARBLE GARDENS

MARBLE GARDENS

Deirdre Purcell

headline

First published in 2002
by HEADLINE BOOK PUBLISHING

10 9 8 7 6 5 4 3 2 1

Cataloguing in Publication Data is
available from the British Library

ISBN 0 7472 6858 4 (hardback)
ISBN 0 7472 6874 6 (trade paperback)

Typeset by
Letterpart Limited, Reigate, Surrey

Printed and bound in Great Britain by
Mackays of Chatham plc, Chatham, Kent

HEADLINE BOOK PUBLISHING
A division of Hodder Headline
338 Euston Road
LONDON NW1 3BH

www.headline.co.uk
www.hodderheadline.com

For my husband Kevin Healy.

Acknowledgements

My most sincere gratitude to Professor J. Joseph Walshe, M.D., Ph.D., F.A.C.P., Governor of Beaumont Hospital, Dublin, and to his colleague, Dr K.A. Abraham, for their invaluable help.

Thank you to my agent, Clare Alexander, of Gillon Aitken Associates, who steers me with empathy and trenchant common sense.

I would also like to thank Amanda Ridout, former M.D. of Headline, and Edwin Higel, publisher of New Island, for taking me on for this new venture. Marion Donaldson is my editor at Headline and I thank her for the depth and breadth of her observations and not least for her flexibility and understanding of her author's personal circumstances. Thanks, too, to Hazel Orme, my indefatigable copy-editor, who catches the lapses in concentration which would have a car written off in Chapter One and then reappear, whole, in Chapter Thirty-One!

Close to home, sincere and heartfelt thanks for continuing support to a large circle of friends and family, especially to Kevin, Adrian, Simon and Laly, all of whom have, with great good humour (and sometimes through gritted teeth) put up with my bizarre work schedules for many years now.

And as always, thanks to Pat Brennan, on whose clear-eyed judgement I rely so much.

CHAPTER ONE

It's still not too late. Make a telephone call and say there's a bomb on the plane. Use a public phone and then leave. They'd never find you in these crowds.

Or pretend there's a family emergency and they have to be taken off immediately. Or something. Do something!

Sophie fights to suppress the insistent inner voice. She had taken the morning off to drive Riba and her daughter to the airport and is due back at work immediately after lunch. Then, having shepherded them through check-in – and managing to stay supportive right up the last cheery, smiling wave – she found she could not leave.

She shifts on the high, hard stool at one of the coffee counters in the departures area, staring into the pallid depths of the dregs in her paper cup. Although Dublin airport is in a state of constant expansion, the crowds increase quicker than the extensions can be built and it is an uncomfortable place in which to linger, especially for someone like her, who hates hustle and noise. Yet here she remains. It is as though she has been tethered to that plane out there with a hawser.

Come on, come on. There's still time. There's a set of public telephones right over there . . . They won't have taken off yet . . . Or go over and say something at the ticket desk . . . Pretend they've forgotten something crucial . . .

Although she does not notice it, she is attracting attention, and not because of her stress. Naturally elegant, and as unselfconscious as her best friend is flamboyantly self-aware, Sophie is one of those women who can wind an old sheet around herself and look as though she has emerged from a top designer's boutique. Having left her coat in her car, she is wearing only a simple navy dress under a rust-coloured jacket from Dunnes Stores, which, on anyone else, would look as cheap as it had been.

Where her friend is lush, Sophie is lean and lissom. Taller than average, with a delicately featured, heart-shaped face, she wears her fair, uncoloured hair cut boyishly short because it is easier to manage that way. She uses mascara and eyebrow pencil only because, in her opinion, without them her blonde eyelashes and eyebrows make her look as pink-eyed as the White Rabbit in *Alice in Wonderland*.

Although it is now second nature to use the name Riba when they are face to face, in Sophie's mind her friend will always be Eily. The two have been together since early childhood; side by side, their mothers wheeled them out in prams at a time when the Dublin suburb to which they had moved from the inner city was still surrounded by agricultural land, and when birds still outnumbered cars on the brand-new grid of mucky, unfinished roads and avenues, drives, crescents and groves.

Even after Eily's parents died, and throughout the vicissitudes that followed, she and her best friend had played – when Eily had been allowed to play – squabbled, competed for school honours and boyfriends, shared traumas, real and imagined, whispered thrilling secrets to one another, taught one another how to kiss properly and bedded their lives in the substance of friendship. Each stood for the other at their weddings, and Sophie was godmother to Eily's daughter, Zelda.

And when, five years later, Eily had given birth to a son, Sophie had fought hard to be delighted and won – just about. Still, her own childlessness is by far the most difficult cross she has to bear and there is not a single day when, privately, she does not mourn.

So Eily and her brood are as close as family for Sophie, whose mother and father have emigrated to New Zealand to be near one of her twin brothers, married there with a large family, and close-ish, but not too close, to the other who lives an openly gay lifestyle in Sydney. Although she had tried not to resent it, their migration towards their grandchildren seemed like further censure of her own barrenness.

Enough! Sophie uncrosses her legs and sits up straighter. Just two weeks into the new Millennium, and her resolution to stop moping about – to blow away the cobwebs of her life – is already broken.

'Hello! Still here?'

She whirls on her stool to find Brian McMullan standing behind her.

Eily's husband had fought through every last ditch of this Caribbean 'nonsense', as he calls it, a rolling war that had culminated in a refusal to drive his wife and daughter to the airport. But here he is.

The Air Arda flight attendants, women's hair backcombed into sophisti-cated but unflattering French pleats, men's shirt collars as sparkling as their teeth, drift up and down the narrow, humming aisle, managing to look simultaneously competent and bored as they signal to each other with eyes and eyebrows.

'Are you all right, darling?' Riba reaches across the aisle to her daughter. 'Comfortable? No pain?'

'Stop fussing – please!' Nineteen years old and as bolshie as any normal girl her age, Zelda throws off the encroaching hand and, angling her face away from her mother as far as it will go, presents the back of her head. Withdrawing, Riba sighs – then catches the glance of a woman in the seat directly behind her daughter and throws her eyes to heaven. The other woman smiles sympathetically and, rejoicing in the complicity of mother-hood, Riba sits forward to pull out the elasticised seat pocket in front of her, double-checking on the single-use syringes she has stowed there. Yes, they're safe. The medication itself is stored in the refrigerator of the galley. It had been quite a palaver getting everything through the security systems at the airport, and she had had repeatedly to show the prescriptions and authorisations.

Multiple myeloma. The words could refer to flowers. Such a musical name for such a horrid disease. She shudders with distaste as she lets the elastic twang back into place and settles into her seat.

It's so unfair. If you have acute appendicitis your choices are clear. You don't get it treated? You die. It is as though Zelda's illness, a cancer of the bone marrow, is having fun with the human race. No two people suffer identically, or respond identically to any treatments, whether that is bone-marrow transplant, or the most potent drugs, the very newest of which include the so-called 'analogues' of Thalidomide. No way is Riba letting any of *that* near her daughter's delicate body. She is sick of conventional medicine, of all medics; sick of hearing about the balance of probabilities and about everything being a matter of trial, error, and the weighing up of acceptable risk. No one will risk giving even the smallest of guarantees. When you try to press them for time scales, or even long-term hope, their eyes slide away.

While she is waiting to die, all the treatments are having terrible side-effects, illustrated by poor Zelda's thin, tortured body.

Would anyone blame Riba for taking matters into her own hands? Jay's hands?

She and her daughter are in the second last row of the charter aircraft, in place for quite a while now; they were boarded by seat-number from the rear. Around and ahead of them, in cheerful cacophony with Enya's crooning through the PA system, their fellow travellers continue to sort themselves out, cramming carry-on bags into the already stuffed overhead lockers, squeezing themselves into their seats. The lockers above Riba had already been too full to take either her large handbag or her flight bag and since the latter is taking up the entire space under the seat in front of her, she has had to wedge the handbag between herself and her armrest. To keep it snug, she wears its shoulder strap bandolier-style across her chest and abdomen. She is determined not to let even this little discomfort bother her. Nothing is going to go wrong today.

Having booked so recently, they had been lucky to get these seats at all. Mid-January to mid-February has become high season for all transatlantic travel, the travel agent had explained, what with all the Tesco, Superclub and Super Valu half-price, two-for-one and coupon offers. Time was when Miami, where they are bound on their first leg, was Shangri-la for Irish people. Now, as she looks around her at the groups of ear-ringed (on the dole?) lads, the gangs of fiercely bleached women breaking out the booze from their capacious handbags and taking sneaky mouthfuls, Riba thinks ruefully that America has become an affordable Disney World, so that taking the trip has to have lost some of its cachet. Time was when you would have boasted about going to New York, but no longer. Not that she should talk, of course, twopence ha'penny looking down on twopence.

Brian McMullan had spotted Sophie by chance. He had been on his way into the Departures area, hoping to blag his way in through security, when he had seen her sitting at the coffee counter. He runs a small car-hire firm from a depot in Finglas and a concession desk at the airport and therefore has ID. 'How did it go?' He slides on to the stool next to Sophie. 'I suppose they're on board by now and I'm too late?'

'I – I thought you wouldn't – Eily said you were taking a car to Shannon today.'

He is not surprised that she is off-balance. Although it is a free country and he has been able – just – to tolerate Eily's infatuation with Jay Street and his organisation, from the time this trip was first mooted, he has been adamant that hauling Zelda half-way round the world is a fool's errand. His failure to put a stop to it is a source of deep distress.

Yet, when barely ten miles out of Dublin on the Naas dual-carriageway, he had screeched into a U-turn and raced back to see them off. 'I changed my mind – but I knew I'd be too late.' He stares straight ahead at the hapless girl behind the counter who, swamped with orders, has decided to make her protest by reducing the speed of her leisurely activities from slow to crawl. 'I decided to come in anyway, just in case they were delayed or something – I didn't expect to find you still here.'

'I shouldn't be. I'm due back at work in an hour, and if the traffic is bad . . .'

'The traffic is bloody murder.' Brian tries to catch the eye of the waitress, who is taking plenty of God's good time to open a blister pack of paper cups with the aid of a thumbnail. 'Seriously, though, they'll have to do something about access to this airport. Talk about a banana republic! The only bloody capital city in the E.U. without a train link to its airport. I would have thought January was safe enough, but I couldn't get into the concession spaces and it took me nearly twenty-five minutes to find a bay in the short-term car park.' He glances at Sophie then stares at his hands. 'I'm chattering, amn't I?'

'Go ahead. Chatter all you like.' Sophie puts her arm around his shoulders and squeezes, like the good friend she is.

Hemmed in for a moment by the sleek navy backside of an attendant who is making herself small to let another pass, Riba stares at the tweed of the seat back in front of her and worries about the effect of economy-seat syndrome, or whatever they call it. The papers have been full of it lately. Embolisms. Deaths. With Zelda's blood in the state it is, should she have splashed out and booked business class on a proper airline? Although money is a bit less of a problem than it was when they were starting off, they still have to be a little careful and it did not occur to her.

Oh, for goodness' sake. She arrests this latest strand of the negativity that is bothering her today and, as the attendant moves off to tidy coat sleeves and bag straps into the overhead bins, scolds herself: *What's the problem? Everything is working like a dream.*

For instance, just look at where they are sitting. Having initially been dismayed that they couldn't be seated together, she understands now that she should have had more trust. Their location is actually a blessing, if there really is such a syndrome as this economy-seat thing. It will be easier to stretch their legs from these aisle seats, to move around without disturbing their sleeping or eating neighbours. Oh, yes, Zelda will probably huff and puff about being forced to stand up and walk about a bit. She'll say she's too tired to move, all the rest of it, but Riba will prevail. Serenely. No fireworks. Just patience.

She had not fully taken in the implications of Zelda's illness for the first two months after the diagnosis, which was a long time coming. Myeloma, the doctors had told her eventually, was usually a disease of later life. It had been small comfort to Riba to be told that her daughter was a phenomenon, that before her, only three cases in the world had been reported in a patient under thirty.

She had overcome her fear with serious outrage: this could not be happening to her own lovely, lively daughter. During those two months, while the extra tests were done and the chemotherapy started, she had buried herself in frantic activity. She had read everything she could find on the illness, all the fact sheets and newsletters; she had hawked poor Zelda round acupuncturists, reflexologists, seventh sons of seventh sons, even to a Chinese couple who practised *qi gong*. She had sat at Donny's shoulder while he trawled the myeloma websites for the latest developments. She had seized on every (rare) story of survival, and had written away for further information. Yet even here she had found little comfort because underlying the long and pathetically hopeful essays she had received from these victims was resignation to their fate.

Riba can remember every second of the turning point – that critical meeting with Zelda's medical team when all the test results were in. It had taken place in the inappropriate surrounds of the hospital's coffee shop and her nostrils are still lined with the smell of the lemony disinfectant used to wash the floors of the place.

While all around them, people did normal things like chat, drink tea and eat limp sandwiches, Riba survived the terrible things the consultant was saying by dint of registering the crumpled Cellophane from the staff nurse's Danish pastry on the table in front of her, the insipid flower prints on the walls, the dangling stethoscopes, her husband's ashen colour. She can still feel the chill emanating from Brian's sturdy body as, dumb with incomprehension, fear and misery, he had gazed around at the circle of faces, grave over limp white coats.

When, towards the end of the meeting, she understood the reality that her daughter was under sentence of death, the sensation was like piling full tilt into a high blind wall made of concrete and she felt dizzy with pain. Why them, why her? Why this lithe, beautiful girl above all others?

She fought the pain and refused to wallow in defeatism. Even as the head buck consultant continued to murmur about T-cells, new vaccines going into clinical trials and all the latest research from America, Riba was pulling herself back from the precipice and turning round to throw herself wholeheartedly into Jay Street's embrace. If medicine, even alternative medicine, thought it could shovel her beautiful daughter into an early grave, it had another think coming and she, who already had unquestion-ing faith in Jay's ability to marshal the forces of healing inherent in all of us, now inflated that belief until it became ironclad certainty.

It was inconvenient that Jay lived in the Caribbean, but so be it. If necessary, she would have taken Zelda to the moon.

'Is there a way I can ring them, maybe on a courtesy phone?'

Sophie stares at Brian. This is not the capable, confident, rugby-head of her acquaintance. A very big man, with neck and shoulders as strong as a bull's and a thatch of strawberry blond hair, Brian McMullan has always radiated strength and certainty, so his tremulousness is unsettling. She averts her eyes: 'You know better than me that it's not on, Brian, once they've boarded.'

That he is echoing her own desire to use the phone to stop this insanity is unsettling but now that someone else is astride the situation, someone with a greater claim to ownership of it, her inner voice has muted and for this she is grateful. 'Look,' she says, on impulse, 'why don't we go and park at the perimeter and watch them take off? If we go now we're sure to see them. You know her – she's sure to "feel" you're there, even if she doesn't see you.'

He flashes her a brief, knowing smile but then suppresses it.

Sophie is brisk: 'Do it for your sake. At least it might make you feel better.'

He does not get off his stool. Instead he continues to look at his hands, pressed into his lap. 'I should have driven them.'

She pushes aside her coffee cup and gets down from her stool. 'Hurry, or they'll take off without us.' She is certain that in this, at least, they are about to do the right thing. 'We'll go in your car – if they look through the window, even for a split second, they'll recognise it and then they'll know you've come.'

At last Brian's expression clears. Although he deals every day in little Corsas, Puntos and Fiestas, his personal chariot is a flaming red Mustang convertible, imported from America and lovingly maintained at appalling expense. Brian and Eily's marriage may have begun to crack under the strain of Zelda's illness and – more significantly – as a result of the spell cast by Jay Street, but in the matter of the Mustang, Brian has his wife's enthusiastic support. She loves driving through Dublin with the wind tugging at her clothes and hair. It makes her feel very feminine, she tells anyone who'll listen, adding that it's surprising how many days it does not rain in this country. Only once has she mentioned to Sophie that Jay Street, too, drives a convertible. No comparison, of course. Jay's is a Roller.

'All right, I'm glad I saw you. Let's go.' Brian gets up and hurries away from the coffee counter towards the exit, leaving Sophie to gather up her handbag and catch up.

Uh-oh! What she sees on the watch face pulls Riba up a little: past their departure time already by about twenty-five minutes. She looks up the aisle. Not too bad. Almost everyone has taken a seat.

Please God they'll make their connections. It'll be tight, though. She couldn't get a direct flight from Miami to anywhere in the Caribbean – all full – so after this one they've to fly from Miami to Nassau in the Bahamas, then, another long flight to Barbados, followed by a quick connection for just a few minutes on some kind of tiny wave-hopper. They'll be basket cases by the time they arrive. It is better, however, Riba feels, to make the journey all in one go, rather than to have to lug their bags in and out of taxis, check into and out of an unfamiliar hotel. That would be a killer for Zelda.

Leaning out over the restraining belt to see past her seat companions through the window, she purses her lips. Well, look at that! Those baggage-handlers are throwing the luggage any old how into the hold. Their own new suitcases, so proudly bought, so carefully packed, might easily be damaged.

She turns towards Zelda to share this with her, but still sees only the back of her head. The navy bandanna has slipped a little, allowing a few wispy question marks of weakened hair to straggle out from under it.

Zelda had always been proud of her thick, naturally blonde curls, so like her father's. Of everything she had gone through, all that horrible sickness and weakness and fear, the loss of her hair had been hardest for her to bear. Riba wouldn't mind but she herself had fought strenuously against the use of chemo right from the beginning. Through panic, she had allowed herself to be overruled and poor Zelda had paid the price.

She sits back. Everything is under control now. She conjures up a picture of what awaits them on Palm Tree Island. Relaxation. Health. Freedom. Her daughter's waxen cheeks blooming with roses, her wasted limbs filling out. Visualisation is a great weapon in the arsenal of influence. Jay is big on visualisation.

The thought of Jay spreads a broad smile over Riba's handsome face. Her wide brown eyes narrow with pleasure and anticipation as she fluffs up her dark hair, lustrous and undyed although she's only six months off forty. She deflects all worries about clots and syndromes, about her husband, her doubting friends, even about Zelda's illness and the damage done by the stream of chemicals poured into her by hardened, disbelieving medics. Concentrating hard, she maintains the image of a healthy Zelda and opens her mind to a joyful flow of positive influences. Nothing bad can happen now. They are on the path, Zelda and she. Leaving aside the Good Lord, if anyone can look after Zelda, Jay can.

Riba closes her eyes and daydreams of the reunion with Jay on his Caribbean Island of Eden.

Outside the terminal, the wind opens icy jaws and pounces, flinging sleet. 'Jesus – where did that come from?' Brian takes off his sheepskin jacket and shoves it at Sophie: 'Here, take this, at least I've a wool suit on.' Turning away, he throws coins into the machine, grabs the parking ticket and sets off at a run through the multi-storey car park, again leaving her to follow.

He had parked illegally – against a wall, right on the criss-crosses of a yellow box – but his luck has held and the Mustang has not been molested by clampers. It is near an exit and they zoom out quickly enough.

They are lucky with the run of traffic lights, and, less than ten minutes after their first encounter in the terminal, they are squeezing into a vacant space between a Hiace and an Audi in the lay-by provided for plane-spotters just outside the airport's perimeter fence.

'Will you drive me back to the car park so I can get my own car?' Sophie has to raise her voice to be heard against the thunder of a jet taking off directly in front of them. Caught up in the whirl, she has almost forgotten that she has to get back to her job and reflexively pats the pocket of her jacket under the sheepskin, only to find it flat and empty. No reassuring bulge of her mobile phone. This is production week at *Wild Places*, the monthly nature magazine where she works as general journalistic dogsbody and occasional illustrator, and her editor had given her the mobile so she could be available. She must have left the damned thing in the car. Again.

'Of course, of course, no problem.' Brian is peering through the vertical, crescent-shaped waves of sleet blowing past the bonnet of the Mustang. 'God, it's really coming down. This is a disaster – they won't see us.'

'They will. She'll be in a window seat. Won't want to miss a moment of the experience so she'll definitely be looking out.'

'Even if one of them is in a window seat,' Brian continues to fret, 'who's to say they're on our side of the plane?'

'Brian, hush.' She reaches out to put a hand on his arm but withdraws without doing so. That would be patronising. Instead, she smiles encouragingly. 'What more can we do? We're doing the best we can.'

He deflates. 'Sorry.'

'Busy these days, I believe?' According to Sophie's husband, Michael, who works as Brian's deputy, they are run off their feet. Michael certainly puts in long hours.

Although Brian will never be rich, in its own small way, his company holds its own in a fiercely competitive market because it is the only one, apart from the giant Hertz, that offers vehicles with hand controls. Some years ago Brian had acted on a hunch that there had to be some disabled tourists, even locals, who are rich – they would have to be so they could pay the huge insurance premium: he had had one of his start-up fleet adapted and then, waving an anti-discrimination banner, had enlisted the interest of a sympathetic newspaper columnist. The article had snowballed into a spot on a radio talk show and from then on he did not have to advertise the facility. Disabled people are serious networkers, and although looking after them is labour-intensive, this niche in the market is lucrative and the three disabled-friendly cars he runs now are almost constantly on the road, in use not only at holiday time but year round. He fidgets now with the spotless chrome spokes of the Mustang's steering-wheel. 'Yeah, we're busy all right. But I could have taken a week off, there would have been no problem with that.' The soundwaves from the wake of the receding jet continue to thud through the cloth roof of the Mustang into its sturdy frame as he looks across at her. 'Do you think they'll come back?'

Sophie is astounded. 'Of course they'll come back. Are you afraid they won't?'

He stares through the windscreen. 'Stupid name for an island, anyway. What kind of a name is Palm Tree Island? I mean, doesn't every goddamn island in the tropics have palm trees on it? Is it the Atlantic or the Caribbean, by the way? The Bahamas are in the Atlantic, aren't they?'

'Palm Tree Island isn't remotely near the Bahamas – it's hundreds and hundreds of miles further south. Very near the Equator in fact. And before you go on to your second question, yes, they do speak English. Thanks to the Americans.' Sophie stares at him. It isn't the first time he has made this error. It is as though by refusing to acknowledge even the correct location of Street's hideaway island he can somehow wipe it away. He is also afraid that his wife will fall so completely under Jay Street's influence that she will settle with him for ever in his tropical paradise and that his beloved daughter will die out there. As a result of his own stubbornness, he may not see her again. Now Sophie does touch his arm. 'It's in the Caribbean,' she says gently.

He runs his hands around the rim of the wheel. 'Things have been a little, well, tense, lately and details don't stick.'

'At least you know one thing for sure. No one would doubt that Eily has anything but Zelda's best interests at heart.'

His expression remains bleak as he continues to run his fingers around the wheel. 'I know that.' Softly. 'Yes, I do know that.' He turns to face her. 'Was I wrong? Do you think I should have gone with them, Sophie?'

She is at a loss now. How does she answer this without betraying either him or her best friend?

He lets her off the hook, turning back again to the windscreen. 'I'm sorry. Don't answer that. I don't know what we'd do without you, Sophie. All of us.'

'For goodness' sake, Brian, what are friends for?'

Something in his tone – or his eyes? – has made her uncomfortable. Or perhaps she is reacting to the slight claustrophobia engendered within the dim, airless confines of a car which, closed up like this, reeks with a sweetish complexity of leather, warm metal, the faint tang of Brian's cologne and the nose-tingling pong of the high-octane afterburn washed over them by the departing jet. She turns away and opens her window an inch.

Just as well. Otherwise she might have missed, above the rim of a depression in the airfield, the sight of a big white tail emblazoned with the logo of Air Arda – a wavy circle in bottle green representing a torc – gliding slowly towards the holding area at the end of the take-off path. 'Look,' she points, 'there they are. And the weather's clearing up just in time too. See?' She is triumphant.

Indeed, it is brightening up. Although it has not yet cleared the airport and has now obscured the aircraft's tail, the sleet shower is scudding away from them across the whitened fields. And directly ahead of where they sit, they can see the sun's disc, as thin as an old silver coin, skimming through frayed grey mittens of cloud above the runway.

CHAPTER TWO

It is lunchtime and, isolated from the chaotic ebb and flow of the desultory football games, shoving matches and raucous yelling of their schoolmates, Donny McMullan and his best friend Trevor Jameson are lurking behind a builders' skip in the schoolyard. They are sucking greedily on the butts they have saved since this morning when they walked to school together from the bus stop. Only sixth-years are allowed to smoke – on sufferance. Donny and Trevor, both fourteen, are in the Junior Certificate stream.

After a shower of sleet that served merely to wet the uneven surface of the yard, the leaden sky is lifting and the sun is trying to come through. Both boys shade their eyes against its sudden brightness to watch a pair of seagulls swoop and dive around a third, in an effort to intimidate it into dropping a scrap of food. They watch the aerobatics of the three birds until, still squabbling, they fly out of sight across the roof of the school gymnasium. Then they return to the business in hand.

Physically, Donny takes after Brian. He is tall for his age, tall enough to pass for seventeen or even eighteen, which has served him and his friends well in the matter of false IDs, the purchase of alcohol and cigarettes, and even in gaining admission to discos. The impression is enhanced by his executive-style steel-rimmed glasses. He hates having to wear them but, as he is very short-sighted, cannot do without them.

The give-away about his real age, however, is the awkward, coat-hanger shoulders that will fill out only with maturity, and the hands and feet that have become liabilities as they outgrew his ability to manoeuvre them in an orderly fashion.

Trevor, an undersized, weedy foil to Donny's lankiness, carefully pinches out the remaining half-inch of the butt and puts it back in his trouser pocket. 'So, how long are they going for?'

'I dunno.' Donny shrugs. He adds, 'A couple of weeks, I suppose. Maybe a month. Depends.' He makes great play of examining the tip of his own rapidly shrinking cigarette.

Trevor, whose sharp intelligence compensates for lack of bulk, glances quickly at his friend then drops his eyes. 'Look, she'll be all right. She will.'

Donny shrugs again. 'Yeah.' He drops the butt and stamps on it, looks around quickly to make sure he is unobserved then bends to scrape it off the ground to drop it into the skip. Briskly, he rubs his hands together and makes a passable attempt at cheeriness. 'So, what are we going to do tonight, then, Trev? The two of them are gone, my da isn't coming home for his tea, he has a business meeting at seven o'clock, apparently, so I'm clear until about eleven.'

Trevor plays along. 'Sounds good, bro! How much have you got?'

Donny waves airily as the bell for return to classes clangs. 'I've a twenty. And I can probably score another few in loose change. At least.' He jangles the coins in his pockets as, followed by his friend, he moves out from behind the skip and joins the streams of boys of all shapes and sizes idling their way towards the classroom block at the far side of the yard.

'Cool!' Trevor sounds enthusiastic. 'I've got at least sixteen. The sky's the limit, bro.'

'Hey, I've got an idea.' Donny stops so abruptly that his friend almost cannons into him. 'You want to cut the afternoon?'

'How can we? The bags are in the classroom.' Trevor looks doubtful.

'No worries. I can pretend Zelda's got real sick again and I've got to go to the hospital.' He taps the mobile phone in the breast pocket of the shirt under his uniform jumper. 'Well, it wouldn't be a real lie, would it?'

'No,' Trevor hesitates. 'But where do I come in?'

'I'm so upset you have to come with me.' Donny's expression, usually so guileless, crinkles until it parodies tragic young boyhood and Trevor, whose voice has not yet broken, giggles. 'Worth a try, I suppose.'

'Right.' Donny is decisive. 'Come on, Trev, nearly eleven whole hours. The town is ours.'

Inside the Arda jet, which has rocked to a halt in the holding area prior to take-off, Riba is on chatting terms with the passengers in the two seats between herself and the window: an elderly American couple, returning to the States following an extended Christmas visit to their daughter and her family. The corpulent, sweating husband pulls out his wallet, extracts the grandchildren's pictures and passes them over. 'Yeah, we were pissed when our son-in-law was transferred to Ireland but, hey! What can you do? We're the old farts now and we just gotta put up with it, let the young folks take over.' He sees that Riba's smile has become fixed. 'Don't get me wrong, ma'am. Ireland's a nice place.'

'So green!' the wife contributes.

Riba hands back the snapshots and the grandfather, after a last doting look, replaces them in his wallet. 'Yeah, real green, just like the brochures. Too cold, though. Your idea of central heating sucks, honey.' He jerks a thumb towards the window, through which can be seen a kaleidoscope of tiny greyish flakes. 'I mean, nobody told us it snowed here, we thought we'd left that behind for a while, for God's sake – but let me tell ya, Riba, you guys over here don't know from snow. You wanna be out in your driveway in twenty below!' He reacts to a dig in the ribs from his wife's elbow and changes the subject without changing tone. 'Riba, eh? That a Gaelic name?'

Fleetingly, Riba debates whether to tell them about her name-change but decides against it. 'Yes.' She nods vigorously. 'It's the name of an ancient princess.'

The captain's lazy tone crackles through the PA cutting off the American's reply. They are second in line for take-off, it seems, but there are two to land. They should be . . . aah . . . moving in four or five minutes. In the meantime they are to make sure their . . . aah . . . seat-belts are securely fastened and they are to relax and sit back. He'll talk to them again after they are . . . aah . . . airborne.

Riba turns to check on Zelda and finds her daughter at last facing front but with her eyes closed. To stave off further conversation with her seat companions, she shuts her own eyes and relaxes deliberately, starting at the toes and feeling the delicious warmth spreading upwards through her calves and thighs and into her midriff. Riba was the name of an ancient princess all right, but not Gaelic or even European. While he was working with her on her regression therapy, Jay had discovered that in a past life she had been an Ethiopian of royal birth, the second daughter of a regional king. Riba was the name that had come up.

Thrilled by this discovery, the new princess scoured the encyclopedias and trawled the Internet to find details of her former entity but had come up with nothing, even with the help of the librarian in her local library. Jay had an answer for this: he explained that there was little in the way of written records for prehistoric times and she shouldn't be surprised if she couldn't find anything on these particular royals. 'Dig deep into your own core,' he had told her gently. 'Does the name feel congruent? Does it feel right?' So she had probed as instructed and, yes, indeed, the name felt absolutely right.

At home later, she had stared at herself in a mirror, at her dark eyes and hair, her smooth, olive complexion, excitement building as she realised why she had never previously felt at home in her skin. For instance, look at the type of clothing she has always instinctively favoured – colourful kaftans and kimonos. That preference had been no accident, she now saw.

Even that small discovery was terribly exciting.

No – Eily had never felt right. She had never been an Eileen. Never.

Names are terribly important to the subconscious, aren't they? In calling her daughter Zelda, for instance, she had tapped into Jay's, years before she met him and when she could not have known how significant this was. She had not read F. Scott Fitzgerald and had named her daughter, not after the novelist's wife, but out of a baby book, because 'Zelda' sounded so exotic.

Zelda was nearly thirteen when Riba discovered Jay's admiration for *The Great Gatsby* and that he had even nicknamed himself after the book's hero. Coincidence?

Hardly.

Try to get Brian to accept any of this? Strapped into her seat, Riba feels her muscles stiffen at the memory of the fights and arguments she and her husband had had about her wish to be known by her rightful name. Not only about this, but about something much more fundamental: about the struggle to get him to accept the whole, no, *holistic* direction her life had taken since she had joined Jay's organisation. She was sure that if she could get him to meet with Jay face to face he would change his tune. But no dice. 'If I need advice on how to lead a healthy life, I'll go to a doctor, or a psychiatrist, or a priest,' he had scoffed, during one bruising argument. 'Or I'll go for a walk in Phoenix Park and ask the pigeons and the squirrels. That fella's only a jumped-up carpenter.'

In vain did Riba point out that Jesus had been a carpenter.

Although she had consoled herself with the knowledge that prophets had traditionally cried in the wilderness, as the months and years passed, her tolerance of her husband's closed mind had weakened and she had become quite aggrieved. Now she feels that Brian's problem may be as simple as ordinary male jealousy. It is more than probable that, childishly, he resents the time she spends on the organisation and therefore the diverting of her attention from himself.

He had even gone so far as to imply once or twice that she was having an affair with Jay but Riba had never lowered herself to respond to that.

One fallout from the distrust and constant carping, however, is that to fund her new life, she has to find money without Brian knowing. Jay Street's courses, vitamin supplements and health products are not cheap and to afford them she has to resort to serious subterfuge. For example, by paying cash for her day-to-day grocery shopping, she is able to cream a little off the top. She has also got into the habit of reporting inflated prices on clothes or anything she buys for herself, the family or the house, and quietly pocketing the difference. It is irritating that she must always remember to remove any price labels or stickers but that has now become a habit, as automatic as setting the alarm clock every night.

If Brian asks where she is getting the money for any particular event or course, she lies to him. Everyone within the organisation gets these things free, she tells him, not remotely guilty about her evasions. Money is merely a commodity after all, and since Jay started to develop his methods, his philosophy has been that his organisation and its techniques would not be valued unless top dollar is paid by those who benefit.

Riba relaxes again and focuses on a mental picture of Jay working his magic on her daughter. She has never seen him heal anyone – that is all done one-on-one and in private – but you only have to read all the personal testaments in the organisation's newsletter the *Inner Door*, to know that he has very special powers. People have been cured of lifelong illnesses, like arthritis. They have lost weight, recovered from serious depressions, come back from the brink of cancer. They have even achieved major business successes, and although the nature of these businesses is never spelled out, Riba does not care because she has never had the slightest interest in becoming a business person.

As soon as she had decided to entrust Zelda's healing to Jay, she had winkled out of the organisation the address of a woman who had been cured of a tumour in her breast. The woman, a middle-aged blonde with tired eyes, dark roots and a husband engrossed in Sky Sports, lived in an untidy, rundown cottage in the middle of rural County Dublin.

In response to Riba's eager questions as to what Jay did or said and how he went about effecting the cure, she had been diffident but anxious to help: 'All I can tell you is that he sat with me and directed me to think in a certain way. He spoke to me for a long time, it could even have been hours – I remember that because it was dark when I came out of the room. I'm sorry, I can't remember what he said.

'I do remember his voice, though,' she added, with a faraway look. 'He has a lovely voice. And the feelings. I can still remember how wonderful I felt, so peaceful and free and young again. I'd do anything for Jay Street,' her sagging cheeks flared with sudden passion, 'anything!'

'He didn't put his hands on you?' Riba had always imagined Jay's healing powers had resided in his hands.

'No.' The woman had hesitated. 'At least, I don't think so. I've tried to remember but it was like I was in some sort of trance all the time I was in there.'

'He hypnotised you?'

'I asked him but he said he doesn't use hypnosis. He said all he was doing was reaching into my mind. That the power was mine.'

She bent watery eyes on Riba. 'What's wrong with you, dear?'

Riba, seeking assurances, had ignored the question. 'You're definitely cured? Your doctors have said you're cured?'

'They're amazed. Of course they won't say for definite, you know what they're like. But they're amazed. It was worth it, I'll be saying that until my dying day, although he—' the woman had jerked a dismissive thumb in the direction of her partner, who was asleep – 'said it was all a waste of money. I didn't think so, and I'm the one that had the cancer, not him. I went to the bank myself and the manager gave me a loan against my ma's house.' She made a small '*So there!*' *moue* in the direction of her husband.

Riba has kept in touch with the tired blonde woman whose shrunken tumour continues to amaze, thank God.

Thank God, too, for the friends Riba has made within the organisation. With people around her who understand, she finds it easier to tolerate the cynics' scoffing, voiced or unvoiced.

The floor under her feet trembles in the abrupt gush of air as the jet in front of them in the take-off queue roars off down the runway. Her stomach fluttering with excitement, she glances at her sleeping daughter, so wan and exhausted, poor little sparrow.

Now the engines rev up to full throttle. Fantastic! They are on their way at last! She relaxes and focuses again on the vision of her daughter restored to rosy health. She and Zelda are under Jay's protection and on a trajectory that will bring them straight into his physical presence. Everything is going to be wonderful. That hair will grow, that face will bloom, and those draining, caustic painkillers and drugs will be thrown down the nearest toilet.

She cannot prevent herself smiling. 'Here we go.' She turns to include her seat companions in her joy. The Americans are holding hands.

'Here we go,' Brian says to Sophie, as they crane towards the eddies of sleet veiling the holding area and the Arda jet. Beyond the perimeter fence, they hear a ground-shaking, muffled roar. He rolls down the Mustang's window. 'It's turning to snow.'

'That doesn't matter a damn.' Sophie is unsure about this but who's going to challenge her? The most important thing is to keep Eily's husband calm. 'With modern aviation equipment, a little snow is nothing. Anyway, it's moved off from here already and it'll soon be gone altogether.'

They both listen hard for a fresh swell of engine noise, now that the deep bass notes of the preceding take-off are fading into the distance. Sophie's eyes hurt from the brightness and the straining and she rubs them. 'Try not to worry. They'll be home to you, safe and sound. You'll see. The little holiday might even do Zelda some good.'

She darts a quick glance at him. She can see he is less than convinced.

For something to do, despite the temperature outside, she too rolls down her window to watch the plane. It is always a miracle, she thinks, how these huge heavy bundles of metal, fuel, human beings, equipment, cargo and suitcases hoist themselves into the air as though they are as hollow-boned as swallows. When she is strapped into an aircraft seat beside Michael, she always has to grip the armrest during take-off, making herself as light as possible to help with the lifting.

As for the interminable race down the runway, her fear, each time, is that the groaning, overloaded aircraft will run out of energy before it breasts the air. The airlines don't seem to care about baggage weight the way they used to and at check-in, when she sees the size of some of the cases being heaved with such difficulty on to the conveyor belts by their owners, her heart always starts to thump.

It thumps now as Eily's jet comes into sight at last and thunders towards them, engines screaming, rivers of moisture streaming off its back. She can see the wings flexing as the wheels bump over the joins in the runway.

Suddenly Brian is outside the car and, a stick figure, legs and arms spreadeagled against the sky, is plastered to the fence. He is waving frantically as the series of pale, blurred ovals along the body of the aircraft whoosh past. Her arm out through the open window, Sophie waves too, feeling a little foolish as she forces her eyes to focus in an effort to distinguish faces.

Now the huge package of unleashing energy has raced past them on impossibly tiny wheels and the faces, if that is what they were, have been borne away. They must have faith: she and Brian − and the Mustang − were seen during the flash-past. Partly for solidarity, but mostly for no reason she can think of, Sophie jumps out of the car to get a good view of the plane's ascent.

Tail on, she thinks, as she crosses her arms across her breasts to retain her body-heat against the onslaught of cold, damp air, an aircraft is aesthetically ugly. A squat, shortened shape trailing vapour and what looks like smoke. All that pollution to be ingested by the rabbits, foxes, voles and fieldmice, which have to share their grassy spaces with these belching, bellowing behemoths.

Another sleet shower threatens and, without waiting to see the wheels leaving the ground, Brian turns to come back to the car, slithering on the melting crystals still clinging to the spaces between the tufts of scutch. He shouts above the hullabaloo: 'Do you think they saw us?'

'Of course they did, they—'

She and Brian pivot simultaneously. It might have been the pop of the airport's bird scarer but it seemed louder, deeper than that, louder even than the engines' roar. A millisecond's silence, then a second boom, unmistakable, explosive, followed by a tearing, screeching series of blasts and squeals that goes on and on and for ever on . . .

Then a shooting, flaming mushroom of something viscous and black. An object spinning towards them, a massive, misshapen Frisbee, green and white, green and white—

Instinctively, Brian leaps towards Sophie and takes the two of them flying backwards into the ditch and flat against the base of the fence, just as part of the Arda tail cuts through the chain-link a few feet away and crashes on to the Hiace, the Mustang and the Audi. With a ringing, rattling wrench, their section of the fence comes down on their heads and they are buried in metal and wire, and a hard rain of debris.

CHAPTER THREE

Riba's expression has frozen in a big round O of surprise.

As it went on, she did not immediately assimilate what was happening and could not find enough breath to cry out. They had been surging along pleasurably – she always found this quite a sexual turn-on – when, without warning, she heard a tremendous bang. Then a second, even bigger than the first. Then it went pitch dark.

Something had happened to the air: dense, freezing, it had rushed up to her, bussed her face with a fierce, enemy's kiss, then grabbed her from the side, as if attempting to tear her head from her neck and her ribs from her spine. She had flown sideways until she had hit something hard yet yielding and then she had toppled over, still strapped into her seat. She had come to rest on her side with her head and shoulders buried in the remains of the locker that had so recently been overhead.

Now, as if through thick layers of cloud, she hears the sound of the world breaking apart and her mouth, filled with the burning taste of whiskey, is prickling. Someone's bottle has smashed. She tries to shake her head but cannot: she is tangled in something soft. A coat, probably. Her left eye throbs as though impaled on a spike, her breathing is constricted by the choking, acrid smell of fuel and smoke and under her weight, her right shoulder feels peculiar, as though it belongs to someone else. She can move her legs and her left forearm and that is the extent of it.

Is this what her parents went through in the moments before they died in their car wreck? Would the noise have been as bad?

Because the noise, although her hearing is muffled, is beyond all things natural.

All these things she feels individually in the split second it takes to realise she has been in an air crash. Consideration of that can wait until later, however, as can the cataloguing of any injuries she may have sustained. For now she feels no real pain, or even fear. She is fully alert. She has to get Zelda.

★ ★ ★

Within Sophie's limited field of vision, the world has changed. Instead of an orderly set of angles, planes, scents and sounds, all is disturbance and confusion. Daylight is distorted by blowing, ruddy darkness; the air is contaminated by stench and howling. Pinned under the body of her friend's husband, she is buffered from the full force of the blows that continue to rain on them for what seems like minutes but is, in fact, less than thirty seconds.

Brian has not stirred. His head is twisted away from hers at an unnatural angle, his ear ground into the mud, the point of his left shoulder digging into one of her breasts. His considerable weight, combined with that of the fence and whatever has come down on top of it, is crushing her so heavily into the ground that her spine feels as though it may snap. She is afraid to move in case the pain of this and all the other pain increases.

The crashing stops, and after an eerie hiatus, other noises combine to become bedlam. Whooshing, crackling, a distant male scream, terrifying in its length and pitch. Then, distantly, the sound of sirens, as though from a television many rooms away.

She is afraid to call Brian's name in case he doesn't answer.

The enormity of what has happened has not yet sunk in. Eily's plane has blown up. This is preposterous. This could not happen.

But the smells, the smoke, the glimpses and puffs of fire, the pop-pop-popping nearby and the gathering squall of sirens seem real enough.

'Brian?' At last Sophie finds the courage to say something. 'Brian?'

Brian does not move.

Now she panics. He is dead. He is dead because of her. It was her idea to bring him here. What will she tell Eily?

Is Eily dead too? Where is Eily? And what about Zelda? Are they all wiped out? Who's going to tell Donny?

Sophie's frenzied mind races off through the future before coming full circle to rest on her own predicament. Jesus, Jesus – suppose everyone around here is dead too and she is the only one alive? The rescuers will be concentrating on the aircraft and the runway. Who'll give a thought to a bunch of loony spotters outside the fence? Perhaps no one will think of coming to look. She will smother and die for want of being heard. A scream gathers at the back of her throat but she chokes it off. Who'll hear one small, buried voice against the mayhem outside?

She shuts this out and focuses as precisely as she can on her own body. She is alive and must use that to her advantage. *Concentrate, Sophie!* Under the weight, she tests her limbs, moving them infinitesimally one by one. Nothing broken, as far as she can tell.

She cannot move her spine, but that is surely because she is so heavily pinned. She can move her neck. Surely she wouldn't be able to do that if her spine was damaged.

She tries again: 'Brian?' Her voice sounds like the remote cawing of a rook.

She waits. Still no response. Not a twitch.

Using as much as she can of her left arm to push hard at what constrains her face and neck, Riba finds she is locked tight and the best she can do is move her head an inch or two upwards and sideways to where she can gasp for oxygen – or whatever oxygen her lungs can find. As she moves, she finds there is more than the coat against her face, there's a sort of mesh. Then she remembers the inner cages within the lockers, designed to stop the contents shifting. Her head must have smashed through this – although she cannot feel pain from any specific bumps or bruises.

Little by little, the clamour outside her closed world filters through to her. No light, of course, because her eyes remain blind, but she can hear a dissonance of sounds: cracking and wrenching of metal, repetitive small reports, like corn popping, and in the distance, the dim wails of multiple sirens. No human screams, just the barely perceptible but continuous moaning of one person somewhere nearby.

She can feel gusts of heat laced through freezing shafts of wind playing on the bare skin of her legs. This is a puzzle. She had been wearing comfortable sweat pants for the journey. Have they been torn off? She reaches blindly to check – and, yes, her thigh is naked. It is wet.

Riba strains to move her head to the maximum degree that her confinement allows. 'Zelda?' she calls, but her voice travels only as far as her gag. She makes a supreme effort, pulling air from everywhere she can find it. 'Zelda?'

She listens hard. There is no answering call of 'Mum'. But the nearby moaning goes on until it is buried in the gathering disharmony of the approaching trucks.

Riba starts to shiver, not ordinary shivering but a monumental, uncontrollable jolting that threatens to bury her again in the thickness of the coat, or whatever is against her face. It would be too, too hard to bear, after all Zelda had been through, all the chemicals and drugs, all the psychological warfare conducted between her parents about these interventions, if she were to die just at the point when she was about to be saved.

As the sirens come close, as she continues to shake and rock in her prison, Riba prays urgently, more urgently than she has ever prayed in her life, to Jesus, to Mary, to her hard-pressed guardian angel. She prays that her pleas will be carried to Jay on his island and that he will turn his benign gaze on her circumstances. She prays that her life be taken in lieu of Zelda's.

Carefully, using the fingers of her right hand like spider legs to crawl across her chest under Brian's, Sophie manages to move her right arm across her body to reach the left, which is by her side. It helps that they are lying on wet earth and the grass of the ditch, rather than something hard and unyielding, like a blazing runway . . .

Jesus . . .

She dismisses the image and uses every ounce of strength to push as hard as she can against Brian's chest with her fists, forearms and upper arms, thus managing at last to shift herself a little to the right and out from under him so that her head, neck, right shoulder and both arms are free of him. Then, counterbalancing the strain by raising her knees a little, she can use most of her body. It is only then it occurs to her she should probably not have moved him. Too late. Slowly, testing each inch to see if her back and hips can take it, she wriggles the rest of herself free until, panting and gasping, she lies beside him, with only the chain-link and something huge blocking out the sky.

Sophie gathers her strength and pits her voice against the commotion outside. 'Help! Help!' She waits a little, straining to pick out some response. All she can hear now is a huge, blended roar, sirens, continuing small explosions, men shouting. Nothing happens to the load above her.

It's still up to her.

So, pushing hard with her knees and ankles, using the groove underneath her as a sort of lifting bench to help her create a tiny space above her face with both forearms, she propels herself backwards until her head is clear. Then, gain by tiny gain, she slithers free and scrambles to her feet.

The ruckus around Riba is getting worse. The multiple sirens, muted though they are by the wrappings around her head, are upon her now. Surprisingly, even though she continues to shake and tremble, she is aware of no fear. It is as though normal traffic through her brain has been suspended until a full picture is available. She concentrates on Zelda.

Zelda, Zelda, Zelda . . .

By force of will, she must cast a protective web around Zelda.

Zelda . . . Zelda . . .

She conjures up an image of Zelda wearing gold. The golden, flowing gown of a royal bride. Zelda is wearing a crown of flowers in her hair. She is roseate, shining. Her smile is incandescent, reflecting the light of a million glowing candles . . .

Riba has no worry, now, that Zelda has gone to a better place. Nor that she is destined to. Not yet. That wouldn't happen to her, not when she is under Jay's protection. No need any more to make foolish, arrogant bargains with God.

The only difficulty that may arise is if Zelda is injured. What consequence will that have on her illness? Suppose she has broken one of those brittle, porous bones? Or has been cut, and some of that precious blood been lost—

Stop this, stop it.

Have faith . . .

The reason for the slip in concentration is because she has heard, very near, a huge engine, the squeal of brakes. She must make herself heard, or at least seen.

She changes the focus of her attention and concentration, channelling every inch towards the throbbing engine: *Me . . . me . . . come and rescue me . . .*

As her legs are less than perfect – dumpy, if the truth be told – they are the only part of her body that Riba never exposes to public scrutiny. Right now, however, along with the restricted way in which she can move her left arm, they are a means of communication and, almost for the first time since childhood, she does not care who sees them or what they think of them as she kicks with all her might. Again and again and again . . . bending her knees, flexing, bending, booting, using them as semaphore. *Here – here – over here . . .*

Seconds later, although she cannot hear what is being said over the engine's throb and the pillowing effect of her confinement, she knows that someone is standing beside her and talking to her. She gives what she hopes is a cheery thumbs-up with her free left hand. The packing around her head and face shifts a little and she feels a rocking sensation as someone grabs a piece of the restricting metal around her head. Faintly, she hears a man's voice. Although he is probably yelling, she is not quite sure what he is saying but she thinks it is, 'Easy, missus, easy, missus.' He is gone and the gag is total again.

An eternity passes, with nothing to keep her company except the pulsing of the huge engine.

Then he is back again. They are back again. She feels more than one set of hands on her torso. Nearer than the engine, much nearer, she hears a high-pitched mechanical whining and tearing. *Cutting equipment.*

Instinctively she recoils but the hands hold her steady. 'Easy, missus.'

★   ★   ★

In self-protection, Sophie, feeling nauseous and dizzy, keeps the red and black tumult along the runway to the periphery of her vision, but cannot avoid the devastation in the immediate vicinity. All the spotters' cars have been damaged to a greater or lesser degree but the fragment of tail, immense from this perspective, has flattened the Audi and the Mustang and left little of the Hiace. The shocked, mostly middle-aged drivers of the other cars are stumbling around these three vehicles through a battlefield of shattered metal, wires, cabling and some sort of padding or flock, which, as though mimicking the departed sleet, is drifting around on the wind before settling to the ground in thick grey drifts. Two would-be rescuers, weeping and mumbling into mobile phones, have reached the Hiace and, with their free hands, have started to scrabble at the distorted door on the driver's side.

No one has noticed Sophie.

Through the dense, blowing smoke, she can see that the men at the van are wasting their time. The roof has been crushed into a deep V by a twisted segment of the Arda logo, and has collapsed on to the head and neck of the driver, who is slumped over his mangled steering-wheel. All that can be seen is his gaping mouth. Clearly he is dead.

Sophie believes she might be sick but her first priority is Brian. 'Over here!' she calls weakly, to a man who is trying to prise off some of the wreckage covering the Audi. 'Please help me, there's somebody trapped. I need help.'

By some miracle, the man hears her and rushes over, catching her just in time as her knees crease like an accordion. 'Sit down, miss,' he orders, trying to sound authoritative, but Sophie shakes him off. 'No, I'll be all right but we have to get him out. Please.' She swallows hard and, lowering her head between those treacherous knees, takes several deep breaths, waiting for the dizziness to pass.

The man looks around desperately. 'Over here,' he shouts to no one in particular. Recognising that someone has taken charge, the others abandon the crushed cars and rush to pull at the chain-link imprisoning Brian. The fence has been sheared through at only one place, about eight feet to the right of where he lies. A little way to the left, it curls back upright and runs onwards round the airfield as though nothing has happened.

By the time Sophie has recovered sufficiently to lend a hand, the men, six altogether, have succeeded in removing some of the shards of debris and, while two push with their backs against the part of the fence half standing, the rest, led by Sophie's original helper – 'One! Two! Three!' – heave at the section covering Brian, who has still not moved.

Sophie plays her part: as a space appears under the fence, she crawls back under it to the inert body, clutches the jacket, making tight fistfuls of the fabric, and drags at it. Brian is careless about dressing and she prays that this suit is one of his sturdier purchases.

The screech of the cutting equipment so close to her head is by far the most frightening of all the dreadful noises Riba has endured. Up and down a tortured musical scale it goes as the aircraft's skin yields reluctantly to its bite. She has to use all her willpower to stay still and not kick or writhe against the vice-like grip of the hands pinning her legs together and restraining her.

Her repertoire of visualisation tricks and relaxation aids is exhausted. Try as she might, she can no longer summon images to distract her from the ordeal and instead she feels every gust of heat, hears every piercing shriek of sundered aluminium, lives through every shake and shudder and scream. For the first time she is almost out of control. Suppose those blades slip. Or jaws. She thinks they must be jaws. Sees them gaping crocodile-like, snapping so close . . .

Then . . . Zelda. Is Zelda going through the same thing?

Please, please, she prays to no one in particular now, fighting the rising waves of hysteria. *Please, please.* Incoherently. *Please* . . .

Just when she thinks she can bear it no longer there is an almighty crack. The gagging softness falls away from around her head and, dazzled by the contaminated, snowy daylight, she is gasping and retching in the fetid air. Hands are busy with her, she has no idea how many but yields to their firmness as she is half carried, half supported away from her prison.

They are putting her on to a stretcher, forcing her down, covering her . . . Their faces are black and grotesque under the oversized helmets. Her own hands are flailing, beating against the greasy unpleasantness of the rubbery uniforms. All around her the sirens continue to screech and there is a burning, chemical stench that overpowers even the acrid reek of aviation fuel.

Turning her head, struggling against all those hands, she can see arcs of foam being sprayed over what used to be the aircraft, already an enormous white-covered mausoleum about fifty or sixty yards away. Incongruously, maybe undamaged, the cockpit of the plane has turned sideways and is pointing slightly upwards, a perky little face peeking archly from the giant, crippled body.

'No-ooo!' Riba screams and pushes herself off the stretcher. She has to find Zelda.

They try to restrain her again but, ignoring pain in her shoulder and neck, she evades them, running back to the place they took her from. She has to get to Zelda.

They catch up with her just as she reaches the broken cocoon where she and Zelda sat so recently only inches apart. In front of where they were, there is nothing but emptiness. The tail section, zigzagged like a broken eggshell, has skidded clear of the rest of the plane. Zelda's seat is vacant. All the others are missing or unoccupied.

Except the two seats beside her own. Riba forgets Zelda for an instant because her limbs turn to mush.

Upright, side by side in their back-tilted seats beside their bent, distorted window, the Americans' hands are still clasped. The wife's face is only half missing but where the husband's fleshy head once was there is now only a bloody, lumpy ring.

As Riba stands, frozen, two firemen are running towards them carrying sheets. Now her own minders have caught up with her. 'Come on, missus.' The hands are strong, will not be resisted. 'We have to get you to a hospital – and let's get this bag off you.' A pair of hands grasp at the bandolier across her chest.

'No-o!' For some reason, Riba believes that if she gives up her bag, she will give up everything. She guards it with her life, and with what remains of her strength. But this gives out and finally she yields to the gathering blackness.

As it descends, they catch her before she hits the ground.

At least Brian is breathing. They establish that when they have him clear of the fence. But what ensues now is a babel of confusion:

'Don't move him.'

'Did anyone dial 999?'

'Someone should get him up off this wet grass.'

'No. For God's sake, you're not supposed to move them – wait for the ambulance.'

It is as though all the shock and fear can be dealt with only by focusing attention on this one person. Maybe this way they can all stem the slide into the abyss. Maybe by dealing with something – or someone – right here, right now, they can bring order to this chaos and stave off their own terror.

One of the men turns to Sophie. 'Are you his wife? Should we move him or not?'

They all fall silent, waiting, giving way to moral superiority in the making of the decision. Sophie stares back at the circle of anxious, hopeless faces. 'No, I'm not his wife. His wife is – or was—'

The bile that has threatened rises close to the back of her tongue and she has to cough. She swallows hard. 'Sorry, his wife *is* on that plane. And so is his daughter. We were seeing them off.'

Silenced, they all swing round towards the horror on the runway to gaze at the conflagration of colour: the red, the black, the ruddy brown, the flickering arcs of blue and amber from the lights of the emergency vehicles and, through the smoke, the swathes of white as the hoses of the firemen spray cataracts of foam on the inferno. As stupefied as the rest, and forgetting Brian for a moment, Sophie gazes, too, until one of the men voices the thoughts of all the others: 'Jesus, Mary and Joseph! No one could have got out of that.'

For Sophie, the first real stabs of anguish. Eily is dead. That infuriating, sprawling, vibrant life has been extinguished.

And Zelda. Poor, blameless Zelda, the pawn on her mother's well-intentioned chessboard. She is dead too. Nineteen years old, facing death in a different way but taken before she had had a chance to come to terms with it.

Sophie's knees buckle and, before any of the men can catch her, she slumps to the ground.

It is teatime. Donny and Trevor are watching the dénouement of *American Beauty*, a rerun of which is showing in an art house in town. They are not all that interested in art. They say yes, though, to American beauty . . .

They have had a good afternoon. They took a trip on the Dart all the way to Howth and walked to the summit, looking out to sea and telling one another how wonderful it was to get some fresh air, giggling at the plight of the poor sods still trapped in the fuggy classrooms. The only problem was that, with all the wind up there, they couldn't light their cigarettes. They were also freezing their arses off. So they scuttled back to the village and into a smoky chip shop where they spent a happy hour cramming themselves full to bursting with batter burgers, curry chips, and Styrofoam beakers of tea.

The eating binge continued when they arrived back in the city centre and decided to go to the pictures. This is a tony cinema that doesn't sell anything as vulgar as popcorn but around their feet lies the evidence of a sugarholic feast: chocolate wrappers, straws, crumpled plastic bottles. They are both in seventh heaven in this palace of dreams, with its lovely, musty smell of flock, dust and old velvet. With only a handful of others around them, they might as well be having a private showing. Sheikhs of the Dublin matinée circuit.

Now, however, they are neither eating nor drinking. They are so involved in what is going on in the film that they are sitting like obelisks: Kevin Spacey is about to have sex with the most beautiful blonde girl either boy has ever seen. Her skin. Her mouth. Her hair. That body . . . Afraid to break the spell, Donny allows beads of sweat to fall unimpeded into his eyes behind his glasses.

Oh, God – his hands are on the waistband of her jeans, he is opening them, he is going to pull them down . . .

Oh, God—

'Shite!' Both boys exhale on the simultaneous exclamation. They are disgusted. Kevin Spacey has bottled out. They're so mad at Kevin Spacey that they don't bother to stay for the end of the film.

As they come out into the evening darkness, populated by swirls of office-workers hurrying to catch buses and trains, Donny turns on his mobile phone. Anxious not to waste his free house, he and Trevor – who has told his mother he is staying in school to attend a debate – have been organising a 'session'. He peers intently at the small glowing face on the screen. 'Hey! Cool! Five messages!'

As he listens to his voicemail, Donny's attitude changes so drastically and obviously that his friend becomes alarmed. 'What is it? What's wrong?'

CHAPTER FOUR

Riba's faint was brief and she regained consciousness as her stretcher was being lifted into the back of the ambulance. Although her shoulder hurt and her face was bleeding copiously, she did not need to be told that she was not badly injured and her focus remained fixed on Zelda. Even as the ambulance screamed towards Beaumont Hospital, she was pressing the attendants frantically to find out where her daughter was and what had happened to her. The airport's major-disaster plan was in effect, however, and every hospital in Dublin and the surrounding areas was taking casualties and bodies, so it wasn't easy to track her down.

By seven o'clock that evening, she was despairing in the waiting area of Beaumont's Accident and Emergency Department because not only God but Jay Street, and all her training in positive thinking, had deserted her. She was now ready to make a bargain even with Satan for her daughter's safety.

Then one of the staff nurses came rushing out to her from behind the glassed-in staff area, offering her the use of her own mobile phone. Zelda had been located in Our Lady of Lourdes Hospital in Drogheda, twenty-five miles from the capital.

Joy so suddenly exposed feels the same as grief, and Riba's customary control deserted her as, blinded by tears, she took the mobile and pressed, mis-pressed and pressed again the numbers given her by the nurse. Dumbly she handed the phone back to the nurse, who made the call for her.

When Zelda finally came on, Riba was still unable to speak. Every shred of every nerve seemed to come together behind her throat, strangling her as she listened to her daughter's weak, distant voice – 'Hello, Mum? Are you there? Mum?' – until finally she managed to choke out a few words.

Even minutes afterwards, however, she could not have repeated to anyone what she said because she could not remember. Indeed, when she thinks about it now, she has the impression that she probably whispered

Zelda's name over and over again, leaving it initially to her daughter to run the conversation, what there was of it: 'Don't cry, please don't cry. I'm fine, Mum, honestly. Not a scratch.'

Eventually she calmed down for long enough to discuss what was to happen. In the morning Zelda was to be transferred to her own consultant at the cancer hospital but was being kept at Our Lady of Lourdes for the night. 'If I put them on to you, Mum, will you tell them what drugs I'm supposed to have? They can't get through to my doctors. I tried to ring home, but there's nobody there. Is Dad with you? Are you badly injured?'

'Not in the least. I'm fine.' Riba was still finding it hard to frame coherent sentences but she managed somehow. 'I don't know where Dad is – he's going to get an awful shock. He probably knows by now. He was going to Shannon today. He'll find us, though. He's probably looking after Donny.'

That set Zelda off again, wailing this time like a four-year-old waking from a nightmare. 'I thought you were dead, Mum, I thought you were dead.'

'Thank God for both of us, darling,' Riba had got out.

'Oh, God,' Zelda sobbed, 'I'm sorry I was such a prat. I know you were only doing your best – and then when I thought I'd never see you again . . .'

'Stop, Zelda, please stop. You are the most wonderful, the most beautiful daughter a mother ever had.' Riba knew that the other people in the crammed A and E waiting room were staring at her but she didn't care as she and Zelda wept together through the twenty-five miles that separated them.

Four of the five messages on Donny's telephone had been from pals who were taking him up on the offer of the free house that night. The fifth, over some sort of chaotic background noise – which subsequently proved to be the din in the entrance hall of the Mater Hospital – was from his father and was barely comprehensible. It included a telephone number: 'Call me the moment you get this message, sport, OK?'

The next couple of hours were gruesome but, luckily for Donny, he had Trevor with him. Because right away, while the evening traffic honked and crawled all around them and he was reacting to the shocking news about what had happened, Trevor was talking to his own father.

Mr Jameson, who worked in town, had come straight from his office to collect the two of them. A quiet, logical man, he set about organising things in sequence. First, while driving his son and Donny to the Mater, he found out, through listening to the news on the radio and making calls to the helpline number that was being broadcast every five minutes, that the boy's mother had survived the crash and was in Beaumont. Apparently she was waiting for a cut above her eye to be stitched. That didn't sound too bad. Even at that stage, Donny could feel relief building. By the time they got to the Mater, Mr Jameson had also located Zelda. She was OK too.

Then something weird was happening. Mortifying. Donny knew he was going to be sick. He didn't want to destroy Mr Jameson's car so he blurted out that he'd like them to pull over. They were in Gardiner Street and there were a lot of people about, but what else could he do?

He got out just in time because it all came spewing, all the tons of food and drink, in one long, shame-making gush, while Mr Jameson stood beside him and held his shoulders. People were looking and he was doubly humiliated. At least he had managed to keep it to the gutter.

'Better now, son?' Mr Jameson had had to help him back into the car because his knees were suddenly very shaky. Thank Christ Mr Jameson hadn't made it worse by going on and on about it. He was quite cool, actually. Donny never would have thought that up to now.

He would never forget the next couple of hours as long as he lived. Especially the waterworks. Even from his dad, who turned out to be in the X-ray department, waiting for X-rays of his head, neck and shoulders. He didn't look all that bad, just dirty and bruised, with one arm in a sling and his clothes all torn. But when Donny told him about Mum and Zelda being OK, he started to blub like a baby. It was really hard not to join in.

That was bad enough, but then there was Beaumont. Donny, who would not let anyone see him cry if you paid him a million pounds, felt the tears get as far as his eyes when he saw his mother's blood-smeared face. 'Don't, darling.' His mother, who was lying on a trolley, lifted one arm – the other seemed to be hurt – to try to hug him, which of course he resisted with all his might, pulling away from her and dashing towards the Coke machine to get himself a drink. Glad as he was to see her safe, he hated that she was like this. The world he had known all his life was deserting him.

By the time he got back from the Coke machine, though, he had things more or less sorted, and when she told him Zelda was OK, he was able to tell her, calmly enough, that he knew already. Then he told her about his dad.

This was news to her. Actually, she seemed shocked, completely gob-smacked, waterworks working overtime. 'He was there? And he got injured? How badly? Is he all right? Have you got a number I can ring him at?' Donny, who remembered only too well all the shouting between the two of them about the trip, knew, of course, that now was not the time to go into it. He hated that he was the only one in this family who wasn't losing it and lying in a hospital.

At least, he thought he hated it but as he answered her questions about his dad and she calmed down, a strange thing happened. He began to feel a bit better and discovered that to be the one with the information, to be the person in charge, wasn't all that uncool. It was unusual to be in this position, especially where his mother was concerned – where anyone was concerned, really – but Donny could feel himself straightening his shoulders without being told. Although he got a bit alarmed by the way her chin crumpled up again just as he had thought they were in the clear, dammit – he'd had enough of the crying. He rushed on to tell her the news about his aunt Sophie, whom he hadn't found yet. 'But she's OK,' he added earnestly. 'Dad says she's OK. I think she's in the Mater as well, because he said he'd seen her, but I didn't wait to look for her.'

This was more news, apparently. 'Sophie too?'

At least she'd turned off the waterworks. 'Yeah, she was with Dad, waving at the plane.'

'And she's all right?'

'A few cuts and bruises but, yeah, he says she's OK.'

'And Dad's all right? You're sure about that?'

To his consternation, this led to total meltdown, just when he'd thought everything was under control. This was desperate, desperate, because as she continued to cry and carry on – like a kid, for God's sake – he was finding it hard not to melt down himself. That couldn't happen. Not here with all these people bleeding all over the place and moaning and lying on mattresses on the floor. 'There there!' he said, patting her, the way a cowboy might pat a spooked horse. He could feel his face going bright crimson. 'Don't cry, Mum. I'm here.'

Actually, although he was ashamed of this, he couldn't wait to get out of the place. It was all very well to be the man, but it was hard to keep it up when you weren't used to it.

She was still crying, but more quietly, when Mr Jameson came in to rescue him and take him home to Trevor's house, from where Donny managed to talk to his sister while Mrs Jameson deep-fried a mountain of chips for them all.

It was only then that he realised four of his mates were probably throwing stones at his bedroom window at home, trying to get in for the session.

'Sorry! I'm really sorry!' Four days after the crash, at the corner of the Quays and Church Street, Sophie has rolled down the window of her

Mini to apologise to the motorcycle courier she has inadvertently cut off, causing him to swerve and almost come off his bike. Although it is a mild, almost spring-like day outside, she has wrapped herself in layers of white wool and has to pull down her scarf to be heard.

Through the thick visor of his helmet, the kid's reply is unmistakable: a string of four-letter epithets impugning her parentage, her competence to handle a car and her entitlement to exist. He starts the machine again and zooms off like an angry wasp, but not before flourishing a final series of finger signals at her. Tiredly, barely able to summon the strength, she rolls up the window. She doesn't blame the kid for his fury: the incident was entirely her fault. She had not been concentrating and could have killed him.

She has never felt so exhausted in all her life. Although the fainting spell immediately after the crash had been brief and, remarkably, she has escaped with nothing but minor bruising to her back and to one side of her face, she is emotionally fragile and has been finding it difficult to sleep.

She is on her way to visit Eily but is not looking forward to it. It is not that she is afraid anything overtly dreadful will happen. On the surface it is simply that she is not in the mood to tolerate another tutorial on Jay Street and his beliefs and, as a result, might blow the friendship altogether. Also, she doesn't want to discuss the crash. If Eily starts once more to go on about miracles, the way she's been going on about them on the phone, Sophie is afraid she will hit her. She can't articulate why. Although she accepts intellectually that their escape was close to a miracle, it doesn't *feel* miraculous. Personally – and extraordinarily – she doesn't even feel lucky. As a result, her telephone conversations with Eily have been fraught, at least on Sophie's side.

The accident seems to have thrown up something in high relief, something Sophie has been trying to ignore for quite some time. At heart, she believes that somehow, somewhere, she has lost some part – quite a large part – of her old friend. It is not only that: the loss has affected the ease within their long-standing foursome too. She and Michael, Brian and Eily had been so comfortable with each other, individually and collectively, until the last few years. She misses that easiness and wants it back. Which is why, she supposes, she keeps plugging away. Cautiously, she turns left at Doyle's Corner. Her foot-dragging at visiting Eily feels disloyal somehow. Friends should accept one another, warts, wacky beliefs and all.

She can pinpoint exactly when the friendship struck a subterranean reef, although recognition was a long time dawning on her.

On a rainy weekend seven years previously, she and Eily – when Riba was still happy to be known by that name – had decided to Do Something

Positive about the rut in which they found themselves. So, leaving Zelda and Donny in the care of the two husbands, who promptly took them to watch a rugby match and allowed them to catch colds, the pair headed off to the annual Mind Body Spirit event held in the exhibition hall of the Royal Dublin Society in Ballsbridge. There was no way either could have known that this first encounter with Jay Street would have such a seismic effect.

The place was jammed. Most people, including Eily and Sophie, were perspiring heavily and carried, rather than wore, their heavy winter outerwear. This further depleted the space between the colourful, amateurish stands as the crowds lined up to have their auras read or their allergies tested, swarmed to buy healing crystals, light boxes, pills, powders and dietary supplements, or made appointments for consultations and therapies. To Sophie, who queued for more than an hour for an Indian head massage offered by a beautiful, bald young woman wearing leather chaps and a fringed shirt, the nearby stand occupied by Jay Street's people was one of many curiosities although, as far as she could see, it was the most slick on offer. Candlelit, festooned with glossy posters, it was dominated by a huge colour photograph of Street, framed in gold and surrounded by dozens of votive lights.

The handouts gave a little of Jay Street's history: born in Chicago of Irish parents, trained as a carpenter, but at the age of twenty-two, after a lecture by a Korean mystic with an unpronounceable name, 'was moved' to give up the building sites to study under his new master, following him all over the globe and settling down for a number of years as the man's acolyte in a remote area of South Korea. In 1981, when Jay was forty-five, his guru died and he came back to Chicago to set up his own organisation. He quickly found a clientèle hungry for answers to their 'life-questions' and alternatives to the 'arid lifestyles' into which they had been shoe-horned. The organisation bloomed and spread and, because of 'phenomenal results', had quickly diversified into products and services such as were on offer that day on his stand. Now, people in sixteen countries, including Ireland, the country 'closest to his heart and heritage', which he had visited eleven times in as many years, followed his holistic regime.

Et cetera, et cetera . . .

From her position in the slowly moving queue, Sophie could see right from the start that her friend was smitten, not just by Street's basic message (*You Can Do Anything If You Believe*) but by the charismatic man himself. After her head massage, Sophie lost her friend from time to time, and always found her back at her newly discovered Valhalla, deep in conversation with one of the attendants or gazing into the clear, celluloid green of Jay Street's eyes.

Eily had already planted both feet firmly on her irritating path.

Sophie stops at a red light in Cabra, envying the driver of the red Mondeo in the outside lane. The man, with the belly of a beer drinker, is slapping his steering-wheel in rhythm with the heavy rock beat emanating from his stereo, all too audible even through his closed window. He looks as though he hasn't a care in the world.

One of the many emotions she finds she cannot escape since the crash is guilt. She feels guilty all the time about everything – the plane, the people who died, the suffering of the bereaved relatives – as if the crash had somehow been her fault. The current speculation is that the aircraft might have hit something during its take-off run and Sophie feels as though she should have seen it and warned the pilot. Or that she should have acted on the urgings of that little voice at that coffee counter telling her to place a hoax bomb call. She might have been arrested but no one would have died. Of course, she can't say anything about guilt to Eily. That would afford too big an opening.

Maybe the breach in their friendship is not entirely Eily's fault, because there is something new, something Sophie would not dream of analysing and whose very existence she finds difficult to acknowledge. Even here, alone, in the safety of the Mini. This is the subtle change in her attitude to Eily's husband, with whom up to now she has been as relaxed as if he were another woman or gay.

She is grateful that he saved her life. But more. Although in waking moments she tamps it down, her fragmented dreams of the past few nights include the sensation of Brian's bodyweight on hers after he tackled her to the ground. With shocking inappropriateness, right through its vivid, detailed recall of Armageddon raining from the skies all around them, her body retains the imprint of his.

This rubbish must be the effect of the crash. The accident seems to have cracked her open, spilling emotions and thoughts topsy-turvy all over the place so that even finding them again, never mind fitting them together in the old familiar order, is proving tough. Nothing seems to be as it was. Because now she fancies that, even before the crash, when he had come to sit beside her on that stool in the coffee shop at Dublin airport – and again in the Mustang while they watched the snow – she had been conscious that she was in the presence of a powerful male.

This has to be the invention of a mind knocked out of kilter because she certainly had not registered it at the time. Yet even now she can feel his shoulder touching hers.

The lights change and Sophie lets the Mondeo cut in front of her before moving off.

★ ★ ★

'Please don't tell my mother – at least not yet.' Zelda, a paper hospital gown covering her thin frame, is sitting on the side of a plinth, on which she has just undergone tests for kidney function. Normally, the woman who takes these tests would not dream of hinting at the results to the patient, leaving this to the omnipotent consultants, but she has taken this little girl under her wing and feels for her. She has also developed a good relationship with Zelda's mother. 'The news is good, dear,' she says.

'I know. And that's great. But you know her. If you give her even the slightest encouragement, she'll take it that I'm cured and go telling everyone. That'd be terrible pressure. I'd prefer it if you wouldn't tell her, please.'

The expression in the technician's faded blue eyes is quizzical. 'You're the boss, young lady. You know I wouldn't tell her anyway without your permission. I'm not supposed even to tell you. Now, put your nice nightie back on and I'll get the porter back in here with the wheelchair.'

As she bustles out, Zelda lowers herself slowly off the high table and bends to put on her slippers. Although she has her good days when she feels positive, she is weary of the constant testing of her blood, her bone marrow and every damned organ in her body. Her fingers and arms are like pincushions from the daily needles.

It had all started so innocently – just a pain in her knee that was sometimes excruciating, sometimes no trouble at all. She had put it down to muscle strain caused by carrying her heavy bag of books to and from school. Then, before she had even gone to the doctor to see what was causing it, the other leg had collapsed under her when she was crossing the road right outside the house.

At the hospital where she had had the fracture plastered, the doctors had been soothing – 'Let's get you a few blood tests, Zelda, see why this leg broke so suddenly' – but now, in hindsight, she can see that already they were being evasive about what they had seen on her X-rays.

Eighteen months down the road, there is little she does not know about the rogue plasma cells that continue to increase and spread, releasing their horrible enzymes, gobbling her bone. She tends to see them as an enemy army that continues to march and will not be defeated, despite everyone's best efforts or small temporary triumphs like today's improvement in her kidney function.

At first, she responded positively to the urgings of her mother and well-meaning friends who tried to convince her that if she bent her mind enough to the task of defeating this army, she would be victorious.

However, her will to fight gradually waned, as the gobbling army marched on and now the dominant feeling is one of weary acceptance. When she wishes that the enemy would hurry up and do its job properly because she is so deeply tired. Day and night, sleep hovers over her head like a warm duvet and it is becoming more and more of an effort to stave it off when the prospect is so attractive.

In the nervy, almost hysterical first days after her diagnosis, Zelda tried to explain the details of her disease to anyone who asked, but soon became fed up with the torturous explanations, misunderstandings and questions. So now, with the exception of close family and friends, she tells anyone who asks that she is suffering from leukaemia. People can get a handle on that. Weepy films have been made about it. Fund-raising is creative and eye-catching, people have friends with it, or whose children have died tragically from it.

Yet the main difference between leukaemia and multiple myeloma is the most relevant of all. People survive some forms of leukaemia, can even eke out their lives to an almost normal length, but in January 2001, there is still no cure in sight for what afflicts her.

All right, the progress of the disease can sometimes be temporarily arrested but so far no one has found a foolproof way to stop the attack of the busy plasma and its devouring of blood, bone and organ.

Zelda knows she might die from a stroke because her blood has been thickened by an overabundance of proteins caused by the osteoclast enzyme being manufactured so enthusiastically by the proliferating plasma army. Or, because her particular cancer can cause a shortage of the clotting factor, she might even bleed to death, should her pelvis or a femur fracture.

Chances are, though, that she will die from renal failure because her kidneys will become overwhelmed by the excess of calcium being released into her bloodstream from her dissolving bones. Or, even more likely, she will succumb to an 'ordinary' infection, because not only are her poor old blood cells being efficiently picked off by their voracious opponents, the chemotherapy is killing them off too. A simple cold, perhaps, or flu, may lead to death from pneumonia.

The porter, a young fellow of about her own age, arrives with the wheelchair and she climbs into it. There was a time when she would have insisted on walking, but no longer. What's the point of exercising her wasting muscles, when they are going to waste anyway? He tries to chat to her about a disco he was at the previous night but takes her non-response as a warning to shut up and wheels her without a further word along the bright corridor and into the lift.

Discos. Yeah. She should be so lucky.

They will all be devastated when she does die. It is a terrible responsibility to have to bear – she was given a taste of what they will go through during those terrible hours she was in the Drogheda hospital, couldn't find her dad or Donny, and was sure her mother had been killed.

Her overwhelming feeling during the crash was not of fear but surprise. She was woken from a deep sleep by an explosion and, before she was fully awake, felt herself caught in a whirligig of screaming noise and of painful motion, followed almost immediately by a tremendous jolt that shook every bone and muscle. She knows now that this was the tail of the aircraft coming to a halt.

Still strapped into her seat, with confusion and screaming all around her, she had looked across to where her mother should have been but all she could see was her naked legs. This upset her but, in retrospect, Zelda realises now that she hadn't even screamed. It was only as she was being pulled out of her seat by the man next to her and led away into the field beside the runway that she had reacted. She had tried to run back towards her mother but her legs wouldn't carry her – and then the fire crews and ambulances had arrived to take charge and she had let them.

During the long trip to the hospital the full impact of what had happened began to dawn on her and she had panicked, shouting at the ambulance men that they had to stop, that she had to go back to find her mother – until the driver had discovered, via his radio, that many passengers in the tail section had been pulled out alive.

Nevertheless, the hours between then and the phone call from her mother had been hell.

At least her ordeal had lasted only a couple of hours. For the rest of her family, her dying is an elastic thread that has drawn itself out so thinly and for so long that everyone's spirit is stretched to the limit. It is easier for her than it is for them because she now sees her death as a permanent yielding to warm sleep. For them, though, the imagining, the constant fear, the watching and waiting must be awful. Worse than the reality when it comes.

Especially for poor old Donny. What a time he is having when he should be heading into the most interesting part of his whole life. Although he tries to hide it, waffling on about school and the dweebish Trevor, she can't help but see how much he is suffering underneath.

What they don't see is that she feels everything that they're feeling – and more.

People talk about acts of God. Well, why didn't He act when He was handed a golden opportunity to get them all off the hook? It would have been clean and quick, probably painless and, outside her control, would have absolved her from responsibility for other people's misery. Why had He decided that she of all people should survive a plane crash? Especially when there were so many people on board with long lives ahead of them. Even little children.

Sometimes she gets quite angry with God.

This disease is going to get her sooner rather than later, she has accepted that, even if others, particularly her mother, have not.

CHAPTER FIVE

In her bright kitchen, where the walls are a healing aqua colour, Riba checks her watch and is brought up short once again as she sees that it still shows the time as it was when it stopped at one thirty-four last Monday afternoon. Superstitiously, she will not take it to a jeweller's until Brian and Zelda get home.

She moves around, adjusting a saucepan lid, checking the vegetable rack to see if anything needs to be thrown out. Her injuries are healing well: the dislocated shoulder, while not back to normal, is on the mend, the tapes on the cut over her left eye are pulling and itching, which means they should probably be removed, and any residual muscle discomfort has become little more than a background ache. Even the superficial gashes in her lips and on the inside of her mouth don't hurt much this morning. Her GP has been marvellously attentive but she has refused all offers of pharmaceutical help. Instead, she has been treating herself to vitamin and mineral cocktails, plenty of the Bs and E, of course, but also including a little extra zinc, selenium and magnesium, with a tiny dash of phosphorous. She has been drawing successfully on all the mental and emotional resources Jay and her courses have given her. She is not at all surprised that she is doing so well.

She woke early this morning and actually had enough energy to blitz the house, so that by around a quarter past nine, a pile of tea-towels, ironed, folded and piled as neatly as paving slabs, congratulated her from the polished granite worktop, while the chrome rail on the Stanley range gleamed in the light streaming through the window over the sink. She has baked: two dozen buns are laid out on the cooling rack, ready for icing. Riba is famed for her baking and loves to bathe in the warm yeasty smell that impregnates every room in her house with its promise of plenty.

She is restless now. It is so silent she can hear the small electronic *thuk!* *thuk!* coming from the clock on the cooker. She twiddles with the dials on the kitchen radio, searching for nice music, but can find only news: '. . . and at a press conference today, the Directors of Air Arda . . .'

'. . . this investigation, already into its third day . . .'

'. . . and this evening, President Mary McAleese will attend funerals of another six of . . .'

One after the other, the newsreaders, voices brown with import, intone variations of the same story and, unbidden, the image of those bleached-blonde, exuberant women, lashing surreptitiously into the vodka before they had even fastened their seatbelts, erupts in her mind. Riba snaps off the radio. Lord have mercy on their souls.

It is not as though she is unfeeling, but God – with Jay's help – had spared her to live and enjoy Creation. So that is what she should do. Enjoy Creation.

She turns instinctively towards the light coming through her kitchen window, and God rewards her with the sight of two starlings, backs gleaming like copper in the austere sunlight, teetering like circus artistes on the tendrils of a leafless weeping birch while they probe for insects in its rough, silvery bark. Riba planted that tree as a gift to herself when she graduated with honours from the first of the organisation's courses.

Thank God she met Jay when she did. Some people – like Brian and Sophie, for instance – have hinted to her that she is involved in a cult. That she has even been brainwashed. That what Jay preaches is the dogma of selfishness or that it is against religion – but Jay is at one with Jesus, whom he loves as much as she does.

Show her where in the gospels Jesus preached anything different in principle from what Jay teaches. Did He say it is sinful to develop your own talents and potential to the fullest possible extent? To plumb then liberate your personal resources so you can live the fullest and most successful life possible? Didn't His Father give us this life and this beautiful world to enjoy? Why should anyone begrudge her the few hours she spends on the good work for high goals?

If only they would come along with her, life would be perfect.

Riba sighs. So, what to do now? It is only just after eleven, too early to see Zelda. Because of consultants' rounds, the hospital does not encourage visitors before lunchtime. She has already told Brian, who is still confined to hospital with internal bruising, that she will be in to see him in the afternoon.

She sits down abruptly. *All right. Face it, Riba. Why haven't you been in to see your husband? You made excuses. You weren't up to leaving the house yet, you said. Yet you managed to go in to see Zelda – and he knows it.*

The other half of her brain answers: *You're afraid he'll see through you and guess what you're planning, aren't you? You're afraid he'll freak and do everything in his power to stop you and Zelda taking that trip again?*

When she had got through to Brian's bedside in the Mater from her own in Beaumont, in the first flush of relief and gladness she had foolishly mentioned Jay's protection. Even at that distance, however, and with the brouhaha all around her in A and E, she had felt him freeze. When she had hung up she had been upset all over again. That was typical of Brian. His stubbornness about Jay is total and he will never admit she may be right, even when the proof is glaring.

She feels like shaking him – and not only him. She feels like catching everyone by the throat. She feels like standing on a soap-box outside the GPO and shouting at passers-by: *See? See? What did I tell you? Not one major injury to anyone connected through me to Jay Street. Explain that if you can. Explain to me why all of the eleven who survived were sitting in the tail section near me . . .*

What's more, Jay's influence had even extended to the spotters' car park where Brian's car had been a write-off. If he and Sophie had been sitting in it, they would have died, just like the drivers of the two cars parked at either side of the Mustang. *So why did he get out of that car seconds before the crash? Why did Sophie?* If proof were needed of Jay's protection, of miracles, what more could anyone ask for? She had attempted to broach this idea with Brian on the telephone, but, predictably, he had pooh-poohed the notion, had even been nasty about it, pointing out that if she had gone on another aircraft she wouldn't have crashed at all. 'Why didn't your precious Jay communicate that to you, or tell you not to embark on this crazy expedition in the first place?'

Riba had ignored this and had not brought up the subject again. No harm in trying, though, and she will probably keep trying until the day she dies.

As for Zelda, although 'they' are keeping her under their beady observation in that oncology hospital, even 'they' acknowledge that Zelda's escape unscathed from the doomed plane had been the most outstanding event of the crash. Riba has no doubt now that her daughter has been earmarked for a complete cure. The sooner the two of them can get on to another plane and fly to the Caribbean, the sooner she can get properly healthy again, and they can all get back to their normal lives.

It will take a little time, of course, even for herself. Riba can accept that, at the moment, mental rigour or no mental rigour, she is as vulnerable as the next person to flashbacks and uncharacteristic behaviour. The previous evening, for instance, she found herself bursting into tears while she was watching Michael Douglas's final patriotic speech in *The American President*, which is a funny film with a few emotional moments. Yet as soon as those tears started, they would not stop and she found herself weeping on and off for almost half an hour. She heard herself calling for a mother of whom she did not have a single memory; she heard words coming out of her mouth, meaningless stuff like 'I'm so sorry' and 'please', repeated and repeated until her mouth bubbled so badly that she could not form them any more.

There are also the smells: even ordinary household smells – bleach, polish, rashers on a heated grill – resurrect the stench of the crash's aftermath, of chemicals, kerosene, incinerating flesh and fabric.

The worst and most vivid memory, however, is of her unfortunate seat companions, the Americans. She sees them – or, rather, what became of them – not only in her waking moments but in her disjointed dreams. That violent trembling starts up again each time.

Here she is, getting upset again, just thinking about them.

After she had been fixed up in A and E, she was told that there would be follow-up visits from counsellors.

She can counsel herself, thank you.

Scrabbling through her collection of tapes, Riba forces herself to take four deep breaths, yoga-style. Then, calmer already, she stands still and allows her spirits to soar along with the gay, lilting rhythms of a Strauss waltz.

That's better. She feels grand now.

She is casting another approving glance around the glittering kitchen, just as the wall telephone beside the back door shrills. Riba hesitates, debating whether or not to answer it because the telephone is a tyranny she has overthrown. After all, what did people do before the telephone was invented?

The phone rings again, she decides to answer, and turns down the music. Her heart jumps when she puts the receiver to her ear. Even with modern cables or satellites, or whatever, there remains that split-second interval indicating an overseas call. This has to be Jay. 'Hello?'

'Hello, Riba?'

Her joy evaporates. The voice is female. 'Yes?'

'This is Monica. Jay asked me to give you a call.'

'Oh, sure! Great! Hi, Monica, how are you?' This is one of the coterie of women, mostly American like himself, who work for Jay *in situ*.

'I'm fine.' The voice, with its open Californian vowels, is younger than its owner and lilts upwards at the end of most sentences as though they were adorned with question marks. 'But what we want to know is how're you doing? We're very concerned about you, Riba? And Zelda, of course? We saw it on the news' – she pronounces it *noos* – 'on CNN a couple of nights ago? We decided not to call you direct. We called head office in

Dublin and they filled us in? All those poor people? What a dreadful thing, Riba?'

Despite all her training, despite even the aftershocks of what she has been through, Riba has to work hard to curb a quick upsurge of envy – indeed, jealousy. It's the proprietorial 'we' that does it. California Monica, as Riba calls her privately, is a blonde, small-waisted, long-legged and toothsome specimen of gorgeousness; she is also very tall, so gorgeously tall that in her presence, during the one time they had met while Jay was touring his franchises in Ireland with his entourage, Riba had felt shrunken, almost deformed. 'Yes, it was quite awful,' she says, managing to sound sober and reflective. 'I wouldn't want to go through that again in a hurry.'

'How's Zelda doing? We're working on her daily, Riba? You need have no worries about that – but Jay wants to know, are you still going to come on over? He's concerned.'

Riba's heart starts to sing. 'That's really sweet of him, Monica. Tell him that he'll see us out there as soon as it is physically possible.' *As soon as I can manage to pull the wool over my husband's eyes.* 'That should be quite soon, actually, Monica,' she says firmly.

'I'll tell him. He'll be delighted. He said to make sure to send you his best love?'

'Love to him too, Monica.'

Riba's heart sings louder as she hangs up. Jay is always so busy but he is obviously thinking about her. She had known this already, of course, but here's confirmation from the horse's mouth. Almost. Well, the next best thing. Like shaking the hand of the man who shook the hand of the Pope.

'Oh, for God's sake, *woman!* Get a *grip!*' She is startled to hear her voice ringing around the silent kitchen, then finds the resources to laugh at herself.

She turns the music up again.

Now the doorbell rings.

As the faint reverberations of the doorbell die away inside Eily's house, Sophie admires the tidy lawn, neat flower-beds, the spotless white-painted gate and kerbstone, the sheen on the black and white tiles of the porch. While she continues to prefer the vaguely seedy atmosphere surrounding her small, gardenless house near the city centre, she can appreciate why the McMullans continue to live in this sprawling north-side estate. Filled with families, Marble Gardens is a good place to bring up children.

She can remember when all four of them came to look at the estate under construction – Eily and Brian were scraping together the deposit to buy – and how they had laughed and made jokes about the name, trying to find some connection between it and the wasteland of rubble and concrete in which they stood. Pretentious names, many owing much to the castles and estates of the British royal family, were endemic then in Dublin's new suburbs, with developers hoping that, with their echoes of pheasant shoots, misty mountains and bluebell woods, they would distract residents from the half-finished footpaths, and gardens laid with less than an inch of topsoil. She stares at Eily's brass bell-push. Should she wait a little before pressing it again? Should she wait at all? Maybe Eily is still in bed.

There was a time when she would not have hesitated for an instant. She would even have shouted through the letter-box.

She decides she will ring the bell just once more and if there is still no answer she will leave.

This proves unnecessary because the door is pulled open, and there is her friend, large as life and glowing in her red kaftan. From behind her, Sophie can hear the lush sounds of a waltz. 'Hello.'

'Sophie!' Eily is clearly delighted. 'What a great surprise. I must have known you were coming – I baked. Come on in! I'll put the kettle on.'

As she passes the sign, WHEN THE PUPIL IS READY, THE TEACHER WILL COME, hand-painted directly on to the wall in curly black letters around a giant photograph of Jay Street, which dominates Eily's hallway, Sophie wonders how Brian reacts to it every time he comes home. Then she suppresses the thought. It is none of her business. Instead, she asks the name of the piece of music being played. 'Strauss.' Eily smiles over her shoulder. 'That one is "The Emperor". It's good, isn't it? I'm celebrating today. Celebrating that we're all alive—'

'This is just a quick visit,' Sophie cuts her off. They are in the kitchen now and she peels off her bobble hat, gloves and scarf, then sits in the chair she has occupied for years at Eily's table. 'I've decided to go into the office for a few hours. How are you feeling? Your eye's certainly doing well – I was expecting to see you looking like a boxer.'

'Never better!' Eily grins. 'I see your own bruises are coming along nicely – that's a grand shade of yellow. Is it painful?'

Sophie touches her cheek. 'Not too bad. Not as bad as it was. Sometimes I forget and when I catch sight of myself in the mirror I think I'm looking at a cartoon.'

'Lots of vitamin E cream, Soph. You should try it.'

'Mmmm.' Although she is aware that vitamin E is a mainstream remedy, Sophie is noncommittal. In the early days of Eily's infatuation with Jay Street, she was open-minded, going along with a lot of it. Now, though, she automatically boycotts her friend's suggestions, in the faint hope that some day the lightbulb will go on. It is a useless protest but helps her feel she is doing something.

If she has noticed this latest twitter, however, Eily doesn't show it. 'Just a suggestion, honey,' she says cheerfully, as she turns away to fill the electric kettle. 'I've plenty here, all you have to do is ask. Never mind. Give it a week and we'll both be back to normal. I'm delighted you came. As a matter of fact, I was just killing time until I could go and see Zelda.'

'How is she?'

Eily turns, letting the water pour down the plug-hole, and her expression floods with delight. 'Oh, Sophie, if you saw her – there isn't a mark on her! I can't wait to—' Abruptly, her face tightens and she turns back to twist off the tap and plug in the kettle. 'I can't wait to get her home again.'

Sophie plunges through the awkwardness as, from practice, she has learned to do. 'Is Brian doing OK? I thought I'd slip in to see him at lunchtime.'

'He's grand. But you know men! And Brian would not be a great patient at the best of times! They're having difficulty keeping him quiet!'

'You haven't managed to get in yet?' Sophie forbears to mention that she thinks it peculiar that Eily had not beaten a path immediately to the Mater. *Shut up, shut up. Didn't I tell you it's none of your business?*

'No.' Staring through the window into the garden, Eily warms her hands on the kettle. 'I just wasn't up to it, Sophie, as I told you. He understands. I'm going in this afternoon. I was on to him this morning but . . .' For the second time, to Sophie's super-sensitised ears, Eily seems to have changed her mind as to what she was about to say.

'I'm dreading the memorial Mass at the Pro-Cathedral on Sunday,' Sophie offers, to bridge the gap. 'Maybe we could go together?'

Eily tenses ever so slightly. 'I might. I don't know. I'm not sure I'd be up to being in the middle of all that drama and distress. I'll see . . .'

Then, through the music, they hear the front door slam. Eily glances at the cooker clock. 'It's only a quarter past eleven.' She frowns at Sophie. 'Donny?' He is not due home from school until half past four. She switches off the music and Sophie hears the unmistakable thump of a heavy schoolbag hitting the hall floor.

'It's him all right – little tramp!' Eily smiles fondly. 'I suppose I should kill him for all this mitching but, God love him, he's still in shock. In here, darling!'

Sophie hears further thumping, then Donny appears in the doorway, filling the frame. 'Hi.' Without meeting the eyes of either woman, he walks straight to the fridge and pulls open the door.

'How come you're home?' Eily continues to smile understandingly as she watches him pooch around in the fridge. 'There's a little bit of salami there, would you like me to make you a sandwich?'

'I can make it myself. I don't want salami. Thanks.' Sullenly.

Suppressing a sigh, Eily sits down, 'Sure, honey, take what you like. There's lots of stuff there,' raising her eyebrows at Sophie as though to seek affirmation: *Teenagers!* Sophie, ignoring the invitation to take part in this adult deal, is uncomfortable. It is not just the awkward, overwhelmingly dominant male adolescent presence, it is that she has the impression that although Donny is hopping mad his mother hasn't seemed to notice.

As both she and Eily watch the boy's wide back, she hears herself talking brightly: 'So did you get a day off or what, Donny?'

'There was no school today,' he mutters.

'Oh?' As Eily, at peace, continues to wear her indulgent smile, Sophie, curbing her increasing and irrational irritation, tries to maintain her tone in the higher, lighter register: 'Why was that?'

Donny takes his head out of the fridge and, although only one of his hands is occupied – with a jar of peanut butter – crashes the door shut with a canal-barge foot. He turns to stare at the two of them. 'Me and one other fella were the only ones who showed up this morning. I felt like a right dork.' Then he turns on his mother and Sophie is taken aback to see Brian's grey eyes so furiously alight in his son's head. 'There was an air crash, remember?'

'Don't be silly.' Eily darts another look at her friend, this time long-suffering. 'Of course I know there was an air crash, Donny. I was in it.'

'You're not the only one, you know.' He is so angry he is shaking. 'One of my teachers was on that plane. I told you. But of course you don't remember *that*.' He takes a step towards his mother, so quickly that Sophie fears he might even hit her. He desists, however, but his voice, so newly broken, cracks up and down the octaves like a bad trumpet solo as he adds, 'And before you ask, the reason I'm not home until now is that we went to Dr Quirkey's. *Okay?*'

Sophie knows that he has been expressly forbidden to frequent Dr Quirkey's Emporium, an amusement arcade that calls like a siren to every schoolboy in the inner city, but she is glad that Eily is not challenging him. 'No problem, darling.' Her friend's gaze remains steady.

Donny doesn't want his mother's tolerance, he is beside himself, yelling at the top of his voice, 'Mrs Richmond was killed. She's *dead*! Trevor was ringing here all night last night to tell me that her funeral was this *morning* but the phone was off the *hook*.' His fury conceals genuine grief. He storms out of the kitchen and, taking the stairs two at a time, blasts up to his room, knocking over a chair on the way.

On the surface Eily seems unperturbed. 'Sorry about that. He's been going through a phase, of course, but since the crash – we'll have to have patience, I suppose. He lost his mobile, poor lamb, in all that dreadful excitement. I've got him a new one but I haven't given it to him yet – it just slipped my mind, I'm afraid.'

Sophie, who is nearer, stands up to right the chair. 'Poor kid.' She peers at Eily, wondering why she herself seems far more upset by Donny's distress than his mother does. Then, a bolt of anger – unexpected because of the tranquillity of only a few minutes before – strikes at the back of her throat, almost winding her. She struggles. This has nothing to do with her. How Eily treats her son, whether or not she visits her husband in hospital, is her affair.

Yet she continues to pull on her gloves and wind the scarf around her neck, thinking that it was hardly worth while taking the whole lot off in the first place. She picks up the bobble hat. 'I'll be off. As I told you, I just popped in. Don't bother to see me out. I'll call again – glad to see you're on the mend.' She hurries towards the kitchen door.

'Of course I'll see you out, Soph.' Eily stands up and walks after her through the doorway and into the hall. 'How are you coping yourself? Any reactions?'

'I'm absolutely fine.' The anger that surprised her so much has now retreated as quickly as it had attacked and she is bewildered by it, even ashamed. On the doorstep, she turns impulsively and hugs her old pal, mindful not to put pressure on the damaged shoulder. 'I meant it, Riba. If there is anything at all I can do or if you just want to talk, all you have to do is ask. You're as odd as two left feet, you know that? But I love you.'

Eily laughs. 'I love you too.' The big warm face is wreathed in its damaged, lopsided smile as Sophie sets off towards the gateway and turns back to wave. How could anyone not love that oversized, open-hearted personality, so obviously vulnerable beneath all the assumed certainties? If Sophie were ever in serious trouble, if she was facing bankruptcy or arrest for moral turpitude, this woman would be the first person from whom she would look for help.

She waves again, then lets herself into the Mini, but although she inserts the key in the ignition, she does not turn it. Instead, she stares at the drab, meagrely equipped dashboard. The burst of anger that caught her so off-guard in the kitchen was not an isolated occurrence within her friendship with Eily. If she is honest, she finds that more and more she has to suppress puffs of irritation at the most trivial things.

She pulls her mobile phone from her handbag and speed-dials the office, telling Nancy, the receptionist, that she is on her way in. Then, after a small hesitation, she dials Michael on his mobile.

Sophie's husband has been sweetness itself since the crash, doing all the right things, hugging her, feeding her, dancing assiduous attendance, making sure she is not bothered by reporters or anyone else. Yet all this care and attention is somehow cloying.

'Hello?' His voice is rushed, breathless.

'Hi, it's me!'

'Hi, Soph, how are you? Are you at home?'

'No, I've decided to go into the office for a bit.'

'Oh, darling, are you sure you're up to it?'

'I'm fine. Honestly. I was going mad at home with nothing to do. It'll do me good. You sound out of breath, am I getting you at a bad time?'

'Not at all – the mobile was on the dash of one of the cars, though, so you're lucky I found it. Me too. I would have rushed off without it. I tell you, it's mad around here.'

Sophie's own mobile beeps. Someone is ringing her. Michael hears the brief break in transmission: 'That someone trying to get through?'

'I'll pick it up later. Listen, I thought I'd go in and see Brian for a bit at lunchtime. Do you want to come?'

'I can't, darling. As I said, with him out of action it's like a circus here. I'm just chasing my tail. Give him my best. Tell the old shagger I'll try to come in this evening after tea, or if not, definitely tomorrow.'

'Right.'

'Are you sure you're OK, Soph? You sound odd?'

'Do I? I don't mean to.' Sophie did not want to pursue this. 'I'm grand, truly. I'd better go too, actually, this is production week and, to put it mildly, I haven't pulled my weight.'

'Right, darling.' She can hear he has already mentally disengaged. 'See you this evening. I love you.'

'Love you.'

After they disconnect, she stares for several seconds at the small green trapezoid above the keypad of her telephone with its seductive italic lettering: *1 message received*. Whoever it is will have to wait.

CHAPTER SIX

Dublin is wearing widow's weeds. The tall lines of flagstaffs along both Quays of the Liffey carry leaden black rectangles; the tricolour droops at half-mast on the dome of the Four Courts, the civic offices and other public buildings. Even the traffic seems to move more slowly as these days of communal mourning continue to lie like deep grey ash over the normally rambunctious city streets.

It is almost too sad to bear and Sophie, who has to traverse the Quays on her way to work, is glad to get out of the more public parts of the city and into its pockets where, at its midpoint in the sky, the January sun penetrates like a laser into the tiny back-streets and alleys. As she and the Mini, like the old pals they are, chatter across the potholes, broken cobbles and half-repaired utility trenches that serve as thoroughfares around Arbour Hill, she is glad once again that the circulation of *Wild Places*, although steady and largely by subscription, is too small to support a move to a more upmarket location.

She has always loved this area, the rows of garage workshops and tiny one-man industries, the unthemed pubs and small, higgledy-piggledy shops, the efforts made to individualise the gardenless terraces of houses: here a startling, canary yellow canopy, there a window-box of polyanthus in unlikely Technicolor, or an elaborate window grille of wrought iron, totally inappropriate for these plain, flush façades of red brick but wonderful in its garish eccentricity. She has always been most comfortable in these unshowy parts of old Dublin where good taste is not yet a matter of conformity, where neighbours still know each other by name, and where you can still get a pint of milk on tick until you get paid on Friday.

Sophie has mixed feelings about the accelerating pace of change in Dublin. It is not so long ago that the name of Boots rang like an alien but tantalising cornucopia for people in the Republic, when Monsoon, Benetton and Marks & Spencer were the target of London and Belfast shopping trips. Although, like most people, she appreciates the new convenience, variety and cheapness on offer in Dublin streets and shopping malls, she misses the chat and the friendliness, the local knowledge that led the woman behind the shop counter to reach for what you wanted before you asked for it.

She does not bother to lock the car when she parks outside the peeling door of the magazine's two-room premises: the Mini is hardly worth a thief's time and, in any event, although there are signs of encroaching gentrification, the district has escaped, so far, the worst of the drug-related rash of robberies and burglaries infesting the adjacent but newly affluent areas such as Stoneybatter, Smithfield and the Blessington Basin. She gives the bonnet an affectionate pat as she crosses in front of it to go into the office. Time and again, both Michael and Brian, who always have something from the fleet to recycle, have urged her to trade up to a better vehicle but she has resisted. She loves the lawnmower sound of its engine, the round headlamps with their air of surprise, the high-pitched, tinny honk on the horn.

'Hello, Nancy.' She pushes open the door and greets the tiny woman sitting at a keyboard in the depths of the debris on what purports to be *Wild Places'* reception desk. Since she spends a lot of her time alone in the office, Nancy, who favours country and gospel music, has a free hand with the choice of radio station or tapes, and the current offering is a loud, joyful ditty affirming that Jesus Loves Us. Just as well, Sophie thinks, not for the first time, because only someone like Jesus could find His way around Nancy's domain, which resembles nothing so much as Dorothy's house in Kansas at the instant of encounter with the twister.

Nancy Madigan is of indeterminate age and resembles a peanut topped with aggressively permed fuzz. Her enthusiasm and unflappable good-humour make up for her lack of prowess in the business of filing and new technology, and are at odds with the drama with which she views her life. Everyone she knows is in permanent crisis – illness, death, divorce, illegitimacy, you name it, Nancy has the full details. An air crash is all her birthdays come at once, and on seeing Sophie she immediately turns off the music. 'Oh! Oh, my God, you poor thing – does it hurt very much?' She jumps up, scampers around the desk and throws her arms around Sophie's neck. 'God! Youse were so lucky!'

Sophie, who has had to bend to accommodate the hug, extricates herself and fingers her bruised face. 'It's not as bad as it looks, honestly.'

'Thank God.' Nancy bursts into tears. 'Thank God! I was down on me knees for yiz all thanking God youse were safe. All those other poor people – Lord have mercy on them.' She wipes her eyes with the backs of her hands. 'It's terrible – I don't think it's natural, this flying.' She glistens earnestly at Sophie, who, touched but somewhat alarmed, deflects the possibility of another hug by glancing away from the round red face towards the closed door of the editor's office. 'Is Imelda around?'

'Nah!' Nancy blows her nose thoroughly. 'Sorry about this blubbing. No, she's not here. Said she had to go to some meeting. C'mere.' Somewhat recovered, she turns back to the desk and starts to burrow through the hillocks of paper. 'Wait now, wait a minute – there's a million messages here for you somewhere. Hold on.' She turns back again. 'Are you sure you're all right? Are you up to it? Shouldn't you take a bit of leave or something?' She jerks a thumb towards the editor's door. 'She'll just have to get in a freelancer.'

'I'm fine, genuinely.' Sophie, shy by nature, hates the spotlight being turned so potently on her. 'So,' she forces a wide smile, 'these messages? Are any of them urgent?'

'Nah – a lot of sympathising, a few of the usual cranks and harpies . . . but there's one here somewhere you'll probably want to see. The twitchers are on. Something amazing on the Wexford Slobs, apparently – can't remember the name. A hoop or a hula or something.'

Sophie has no need to call the bird people. The *Irish Times* has already covered the sighting of a hoopoe in Wexford and, unless Imelda sanctions a trip down there, *Wild Places* would not have much to add. She'll simply add a line to her column.

She makes her way to the layout boards at the back of the office. *Wild Places* has not yet got to the stage of being composed on computer, although this technology is cheap and widely available. The magazine's editor, an eccentric, somewhat grumpy woman in her middle sixties, prefers to do things in the old-fashioned way.

Sophie examines one of her watercolours – of a pine marten balanced on a branch. It has been placed dead centre of a general piece on native Irish wildlife and she is pleased Imelda has captioned it with the animal's Irish name, *cat crainn*, literally, the cat of the tree. When she examines it closely, however, her work, as usual, disappoints her severely critical eye. Although she admits she has been partially successful in catching the alert, cat-like stance and general beauty of the animal, the dark brown fur is not sufficiently glossy, the white throat patch and lovely pale insides of the large ears not enough of a contrast. When she is challenged on all this self-criticism, as she is frequently by her husband and friends, she acknowledges that she sets impossibly high standards for herself.

She walks across to her desk, normally an island of order in the midst of the chaos but which has become in her absence a satellite to Nancy's. She sits, pulls a batch of the newspaper clippings, faxes and Internet pages towards her and starts to read: fears about an oil spillage threatening the Galapagos, reports of an archaeological dig suspended because of a threat to the habitat of an endangered moth . . .

Then a peculiar thing happens. As she tries to concentrate, the print blurs and swims before her eyes and what she can only describe as a buzz begins somewhere in her solar plexus. It is as though something tightly wound is unravelling noisily. What is worse, the imitation panelling nailed to the walls seems to advance towards her from all sides as though to crush her, as does the bouncy gospel music, restored to its original volume but now seeming to grow louder and louder . . . Something is spiralling out of control. This 'something' is a swelling, filling sensation, threatening to explode in her head. Sophie starts to sweat. Frightened, she extricates her desktop telephone from under a heap of the cuttings and punches out Michael's mobile number. His recorded voice cuts in immediately: 'This is Michael Dolan of EconoCar Hire. I am unavailable at present . . . please try our main number at . . .'

Sophie hangs up. Deadline or no deadline, she cannot stay here a moment longer. She looks across at Nancy, still searching and adding to the collecting of message slips she clutches in one chubby little hand. 'I just remembered—' She jumps up and makes for the door. 'Sorry, Nancy, tell Imelda I'll ring her.' Before the other woman has reacted, she is outside and has jumped into the Mini. She glances into the rear-view mirror just before she turns the corner at the end of the street and glimpses Nancy, framed in the doorway of the office, the sheaf of messages still in her hand, staring after her. Shocked she might be, but not as shocked as Sophie herself is by her behaviour.

Within a few minutes, not remembering by what route she got there or how long it took, she finds herself out of the car and running hard through a colonnade of bare horse-chestnuts set in parallel with one of the side roads in the Phoenix Park. Too soon, she reaches the end of the avenue and halts, leaning against one of the knobbly trunks. She is no athlete; her chest hurts and her lungs are on fire, so she has to lower her head, hands on knees, to catch her breath.

She first encountered this regal avenue as a child. Her parents had brought her, her brothers and Eily – who was treated in their family as a sort of surrogate extra child – to the zoo in the surrounding park, an exotic gem in the palm of a huge hand, as a Sunday or birthday treat. While the boys romped and did their secretive twin things together, and Eily's interest was excited by the strangeness and rarity of tigers, cheetahs and flamingos, Sophie tramped obediently round the cages and enclosures like the compliant little girl she was. She had never revealed that she hated the iron bars, the bare floors splintered by claws, the cavorting of sea-lions and penguins who performed for their supper, the endless head-shaking of the mangy polar bear, nor that her soft heart bled each time her eyes met the resigned gaze of a caged chimpanzee or the weary gorilla.

At least nowadays the zoo has developed and expanded so it more resembles 'native' habitat: for instance, the big cats can roam freely – or relatively freely – in grassy, bush-like territories with real trees on which to sharpen their claws. During the old days of relatively small cages, it was always a huge relief to her when, after their visit to the animals, they walked in the huge open spaces of the park where the squirrels were as free as the birds. Depending on the season, they went to admire the trim spring flowers and scalloped borders in the People's Park, to run up and down the wide, sloping steps of the Wellington Monument, to roll down the grassy hills near the Magazine Fort, or to tiptoe close to the herds of deer on the wide, windy ranges of the Fifteen Acres.

Sophie's favourite season was late in the year, October usually, when all the trees had turned and the park seemed on fire. This relatively secluded area, where she is now, with these particular chestnuts, has always been her favourite. While her parents strolled, or sat chatting on the benches, and the twins and Eily threw sticks to dislodge conkers, Sophie kept herself a little apart, listening to the way these giants whispered to one another about love affairs begun or plots hatched within their cloister.

After a few moments she sits on a bench nearby and looks at the ground so as not to encounter the curious eyes of the elderly man towing an overweight, wheezing boxer dog along the footpath in front of her.

She waits.

Then, when the man and his dog are well clear, she tests. That frightening, rubbery, unwinding sensation has subsided. She looks at her watch. She had said she would drop in to see Brian . . .

Quickly, she pulls the mobile from the pocket of her jeans, turns it on and dials Michael's number, but, once more, his electronic voice clicks in. She disconnects and the screen reminds her of the message, but she puts off listening to it. She gets up and walks back at a normal pace towards where she has parked the Mini. Before she reaches the car the mobile, still in her hand, chirps. She looks at the caller display. It is the office. She punches. 'Hello?'

'Sophie!' The editor's voice is brisk. 'Glad to hear you're on the mend. You didn't get my message earlier?'

'Sorry, Imelda.'

'Not to worry. I'm delighted to hear you're out and about. Best thing for you. Well done – it's a terrible business. Now, do you think you'll be able to come in this afternoon? We need to have a staff meeting.'

'Oh – sure.' Sophie is astonished. In all the years she has worked for the magazine, she has attended perhaps three formal meetings. She knows better, though, than to quiz her boss. 'Sure,' she says again.

'Around three? That'd suit?'

'Sure.'

As they disconnect she is perplexed. Meetings are not Imelda's style. One talks as necessary about articles and layout, one does one's work as one is hired to do it. Everyone – staff, contributors, twitchers, mammalians, flora and fauna enthusiasts, insect and fish people – within the eclectic circle connected to *Wild Places* knows exactly what they have to do and when.

The three-person hierarchy is simple. Nancy is the factotum. Sophie, one step up, collates wildlife news from all sources and assembles it into a long, round-up column, spreading over several pages, which serves as the heart of the publication and is the reason most subscribers continue to send in their annual or quarterly cheques; she takes photographs, or draws and paints her illustrations. Then there is Imelda, who sifts through the contributions – commissioned, regular and unsolicited – lays out the magazine to a format that hasn't changed in decades, negotiates with printers and advertisers, pays bills. Imelda's decisions are quick and final. *Wild Places* has appeared on the first Monday of each month for the past twenty-four years. The deadline is four o'clock on the Tuesday before that. End of story.

With such a simple structure, Imelda can rarely see the point of a meeting. To her, meetings are time-wasting exercises designed to make people feel important about themselves and enabling them to put off the real work. Today, however, if Nancy's take on the story is to be believed, she is having two meetings within the space of a few hours. What on earth is up?

Sophie tucks the phenomenon into the back of her mind. She will deal with it when she has to, at five minutes to three when she is walking back into the office. She has had enough agitation so far today to last her several months.

Her self-criticism does not go hand in hand with ambition: she recognises that she should probably have moved on long ago from the fusty environs of *Wild Places*, and feels vaguely guilty from time to time about her sloth. If she was any kind of a decent journalist, she should be longing for a way to exercise her brain and her professional skills. What fuels the good journalist is wildfire curiosity, a trait in which she was born deficient.

She is not even a proper wildlife enthusiast; if she was, she would be jumping out of her bed every day before sunrise, tramping through muddy fields to hear the dawn chorus, to catch the perfect shot of a feeding hare or of a bloody-jawed vixen slinking home. Instead, she rolls over on her mattress.

Although she knows she could do a lot better if she tried, she has been contented to clip along exactly as she is. To work at *Wild Places* is to lead a peaceful life filled with small satisfactions.

Or it was until the air crash, when everything tipped askew and, so far, has not righted itself.

According to its official website, the Phoenix Park – the clear eye in the head of Dublin city – is 'a centre for pastoral recreation and learning, Gaelic football, sport, polo, cricket and concerts, 1,752 acres of wilderness and landscape gardens'.

Less than a mile from where Sophie is letting herself into her Mini, 'pastoral recreation' is going on in the hidden, shrubby byway near the Ashtown Gate where her husband and one of his EconoCar co-workers are hard at it in the undergrowth.

Joined together in unconnubial physical bliss, Michael Dolan and Yvonne Leonard, an exuberant, lush twenty-year-old, whose philosophy embraces concepts such as *I'm Worth It!* Or *Just Do It!* are reaching the climax, so to speak, of today's event. Or, at least, he is. Yvonne is not all that bothered today and, if the truth be told, is only going through the motions. Today's coupling feels to her like an extension of a visit to the gym. A grand bit of exercise but with a few illicit thrills thrown in. She wishes he'd hurry up, actually, because even though there's a bit of sunshine trickling through the tangle of branches above their heads, her bare knees are freezing.

She and Mick have been having it off for about three months now. She had set her cap at him as soon as she saw him the previous September when she joined the company as a reservations clerk. After a period of delicious flirting, private looks and tingling *double-entendres* – the best part of any affair really, Yvonne thinks – they got it together after a night in the pub. She knows it is not going to last for ever and she is already getting a little tired of coming here to this bloody uncomfortable – and cold – *forest*, for God's sake. Mick insists it's not safe to go to a hotel because the tourist industry is peppered with people he knows.

Yet even though his repertoire begins and ends with the missionary position, the sex is still moderately exciting, and while it lasts, well, what the heck? He's a good-looking guy, he's good at it – as far as he takes it – and he knows the score. If there's any messing, though, for instance if he gets serious or if the wife gets involved – *Jesus wept!* – Yvonne is out of here like the clappers. In the meantime, *carpe diem* and all of that, as Robin Williams might say. Yvonne and her friend Collette just love those feel-good videos.

Yeah, Mick is all right. Pity he's married. Yvonne has found herself wondering recently what he's like at home with his wife.

Like, a few times lately, she has found herself playing with fire by dialling his home number late at night. Only if she has nothing much else to do, of course. Just to hear him answer. Because even when he does answer, she hangs up immediately.

If he sounds sleepy or detached when he says hello, she starts wondering if he and the wife are at it.

Don't go there, Y! Don't go getting mushy. This is what it is and that's that. A bit of gas.

Was that *carpe diem* thing in *Good Morning Vietnam* or was it *Mrs Doubtfire*? While she is giving her lover little encouraging pats and ear-bites, Yvonne amuses herself by trying to remember.

If their boss could see them now! It doesn't hurt that this is one in the eye for that stuffy Brian McMullan. As Mick pumps and groans and gasps, Yvonne's smile widens. That fella doesn't know what end of him is up. He never even comes to the pub. He should learn to live a little.

At an early stage she had toyed with the idea of a foursome, to include her friend, Collette – who thinks Brian is quite a piece of stuff – seeing it as harmless fun for all of them. She even threw out feelers, casually suggesting that, for a bit of craic, they all go to one of the new lap-dancing clubs some night. Brian hadn't copped on. He had frowned at her like she had two heads. 'Oh I don't think my wife would go along with that.' What a dweeb!

Hey! No. It wasn't *Mrs Doubtfire* – she gives Mick an extra-special jolt from her thrusting pelvis and squeezes hard. She has it. It was *Dead Poet's Society*.

'Ah – ah – ah – ah – aaaaa-hhh!' Fearful of attracting attention, Michael, unaware of the small triumph of memory achieved beneath him, cuts off the last 'aah' as best he can. He allows himself a few moments of feeling good, then kisses Yvonne appreciatively. Her eyes are still closed, the gorgeous little poppet, but she is smiling that smile of satisfaction he has grown to know. No need to ask how it was for her. 'God, that felt good,' he breathes into her ear. 'You're brilliant, do you know that?'

Yvonne nods a little. 'Don't I know it!' She raises an arm, checks her watch. 'We'd better be getting back, hon.'

Michael lifts himself off her and adjusts his clothing. They always carry with them a roll of kitchen towel, to deal with the messier side of the business, and both set to work with quiet efficiency. They have it down to a fine art, actually. The only thing that bothers him is that someone else will discover this little glade and they'll have to look for another location. Mindful of this, he takes a different car on each occasion and parks it in various places and at different distances so it won't act as a signpost.

Yvonne's present dump of a flat is out. He's been there once or twice, but she never puts out for him there because the walls are paper thin and her room is next to that of the landlady, a shrew who prides herself on renting only to respectable people and who would evict in a minute if she suspected any hanky-panky.

'How's your wife bearing up after that awful crash?' Yvonne, whose cloud of blonde hair has already been combed and teased back into the tousled *Charlie's Angels'* style she favours, is looking at her reflection in a powder-compact mirror while reapplying her lipstick.

'She's good. Amazing, actually.' Michael's admiration is genuine. 'To tell you the truth, I wouldn't have thought she had it in her to be so strong.'

'Makes me feel funny in a way, you know, us like this and all.' Yvonne slips the compact into the pocket of her down-filled body-warmer.

Like an uncle, Michael leans forward and kisses her forehead. 'Don't you be worrying yourself. It's me should be thinking things like that. You're far too young.'

She smiles absently at him. 'Come on, we'd better get back before we're missed. Some day we're going to be caught – you know that, Mick?'

'I don't see why. We're very careful.' He takes a last look round to make sure they have left none of their belongings behind and kisses her again. 'Back to the mill.'

As they walk to the car, his mind is conducting a small survey. As far as he is concerned, there is no reason why this can't go on for ever, or at least until it doesn't suit one or other of them any more. No one is getting hurt – Sophie would never suspect, never mind find out – and the business of EconoCar is under no threat. They are entitled to a lunch hour. Everyone is entitled to a lunch hour.

Actually, they're doing the company a favour. The work-experience kid they've taken on for a couple of weeks is getting good experience, isn't she? He keeps forgetting the girl's bloody name. She is a bit of a looker, too.

For now, Michael is happy enough with what he's got. Good old Yvonne – she's such a little goer, isn't she?

CHAPTER SEVEN

S itting by Zelda's bed Riba, careful not to wake her, gently arranges the tendrils of fluff, all that remains of her daughter's mass of curls. 'For the moment, darling,' she whispers tenderly. 'It'll all grow back very soon.' She covers the girl's bony shoulder with the coarse sheet, recoiling a little from the heavy pong of detergent that, like spores, seems to invade the most sensitive parts of her nose.

She pauses, caught by Zelda's beauty. The bluish skin of her face and neck is as smooth and unblemished as new satin, the pale mouth is still full, the dainty tracery of veins in the eyelids could have been drawn by a precise watercolourist. She swallows hard, forcing the constriction in her throat to yield. If anything was to happen to her . . .

Firmly, she blinks back the tears and settles against the hard, high back of the hospital-issue chair, just waiting and looking. Everything is going to be grand.

She is itching to get her hands on this room. They do their best, of course – the walls have been painted in a pale peachy colour and the curtains at the window are sprigged with lavender – but the sick need candles and incense and comforting, sensual objects around them to help them get well. Here, however, they prefer that you don't bring in this kind of thing, not even flowers. Zelda's condition, they say, requires sterility and rigid control of everything in her immediate environment.

For once, Riba has acquiesced without a battle. She cannot wait, however, to get her into more holistically healing surroundings.

At one stage, the medics in this hospital had broached the subject of moving Zelda to a hospice. Riba had kicked up blue bloody murder. Although, to be fair, she has heard nothing but good things about both Our Lady's in Harold's Cross and St Francis's in Raheny, this is not an option, never will be, no, no, no. Imagine! Even if the time ever came when Zelda needed that kind of care – and Riba does not concede that – she would certainly *not* put her into a place surrounded by dying people.

While she watches her daughter sleep, her mind wanders back over the earlier scene in the kitchen with her son. She is contrite now. Taking the phone off the hook so soon after the accident maybe hadn't been such a good idea.

How could she have known?

In her defence, she had had enough of the urgent parade of reporters and well-wishers and sympathisers, everyone agog for first-hand information and all the gory details. *It must have been awful – can you remember much? What happened – how much could you see? How did it happen? Any news about the investigation yet? Are you going to sue?* It should be perfectly understandable why anyone would take the blasted yoke off the hook to get a little relief from that kind of stress.

When the investigation officials come calling to record her account, she will be truthful and no more. No histrionics. Her considered and deeply held view is: what does it matter how it happened? It happened, didn't it? There is no going back from that so what is the point of digging endlessly through the terrible details?

After all, what can she tell them? Two loud bangs, a brief sideways flight through suddenly frigid air, and that's all she knows because after that she was buried up to her neck. Then she was pulled out and brought by ambulance to a hospital.

So, for the moment, let others feed the insatiable media with what grim details they feel they need to share. Riba is biding her time. She will speak out about the real story, the story of the miracles, when the time is right, when all the distress and headlines have abated and people might be a little more receptive.

As for suing and investigations and horrible insurance companies, she is going to leave that kind of hassle to Brian as she always does. The corners of her mouth turn down with distaste. All right, the time will come when the subject of compensation and claims will have to be faced but she is going to do her damndedest to stay above the more sordid side. Brian, who of course will have claims of his own, can do all that for both of them. She'll sign anything she's asked to sign and that will be the extent of it.

She is determined to look after herself properly and so far, she thinks, she has done a pretty good job of it.

She admits, however, that she should have given more thought, more attention to Donny. On top of the shock of what had happened to every member of his family, his upset about his teacher, whom Riba had never met, is deep and genuine.

He was so terrific in the hospital, wasn't he? So manly. The reality of the whole thing is probably only now dawning on the poor kid.

Now that she is examining things, she can see how seriously he has been acting up since Zelda's illness was diagnosed. Riba has to acknowledge that, in the general run of things, poor old Donny hasn't had much of a look-in lately. Yes, she really will have to pay him some quality attention. For now, though, all she can do for him is to listen and maybe perform small services. For instance, she'll make him a nice sandwich and a cup of coffee when she gets home and the two of them will head off together to see Brian.

That'll be great for both of them, as a matter of fact. Brian probably won't be able to resist having a go at her for taking Zelda on the plane but he won't want to look too unreasonable in his son's eyes.

Behind the locked door of his room, Donny is lying on his bed and staring at the ceiling. He does not have the heart even to turn on his stereo. With the exception of one or two small outbursts, such as happened downstairs earlier, he and his room have been silent since the crash.

Donny does not talk much at home. He certainly doesn't show his hand – at least, he hasn't since the onset of his own adolescence collided with the discovery of Zelda's illness and all adult attention swung to focus on her. Nowadays, when he emerges from his room, he tends to go about the house in a simmering, silent fug of grudge. Or that is how he knows he is perceived and he doesn't give a fuck.

In reality, he is desperate. While he has never admitted this to a soul, he has loved and admired his beautiful and academically brilliant sister since he could toddle. Although he wants to be like her in every respect, and despairs of his inadequacies, he has rowed back in every area, afraid to compete in case he fails. It was too much of a risk to aspire to her 525 points in the Leaving Cert, so he simply stopped trying and is slipping further and further towards the bottom of the academic league in his class.

In fact, his high-octane family has been a long-term trial for Donny, who was born quiet. As soon as he was old enough to think about such things, he felt he had arrived as a sort of appendix, that his strong-willed, volatile parents had been perfectly happy with one gorgeous daughter and would have been just as pleased if he hadn't made his unexpected appearance. As he was never demanding or prone to tantrums, he was left to fend for himself a lot of the time, building dream castles with his Lego then graduating to Meccano and now spending hour after hour locked into his room trawling through the Internet or playing computer games.

His parents love and care for him, he knows that – and materially he has been deprived of nothing – but the love is somehow absent-minded and the care automatic, especially since his mother started down this stupid, so-called Path of hers seven years ago and the rumblings and hissings began between her and his dad. Donny always slams around a bit when he hears them – to show them he's there – but they never seem to notice.

His father tried hard, finding the fees to place him in a rugby-playing school and concealing his disappointment when Donny (deliberately) flunked out of the school sports teams. As for his mother, there are a lot of reassuring endearments – 'Are you all right, my beautiful, darling son? You know your Mamma loves you very much, don't you?' – that sort of thing, but Donny recognises scornfully that even when she is at her most fulsome, his mother is away in her own head.

The awful thing is, he loves her too. Even in the middle of a row, when she is at her most infuriating and he feels like throttling her, something in the middle of his chest seems to bleed with love.

He dealt with all of this well enough until Zelda was hospitalised for the first time when he was just thirteen and his hormones went into riot.

Then the crash happened.

Some of that day is a blur but the rest is so vivid and real that it still shocks him. Somehow, Kevin Spacey and that girl covered in red roses have become part of it. Red, like blood.

All right, he admits it, he was seriously emotional for a few hours that day, especially when he heard from his dad and thought his mother and Zelda might be dead. He might have become an orphan and had to go in to a home.

That was just a blip, of course: he's not emotional any more. He is angry, though. For some reason, the fact that everyone turned out to be OK doesn't make him feel lucky, only furious – at them. He can't figure out why this should be.

Actually, he doesn't want to know why. Being angry with them, especially with his mother, is easier to deal with and feels better than trying to understand other stuff.

Like, he has every right to be livid with her, certainly at the moment. As if it isn't bad enough that she turns up at the parent-teacher meetings looking like something out of *Star Trek*, or that she says and does these totally mental things like taking telephones off hooks. The main thing that's bugging him today is that here he is different from everyone else once again, one of the only two frigging kids in the whole school, probably, who is not at the funeral.

At least there is one person on the planet who understands and that's Trevor. Trev's mother is a drip too, Trevor says, but Donny can't really see it. She's boring all right but, on balance, Donny would prefer to be living with the colourless Jamesons than here in this house of horrors. They'd leave him alone at least and wouldn't be looking at him all the time and asking if he's all right.

All right? What does she expect? He just walks out of the room when his mother starts that.

He springs off the bed and turns on the stereo. Loud.

Then he doesn't know what to do next so he flops back again.

Until the air crash, his remedy for everything had been to bury himself in his headphones, but over the last few days everything has seemed different. More Technicolored, like Kevin Spacey's hallucinations in *American Beauty* – only Donny's hallucinations aren't delicious, they're mental.

Listlessly, he pulls the duvet out from under him and, shoes and all, wriggles under it, tucking it in above his ears and allowing only the tip of his nose, his eyes and the poll of his head to show themselves to the world. He feels something burning and pushing behind his eyes and the bridge of his nose. Under no circumstances will he cry.

Brian's eyes widen with delight when the door of his hospital room opens to admit Sophie, who hesitates on seeing that a doctor is with him. 'Oh! Sorry – I'll come back.'

Irrationally fearful that she will vanish, he calls out to her: 'No – Sophie! Come on in!' He pulls himself up on his pillows, wincing at the sudden pain that strikes under his ribcage. 'We're just finished, aren't we, Doc?'

'Yes.' The doctor, who is Asian, smiles sweetly. 'This is one of my success stories,' she says, encompassing both patient and visitor. 'He is wonderfully well! He is constructed like a Sherman tank!' There follows one of those little gavottes in which one person relinquishes control of a space while the other waits to claim it. The doctor leaves, closing the door softly behind her.

'I didn't know what to bring in to you.'

As Sophie sits in the chair by the bed, Brian becomes conscious that she won't meet his eyes. Something odd has happened between them and for him it happened less than a minute ago when she pushed open the door and faltered on the threshold. Since the crash, he has been so caught up in worry about his family, particularly Zelda, that it was not until he saw her that he recognised how distressed he would have been had anything happened to Sophie. He can't sort this out while she's here, though, can he?

He tunes in and realises she is gabbling. '. . . so that's a lie – I didn't try

to get you a thing, so here I am with one arm as long as the other. Sorry.
I don't know which way of me is up at the moment – as a matter of fact,
I can't stay long. My boss has called a meeting, would you believe? Must
be serious. We haven't had a meeting in that place since old God's time.
And I've the whole column to do – how are you?'

This verbal spewing is unlike her. 'How am I?' He stares at her for a
second, then grins. 'That doctor's right. I'm a complete bloody sham,
taking up a bed in a hospital when there are so many more deserving
cases. They say I'll probably be able to go home on Saturday at lunchtime.'

'Good. That's great.' Sophie nods vigorously. 'Eily will be delighted. I'm
sure she misses you terribly.'

'Yeah.' Brian's feelings about Eily are mixed at present, to say the least.
'Listen,' again he pulls himself up. 'I get reports about Zelda and I've talked
to her on the phone, but how is she really? I'm going mad because I can't
see her for myself. I'd trust your judgement, Soph.'

'I haven't been in.' Sophie looks chagrined. 'Sorry. I've been sort of
caught up in my own stupid little life.'

'Don't say that.'

There is an awkward pause as neither seems able to find a way to
continue. Eventually Sophie, speaking quickly and loudly, tells him that
she believes Eily. 'Honestly, I really do this time. Apparently Zelda didn't
have even a mark on her.'

'I can't stop thinking about her.'

Although this is true, although a great deal of his waking moments have
been concerned with his daughter, he can't take his eyes off Sophie now.
She looks so adorable, all dressed in white. 'You really do look great,
Sophie,' he says warmly. 'Eily told me about those bruises on your face,
but you don't look half as bad as I imagined.'

'You should see it from my side!' Despite the light tone, she surprises
him by getting up abruptly and walking to the window, although the drab
street outside is hardly inspiring. 'Nice room,' she says, without turning
round. 'Is the food good?'

'It ought to be at the prices they charge.' Brian is aware of the tension
between them as, still with her back to him, she carries on as though she
has not heard him.

'I was thinking earlier that I should probably go to the service in the
Pro-Cathedral on Sunday for the victims. I couldn't bear to go to any of
the individual funerals.'

'Oh, no.' Brian, who has been glued to the news bulletins on radio and
television and who keeps reliving the events of the crash, is appalled at the
suggestion that she – or he – might consider going to the gravesides of

those who were killed while he survived. 'Nobody would expect you to, Sophie,' he says quietly. 'It's tragic, of course, but we didn't know any of them.'

'I can't help feeling guilty, though.' Now she turns round.

'Me too.' Brian drops his eyes.

Sophie can have no idea just how guilty he feels – about not being firmer, about not putting his foot down to prevent his wife and daughter taking that fatal flight. If he hadn't been such a wimp, none of the people he loved would be in this situation. Sophie wouldn't have been with him at that perimeter fence.

He looks up at her. 'I'll be out at the weekend, as I said, and, on reflection, you're right. I should probably go to that service too. We should all go, I'll have a word with Eily.' *Lots of luck with Eily*, he thinks, but does not share this. 'How about Mick?'

'I don't know. I'll ask him.' She comes back to sit again at his bedside and pulls off her hat, shaking out her hair.

He has always liked Sophie's hair, always so shiny, like a baby's, newly washed. In fact, he has always admired her casual, almost careless attitude to her looks and grooming. Unlike his wife's. The bathroom after Eily's lengthy ablutions, he thinks darkly, must resemble a Turkish brothel, such is the overpowering smell of perfumes, lotions and scented candles.

He realises that Sophie is staring at him. 'Too much time on my hands, Soph,' he forces himself to sound light-hearted, 'too much thinking. The sooner I get out of here the better because the whole thing keeps going round and round in my head like a repeating horror movie.'

'Me too.'

Through the thick wooden door they can hear the clink of glasses or crockery being wheeled past. To fill another silence in the room, Brian begins to chitter-chatter and hears himself going on about his wife. 'According to her, I'm to look forward to the arrival of Frankenstein's monster. I'm not to say anything, no matter how mutilated I think she looks. She's an extraordinary woman,' he adds, meaning this in many ways.

'Indeed she is.' Sophie chooses the most benign interpretation. 'When they made your Eily, they threw the mould away – but what would we do for entertainment without her?'

They laugh their affection for Brian's wife, easing the pressure between them. However, as the banter about Eily's personal traits continues, Brian begins to feel uncomfortable and again they run out of things to say. 'I know we said we shouldn't talk about it,' he says quietly, 'but I can't stop thinking about all those coffins, all those funerals and bodies and tears. That's really why I feel like such a fraud. Why them and not me? I swing between feeling like the luckiest guy on earth and the most undeserving.'

'I know what you mean. I've been going through that a bit myself.'

Then this conversation fails too.

Brian faces up to it. 'Look, Sophie, we have to talk.' Then, as Sophie drops her gaze to the floor, 'She hasn't said it directly, but I know by the way she is behaving that she's still determined to go. To put Zelda through it all again.'

'Well, she hasn't mentioned it to me.' Sophie raises her eyes, then says, 'You know Eily would give her last breath for Zelda. Please, Brian, you know she wouldn't do anything to harm her – she's always had Zelda's best interests at heart.'

He had assumed her to be an ally, and is taken aback by her vehemence. 'I know that,' he says, slowly and carefully. 'I accept that. Why are you defending her like this? In your heart you know as well as I do that she is, to put it charitably, misguided. You talk about Zelda's best interests. Do you not think I have her best interests at heart?'

'Of course I do – of course—' She falters. 'I didn't mean—'

'Where Eily and I differ,' he interrupts, his desperation rising, 'is in the definition of Zelda's best interests. I think – or at least I did think – that you're with me on this, Sophie.' It is against his nature to plead or to beg, but he begs now: 'Please, Sophie. Please. My only daughter is dying. She is my flesh. I can't explain it to you, but in the deepest part of me I need some time with her, as much as is left. Can we work together on this to keep her away from that fucker in the Caribbean?'

Sophie stares back at him. 'This is so unfair,' she says softly. 'You're asking me to collude with you against my best friend. You're asking me to choose between my friendship with you and my friendship with her.'

'Someone has to talk sense into her. She won't listen to me – please—' He breaks off as the door opens and Eily comes in to the room.

Sophie instantly leaps from her chair. 'Eil– Riba! Here, take this seat – hi, Donny!' She smiles brightly as the boy mooches in behind his mother.

'Sophie! You're here.' Then Eily turns to him. 'Hello, darling. My God, aren't you a lovely sight?' She crosses to the bed, plants a lingering kiss on his cheek, then sits beside him with one arm around his shoulders, overpowering him with Chanel No. 5.

Brian, obscurely embarrassed, looks away from her to his son, who has turned towards the window and is already hitting buttons on his Gameboy. 'Howdy, sport.'

'Hi, Dad.' Donny does not look up. 'Can I have money for a Coke?'

'Of course, darling.' Eily unclasps her handbag and takes out her purse. As Donny grabs the proffered fiver and makes his escape, Brian is upset to see Sophie glance at her watch: 'Actually, if you don't mind, I'd better be getting back to the office. I only dropped in for a minute and you two have a lot to catch up on.'

'But you've only just got here.' He pushes himself higher on the pillows, wincing again.

Sophie picks up her hat from the bed. 'I know.' Her tone is brisk. 'I'll come in again very soon, I promise, although if you're getting out on Saturday . . .' She leans over to peck him on the cheek, then says to Eily, 'I owe this husband of yours a lot, you know – if it hadn't been for him I'd be just a happy memory to you all.' Crab-like, she edges towards the door and it's clear to Brian now that she can't wait to get out. She opens the door, but then pauses. 'I forgot to ask you, Eil– Riba, how's Zelda? Did you go to see her?'

Brian sees his wife's face soften. 'She was asleep and I didn't want to wake her, but that's the best thing for her now. She needs as much sleep as she can get. It's a great doctor.'

'Did you talk to any of the real doctors?' He can't prevent the edge creeping into his voice. Sophie reacts by pulling her hat hard down over her eyes, but his wife does not seem to notice.

'No, not this morning. But I did see some of the nurses and they're pleased with her.' She moves to the chair vacated by Sophie, sits in it and folds her hands in her lap, looking from one to the other. 'They're feeding her as much as she'll take, day or night. As a matter of fact, I gave them a pack of the liver formula. Jay recommends it.'

For an instant the room seems to shrink-wrap itself.

Sophie blows them both a quick kiss. 'That's great, Riba,' she says. Then, 'I'll leave you two to chat. I've a lot to do, as you can imagine, and I'm not finding it that easy to concentrate.'

'See you soon again, I hope.' Brian lifts a hand to wave. 'Yes, see you, Soph.' Eily, too, waves but Sophie has already vanished.

As she hurries down the corridor to punch the lift buttons, Sophie feels like Brutus caught red-handed by Caesar before the Ides of March.

Just as the crash seemed to have stirred up the sludge at the bottom of her soul, conversation between herself and Brian had felt weird, disconnected: it was as though a barrage of words had risen into the air between them and drifted back to earth in any old order like a shower of confetti.

This has got to stop, right here and now, whatever it is. What age is she, for God's sake? How long has she known this man – *and this man's wife*? What about their daughter, her goddaughter, poor darling Zelda?

She will have nothing more to do with any discussions about trips or no trips. They have to work it out between them.

Yet that isn't the only thing that is bothering Sophie: there is something else, even deeper and darker. By referring to Zelda in the way he had, flesh of his flesh or whatever he had said, Brian had exposed Sophie's most secret agonies. For she has longed for children, for a child, singular.

She and Michael had tried for years. They went through the indignity of the examinations, probings and tests; they were told that nothing was physically wrong and were sent home to try again. Adoption was out, because Michael wouldn't hear of it. He had been through enough psychology, he said, and would not countenance any of the personal shit potential adopters had to expose to social workers while so many shysters and morons who are obviously not fit for parenthood are allowed to carry on procreating regardless.

For a while she had tried to fight him, but then, little by little, lost heart until the longing was tamed and locked away. It seemed Michael hadn't cared all that much, really, but to Sophie, his casual relinquishing of the dream was the end of a passionate relationship and the beginning of a polite one. At this point, she could not say one way or the other how her husband feels about children.

From her perspective, Michael's insensitivity to her feelings of loss, and intermittent jealousy of Brian and Eily, increased her sense of distance from him. She certainly now believes he would not understand her inward rage at Eily's seeming carelessness with the gifts of her daughter and son, at her placing of Street on a pedestal far above theirs – at least until Zelda's illness. In Sophie's opinion, her friend should have been casting around for all means to serve them; she should be on her knees day and night thanking God for them. If Zelda and Donny were Sophie's children, she would be as vigilant and protective with them as a lioness is with her cubs.

The lift deposits her in the plush, hushed lobby of the hospital and she almost runs through it, welcoming the dampness of the grey air of Eccles Street when she gets outside. When she reaches the car, she sits in it without engaging with the traffic warden who, ticket pad at the ready, is leaning over the Mini's bonnet to examine the tax disc on the windscreen.

Sophie zooms off, leaving the frowning woman staring after her.

Any distraction is welcome. She has swum alongside Brian, Eily and their children in shallow waters for years, but since the crash they are all floundering around with nowhere safe to place their feet.

Except Eily, of course. Eily's feet, despite the traumas she has undergone – and is still going through with Zelda – seem to rest immovably on a thick continental shelf of certainty.

★   ★   ★

For a moment or two after Sophie's departure, Riba and her husband continue to gaze intently at the mahogany veneer of the door as though expecting it to reveal the Fourth Secret of Fatima.

Brian's tone is determinedly upbeat: 'You look well, Eily, much better than I expected.'

Riba, pleased by the compliment, smooths the sleeve of her shantung jacket. 'What did you expect?'

Brian shrugs. 'I dunno – maybe a mummy? Bandages top to toe? You look good, Eily, that colour suits you.'

'I've seen enough bandages to last me a lifetime.' She shudders a little at the memory but agrees with his assessment. Today, to divert attention from the bruising on her face, she has made a special effort. Her top is a deep shade of red under a jacket in toning pink and with her straight dark hair, sallow skin and magnificent breasts, her reflection had reassured her. In fact, no bad thing: she might have emerged from a fortune-teller's caravan or wandered into the hospital from a souk.

She leans forward to allow him full view of her womanliness. 'Let's talk about you. How are you?'

His expression is opaque. 'I'm fine. Actually, I could just as easily be at home. I feel I'm here under false pretences.'

'Oh, for God's sake, we pay squillions to the VHI. What's the use of health insurance if you can't avail yourself of it?' She tosses her mane, conscious that Brian is studying her. His tone changes as he asks her, in a soft voice, 'just as a matter of interest', why she has not been in before to visit him. 'What's the real reason, Eily?'

Riba raises her chin. 'I'm here now, amn't I? And we've spoken lots on the telephone.'

'Eily . . .' He attempts to prop himself on an elbow.

She seems to sense what he is at and cuts him short: 'Don't spoil things.' She stands up and walks across to the television, placed high on a wall bracket. 'Anything on?' She looks around for a newspaper.

Brian glances at his watch, a Seiko, which, remarkably, had not missed a tick during or after the accident. 'The news.'

'There's got to be something better. Let's see . . .' She picks up the remote control and flicks through the soaps, chat shows, cartoons and business channels, pausing as she comes upon a grainy black and white film on BBC 2. 'Ooh! *Duck Soup!*' She is delighted. 'The Marx Brothers! There, now, what did I tell you? You like the Marx Brothers, don't you?'

She glances over her shoulder: Brian is back among his pillows, his eyes closed. 'Whatever you say.'

Riba returns to her chair and picks up his hand, which is lying listlessly on the counterpane. He does not resist as she warms it between her own, then, eyes raised to the television and chuckling at the slapstick, starts gently to massage it.

This is how Donny finds them when, sucking his drink, he comes back into the room. Riba continues massaging but smiles widely. 'Hello, sweetheart, everything all right? You found the cafeteria, I see.'

'Vending machine. Here's your change.' Donny throws a fistful of coins on the bed-covers and while his mother gathers it up, glances anxiously at his father. 'Hi, Dad. You OK? Want some of this?' He holds out the drinks can.

'I'm fine, sport. Thanks.' Brian pulls his hand from Riba's and reaches for the can. He sips, then hands it back to his son. 'I've been seriously lucky, and so has your aunt Sophie – but you know that.'

'Yeah,' Donny mutters. He places his drink on the window-sill, then stabs again at the buttons on his Gameboy. He quickly loses interest in it, however, and joins his parents in gazing upwards at the crackle-glazed print of the Marx Brothers film on the television.

Riba reaches again for Brian's hand but he has tucked it under the covers.

CHAPTER EIGHT

Contrary to her best intentions to enter the office casually at two fifty-five, Sophie's curiosity gets the better of her. She has dawdled as long as possible over coffee and a sandwich in one of the local pubs, but she arrives just after half past two and finds Nancy agog: 'They're in there with her. They arrived a few minutes ago.'

'Who's in there?'

'I don't know. They didn't say. Two men. She was out here waiting for them and they just went straight in – and wait till you see her!'

'What do you mean?'

'Just wait. I won't spoil the surprise.' Nancy's stout little body quivers with drama.

Sophie is alarmed now. A meeting to include both herself and Nancy? This is so far off the map of Imelda's normal behaviour that it has to be something very serious. Are they about to lose their jobs? At the back of her mind, she has always wondered how the little magazine survives. At one pound fifty a copy, with the same loyal, but small-time advertisers month after month, it has to be a pretty precarious operation. Her own salary is buttons but, as they inherited their shabby little house, she and Michael have no mortgage and small outgoings so it suits her to work as she does, at her own pace, at something she likes. What is she going to do if *Wild Places* folds? Collating and illustrating articles on beetles, shrews and robins is a slow burner where mainstream journalism is concerned and almost everyone else in the field has a much higher profile.

As for any other job, at her age and having led such a sheltered life, she has no appetite for competing with the thrusting, super-confident cubs of Ireland's roaring economy.

Like a danger signal, her bruised face starts to hurt as three o'clock comes and goes with no sign of the editor. 'She said three, she really did.' Nancy begins to pace. 'She did say three to you, Sophie, didn't she?' Unmarried and with a demanding, semi-invalid mother to support, she needs this job far more than Sophie needs hers. What would she do? Who nowadays hires a sixty-year-old woman? And where else but at *Wild Places* would her idiosyncratic approach to office work be tolerated?

'Oh, you're here, Sophie. Good! You too, Nancy.'

Both women turn towards the editor's office as the door opens and Imelda appears.

Sophie stares openly. Nancy's earlier heralding has not been misplaced. Their boss looks flushed, flustered and quite upset which, for someone so self-contained, is unusual. More overtly startling, however, are the bright pink lipstick and the viscose floral two-piece into which Imelda has belted her spare, angular frame. Her iron-grey hair, which has always flared around her features like a frizzy corona, has been gelled to her head under a girlish Alice band. 'Come on in.' Unaware of the effect her get-up is having on her staff, she turns and walks back into the office.

'Well, I did warn you.' Nancy's nervous grin is catching and Sophie grins back: they are in this together and whatever will be, will be.

Followed closely by Nancy, she walks through to the inner office, to find her boss standing behind her big, battered partner's desk, the gelled hair glinting in the light coming from the fly-specked window behind her.

The room smells as though someone has just showered: there is a strong whiff of expensive male cologne. Across from Imelda sit the source: two accountants in their mid-thirties perhaps, one wearing a softly draped suit over a black T-shirt, the other in sharply pressed designer jeans and a blisteringly white sweat top, which does not conceal the roll of spare flesh across his midriff. Imelda sighs and pulls off the incongruous Alice band. 'I'm sure you've gathered, Sophie and Nancy, that the magazine has not been doing well. So let me explain what's going to happen.' Her voice is steady. 'Because we are so far advanced with this month's issue, we will publish as normal, but this will be the last one. Somehow, I will find a way to pay your salaries for a month longer, so we can all tidy up, put things in order, so to speak. And if by some miracle an investor can be found – or even a buyer – well, then, who knows? We may rise again. I haven't lost hope. Please believe that.'

Her expression belies this as she stares at the pitted, scarred oak of the desktop. 'I'm very sorry. I had hoped there'd be some good news on that front today, I'd even planned a little celebration, but unfortunately it was not to be.'

Her face sags and she looks tired, older than she is.

'I am very sorry,' she repeats quietly, as the accountants examine their nails. 'Your PRSI is paid up to date, of course, and I will look into the ins and outs of getting you every statutory penny you're entitled to.'

The silence in the room ticks as loudly as any clock as Sophie discovers, just as she is losing it, how much she wants to keep the job she has undervalued. Imelda's Day-Glo lipstick, she sees, has begun to bleed into the cracks at the corners of her mouth and has formed a circular track of pink cross-hatching around her lips. 'I'm sorry too, Imelda,' she says gently. 'I know this is even tougher for you than it is for us.'

The editor nods. She seems resigned, as if, despite the brave banner-waving, the misplaced attempt to look chic, she had known all along she wasn't going to get away with it. 'Try not to worry. Maybe someone will come in with money.'

Sophie glances at the accountants, who have adopted professionally blank expressions. One smiles slightly in response and twitches an eyebrow, as though to warn her she should not hold her breath. This annoys her. 'It's a valuable little magazine, Imelda,' she says loudly, standing up abruptly. Both men rise, too, as she and Nancy make their way out of the room.

Once she has closed the door of the editor's office behind her, she stops dead in the centre of this chaotic but endearing place. 'Come on, Nancy,' she says, to the other woman, who has instinctively gone behind her desk and is crashing around as if everything is normal. 'Get your coat. We're not going to hang around here. Let me buy you a cup of coffee in the pub or even a drink. We can come back and catch up later. When those two have gone.'

'Sure thing.' Nancy walks to the coat stand and pulls her anorak from one of the graceful wooden curls. As she attempts to zip it up, Sophie sees that the little woman's hands are shaking.

Zelda lies quietly in her hospital bed. Over the past eighteen months she has lain so often like this in coarsely woven sheets, chosen for their hard-wearing quality rather than comfort, that she no longer notices the scrape of the harsh fibres against her thin, defenceless skin. It is simply a fact of her illness, as inevitable as the lethargy, the bald skull, or the way she feels cold all the time.

In general, however, she likes it here, in this small hospital that has become a second home. She appreciates the unfussy, matter-of-fact way that the nursing staff treat her, the unhurried care of the doctors. In truth, she prefers it greatly to being in her own home and having to face her mother's constant reassurances and determined cheer, her father's badly concealed panic, her brother's confusion and distress.

Her mother is the most difficult to handle. Zelda finds it impossible to convince her that there are no breakthroughs or miracles on the horizon. She herself understands completely why the various Somebodies Out

There who make research decisions, and commit their trillions to them, have had to make choices. Understandably, they have concentrated most of their firepower on the commoner diseases of mass destruction.

In broad terms, she wishes people – and not only her mother – would simply face the facts and acknowledge them to her instead of skipping around them with euphemisms. Even her medical consultants, with one exception, slide sideways off the truth, slipping in words like 'remission' and 'quality of life' as if she is a baby and doesn't understand the depth of her own predicament.

The exception is her haematologist, a gentle Palestinian with the smile of an angel. As recently as last night, he had arrived at her bedside to impart the latest news. 'This is if you wish to hear it, Zelda,' he said quietly, as he settled himself on her bed.

'Of course I do.' Although she always liked to hear him speak in his heavily accented but musical English, this was a lie. At some deep level, the air crash had acted like the bell at the end of the fight. It had certainly killed the need for information and in this, at least, she was in step with her mother. Since last Monday, Zelda had concurred with her mother's view – but for different reasons – that there should be no more dashing into every new medical avenue of futile hope.

So far she had not mentioned her wish to be left in ignorance, or what was left of her ignorance, least of all to this kind haematologist, who had been honest with her, who had only her best interests at heart and who, assuming correctly that she was an intelligent adult who had learned the jargon and who knew how to follow the course of her own disease, never patronised her.

'Well,' he began, 'the very good news is that your condition has not worsened but, of course, we must be careful. Lots of rest and vitamins – and sunshine, if we ever get any!'

'Yeah, we will, in the summer. If I'm still here, of course.'

'At present I do not see why not.'

She saw that his expression was open and clear, no fudging. 'But if I'm in remission, why do I still have breakthrough pain sometimes?'

'Do you have pain at the moment?'

Zelda had shaken her head. 'Not right now. And, funnily enough, not as often since the crash. Isn't that a howl?'

'There are a lot of things we cannot answer,' the medic said sadly. 'All I can tell you is that, for the moment at least, all our tests show that your bad cells are not doing bad things. Maybe they are resting.'

'Yeah,' Zelda smiled, 'or maybe they're too shocked to do much! So what's that stuff in your hands?' She indicated the papers.

'I was coming to that.' He shuffled them a little. 'Here we have some of the very newest results from the United States of America, and my second piece of good news tonight is that, in trials, in a few cases, remissions have been obtained by experimenting with very high-dose chemotherapy but only when it is coupled with either some other, very new drugs, bone-marrow transplantation or the removal, education and replacement of primitive stem cells obtained by plasmapheresis. Do you understand?'

Zelda was stung out of her relaxation. 'Yes, of course I do.' She had no need to ask about plasmapheresis − where blood is spun and separated in a centrifuge − but the words that had leaped out at her were 'high-dose chemotherapy'. 'No, thank you,' she said, thanking God that she was over eighteen and the decision as to whether or not she would accept or reject any treatment was hers to take. 'I have made up my mind not to have any more chemo. How long are these new remissions?' She didn't want to rain on the Palestinian's parade.

'Too early to tell, but promising. If you wish, I can tell you how it is thought it all works.'

'Not if it involves chemo.' Instinctively, Zelda had passed a hand over her pathetic head and then, fearing he might think her refusal to consider the therapy was purely from vanity, smiled at him. 'It's nothing to do with how I look. Honestly.'

The consultant had returned her smile with his own enchanting grin. 'To me, my dear, you are a very beautiful young woman.'

Zelda had laughed openly at his kind deceit and he had laughed back. 'I mean it.' Then he had become serious again. 'However, I see that you are not at present interested. In any case, all this is still only in development. These are trials, Zelda, as I said. I am not suggesting that you may receive this treatment tomorrow, even if you were willing. But we will talk again, perhaps.'

'Not if I can help it!' Zelda was still grinning. It was a sort of conspiracy that this particular consultant and she had entered together, whereby he read her all the latest theses on her illness and she pretended, for both their sakes, to react as if any of it would mean anything for her. No matter what they came up with now, Zelda was convinced it would be too late. And she was adamant about the chemo. 'Listen,' she said slowly, 'how much longer do I have to stay here this time, do you think? I'm doing well, you say that yourself, so if I'm as well as I'm ever going to be, what's the point of just lying here?' This was a loaded question. Deep down, she was hoping that she would be allowed to remain here in peace for longer, so she would not have to see others' torment round the clock.

The consultant seemed to understand this. He glanced towards the drip stand beside the bed, then adjusted the valve regulating the flow of the clear liquid into the vein in her hand. Without looking at her, he said, 'It's up to you, of course. Your mother wishes you to be at home so she can look after you. And,' he hesitated a little, 'I have already told her you can go home any time you want to.' He made another adjustment to the drip before looking down at her with compassion in his dark eyes. 'My present advice, however, is to stay here for a little while longer. We need to get your nutrition up.'

'Thank you.' Zelda nodded gravely. 'I'll consider it.'

After a few further remarks of a general nature, including the information that he would not see her for a few days as he was taking his wife away for a long weekend, he bade her goodnight and walked softly out of the room, leaving her with no regrets at having rejected the aggressive treatment he had suggested – and the feeling that someone truly cared about how *she* wanted to spend the rest of her life.

She becomes aware that the sun is setting outside and finds herself drifting into that half-waking, half-sleeping hinterland of images and thought that is so familiar to her and in which it is a toss-up between acceptance and grief. Because when she sees how upset everyone is, her family, her honorary 'aunt' and 'uncle' Sophie and Michael, the handful of schoolfriends who have the courage and loyalty to continue to visit her, even though they have their own lives to lead in the universities around town, she always takes up the fight again for their sakes.

All too often she finds herself projecting into everyone's anguish and sorrow as she is buried. She sees her father and poor Donny, their faces scarred with tears, shouldering her coffin at either side of her head, while her devastated mother follows her down the aisle of the church, having to be supported by an army of weeping friends. She sees her own friends, the nuns who taught her, even Donny's lumpen group, weeping around her grave.

So she hangs on. She tries to normalise the situation for others' sakes, even, during the earlier stages of her illness, to make jokes with her friends about death. She could write her own thesis on death, she used to tell them, but they reacted emotionally and she stopped.

It was a stupid joke anyway, since she is not going to have the opportunity even to get her primary degree.

As she had told the haematologist, the amazing thing is that, although she continues to take her pain medication, the breakthrough pain is largely absent and for this she is truly grateful. It is only since she became ill that Zelda has discovered absence of pain as a separate physical sensation. It is a warm, free, flexible feeling, which no one, including herself, recognises until it is lost.

Her room faces west and, amplified by the glass of the window, the rays of the setting sun play directly on her bed. As she luxuriates in the lack of discomfort, she raises her face a little, inviting the warmth to bathe her eyelids and neck. Now she basks, drifting in and out of a haze, which could be a doze, a dream or simply an increasing lack of interest in her surroundings. It is as though the cogs and wheels within her brain are slowing.

Her door is ajar and, just outside, she can hear someone talking to someone else, but has no interest in what they are saying, even if it is about herself.

The crash, horrific though it was, seems now to be a faraway incident, decreasing in horror and significance, and might have happened to some other Zelda. The instant of collision – the noise and screaming, the juddering, tearing and fright – has been encased in a sort of thick bubble and is safely drifting away.

Is this what it is like to die? To be an airship detaching from your tethers one by one until at last you are free to fly?

How will the actual moment occur, when the knot securing the last tether is untied?

Apart from the agony her departure will cause those she loves, her only other regret is that she has never had a real boyfriend, or known what it is like to make love. There had been plenty of snogging after discos with one boy or another but nothing had ever become serious. She and her friends had roamed Dublin as a carefree, mixed-gender gang, content to remain pals. And none of the girls had surrendered their virginity. This had been a marvel to Zelda's mother, who had taken her aside on her sixteenth birthday and told her she had made an appointment for her at the Well Woman clinic 'to get fixed up'; she had been astonished to find her offer spurned, genuinely mystified at the 'new prudity', as she called it. 'Of course it's brilliant, darling, of course it is, what else can a mother say? But, my God, aren't you all marvellous? We couldn't wait! Young people these days are terrific. So sensible and wise. When I think of the risks we took . . .' Zelda had felt obscurely that her mother protested too much.

And now she wishes she hadn't been quite so 'terrific' because now sex is to remain for ever a mystery. Even if she was able to find a boy who could overlook the jangling bag of bones she had become, she would not be able to summon up enough energy to participate in the act.

So, sadly, like the nuns and spinsters of her mother's youth, she will have to die wondering.

The voices outside have stopped now. She is aware of the door being pushed open. Through the lovely golden light bathing her eyelids, Zelda senses that someone has come in. She is still comfortable. She doesn't want to drag herself back. She will pretend to be asleep.

Then her hand is touched and she recognises her brother's hesitant voice: 'Zel? Are you awake?'

She opens her eyes. Donny's face seems to have got smaller, his glasses bigger. Her heart floods with compassion and love but she doesn't want to make things worse for him by showing it. 'Hi there!' She tries to make her voice sound light. 'Come for another gawk at Kojak, eh?'

He shifts uncomfortably. 'Well, actually, I think a bit of the hair has grown back since I was in.'

'You're such a bad liar.' Zelda laughs affectionately and instantly Donny's expression clears.

As she hoists herself into a sitting position he drags up a chair and proffers a plastic supermarket bag. 'Here, I brought you these.'

Zelda takes the bag and looks inside. 'Hey! Grapes! Just what I need.' She tips the fruit out on the bedspread. 'Where'd you get the money for these? It's a very big bunch.'

'I blagged it.'

'So what's new? You're spoiled rotten, do you know that?'

'Look who's talking—' He stops abruptly, stricken with remorse. 'Sorry I didn't think.'

'Shut up. You're right – lying here like Lady Muck, nothing to do except eat grapes and all day to do it. Help yourself.' Although it has been a long time since she felt hungry, Zelda breaks off a small section of the bunch, detaches a single grape and pops it into her mouth. 'Well, little brother, tell us all the news.'

'I can't stand being at home any more, Zel. I just can't stand it.' His glasses quiver on his nose as he warms to his theme. 'She's driving me bonkers. I don't know how Dad puts up with her.'

'Come on, Donny,' Zelda is pleased the focus is off herself, 'give her a break. She's out of her mind with worry – you know, the crash, me, all of it – she'll settle down. How's Dad? Have you seen him? He sounds good on the phone.'

'That's another thing. He's fine – he's coming out of hospital at the weekend, probably Saturday, but I can't stand being in the same room as the two of them. It's like, it's like . . .' His whole body tenses with the effort of finding an appropriate simile.

'A volcano waiting to erupt?'

He relaxes a little. 'Yeah. That's exactly right. And it's all to do with this Street guy. I hate him.'

'You don't know him, Donny.' In defending Street, Zelda is conscious of the irony and, for all his immaturity, so is her brother.

'Come on, Zel, for Christ's sake. You didn't want to go to do all that mumbo-jumbo. You told me you only went because you got tired of fighting her.'

'Yeah, but . . .' It dangles there, the long-tailed implication that desperate situations call for desperate measures, even mumbo-jumbo. As Donny picks nervously at the armrest of his chair, Zelda tries to move to safer ground. 'How's the girlfriend?'

'What girlfriend? She's not a girlfriend. I keep telling everyone – why won't anyone believe me?' It's a standing joke in their house that Donny's friend, Fiona, is already planning to snare him into marriage. 'Anyway, if she's anyone's girlfriend, she's Trevor's.'

'Oh? Is there something I should know?'

'Mind your own business, Zelda.'

'All right, all right.' Zelda throws her hands up. 'You're right, it is your own business, I was only making conversation.'

'Yeah, it is my own business.' Donny continues to pick at the armrest. 'But I do hate Mum. She took the phone off the hook and I missed Mrs Richmond's funeral.'

'Poor kid. Maybe she did you a favour, though, because it would have been awful for you.' Zelda pops in a second grape. 'Anyway, I thought you hated Mrs Richmond.'

'No, I didn't.'

'You said you did.'

'That was just because of the exams. She was giving me an awful hard time. But I didn't really hate her, not really. Ah, it's all just crap.'

'You're going to have to be a bit more tolerant, Donny.'

'Yeah, right.' Donny's attention is already on something else. 'Listen,' he says, his tone so deliberately casual it is obvious he is going to say something serious, 'I just happened to be reading up about myeloma on the Internet last night and one of the things I found out is new stuff about T-cells. All right, I'm not a suitable match for the bone-marrow transplant – I accept that graft versus host thing or whatever it's called although I half don't believe those poxy tests. But they're doing great work in the States, Zel. Do you want me to bring the stuff in to you? They'd use your own T-cells, you see, or even, if that didn't work, they'd use a donor's. The chances are I could be suitable. It's not the same as the bone marrow. All we have to do is get our cells analysed. It's no big deal.'

Although he is not looking at her, he is sitting as intensely as if he is balanced on the tip of a sword and Zelda, unsure of how to handle this, hesitates. The offer, coming so soon after the haematologist's reference to the new research, is almost uncannily coincidental. 'I do know about it, as a matter of fact,' she says quietly, 'although not all that much. And I've been thinking about it. Thanks a million for the offer. I really appreciate it.'

He takes this as a positive reaction and barges on, 'You see, although it doesn't say in the research how they do it, I imagine what happens is that, like the bone-marrow thing, your cells would have to be zapped and then they'd take some of mine to put into you. Apparently the healthy cells are sort of teachers and they educate the unhealthy ones. Something like that. It sounds simple enough to me. There'd be a bit of pain involved for me afterwards, I suppose, but that's all. I'd get over it. It'd be nothing. Really.'

His expression shines with the offer and he is so sure he is giving her new hope that Zelda could cry. 'You do know that all of this is just research, Donny? That they're probably still doing it only with animals?'

'I could find out.'

'And even if we could access it, it might be very risky. There are no guarantees with any of these treatments, you know, not one of them.'

'Yeah, but there's drugs you take to help you with rejection and stuff. There's a risk with everything.' His voice is rising. 'We have to do something. We can't just lie here, Zelda.'

He is so crestfallen she has to let him think she is taking him seriously. 'Well, that's not strictly accurate. We're not doing nothing. And, in my case, all the advice was to go for the straight chemo – they did consider a transplant at one stage but it wasn't only you, they couldn't find any donor. Remember? Anyway, at this stage, they think it probably wouldn't help me.'

'Why not? Why wouldn't it help you?' He is excited again now and she notices that his forehead is perspiring a little. 'How do they know unless they try? Seriously, Zel, I'm going to discuss this with Dad. He'll understand.'

As she continues to gaze at him, he realises she is not taking the bait and trails off. 'Surely everything's worth a try,' he mumbles. He stands up and walks to the window. 'It's roasting in here. Do you mind if I open this window?' He pushes ineffectually at it.

'It's sealed, I think.'

'Bloody stupid thing – I don't know how you stick the heat in here.' He gives the window sash a vicious thump, then blurts, 'You're dying, aren't you?'

Zelda is startled but tries hard to recover. 'Hey, not so fast! Not yet, little bro. I'm still here, amn't I? And I did survive an air crash, after all, so I can't be that bad.'

He turns round to face her. 'Are you?' His tone is angry now.

He won't be deflected and she sees it. 'Am I what?'

'Dying.'

'Maybe. Probably. I don't know – please, Donny.'

'How long have you got?' He is relentless.

She lies fully back on her pillows and stares at the ceiling. 'I don't know,' she says quietly.

He comes back to the bedside and sits down again. 'Well, is it a week, a month, a year? They must have given you some idea.'

'No, they haven't. Genuinely. But there's no point in pretending that the future is bright.' A huge wave of tiredness engulfs Zelda but she makes a final effort to inject energy into her voice as she turns her head to look directly at him. 'On the other hand, and this is no bullshit, my consultant was in with me last night and he was telling me the same kind of thing that you were telling me just now, about all this new research just out in the States. They're hopeful.' She is already revising the previous night's decision on the high-dose chemo. She is inclined to do anything, anything at all, to prevent that expression in her brother's eyes intensifying.

'How hopeful?' He leans forward so suddenly that one of his feet, uncoordinated with the rest of his body, snags the bedspread and tumbles the grapes on to the floor. Neither makes a move to save them.

'Very. After all, as you know, I am this medical marvel. Youngest ever!'

'Don't joke about this, Zel. This is serious.'

'Sorry.'

'We have no choice, then. You have to go to the States.'

She stares at him. The fatigue is irresistible. She has to close her eyes. And, although she pushes it, she can no longer raise her voice above a whisper. 'I'll mention it. I promise.' Her eyelids droop but she manages to keep them from closing as she puts out a hand to touch the back of his, lying like a lost ham on the bedspread. 'I'm doing my best. I've very little pain at the moment, so that's one hopeful sign maybe. I will do my best, but don't get your hopes up too high, Donny.'

As though it might betray him he pulls away his hand. The prominent Adam's apple in his neck jumps. 'I'll make them send you to the States. I'll make them.'

'We'll talk again about it. Now, I hope you don't mind, I have to call a nurse. Time for my injection – I'm becoming quite the little junkie, you know.'

'Shut up!'

She smiles at him as best she can. 'I really am knackered, I'm afraid. I'm going to have to ask you to go, Donny. Will you press the bell for me?'

He stays seated but grabs the bell at the end of its cable and activates it. She can see he is struggling hard to say something. 'What, Donny? What is it?'

He shoots to his feet and begins frantically to gather the spilled grapes. 'Nothing. It's nothing.' Then he dumps the fruit on her locker, turns and, without looking at her again, walks swiftly to the door, muttering goodbye. She tries to raise herself again to address his back, but the burst of energy has ebbed.

CHAPTER NINE

'Sophie Dolan! For God's sake, concentrate!' Although she is alone, Sophie has spoken aloud in her exasperation. She is in what she and Michael describe wryly as her studio, a tiny boxroom, no bigger than a large closet, tucked into a return at the top of the stairs and in which it is impossible to move more than a step in any direction between filing cabinet, drawing table, stool and bookcase. Working from a selection of agency photographs, she is trying to finish a line drawing of a Minke whale, which, as an accompaniment to a map of recent sightings around the Irish coast, should already have been on Imelda's desk. The complex pleating on the throat, which extends all the way back to a spot between the animal's flippers, is defeating her.

Since Imelda's shock announcement – which, with hindsight, should not have been so shocking – Sophie keeps telling herself there are jobs of all kinds available in Dublin at present. As each hour passes, however, she grows fonder in retrospect of her easy-osey life at the little magazine, its seat-of-the-pants but relaxed routines, Nancy's eccentricities, and most of all the freedom she has had. She admits to herself that she has led a charmed but quite lazy existence.

Also, she realises now that she will miss the boss. Although Imelda radiates self-sufficiency, Sophie has sensed more than once that, underneath it all, the older woman is perhaps not quite such a toughie as her outward demeanour suggests. Should she invite her out to lunch or something? The poor woman is going to need all the support she can get.

She looks at her illustration with disgust. She is tempted to colour-wash the whole thing and forget about accuracy – what's the point in being so pernickety since the magazine is defunct anyway? Who'll care about one illustration in its last edition?

'No. Stop it. This isn't good enough – you're supposed to be a professional.' She balls up the illustration and throws it away. She will just have to start again.

Drawing this animal would usually be a labour of love: she is fascinated by all cetaceans and continues to add further clippings and photographs of them to a box file already bulging with hundreds. One of her major ambitions is to go whale-watching off the coast of South Africa or somewhere else where the climate is friendly and she won't have to sit for hours on some freezing headland in the hopes of seeing a distant blow. Since 1991, some twenty-four species of whale have been recorded in the seas around the Republic of Ireland, officially designated as a whale sanctuary, but Sophie is not satisfied with having seen the familiar pods of dolphins, porpoises and the occasional Fin, Sei or Minke that strands itself or swims near enough to the coastline to be categorised. She wants to be close and comfortable in a boat when the waters heave over the back of a fully grown Sperm whale or hear for herself the mighty slap as a barnacled Southern Right returns to the water after a ponderous breach. She wants most of all to catch a glimpse of the leviathan Blue.

She glances at the travel clock perched on top of the filing cabinet. It is five minutes to midday. In ordinary times, Michael would have rung her by now – just the ordinary spousal check-in call. Of course, with Brian still in hospital, these are not ordinary times.

Since the row over their dinner table last night, the echoes of which still reverberate miserably in Sophie's soul, she shouldn't be expecting him to ring anyway.

The quarrel had blown up from nowhere. They had been discussing the closure of *Wild Places*, and while she had wanted him to ask around in case someone might be willing to put some money into it, he had seen the magazine's collapse as an opportunity for her. 'Come on, Soph, this could be the best thing that ever happened. You're too good for that little rag. They've been exploiting you for years.'

The more insistent he became, the more Sophie had found herself stubbornly retreating into a recital of the magazine's virtues, defending the contributors, the faithful subscribers, the ethos behind publishing an independent magazine devoted to ecology. She could not shake off the image of Nancy's mournful face in the pub that afternoon as the two of them sipped flat beer and tried to think of something positive to say to each other. 'And it is – was – ethical. We're very careful what kind of ads we take,' she said furiously to Michael.

'Yeah,' he was not impressed, 'so ethical that you've gone down the tubes.'

The argument had escalated quickly and, Sophie thought, irrationally. Michael had flushed with anger and become more and more sarcastic. 'Tree-huggers? Save the whales? Spare me!'

The telephone rang and he went to answer it while Sophie continued the argument in her mind. Normally during rows she either froze or did her best to calm things down – anything for peace. On this occasion, however, she was not about to cave in easily. This was her life, her magazine. In fact she was surprising herself with her passion for *Wild Places*.

He had come back quite quickly.

'Who was it?'

'Wrong number,' he had said shortly, and had begun to shovel food into his mouth. Sophie, who had noticed in passing that they had been getting a lot of wrong numbers lately, was concerned nevertheless with more immediate matters. She took a deep breath. 'Listen to me, Michael,' she tried to keep her tone level, 'we need more of these magazines, not fewer. Our planet is choking.'

This merely fuelled his rage and he flung his cutlery on to his plate. 'That may well be – although in my book, the jury is still out on this whole global-warming stuff – but it's not going to be stopped by one mildewy little sheet no one ever read.'

'That's not true,' she had fired up. 'That's simply not true. We have a long list of subscribers—'

'Oh, really? Well, no one I've met has ever heard of the bloody thing.'

'It's not a tourist publication, for goodness' sake, Michael. It's more important than that.'

'Oh, so now we're getting uppity about tourists, are we?' He had leaned across to her until his face was just inches from hers. Stabbing a finger at her, he almost spat, 'May I point out, Mizz Oh-so-perfect, that these tourists who are such objects of derision in the rarefied air of slob lands and eagles' fucking eyries, or whatever you call them, have put the lamb in that fucking stew on your plate.'

'Michael!' Sophie was horrified, not just at the obscenity but at the realisation of how quickly a discussion had flared into this wounding brawl. 'What's eating you, Michael?' she asked quietly. 'This isn't about the magazine. Did something happen at work?' They stared at each other for a moment or two. Her face started hurting and, reflexively, she put a hand up to it.

He sat back again and became conciliatory. 'I'm sorry. I know how you hate bad language.' He pushed a piece of potato around his plate with his fork. 'Look, Sophie, I am genuinely sorry for getting so angry, especially when you're not feeling well. I'm only trying to help. If you want to save *Wild Places*, then save *Wild Places*, but don't count on me. You do whatever you want to do, you always do anyway. I don't give a shit – in any case, the money you bring in wouldn't feed a budgie.'

'That's not fair.' She was stung all over again. 'You always said the money didn't matter.'

'I know I did.' Again he had paused. 'This is getting us nowhere and I don't think you need my advice about anything.' He pushed away the remains of his dinner and placed the cutlery neatly on the plate. 'I don't want to fight with you, Sophie, I really don't. I'm sorry for my part in it. I was out of line with some of the things I said. If you don't mind, I've had enough to eat. I'm going to watch TV.' He stood up then and walked out of the kitchen, leaving Sophie to stare after him, and to face the unpalatable fact that there was some truth in his assertion that she could do better for herself.

The topography of their house was simple; 'two up, two down', was how any estate agent would describe it, a generous classification. When it was built, more than a hundred and fifty years ago, it had been a simple two-room artisan's dwelling, with one catch-all living area downstairs into which the front door opened and where all the cooking was done on the huge open fireplace. The other room, the bedroom, covered the equivalent floor space upstairs and they were joined by a wooden staircase rising from beside the front door to a ceiling trap. An outside lavatory had been reached via the small yard.

Sophie and Michael had modernised the place by constructing a two-storey extension at the back, fitting a proper kitchen downstairs and splitting the space above it into a second bedroom, Sophie's tiny study, and an equally small bathroom. Yet the charm of the original remains, not least because of the way Sophie has used her flair for simplicity and colour. She took little from her parents' home when they emigrated, and, in any case, she is not one for clutter, and the overall feeling in the little house is of ease, order and calm. She has left bare the original flagstones, worn smooth and polished by the hobnails of many generations, but laid on them bright rag rugs from New England. She has covered her couches and chairs with Indian and Mexican quilts and throws; she has whitewashed the walls and hung them with a few of her drawings and watercolours, and one prized oil: a small Charles Lamb, dating from the forties, which depicts a deserted Connemara pier in high summer. Brian and Eily – who had found it in some shop along the Quays before the Quays became trendy – gave it to Michael and her as a wedding present. It was an inspired choice because, whatever Michael thought about it, the muted palette of this most bucolic of Irish painters has given Sophie endless pleasure.

Her house always smells faintly of soap: her one major personal indulgence is always to buy handmade from a speciality shop in town; she loves the clean coolness of it, redolent of childhood bath nights.

There is one exception to all this good taste. Michael, who loves cars, has always insisted on hanging an Audi calendar in pride of place right above the mantelpiece. Since he had taken little interest in any other aspect of the décor and always given her a free hand, Sophie had thought it a small price to pay.

So thick is the stone on to which the kitchen extension was grafted that as she sat last night, staring at the stew congealing on her plate and going over the row that had blown up so quickly, she could only barely hear that her husband was watching *Who Wants To Be A Millionaire?* She felt like crying. Michael had been so short-tempered lately. What was that phrase her mother always used? 'Street angel, house devil'. That described Michael perfectly at the moment. Away from home, he was still the life and soul of any company, with a flippant, quick wit and the capacity to turn even his chauvinism – undisputed even by himself – into droll, self-deprecating entertainment. At home, however, his flippancy now veered towards sarcasm and their joint sense of humour seemed to be sundering. Did they even like each other any more?

What had he meant by saying she always did what she wanted to do? Surely not. Sophie thinks of herself as a compliant mouse.

Sophie shakes herself back into today and today's task, probably one of the last illustrations – if not the last one itself – she will do for the magazine. She pins a virgin sheet of paper to the drawing table and starts again to draw the Minke.

Riba hums as she bustles around her warm, cluttered sitting room, tidying, fluffing, straightening, picking up photographs and dusting them lovingly. She adores everything in here, each fixture and fitting, the miniature chandelier in pink glass, the white marble fireplace with brass firedogs and shining fender, the mahogany television cabinet, which frames the huge set, even the eclectic confusion of ornaments and inexpensive bric-à-brac, all of sentimental value and therefore never culled, no matter how closely they have to jostle for shelf and table space.

She picks up a little hand mirror, framed in blue mosaic. It was a present from Brian in the early days when, coming home from work, he frequently produced a small surprise for her. She smiles fondly as she flicks it with her duster. Those were nice times, when the worst that could happen was that Zelda or the baby would get a few sniffles or Brian had steam pouring from his ears after some encounter with a bad-tempered tourist.

Lately, everything seems to have got larger and more threatening.

She finds herself looking into the mirror. At such close quarters, the bruising on her face and the stitching above her eye are seriously ugly; if anything the discolouration has become more intense. As she examines herself, yesterday's skirmish in Brian's hospital room comes to mind. Sometimes Brian can be so . . . so . . . She can't find the correct word. Unconscious? He can be so *unconscious*.

He'll come round. Time is what they all need – but where Zelda is concerned, time is what they do not have.

She replaces the mirror on the lamp table and flicks it with the duster one last time. *Believe It and It will happen.* She breathes again, drawing oxygen from every corner of the room. *If you believe It, It is already yours.*

The magic works, as it always does, and within a few seconds, her mind has calmed again, and that light, Friday feeling has returned.

For all her life, Riba has always loved Fridays, thinks of them as days of rainbows. She is not by nature or inclination an early riser, yet it always seems easier to get out of bed on a Friday morning. This, she reckons, is probably a throwback to her schooldays when Friday was the prelude to two days of freedom. It was also payday for the uncle and aunt who raised her, the day on which they ceremoniously opened the safe in the parlour and gave one another an amount they considered to be fair and just reward for a week's labour. Friday also meant a good, substantial dinner, even if it was fish.

This particular Friday morning, not even the dank rain sweeping through the empty roads of the estate outside can dim her spirits. The trauma and flashbacks resulting from the crash are at bay, temporarily at least. She is also convinced that her daughter, while perhaps not actively improving, has undoubtedly stabilised. That nice consultant from Palestine gave cause for confidence in this when she spoke to him on the telephone. And although she has her own agenda for Zelda's health that she no longer shares with the medical people, she didn't discourage him when he had said he was going to run some new research by Zelda herself.

Things will only get better today. She felt it in her bones the moment she woke up and had got up immediately to start the day with another baking session, a marathon one: buns, an apple tart and two rounds of soda bread, wheaten and white. The house now smells like a French patisserie as everything cools on wire racks in the kitchen and the air waltzes to one of her Strauss tapes, played at top volume from her player.

Riba loves this. She moves to the centre of her sparkling, chintz-furnished sitting room, about fifteen feet square and carpeted with thick, patterned Axminster in green and crimson. With hands on hips, she looks around to make sure everything is in order. Grand. Everything hunky-dory.

Her instincts will always move her towards light and heat – another proof, if proof were needed, of her previous life in Africa – and as the incessant rain dashes at the house from the low, dismal sky, she moves now towards the radiator under the window, draped with crimson velvet and free of the light-cutting nets beloved of all her neighbours. Insulated behind her double-glazing, she hugs herself, dreamily watching the slow spread of a shallow stream from the overflowing gutters across the full width of the road. It might be selfish of her but she cannot help thanking her stars – and God – that while others splash miserably outside she is cosily ensconced in her nest where the only sounds are the soft clink within the radiator under her palms and the distant thump-and-whoosh as the thermostat on the gas boiler in the kitchen instructs it to reignite.

Her reverie is shattered by the shrilling of the telephone in the hall. She hurries to answer it. This will not be bad news. 'Hello?'

'Good morning, Riba?'

California Monica. Two days in a row! 'Hello, Monica, nice to hear from you again so soon – what time is it there?'

'Oh, it's just a quarter of seven. We get up early here, on PTI.' The woman chuckles deep in her throat.

'Pee-tee-eye?' Riba is confused.

'Palm Tree Island.' California Monica is patient. 'We've been thinking about you, and Zelda and all of you. How is she today?'

'I haven't been in yet to see her.' Riba is now irritated. The use of the acronym, despite the chummy tone, excludes her in some fashion. 'It's just a quarter to eleven here, Monica,' she says flatly, 'and I don't usually go in until around lunchtime. But thank you for asking. Yesterday I thought she was grand. Peaceful.'

The American chuckles again. 'That's wonderful – but why am I not surprised? Have you guys had an opportunity yet to consider dates for your trip?'

'Not yet. You see, Brian is still in hospital and—' She stops. Why the big push all of a sudden? Why should she be explaining herself to this woman? 'I'll let you know as soon as I have a date,' she says firmly.

'Don't make it too long. The weather is awesome just now, not too much humidity, no bugs, no wind, and the ocean is like a polished sapphire today. But then, without the rain you guys have, I guess you wouldn't have all that wonderful Irish green.'

Riba is struck, hard, with echoes of the Americans who sat beside her in the aircraft seat, his fleshy lips, her coiffed head, the snapshots of their family. She fights nausea, barely comprehending what California Monica is saying as the woman burbles on about the beauty of Ireland, of her odysseys through the west. 'So beautiful, Riba, so wild. Well, I must get on.' She becomes brisk. 'We'll talk again soon. Be well, sweetie. Jay sends his love.'

'Me too. Tell him that, won't you, Monica?'

'You bet.'

They say goodbye but as Riba hangs up, pulling a face – *Pee-tee-eye indeed!* – the remnants of her relapse into horror haunt her. And something more. A disloyal, subversive niggle. If Jay is so interested, why doesn't he ring her himself?

As soon as the treacherous question is asked it is answered. Jay Street has more important work to do than concern himself with every individual beat of every individual story. Thousands are on his mind and under his protection, not just herself and Zelda. She is an ungrateful witch to entertain such a perfidious thought.

She is conscious of sudden pain in her right hand. She looks down: the fingers, still tightly fastened around the silent telephone, are cramping. She prises them away, concentrating hard in an effort to regain her rainbow day.

Riba sits down abruptly on her little telephone chair and stares through the porthole window at her bare, stubby rosebushes being whipped around in the wind and rain outside. She must make a plan. What would be the best way to reinstitute the trip? How could she convince Zelda to step on to a plane again so soon? Is it fair to ask her?

Of course it is – the end game is what counts. Of course it's fair to encourage her to seek her own healing. Riba runs her hands through her hair. She worries at it, combing and combing, catching it in one fist at the nape of her neck in a ponytail. Such thick hair, so extravagantly thick – her fingers remember the feathery feel of her daughter's pathetic few wisps. Yet Zelda is so psychologically together, so strong – Riba is lost in admiration for how she is handling everything, not only her disease but the aftermath of the crash. She has dealt magnificently with the situation. Any mother would be proud of such a daughter . . .

The more difficult question, perhaps, is how to make sure she recognises the wisdom of doing this quietly without bringing Brian and the whole world down on top of them both.

She lets her hair drop again. No precise plan comes to mind but she has confidence that she will think of one. Zelda has to be convinced – she has to. What does she have to lose!

Nothing, is the answer.

At the very least, there will be sunshine and ozone and good natural food.

Riba makes a decision. No time like the present. She will go to the travel agent's today, right this minute. She will triumph over all the sceptics with the force of her conviction – and just in case Brian, or anyone else, finds out and tries to thwart her, she will make sure she buys non-refundable tickets.

CHAPTER TEN

A buzzer sounds. Riba is now fourth in line. Alongside half a dozen others, she is sitting in a hard plastic chair, waiting for her number to come up on the electronic message board above the line of agents' heads in the busy travel agency. Rain streams down the huge plate-glass window behind her.

She has buried herself in a glossy holiday brochure to avoid the glances of her fellow punters, curious about the bruising on her face.

Buzz! She is third.

Before she is called to the counter, she hears her name spoken softly. 'Mrs McMullan?'

She looks up from her perusal of the delights of Malta and finds a middle-aged man in shirt sleeves standing in front of her. 'Yes?'

'My name is Peter White.' He holds out a hand. 'I'm the manager here, would you like to come into my office?'

Riba is not surprised. In her view, her all too obvious injuries have little to do with her being recognised: she is accustomed to people remembering her, probably because of her aura. Everyone has an aura, of course, but it is only when you recognise it that you can make it work for you.

She shakes the man's hand, then follows him through a door at the back of the big office, along a short corridor and into a small, windowless cubicle where the desk, filing cabinets and every other horizontal surface are stacked with columns of brochures. He apologises for the mess – 'It's our busiest time of the year, and it's madness at the moment' – and invites her to take a seat. Then, he sits in his own chair, and says, 'I am desperately sorry for what happened, Mrs McMullan. One of the girls outside tipped me off that you were here, she remembered you. As you can imagine, all of our staff is traumatised – nothing like this has ever happened before. As well as yourselves, we had seven other clients on that flight. We've only reopened this morning. But life must go on – Arda's flying again this afternoon, would you believe? We've clients on the plane, going to Lanzarote. How is your daughter? And Brian, of course. I haven't seen him for years, but we go back a long way. I was shocked to hear he was involved too – and him not even on the aircraft.'

Riba decides that the least said about Brian the better, in case this man takes it on himself to telephone him to offer his sympathy. 'They're both fine,' she says quickly. 'Thank you for asking. Zelda's weak, of course, and upset, but she's coming home from hospital this weekend. It was a miracle, you know, a miracle. Of course, we have very good protection.'

'That's very good to hear. The insurance nowadays is pretty comprehensive. Of course, you get what you pay for.'

Riba is about to disabuse him but decides to save her energy. She smiles widely at him. 'Thank you so much for the flowers – they were heavenly!' As it happens, the bouquet from the travel agency had been one of the biggest and lushest. 'I haven't yet got around to sending formal thank-you notes, but I will!'

'Oh, please, Mrs McMullan—'

'Riba, please.'

A brief frown of incomprehension crosses the manager's forehead but he dismisses it. 'Thank you, Riba – what an unusual name! Please, I mean it, don't send any notes or letters, it was the very least we could do.' Then he adopts a more businesslike tone. 'So, I assume you're looking for information – do you have your insurance policy with you? Have you been in touch with the company?'

'Oh, no,' Riba chuckles, 'that's not why I'm here. Brian can sort that out.'

The manager looks relieved. 'Then what can we do for you?'

'As a matter of fact, I want to book the exact same trip again for my daughter and myself. Except for using Air Arda, of course. We'd like to go as soon as possible, and would you check for any special deals in business class?

'That's much better!' Her voice loud in the silence of her little study, Sophie detaches the new drawing of the Minke from the clips holding it to the board and, critically, turns it this way and that under the dappled grey light from the overhead window. Her swan song for *Wild Places*. Whale song.

Good or bad, it will have to suffice because the magazine goes to bed in just over two working days and there is still the column to pull together. She smiles sadly, hearing Imelda: 'I don't want it good, I want it now!' When deadlines approach, the editor frequently talks in clipped, urgent journalistic clichés as though she is starring in another remake of *The Front Page*. Used to talk in clichés.

Carefully, Sophie slides the illustration into her leather portfolio, along with the photographs in case Imelda decides to use one instead.

She gets off her stool and grabs her camera bag. While catching her breath after her mad dash in the Phoenix Park the previous day, her eye had been caught by a beech tree standing alone in one of the grassy plains on the other side of the roadway. Without its leaves, the marvellous structure of its skeleton was fully apparent so if she gets a moment – and if the rain clears – she might nip up to photograph it for future reference.

What future reference? The smug, smooth image of the two plump accountants pops up before her eyes and throws her into an astonishingly bad temper. She is taken aback at its suddenness and strength – what has got into her lately? First with Eily and now this. Is volatility infectious?

For whatever reason Sophie, who had always been the calm one in every group, now finds herself inwardly seething. She rails against her situation. She has been loyal to Imelda, to Nancy, to Uncle Tom Cobley and most of all to Eily, despite her crackpot ideas. What is she herself getting out of any of it, except maybe an ulcer? When is it going to be her turn?

She stares at her camera bag. Will she or won't she?

In the hierarchy of trees, she ranks the beech immediately after her horse-chestnuts, again probably because of childhood experiences. The National Botanical Gardens in Glasnevin had been another destination for the Sunday family outings and here, too, her favourite season was always the autumn when the leaves were turning and she, her brothers and Eily could rob the gardens' red squirrels by gathering handfuls of the sweet beech nuts that littered the ground under one old giant beside the Tolka river. Life then was what you lived outside your classroom – that prison to be endured between endless summers.

Sophie decides to follow her instincts, to take the damned snaps. Nothing to be lost. At least she'll enjoy it.

As she reaches the front door, she sees that the telephone receiver is half off the hook – Michael must not have replaced it properly last night. Furiously, she lifts it and bangs it back properly but as she pulls open the front door, it rings. After a moment's dithering, she snatches it up, 'Hello, yes?' very quickly, conveying from the outset that she is busy and this should not be a prolonged conversation.

'Aunt Sophie?'

Eily's son is barely audible through a babel of yelling and noise and Sophie's bad temper immediately recedes. She closes the front door again and sits on the telephone seat. 'How are you, Donny? More to the point, where are you? You sound as though you're in a pub on Christmas Eve.'

'We can't go outside for our break because it's raining so we all had to stay in our classrooms.'

Sophie can just imagine the scene. She looks at her watch, conscious of her hurry. He has rung like this from time to time for no discernible reason and she believes he may even have a small crush. Remembering her own adolescence, she has always been sensitive to feelings that could crumble so easily and forces herself now to concentrate on Donny rather than on her bad mood, which is rapidly deflating anyhow. 'Is everything all right, Donny?' she asks, when he still appears to be tongue-tied.

'Yeah, but . . .' He hesitates again, then, in a rush, 'Could you meet me sometime after school today, Aunt Sophie? There's something I want to discuss with you. Don't tell my mother or father, all right? You'll understand why when we talk.'

Sophie's fury is a distant drum-roll now and it is her turn to be tentative. Having decided, on leaving Brian's room, not to be pushed any deeper into the psychological swamp of Eily's family predicaments, the last thing she needs now is a further complication. But Donny sounds so young and so desperate that she feels she has no option but to agree, and they make an arrangement to meet in the Kylemore Café in O'Connell Street at five o'clock.

The energy of the temper tantrum has drained. She replaces the receiver and sits for a few moments, toying with her key-ring, to which is attached a little silver polar bear, typical of the tokens Michael used to give her. She remembers the day he gave her this.

It was about four years after their wedding. Brian had not yet set up EconoCar and both he and Michael were working for a charter airline specialising in bringing Americans and American-Irish to Ireland. That morning, the city, which most years sees no more than a few sleet flurries such as last Monday's, woke to find itself covered in a foot and a half of genuine snow.

In that era, long before the economy started to roar its insatiable demands, on such a mad day the citizens drew back their bedroom curtains, took one look at their white streets and gardens and instead of rushing out to work, hopped back into bed and turned on their radios to listen to an excited RTE broadcasting from its hastily instituted 'national weather desk'. They huddled under their warm blankets and listened happily to lists of school closures and train cancellations, to which hills had been gritted or not gritted, and to the news that the entire city transportation system had been paralysed.

That morning she and Michael had got up as normal, but then, turning on their radio like everyone else, had learned that Dublin airport was closed until the afternoon and that all overnight flights from the USA were being held in airports along the east coast. Delighted, they had raced back to their warm sheets and, in naughty, mitching mode, had made tumultuous love. Had scoffed tea and toast among the tumbled bedclothes and then made love a second time. And in the early hours of the following morning, when the delayed passengers had all been soothed, sorted and sent on their various ways, a sleeping Sophie had been awakened with a kiss and given this little bear. 'I just thought you'd like it. To help you remember today's big freeze. It's not real silver, Soph, it's only plated, but it'll last as long as we love each other.'

Superstitiously, she had guarded ever since against losing it.

What is happening to this marriage? Their childlessness is a factor, of course, but in her opinion they had come long ago to an unspoken agreement about this and it is now just a background sadness.

They had been happy for a few years. Deliriously so at the beginning, when sex ruled their lives, and Michael's vigour, wit and scattergun charm had been all that mattered. Hardly believing her luck that someone as reserved and inexperienced as she in matters of the heart could attract such a good-looking, popular and fun-loving person, Sophie had felt she was caught up in a romantic whirlwind. She had loved him passionately, they had loved each other passionately, so much so that it had been no hardship to overlook his less attractive traits: the tendency to pout, for instance, or his impatience with her lack of career ambition. During those first years, he had never complained about her vagueness, now a constant carp.

Lately, the intervals between lovemaking have been getting longer. At night they rarely go to bed at the same time, and if they do, they lie beside each other in a state bordering on nervous tension until one or other breaks it by saying goodnight and turning away.

To be fair, there are two of them in it. If his sex drive has faded, so has hers. Although she is happy to co-operate when – if – he reaches for her, she is usually relieved to be let off the hook to go to sleep in peace.

Well, she *thinks* her sex drive has diminished, although now and then she finds herself fantasising about other people. Like—

She cuts off the thought before it can develop by standing up quickly, leaving the house and closing the door firmly behind her. Sex, of course, has always been the seductive serpent in the garden. It sure was for herself and Michael, and she can see now how it probably blinded them to the negative factors in basic compatibility.

The train of thought persists as she and the Mini splash through the streets. At least there is one problem she does not have to contend with:

she is as sure as anyone can be that he has never been unfaithful. Michael is a laddish type and on nights out without her he is in the pub with the mates he has kept up with since his rugby-playing days or from school, none of whom Sophie knows well or cares to know better. Although she is as much aware as anyone else that 'the wife is always the last to know', she would be astonished to find that her husband was deceiving her. Michael is irascible, unreasonable, and all kinds of things, but he is also straight. His lack of interest in sex may easily have something to do with stress. You cannot live in the pressure-cooker of a childless marriage without knowing your partner inside out and Sophie knows that the breezy air of self-assurance he projects is as porous as a peach kernel.

For instance, faced with the solidity and confidence of his friend, colleague and boss, Michael has to be reminded all too vividly of his own status a step below on the ladder. Although he and Brian get on well together, she knows he resents the fact that, after all these years, he is still second banana and has frequently talked of going out on his own and setting up a classy chauffeur service with uniformed women at the wheel. Yet he has never done anything about this, further fuelling the irrational grudge. But aren't most grudges irrational? She doesn't want to overstate the case and believes that all it would take to collapse this one is a proper heart-to-heart.

A piece of grit has caught under the rubber of one of the Mini's wipers and starts to screech along the glass of the windscreen, setting her teeth on edge. Somehow, although she can never broach any of this, their marital relationship frequently lies between them as redolently as a damp dog.

The day is not going well for Sophie's husband. Apart from the bad taste in his mouth from last night's row, he has lost valuable business for EconoCar.

This morning he had arrived at the airport in plenty of time to service a seven o'clock pickup from one of the transatlantic flights, four category C cars for a golfing party, but the wretched aircraft, driven by tailwinds, had arrived an hour early and the clients, finding no one at the EconoCar desk, had gone to Avis further down the concourse. Because it had been a last-minute booking through an agent in Chicago who had not yet forwarded payment, it was unlikely the company would see a single dollar.

Michael is going in to visit Brian later and, on balance, thinks he will keep that little bit of bad news to himself for a while. The guy will not be amused.

And now Yvonne is flirting with someone else.

The arrivals terminal in Dublin airport is being transmogrified. Again.

As the Irish economy booms, it appears that each refurbishment and expansion of the airport dovetails directly into the next and Michael can barely remember a time when he wasn't tripping over 'pardon-our-appearance' sandwich boards or when the sound of drilling wasn't making it difficult to hear clients on the telephone. A casual visitor would never believe there had been a major emergency here just five days ago. It's business as usual, including the construction.

At least they have a bit of light out here. EconoCar's desk has been squeezed in at the front, just at the taxi exit, where they can grab a few impulse rentals; Michael feels sorry for the poor bastards whose bewildered pre-booked clients have to follow a long series of temporary signposts to find them behind the hoardings, where the scenery is blank plywood adorned with a tangle of exposed wires.

Of immediate concern at present, however, is the way Yvonne is laughing and joking with one of the site workers, a beefy young man with come-to-bed eyes and a mass of curly black hair on his head and on his chest too, to judge by what is showing in the V of his work shirt. She is leaning over the counter on her elbows, her uniform jacket bulging enticingly at the top button, which might even pop under the strain. Michael, who is all too conscious of his own slightly sagging physique and the greying hair in front of his ears, can't intervene. He is caught on the telephone with some elderly dimwit from an agency in a provincial town who seems to have all the time in the world to shoot the breeze over one puny reservation for a Fiat Punto for six days – and thinks EconoCar should be licking his boots in gratitude. Over the man's slow, ponderous anecdote about a previous customer he sent to the company, Michael strains to hear what Yvonne is saying but although their counter is less than ten feet long, the drilling and general clamour within the concourse defeats him. All he can do is glare at her but she either doesn't see him or is deliberately ignoring him.

When was the last time she laughed sideways at him like that? Look at the way she's sort of fingering the telephone. What's she at?

As if he didn't know.

By the time he gets rid of the agent, his gut is so tight it is actually hurting.

The flimsy he is filling in tears under the pressure of his Biro and he has to discard it to start on a new one. At least the building worker has gone and Yvonne is now sitting demurely in front of the computer terminal, the intricacies of which, to his chagrin, Michael has still not mastered. Anyway, aren't women better at typing and that sort of stuff?

She is wearing her blonde hair in a ponytail today, and as this flicks from side to side while she types he is engulfed by the familiar rush. Flick! Flick! Oh, God, that rhythm.

He tries to concentrate on the new flimsy.

He can hardly lash across and interrogate her, especially here – but he wishes now that he wasn't always betrayed by the you-know-what in his pants. Flick! Flick! He can see that lovely smooth back, that gorgeous little bottom.

Stop it, Dolan. Stop it this minute! Get a grip.

But he has the right to know if she is on the move – he has that right at least, surely.

No, the better option is to keep his trap shut. Nothing scares off a woman like Yvonne more than to have a fella breathing jealously down her neck. Even if she is on the move – he presses so hard on the docket he is in danger of ruining this one too – there are plenty more fish in the sea.

On cue, the little work-experience girl comes back from taking a wheelchair client to his car. 'Hello there, sunbeam,' he raises his voice to a pitch he is sure Yvonne will notice, 'God, you're a sight for sore eyes – how did it go?'

Dammit, he still has a mental block about the girl's name. Bernie? Bláithín? He can't ask her, for God's sake, she's been working here for more than a week . . .

Yvonne hasn't turned around.

The work-experience girl blushes, causing an instant rise in his spirits: he didn't know girls blushed any more, certainly not girls under thirty. It's lovely, actually. Before she can tell him about the client, though, they are interrupted by a long-standing acquaintance of Michael's, an agent who used to give EconoCar a lot of business when he was with another firm but most of whose work nowadays involves sending Irish people away. Michael sticks out his hand. 'Peter White, as I live and breathe, how are you? Haven't seen you for a while.' They shake hands. 'Aren't we going great? Are you going to Cardiff?'

As they exchange pleasantries about an Ireland–Wales rugby fixture set for the following month and continue to swap congratulations on how well the Irish team has been doing this season, Michael can see, out of the corner of his eye, that Yvonne is standing up, leaving the desk, going through the exit at the back of the concession.

She could be going to the loo, of course. Or out for a cigarette. On the other hand, she could be going to meet Mr Perfect Pecs.

He realises that the other man has stopped speaking and seems to be waiting for him to respond to something. 'What's that? Sorry, Peter, I got distracted there for a moment.'

'McMullan. I came over specifically to ask you to pass on my best wishes. He's one of the good ones.'

Michael makes sure his peripheral vision encompasses the concourse as he smiles at the other man. 'Sure thing, I'll tell him you were asking for him. As it happens I'm probably going in to see him later in the Mater. He's doing well, I understand. Of course, it's hard to kill a bad thing.'

'Yeah.' White leans on the counter, a fond smile on his face. 'Jays, Mick – will you ever forget those early days training in CERT when we were all young? When we were all going to shake up Irish tourism, become millionaires, run our own shows. Met any millionaires lately?'

'You said it.' Although Michael genuinely likes this colleague and doesn't want to be rude, he wishes now that the man would just go away. He is itching to leave the desk and find out what Yvonne is up to. However, the other man seems in no hurry: 'Funny how we're all still in the trade one way and another. It's addictive, this business, isn't it?'

'Yeah.'

Michael holds his Biro suspended above the docket and, getting the message at last, White straightens up. 'Better go, I suppose, I've a crowd to see off. Lanzarote. I thought it better to come out here myself.' He grimaces. 'They're on Arda – you get the picture! So, anyway, tell the old so-and-so I was very sorry to hear what happened, speedy recovery, all that.' He lowers his voice a little. 'Sophie too, of course – she had a lucky escape too, I hear.'

'Yeah, she's doing fine. I can't believe how lucky they all were. You heard about McMullan's wife and daughter?'

'Of course – sure they were with us. She was in with me this morning as a matter of fact – brave woman. Unusual name. Riba, is it? Although that's not the name we had on the original manifest.'

If Brian McMullan's wife wants to be called Katy the Kitten that's fine by Michael, and he had never understood the fuss his boss had kicked up about it. 'Yeah. Riba,' he says absently. He is getting a crick in his neck with the strain of keeping the concourse under surreptitious surveillance. He wishes White would go about his business but the other man is still ruminating; 'I have to tell you, though, if it was me who'd been in that crash, experienced and all as I am, I wouldn't be in a hurry to try it again. In fairness, though, when she was rebooking, she did specify anything but Arda. Got her an upgrade too, pulled a few strings with BA. They could hardly refuse in the circumstances.' He smiles. 'Well, see ya, head! Onwards and upwards to Cardiff?'

'Yeah, looking forward to it, should be a good one. Take care of yourself.'

As the other man walks off, Michael is not thinking ahead to the rugby match, he is already moving to the rear of the concession space. He stops at the computer terminal where the kid is stapling documents together. 'Listen – er –' *dammit, what is the girl's name?* '—I'll be back in two ticks. Don't sell the fleet on me now, sure you won't.' He bestows on her one of his most brilliant smiles.

Blushing again, the student smiles back.

CHAPTER ELEVEN

B rian, fully dressed in denim jeans, black sweatshirt and white trainers, is lying on, rather than in, his hospital bed. He is still wearing the surgical collar, although the pain has receded to the extent that he believes he will not need to wear it for much longer.

He has decided to discharge himself but has been persuaded by the nursing staff not to go until he has seen his consultant, who has been contacted and will arrive when his schedule allows. In the meantime, chafing at the delay, Brian is flipping desultorily between the four channels his television set can receive without snow but the viewing choice is risible: an antiques-valuation slot on a magazine programme, a game show, a children's cartoon or Sky News. He is bored silly.

Never one to stay still for any length of time, he turns off the television, heaves himself to his feet and walks to the window, a matter of just a few paces.

A waste of energy. Nothing to see. A multi-strand necklace of car roofs. Umbrellas. Wet.

All shite.

Where is that damned doctor? This is as bad as being in prison.

He sees now that for the first few days after the crash he was undoubtedly in a daze, but now his brain won't stop chattering as though making up for lost time. It states cases, then answers itself with opposing points of view on subjects ranging from the crap they're showing on television these days to global warming and back to the stock markets; it sees Zelda and, finding this too painful, plunges into fiery arguments with colleagues and clients as though they are physically present, debates with politicians who don't know their arses from their elbows about tourism in general or car hire in particular but who are intent on taxing and regulating the industry out of existence. It again insists on worrying about Zelda then veers off to talk to itself about his wife and her irritating oddities, about Donny and rugby and doctors. And Sophie.

As in, of course, Mick-and-Sophie.

She did look adorable, though, didn't she? He had wanted to catch her up in his arms and hold her gently for ever so she would never come to any more harm.

Stop this, McMullan. You're talking about another man's wife here . . .

Mick's wife.

Mick. Now there's a bloody eejit. Tomcatting around the airport and further afield too – making no secret of it either, while pretending to himself that he's being discreet. And with scrubbers like Yvonne Leonard, who even had the gall to try to recruit Brian himself for one of her ghastly friends. Brian knows that if he had a wife like Mick's he would never play away from home. Never. Not that he ever does. Not yet, anyway.

The thought makes him uncomfortable. Think of something else. Quick. Restlessly, he walks from one side of the room to the other and back again, over and back, through the only clear space. Where is that bloody specialist?

Brian knows he's not a very deep person. He thinks he's not even very clever, although he passed his Leaving Cert. He never reads books, his favourite singers are James Taylor and Cliff Richard, and he has no hobbies outside his passion for rugby football and an abiding interest in planes, airlines and their schedules. If he'd had the gumption and the smarts at the time, he would have applied to Aer Lingus to become a pilot. He had funked this and instead went training in CERT, the Irish government's training programme for the tourism and catering industry. From that it was a short step to car hire. Next best thing to planes. Sort of. None of this had posed problems in the past because he can hold his own in any conversation or debate.

When Eily's path began to move away from his, he had weathered it with good humour, assuming she would grow out of it. Even as the years passed and she did not grow out of it but became more deeply immersed, he had dealt with that, too, on the basis of each to his own. In any event, her activities, no matter how far-out, didn't impinge all that much on him.

So Brian's life had rolled along happily enough. Until the diagnosis of Zelda's illness.

Lately, though – and, if he is honest, even before Zelda's illness – he has been unable to avoid noticing the riffs of serious discontent that seem constantly to roll towards him day after stifling day and which he has been finding increasingly difficult to surmount.

He stops pacing and moves to stand at the window, again staring at the rain. Right. He checks his watch. He will give this lord of the wards another twenty minutes and then he is out of here regardless.

He fiddles with the toggles at the neck of his black sweatshirt, a Christmas present from Zelda. This new state of dissatisfaction with his lot is a persistent bugger.

It's everything: the clutter spreading over their house as rampantly as fungus, the fact that Eily won't answer the telephone if the moon is in the wrong quadrant or something, the repetitious workload he had once found so challenging. Or that all of a sudden he seems to have no one to talk to.

It's the whole thing, this whole, unfair, claustrophobic world. It is Life. Bloody Life. He needs space, he needs to *breathe*, goddammit.

Brian is unused to analysing his feelings and is embarrassing himself by doing so now. Must be something to do with the crash. What's that they call it? Post-stress trauma? Post-traumatic disorder? Whatever. His attitude has always been that a bloke has to play with the cards he is dealt, while doing his damnedest to stay in the game and get a better hand next time.

He looks at his watch again, eighteen minutes and counting. He reaches for the remote control and switches on the television again. Jesus. They're talking about flowers now.

It isn't even the distress and incomprehension that oppresses him every time he thinks about what is happening to his lovely daughter. Deep down, although he is inclined to blame Eily for all ills, he knows that the problem does not fully lie with his wife and her nutty ideas. As a matter of fact, it's not fair to use Eily as a whipping post. It's just that he can't help doing so, to the extent that no matter how much he scolds himself for being unreasonable, he cannot prevent his hackles rising every time she walks into a room. It's not as though she's a bad person. On the contrary, in spite of the loony tunes, she is probably too good for the likes of him. Like Sophie is for Mick.

Brian's expression softens at the thought of Sophie, all wrapped up like a—

He frowns, trying to think of what she had reminded him of yesterday, dressed up like that in snuggly white. Nothing appropriate comes to mind, unfortunately. A little white rabbit? A gorgeously iced Christmas cake?

They're talking about snowdrops on the television. That's it, she looked as fresh as a snowdrop. Jeez, he'll win the Nobel Prize for that one.

When he hears the door open, Brian, the neck brace constricting his movement, swings round.

'Howdy, pardner.' Mick Dolan pitches a box of Cadbury's Roses from the door to land precisely in Brian's hands. 'Eat a few of those. You could do with a bit of sweetening up.'

Brian takes his time over switching off the snowdrops, pretending to have to search for the off button, although it is the only red button on the remote. Seeing Mick come in like that, just when he was picturing his wife, has thrown him off balance. 'Howya, Mick,' he says, as heartily as he can manage. 'Thank Christ! You're the cavalry. I've to wait a few minutes but then I'm checking out – you can give us a lift? Eily'll be in later, but I can't wait until then. I'll give her a buzz, tell her to meet me at Zelda's place. Take a pew.' He indicates a second chair by the wall. 'So,' awkwardly, he shifts his bulk, 'how're things out at the ranch? Miss me?'

'Like a dose of the clap.'

'Thanks very much.' Brian looks hard at his visitor. Despite the jaunty tone, has he detected that the other man seems jumpy? Even evasive? 'Everything all right, Mick?'

'Why shouldn't it be?'

His friend concentrates on pulling the second chair to the side of the bed and, as he sits in it, Brian knows for sure that something is on his mind. He could simply be catching Brian's own mood. He yawns, stretching it for a little longer than necessary. 'No reason, none at all. Just that I thought you look a bit tense, that's all.'

Mick yawns too and, like Brian, seems to take too long about it. 'Working my ass off, my friend, that's what. Morning, noon and night in the service of the ungrateful – it's funny how you can catch a yawn, isn't it?' He settles down. 'Well, you don't look too bad, I'll say that for you. How's Eily doing? And,' he lowers his voice respectfully, 'poor little Zelda. Haven't seen either of them yet, I'm afraid.'

'I'm going in to see her the minute I get my release papers.' Brian's chest hurts suddenly but the other man doesn't seem to notice his grimace. He rattles on. 'She's a great woman, all the same, I have to hand it to her, she's got great guts – you too, Brian, to let them go again so soon. If it was me now, I'd be terrified.'

'What do you mean?' Brian's blood seems to have stopped moving. 'Go where?' He stares at the other man, then repeats, 'Go where?'

Less than an hour later, Riba stands up in fright as the door of Zelda's hospital room rebounds hard against the rubber stopper fixed to the floor and her husband, looking huge, fills the frame: he is breathing heavily as though he has run a gruelling marathon. Or as though he is trying to control his temper.

'Dad! You're out – I didn't expect you.' Zelda, just as startled as her mother, almost drops the hot drink she is holding midway between her tray and her lips. She is sitting upright, swaddled in a blanket, showing just the hand clutching the cup.

Although taken aback by his obvious fury, Riba recovers quickly. 'Come in, Brian – what's the matter with you?' She hurries across to him, pulling him inside and closing the door behind him. 'Don't stand there – there's a terrible draught from that corridor.'

She drops back a little as, ignoring her, Brian crosses to the bed. His face suffused with tenderness, he looks down at his daughter. 'Hello, sweetheart, how're you doing? Sorry,' he points to the surgical collar, 'I'm afraid I can't kiss you, but I'm taking this damned thing off tomorrow, and when I do I'm going to throw it to kingdom come.'

'I'm doing fine, Dad, really.' Zelda smiles, exposing bloodless gums and teeth too large for her mouth. 'It's lovely to see you.' She puts the thick white cup down on its saucer and retracts her hand under the blanket then lies back on her mound of pillows. 'I was worrying about you, but I needn't have. You look quite OK. Mum here has kept me posted.'

Briefly, Brian touches her thin shoulder but then Riba sees his expression cover over again and is disturbed by the steeliness of his tone when he turns back to her. 'Could we have a private word?'

'What about?' The urge to flee is strong. They've had their rows and lately they haven't been getting along all that well but, like many large men, Brian is generally easy-going and she has rarely seen him as coldly angry as this.

'I'll tell you outside.' He turns to Zelda. 'Nothing to worry about, Zelda, love, won't take a minute, OK?' He touches her shoulder again, then marches away from the bed and, for the second time, nearly knocks the door off its hinges.

'What's this about, Mum?' Zelda's eyes are enormous in her china-white face as Riba, playing for time and doing her best to hide her dismay, tucks in the blanket, covering every exposed area as far as her daughter's chin.

'Haven't a clue, darling,' she manages a smile, 'but I sure am about to find out, amn't I? Men! What would we do for excitement without them, eh? Stay warm under there now.'

Outside, she finds Brian's back to her. He is pretending to examine a framed seascape on the wall but he hears her emerge from the room and whirls to face her.

She quails.

He stares at her from under his thatched eyebrows, but doesn't waste any time. 'What the hell do you think you're doing, Eily?' They are in one of the valley periods of the hospital's routine: the teas have been delivered to the rooms, and while the patients are eating, the staff have, as it were, withdrawn to barracks. For the moment, at least, they have the corridor to themselves.

'I have no idea what you're talking about.' Riba, refusing to show how intimidated she is, keeps her back straight and her tone calm but she is seriously alarmed. He comes very close, towering over her. He is a handsome man but the colour of his face, mottled with temper, contrasts badly with the thick shock of pale strawberry hair.

'I think you do,' he says, 'and it's over my dead body. You move that girl anywhere, *anywhere*, and I'll swing for you. I mean it, Eily. At the very least, I'll get a court order to stop it.'

'She's my daughter,' Riba arms instinctively for combat, 'and I will do what I think is best for her. Don't come the heavy now, Brian, please. Who raised that girl? Where were you when you were needed, with your work and your cars and your football?' Even as she is remonstrating, her brain clicks furiously as it tries to compute how he found out. The manager of the travel agency couldn't have telephoned him to warn him or tip him off – that would be unethical, surely. Anyway, why would he do such a thing?

'Don't start with that garbage.' He is shaking with anger. 'I didn't hear you giving out about the hours I was putting in while you were swanning all over Dublin in the Mustang. I didn't hear many complaints when you went off to the Costa Del Sol with your bloody mates. And now that we're talking about it, I don't hear many offers to come in and give us a hand when we're busy – or notice much belt-tightening going on when business is slack. Where do you think the money comes from to pay your credit card bills, Eily? Do I just stroll out every morning and lift it off the bushes in the front garden?' He is so close she can detect the faint disinfectant smell emanating from his surgical collar.

Although her hand goes defensively to her throat, her tone remains calm. 'Is this all about money, Brian? Are we in trouble financially?'

'Of course it's not about money!' He seems fit to explode and is now actually frightening her with his sheer size and the depth of his rage as, barely managing to keep his voice down, he thrusts his face into hers. 'It was never about fucking money – you know that very well. Have I ever stinted or denied you anything you wanted, any of you? I've never rubbed your nose in it, Eily, and I'm not claiming we're on the breadline, but although it might be news to you, we're not exactly rolling in it either. Why do you think I work so shagging hard?'

'Calm down, will you?' Riba manages to hold her ground. 'This isn't the time or the place for a domestic row like this. We can talk about this at home later. She'll hear you.'

'Does she know about this? Have you told her?'

Riba backs away a little from his huge, convulsed physical presence. 'No, I haven't, as it happens. Because you arrived before I got a chance.'

'Well, thank God for that anyway.'

As they stare at one another, Riba concentrates hard, putting light around him, smoothing the air between them. For a moment it is touch and go but then he backs off a little. 'I meant what I said, Eily,' he says, in calmer tones. 'I wasn't joking. We don't know how much time she has and I'm not having her hauled half-way around the world.'

'We've had this conversation before, Brian.'

'Yes, we have, and this is the last time we're having it because you're not getting away with it this time. I should have stopped you before and I'll never forgive myself – she could have been killed, you both could have been.'

She seizes the opportunity. 'But we weren't killed, Brian!' In her zeal, she closes the physical distance between them again. 'Don't you see why? Nothing bad can happen, nothing – the protection. If you'd only listen—' She sees that this was a mistake.

He steps away from her again, violently, as though she has uncovered a contagious and revolting lesion. 'Don't, Eily! Don't push your luck.'

Riba decides to leave it. For the moment. She has to anyway, because two women, pushing trolleys, have come round the corner at the end of the corridor. 'Let's not fight, honey,' she wheedles, closing the distance between them once again and putting a placating hand on his arm. 'Come on back in to Zelda. She'll be wondering and worrying about us. You know how she'd hate this.'

He looks down at her hand on his sleeve but she intensifies the light around him and again it works. He lifts his head and she is glad to see that the high colour is draining from his face. As they turn to walk back into the room, however, he stops her, dangerously quiet. 'I meant it. Don't think this is just another ordinary spat.'

'Of course I don't, Brian.' She smiles and pats his arm. She is not angry with him. Like her, he is entitled to act on his own convictions, however ignorant. Caught up as he is in so-called reason, despite her efforts to show him a better way, it's understandable why he cannot see that this is Zelda's best – *only* – remaining chance.

He is mistaken if he thinks he can bully or intimidate her out of doing what is best for her daughter: even as she follows him back into the room, Riba is already changing gear. Thank God she hadn't already spilled the beans to Zelda – she had been about to when he had burst in. His timing had been spot on. Isn't it fascinating how the protection works? 'Hello, darling, we're back. Sorry about that.' She and Brian, avoiding one another's eyes, are now rearranging themselves at their daughter's bedside.

'What's wrong, Mum? Dad?' Predictably, Zelda is upset.

'Nothing at all, darling, everything's grand – finished with this?' She removes the tea-tray and places it on the floor just inside the door. 'Silly old money stuff. You know how all couples fight about that.' Confident, as she takes her place beside him, that Brian will go along with this, she smiles. 'I tell you what we do agree on, darling. The priority now is to get you out of this hospital and into your own home where we can look after you properly and build up your strength. Isn't that right, Brian?'

As her husband reaches clumsily for Zelda's hand, Riba is planning busily. Now that she sees how deep his opposition is, she has no option but to work secretly and alone. It wouldn't be fair to involve poor Zelda, who shouldn't know she's travelling until they are within an hour of leaving and Brian is safely back at work. That way, Zelda won't have to lie.

Her brain is ticking overtime now: she will have to make sure he is not at the EconoCar desk at the airport when they are checking in – should she arrange some sort of diversion? She will have to change agencies; she probably shouldn't use the credit card to pay for the tickets.

She notices that Zelda's emaciated hand is concealed in Brian's massive one. He is being very, very careful, holding it as loosely and delicately as though it was a tiny, injured bird.

Riba feels the tears prickling. 'Maybe we should say a little prayer of thanksgiving? After all, this is the first time we've been together after the crash.'

Rich with the layered stench of damp fabric, frying onions, hamburgers, cigarette smoke and coffee, the Kylemore self-service café in O'Connell Street is filled with an eclectic mix of customers, gaggles of students and schoolkids, elderly ladies sitting in pairs, exhausted shoppers and a few workers killing time between leaving their jobs at five o'clock and going to the six o'clock films. It is also a transient refuge for two thin, tattered men, each guarding a jumble of old plastic bags, held carefully between his feet, each sitting alone at his table, bare except for a single cup half filled with tea which, in Sophie's estimation, had long ago gone cold. Although the rain has stopped, the windows are streaming with condensation.

She would love to get her hands on the place, to rip up the tiles on the floor and replace them with something brighter and more imaginative. At least the crockery is real.

It is ten past five now, and still no sign of Donny.

Sitting by a window just inside the entrance, she has a good view of the Anna Livia fountain in the centre of the street outside. This privately donated piece, now due for removal and replacement by a monument to the Millenium, surrounded by stepped limestone blocks, is an object of derision to most Dubliners and used as a dump for fast-food containers, cans, bottles, cigarette butts and worse. Sophie has driven past it a thousand times and never given it more than a glance of disgust because of the litter surrounding it. Yet now that she has time to examine it, the fountain itself is not bad, a graceful bronze sculpture of the river Liffey manifested as a reclining mermaid over whom water flows into a reflecting pool.

She sips her coffee and smiles a little as she remembers how she and Eily, both tottering uncomfortably on platform clogs, had hurried down the street past this very spot on their way to meet Michael and Brian outside Clery's for their first double date. Sophie had insisted on doubling because at that stage she still remained to be convinced about rugby types. All through her adolescence at school, she had been warned by other girls that every rugby player's ambition was to deflower virgins and to boast about this afterwards at a bar counter.

In fact the rugby-club hop, where the previous night they had met the men who became their husbands, was the first excursion either of them had made to the uncharted wilds of the south-side social scene and they had been somewhat nervous about going.

At least, Sophie had been nervous. As ever, Eily had been the one to suggest new pastures. Tired of the tennis clubs they usually frequented, she had suggested they try the GAA. But quite quickly all those ruddy-faced hurlers and Gaelic footballers had proved to be too healthy and wholesome for her adventurous tastes, and she had finally convinced Sophie to move into the unknown arena of the rugby social. 'Don't be such an old cowardy custard,' she had urged, spraying so much lacquer on her hair that Sophie had been in danger of gagging. 'Let's spread our wings a little. We're in a terrible rut.'

This was undeniable and even Sophie had had to admit that boredom had set in. So, tense but excited, perfumed, kohled and TanFasticked, she had accompanied her pal as they clunked forth on their platforms towards fresh fields on the other side of the city.

In the event, the differences at first sight between the ambience in this new club and what they were used to were not apparent. The music was identical, for instance, but then small, subtle variations began to appear. The young people here seemed louder, more confident, better-looking, with clearer skin and thicker hair, taller even than Eily and Sophie's friends, although with the girls, this was hard to decide for sure because of the platform shoes.

Within minutes of their arrival Eily had spotted a quarry.

They were still unsure, hanging around just inside the door, when she clapped eyes on Brian. One of a relaxed group lounging at the bar, he radiated confidence and ease. She dug Sophie in the ribs. 'That's the target for tonight.'

'Which one?' Sophie, still getting her bearings, peered through the fog of cigarette smoke.

'The really big one, the blond. Ohmigod!' Eily's voice rose to a squeak. 'Quick, look the other way – he's seen us looking at him!' Laughing hard, as though Sophie had cracked the most scintillating of gags, she had thrown back her head, extending her neck and thereby exhibiting her cleavage to full, quivering advantage. The ruse worked because it did not take the target long to approach. He had another bloke in tow, darker, not quite so massive but physically impressive none the less.

They all introduced themselves – an astonishing turn of events for Sophie and Eily, who were accustomed to being accosted with a simple jerk of the head or, at best, a muttered, 'Are you gettin' up?'

The second guy, whose name was Michael Dolan, turned out to be the more forward of the two: 'Sophie? What an old-fashioned name – I had an Auntie Sophie once, well, a grand-auntie. Ow!' He had reacted to a kick from Brian, who shot him a deadly look for good measure, but Michael had remained impudent. 'Take it easy, Brian, that's a compliment. We're talking about one of my relatives, for God's sake.' Then, without further preamble and with no fear of rejection, he had taken Sophie's hand. 'Care to dance, Auntie?'

He was a rhythmic, if unadventurous, mover and as dancing at that time was strictly hands-off, Sophie had a good opportunity to examine him. She liked what she saw. And if he was intent on deflowering her, it didn't show. Still, with the horror stories still fresh, she had remained wary. 'Jeez, Sophie,' he had exclaimed, towards the end of the dance, 'you're a hard nut to crack, but I like a challenge. You'll get to like me too, be sure of it.'

Of course she had, being forced to laugh at herself as he set out to puncture her somewhat prim, even ascetic proclivities and, with cheerful lack of pretension, even to scoff at her natural modesty. She had been good for him, too, because in her presence, at least, he had been inclined to tone down his tendency to vulgarity. In fact, as she looks back on it now, on that first night he had treated her as if she were a rare butterfly, charming her into his net.

She is shaken out of these reminiscences by the sight of Donny rushing along the street. He arrives at her table, panting. 'Sorry I'm late, Aunt Sophie,' he is flustered and out of breath, 'but they were all queuing for the computers and I didn't get on-line until half an hour ago. I should have gone home and used my own. Sorry.'

Sophie notices he has a fairly thick wad of A4 paper in his hand. 'Relax, Donny,' she smiles at him, 'you're not that late. Sit down – what can I get you?'

He throws the papers on the table. 'I'll get it myself. I'll just have a Coke.' He hesitates. 'And maybe I'll have a single too, maybe a large one, I'm starving. Won't be a second, Aunt Sophie.'

Sophie smiles. Since he turned twelve, she has never seen Donny without food either on his person or on his mind. She watches him hurrying through the tables towards the service area, rooting in his pocket for money. His hair is sticking up all over the place and he reminds her of an ungainly pony who finds itself growing unexpectedly into a horse. She wants to comb down the shaggy hair, to smooth it for him, to straighten the shirt collar that is sticking up, to pull his anorak, worn draped half-way down his back like a shawl, properly on to his shoulders. His shoes are muddy and down-at-heel – if he was hers, he'd be turned out spanking new every day.

She picks up the papers he has dumped on the table and finds that they are computer printouts, all from sites dealing with multiple myeloma. She starts to read but although she concentrates hard, finds little that is new: until Eily turned her back on conventional medicine, the two of them went up and down every byroad of the disease and all the developments surrounding it but they have always come up against one insurmountable wall. Multiple myeloma remains incurable, despite all of the research, theories and therapies being thrown at it, and the most that can be hoped for still is delay of deterioration and an extension of remission. Skimming through Donny's printouts does nothing to increase her optimism about Zelda's prognosis. One of them is about a newly available family of drugs called proteosome inhibitors that can apparently kill myeloma cells, but are also able to kill even the rogue cells that bind themselves to bone marrow and are protected against chemotherapy. This represents only a development of stuff Sophie knows already and it will probably take years before the treatment is freely on the market.

The word 'Thalidomide' jumps out at her. 'Thalidomide directly kills tumour cells, alters the interaction of myeloma and bone-marrow cells, overcomes resistance of myeloma cells to chemotherapy, and stimulates the patient's own immune response against their myeloma cells . . .'

He has printed out pages and pages about research into vaccines, too. She turns the last page of this section and finds, highlighted aggressively in bright pink, notes indicating that the new treatments were likely to be

more effective and have fewer side effects than currently available therapies, and offered great potential to improve the quality of life and survival
of patients with myeloma.

Still no mention of the word 'cure'. Sophie looks up: Donny is coming
towards her. She tidies the papers into a neat rectangle and sees what he is
carrying – a small mountain of chicken nuggets, chips, apple pie and an
enormous beaker of Coca-Cola. He notices that she is scrutinising this
and blushes. 'Well, I had hardly any lunch.'

She pulls out his chair. 'Sit down, love. And, for God's sake, don't be
defensive, eat as much as you like. You're as thin as a whippet! You should
have let me get it for you – how much did all that cost? If I'd known you
were going to buy so much . . .'

'Oh, things have certainly changed around here – money's no object,
these days,' he says, falling on the food. 'I could probably book myself and
all my friends as many concert tickets as I like using Dad's or Mum's credit
card on the phone and nobody would bat an eyelid. If they even noticed.
It's pathetic actually.'

She waits while he makes heavy inroads into the meal. Then, as quietly
as the surrounding hubbub will allow, she says, 'What did you want to talk
to me about, Donny?'

He swallows what is in his mouth and fires up. 'I want you to talk to
them, Aunt Sophie. I saw you reading the stuff. Did you see the bit about
where siblings can donate their T-cells? I marked it for you.'

'I did, Donny—'

Before she can elaborate, he has rushed on. 'That's new. It could be the
breakthrough we've been waiting for. I've been following it all the time
and this is completely new, it's completely different from bone-marrow
transplants.' He picks up a chicken nugget but does not put it into his
mouth. 'I wanted to donate my bone marrow but apparently nobody
wants to know.' His bitterness is on show, and his desperation. 'So, please,
Aunt Sophie, please would you talk to them?'

Sophie looks at him, her heart breaking. 'If this really is different,
Donny, I'm sure if you were to talk to your dad . . .'

He stares at his tray. 'There's no point. He won't pay any attention – he
can't, because *she's* running everything. Anyway, he's in hospital, isn't he?
That's why I asked to meet you, Aunt Sophie, you're my last chance.'

CHAPTER TWELVE

Next morning, as soon as she feels Brian is safely out of the house and about his own business, Riba swings into action. She has been thinking and planning furiously and everything is in place, in her mind at least. Timing will be crucial.

Over the years, she has suffered in silence as her husband excitedly read aloud to her from the *ABC*, the Bible of airline schedules, finding it hard not to yawn as he marvelled at the symmetry whereby Air India can connect directly at Bombay with an overnight Malaysian from Singapore. Her tolerance has paid off because she has learned by osmosis how to read the *ABC* and dived for it last night as soon as he went upstairs to bed.

She has changed her mind about the air tickets having to be non-refundable. After what they have been through, she and her daughter will need all the reassurance and comfort they can get. They deserve business class. All right, bearing in mind yesterday's row and that Brian has to work hard for everything they have, Riba nevertheless congratulates herself that she has already built up substantial brownie points because all through their marriage she has been prudent with their money – her white lies about the cash she has to spend as a member of Jay's organisation notwithstanding. And after this jaunt, she promises herself to be more prudent than ever.

A quick, surreptitious phone call to her local agency reveals that the best deals at present are via Paris on Air France – and that the connections work. She and Zelda can be rerouted to Palm Tree Island via Paris and Antigua for just an additional £423 sterling – less than £500 Irish. A piffling sum, really. Especially when you consider that there will certainly be compensation at some point as a result of the crash. The letters are already arriving through the letterbox.

So Riba cancels her booking with the original agency – which has not yet issued the tickets – and takes a taxi into the centre of the city. She has chosen Thomas Cook, directly opposite Trinity, because of its size: large enough, she hopes, to ensure that she can rebook anonymously without encountering questions from some ex-colleague of Brian's. As for her bruising, it is not half as bad as it was and therefore should not attract curiosity.

Traffic is very light, exceptionally so. It is her first time in town since the air crash and, sensitive to atmosphere and mood, she feels as though the city is still bleeding after the trauma. Shoppers, even the younger ones, seem to be moving with less bounce, and the old stones of Trinity College, where she has been dropped off, seem to her to be grizzling, despite the bright sunshine.

She peers through the window into the agency. Good. Plenty of staff available. Then, unexpectedly, she is hit with doubt. Can she pull this off? Should she try so soon after the crash? Leaving Zelda out of it altogether, will she herself be able to step on to an aeroplane?

Riba straightens her spine. She will certainly be able to fly. Don't they always say you have to get right back up on the horse when you fall off? She also thanks God – and the protection – for guiding her to keep her handbag strapped to herself like that in the Arda plane, otherwise they might have lost their passports along with all their luggage. No. This is meant to be.

She pushes open the door of Thomas Cook, donning her nicest smile for the agent who invites her to sit. She tries to stay relaxed as she gives the flight numbers and connections she has in mind on Air France and Liat, focusing on sending benign messages to the girl, who is young and attractive, with a soft Scottish burr.

'Yes, madam,' the girl says. 'Those flights are available. Shall I book them?'

'Please do.' Riba nods graciously, Hyacinth Bucket-style.

The girl looks back to her screen. 'How will you be paying?'

This is the tricky bit. Riba takes a deep breath. 'By cheque,' she says firmly.

The clerk immediately looks doubtful and removes her hands from the keyboard. 'I'm not sure about that, madam. This is Saturday and although we have private arrangements to handle cheques the banks are closed, and with the flights on Tuesday – we would need a few days for your cheque to clear.'

'I can see your point.' Riba smiles pleasantly and then, as though it has just occurred to her, 'I know. Suppose you take an imprint of my credit card and then – perish the thought – if anything should happen with the cheque you will be covered.'

The girl is puzzled. 'But, madam, why not put the tickets on the card?'

Riba is prepared for this and lowers her voice so that she sounds as if she is taking the girl into her confidence. 'Well, as it happens, this is a surprise for my daughter.' She leans closer. 'She – she hasn't been well,' she taps her head meaningfully, 'and we think a little sunshine might do her good. Now don't get me wrong, she's no trouble or anything, it's just like a little eating disorder, you know yourself, but one of the manifestations of her illness is that she is a bit obsessive – well, more than a bit obsessive, actually, about money of all things. She thinks we're all on the way to the poorhouse and, as it happens, she's a genius with technology. So there's no fooling her. She surfs the Internet all the time, doing checks on all our on-line banking and credit accounts.' Riba shrugs, trying to mesmerise the agent with her eyes. 'I don't want her to know until the last minute in case she thinks this is costing too much and won't come.'

She knows this is a pretty bizarre yarn but, try as she might, she had not been able to come up with a better one in the short space of time since the row with Brian. She fixes the girl again with a smile and her deep brown gaze, mentally sending her positive messages, determined to get through with sheer force of personality. The girl hesitates. 'Hold on, madam, I'll see what I can do.'

Ten minutes later, a set of tickets in her handbag, Riba is back on College Green. She exhales, slowly, feeling that, like the city, she has been holding her breath for a very long time.

She crosses to the ATM in the wall of the Bank of Ireland and withdraws the maximum five hundred pounds her Laser card will allow. She will take another five hundred from the airport machine just before they board. A thousand should see them through for incidentals. Jay's little island is in the Third World, how much can they spend?

Riba starts dreamily to window-shop in her mind. What kind of present should she bring Jay, as their host? Something substantial, obviously . . .

Winter Saturday mornings used to be relaxing for Sophie and her husband as they dawdled around the house, having a cooked breakfast, reading the weekend newspaper supplements then mooching through the local super-market. In the last year or two, however, as EconoCar had kept pace with the general economy in the country, the pressures had mounted and now Saturday was like any other day of the week.

This Saturday morning had dawned sunny and unseasonably balmy and, with Michael long gone to the airport, Sophie had decided she wouldn't hang around moping about her job. It was a lovely day: she shouldn't waste it. She had several rolls of film to be developed, for instance. She had dressed quickly and, at the last minute, had driven to the Phoenix Park to shoot off a quick roll of her beech. It hardly mattered now, but for some reason, it made her feel a little better to carry on, however foolishly, with business as usual.

By ten fifteen, she had already left it and the other four rolls at One Hour Photo in the Ilac Centre, one of the better proprietary shops in her opinion. She had never aspired to darkroom facilities: *Wild Places* wasn't the kind of mag where the nuances would have been visible and, in any event, why shouldn't she take advantage of the technological advances offered by this new world? As recently as ten or twelve years ago, before the advent of these one-stop shops and postal services, to get a film developed you had to leave it at your local chemist's then wait up to a week.

Having shopped for the weekly groceries on the way home, she is letting herself back into the house when she almost slips on the shower of unsolicited mail delivered in her absence. Sophie enjoys a love-hate relationship with junk mail: she resents its intrusion, hates the wastage of resources involved, yet can never put it straight into the bin. Instead, she always finds herself sitting down shamefacedly to leaf through offers to top her trees, clear her rubbish, build her a conservatory, replace her windows, or give her three for the price of two in everything from chickens to baby-wipes. As well as these offers, today's batch contains two newspapers, a local free-sheet and the *Inner Door*.

After putting away the groceries, she makes herself a cup of coffee, puts aside the newspapers and sits at the kitchen table with the junk mail. She skims through and tears up all but one, an amateurish offer from Handyman Tony – Tiling, Plumbing, Carpentry, Rubbish Removal. No Job Too Small. Then, flashing through the *Inner Door*, which contains all the usual bumf, interviews, blurry pictures and endorsements of the Street machine, she is about to consign that, too, to the garbage when a colour advertisement she has seen before catches her eye.

It features a large photograph of the man himself, barefoot in the sand, dressed in a white suit and standing under a white canopy against an emerald sea. He is smiling gently and his hands are outstretched in a messianic pose. Although Street is clean-shaven and his suit and haircut are modern, the photograph reminds Sophie of the holy pictures of Jesus she used to stuff between the pages of her missal in childhood. Underneath, the caption reads:

Get married, remarried or have your vows renewed in Paradise. Have your union solemnised to the sound of the ocean. Get back to BASICS with a clear, simple, but very meaningful ceremony. NO HASSLE before or afterwards. We take care of all local requirements. All you will need is the

*SAME documents you need for your wedding in Ireland, plus your passport.
Full-board accommodation for up to two weeks in private thatched
bungalows, set in the gloriously exotic virgin forests of this enchanting
island. BUT WITH ALL MOD CONS! All travel, accommodation and
official fees in one easy payment, finance arranged. Limousine airport
transfers, flowers, wedding cake, and traditional WEDDING FEAST for up to
12 people included as standard. Music (steel band), still photography and
video, if required. Also upgrades to Business Class travel and Luxury
Suites. YOU'RE WORTH IT! Ceremony conducted PERSONALLY by Jay
Street, officially licensed by the Bureau of Weddings, Palm Tree Island.*

The Irish contact details followed. The ad is obviously generic because the
word 'Ireland' in its main body is in a slightly weaker type.

Sophie wonders what type of person wants to be married by Jay Street
PERSONALLY. His followers, presumably, the people who will shell out
their hard-earned money merely to stand in their hero's charismatic
presence. People who believe more strongly in him than they do in their
own friends and families. People like poor old vulnerable Eily.

If she is being honest, Sophie has to admit that Jay Street had worked
one genuine miracle in that he had rid Eily of her sense of contrition and
guilt about the pair of shysters who had raised her.

When Eily's parents were killed in a car accident, four of the five
relatives who might have taken her in were unable to do so. Her maternal
grandmother, a widow in her seventies who could barely move because of
serious arthritis, was obviously unable to cope. Her mother's sister was a
nun in an English convent, and the other two were bachelor uncles, her
father's two brothers, who lived together in alcoholic squalor on a
smallholding in farthest Mayo. In any case they would have been unwilling
to take on a small girl, even if they had been suitable.

A third uncle, however, married but childless, lived and ran an
all-purpose grocery-cum-newsagent's in the same new suburb of Dublin
as Eily and Sophie. At first everything had been fine: having a young child
around the place had been a novelty and the pair had basked in the praise
of their friends, neighbours and customers.

'Aren't ye great to take on the rearing of a baby?'

'Sure what else could we do? Isn't she our own flesh and blood?'

As the novelty wore off and the frightened, compliant toddler with the
chocolate-box eyes and glorious head of dark hair had turned into a wilful
pre-teen with a mind of her own, the situation had turned sour. The uncle
had believed in the adage concerning rods and spoiling and the slightest
back answering or cheek was severely punished. Many was the night on

which Sophie and her family had had to comfort Eily when she escaped from her home to bathe her wounds in theirs.

The couple had exploited their charge in their shop, too, insisting that she act as unpaid drudge behind the counter so that Eily had had to fit in her homework between ringing up the cash-register, stacking shelves, lugging sacks of provisions, to the extent that she attracted further punishment in school for slacking. Weekends were the busiest times in the shop, which was the only one open in the neighbourhood on Sundays, but although they made a song and dance about giving their permission, the couple could not say no every time Sophie's family asked to take her out without seeming unreasonable.

If it hadn't been for these respites, Eily would never have had any childhood at all.

The shop is long gone, sold to a supermarket chain, and shortly after Eily's marriage, the uncle and his wife had died within six weeks of one another, the wife lingering just days after a stroke, the uncle dropped in his garden by a heart-attack.

It was subsequently discovered that the pair had bequeathed their estate to the church and, for some reason, although she did not covet the money, this rejection had resurrected Issues, as they are now called, for Eily.

Strangely, to Sophie's mind, Eily had felt that this treatment of her in the will had been her own fault, for no legitimate reason that even she herself could work out. No matter how much they had discussed it and no matter what arguments Sophie had mustered to reason with her, Eily had felt that she had somehow let down her uncle and aunt, and that being cut out of the will was a sign of their hurt. 'It's not the money, you know that, Soph.' She had fretted and fretted, across either her own table or Sophie's. 'I should have visited them more. After all, they took me in, they didn't have to – I could have been brought up in one of those awful institutions – and I wasn't even there when either of them died.'

'How could you have been? It was very quick for both of them and you did visit your auntie on the morning of the day she died.'

'Yes, but she was unconscious and she didn't know I was there.'

'She probably did, Eily – I'm sure she did. You know what they say, that the hearing is always the last to go.'

'And at her funeral,' Eily was not listening, 'I should have been more upset. I wasn't even crying all that much. He must have thought I was a heartless, ungrateful bitch. That must have made him feel awful, having no one else in the world except that pair of alcoholics down the country.'

Round and round the discussions went until eventually Sophie had realised there was no point in arguing or reasoning, or in pointing out that this same uncle had been a vengeful, vicious Tartar who had made her friend's young life a misery. Eily simply could not overcome these inexplicable feelings and all Sophie could do was listen and interrupt as little as possible.

It was not until Eily had stumbled across Jay Street and had started to 'work' with him that this sense of unfinished business had been exorcised and she had found peace. Sophie has to hand the guy that much.

If only it could have stopped there. Sophie has been privileged – if that's the word – with a glimpse of her friend's store of Jayorabilia: every pamphlet and tract he has written, every book he has personally recommended, every scribbled note in his handwriting that she has been able to get her hands on and has carefully preserved between sheets of transparent plastic. Eily's most treasured possessions are the two personal letters he wrote to thank her for some special service she did for him during his visits to his Irish troops. It is just as well the guy travels to this country so infrequently, because who knows what Eily would be like if she had more convenient personal access to him?

Sophie stuffs the *Inner Door* into the bin with all the other junk and looks at the clock – it's almost lunchtime. She has little to do: completion of her column, which only yesterday morning had seemed so urgent, could wait until Monday. She might as well hop back into town and see how the beech pictures have turned out.

Brian finds it painful to drive and wishes now that he hadn't been so hasty in getting rid of the supporting collar. Ironically, the hand-controlled car he is using seems to worsen the situation. It is with some relief, therefore, that he pulls into the kerb in front of the Gresham Hotel in O'Connell Street where, with any luck, the client will be ready and waiting. The great advantage, of course, is having the disabled sticker displayed on the car's windscreen, which means he can argue legitimately with the clampers.

This morning it has been busy at the airport, with a lot of people coming in for a conference – and Yvonne Leonard has called in sick. He would have made this delivery himself in any event because this rental is a freebie, to repay a favour from a regular client who had lost a leg in a site accident many years previously before he became a successful building contractor.

With prosperity for the contractor had come perks, including a box at Anfield. For Christmas, Donny had received, along with his Gameboy and new stereo, a sealed envelope containing an invitation for himself and 'a guest' to this box. The invitation included the information that he and his guest would be picked up at the airport and escorted to the stadium where they would be offered 'refreshments' in their private suite. Plus – the icing on the cake – after the match, they would be taken to the dressing room, where, if fortune smiled on Donny, he and his friend would be introduced to his heroes, Fowler and Owen.

Brian's in luck: the builder and his wife are ready so the chat and formalities take only a few minutes. He sees them safely away then crosses to the taxi rank on the meridian of the street. 'Airport, please,' he says to the driver, then dampens the man's enthusiasm for this lucrative run by ordering him to go the back route, via Ballymun, which is a few miles shorter than using the motorway.

'Whatever you say, boss!' The man stabs the buttons on the meter. Hard. Then he guns his engine and swings into the traffic, causing apoplexy in the driver of an ancient Morris Minor whom he has cut across.

He is even more disgruntled when, on impulse, as they are just twenty yards into Parnell Square, Brian orders him to go straight into Parnell Street, rather than go round the square. 'Stop here and wait,' he says, as the taxi pulls alongside the entrance to the Ilac Centre. 'Won't be a sec.' He has decided to dash into Eason's bookshop to pick up a few tapes for Zelda's Walkman.

Latterly, since it became clear that he was helpless in the face of Zelda's illness, Brian has thrashed around, dealing with his own distress by plying his daughter with material goodies, of which few are of any use or benefit to her – jewellery she does not wear, stuffed animals, a fluffy bedjacket in baby pink, even, on one occasion a pair of tickets for a U2 concert in America, which she was far too ill to attend. His wife has remonstrated with him about this, but to no avail. It is not in his nature to stand by and do nothing.

Now, as quickly as his temporary disabilities allow, he hurries through the shopping centre and gathers music tapes willy-nilly, Britney Spears, the Corrs, an audiotape of the novel *Wuthering Heights*. He pays for them and retraces his steps towards the Parnell Street exit. That yob in the taxi will probably be fit to be tied, but that's his problem.

As he passes the large plate-glass display window of the One Hour Photo premises he stops at the sight of a familiar figure just inside the door. She has her back to him as she checks through a set of photos she must have collected. He moves closer to make sure and, as he does so, she turns round and sees him. It is she.

She hurries out of the shop towards him. 'Brian, what are you doing here? When did you get out?'

'Yesterday – did Mick not tell you? He gave me a lift.'

Sophie frowns. 'I wasn't talking to him last night or this morning – he came in late and he was gone when I got up.' She indicates the distinctive Eason's bag, striped in green and blue. 'You didn't waste time, anyway. I hope you're not overdoing it – buy anything nice?'

He looks down at his purchases. 'Oh, I just picked up a few things for Zelda.'

'As a matter of fact,' she says slowly, 'meeting you like this is lucky. I want to talk to you about something but I didn't want to ring you at home – have you a minute?'

Brian, thinking of the taxi-driver outside, hesitates, then decides that he's such a surly bastard he deserves to wait. If he doesn't, big deal – luckily, he isn't one of the guys Brian knows from the airport rank. 'Sure, why not?' He smiles down at Sophie. 'I'll just give work a shout – we're very busy but they can do without me for half an hour.'

They make their way up the wooden stairs to the café, Jonathan's, above the main rotunda of the centre, but as they reach the top, Brian is still talking to the work-experience girl on his mobile. She seems to be coping well. Mick is out on the concourse somewhere.

Still talking, he nods and smiles when Sophie mimes, 'Coffee?' at him, and waves him towards a table.

'What did we ever do without mobiles?' She is already a third of the way through her own coffee when at last he finishes.

'Yeah,' Brian says ruefully, squeezing himself into the narrow space between chair and table. 'Sometimes, though, they're a bloody nuisance.'

As he and Sophie chat a little, continuing the strand about the merits or otherwise of mobiles then moving on to today's sunshine, Brian is conscious that he is becoming more uptight with every second that passes. He is finding it hard to look Sophie in the eye. Her white woolly scarf is wound around the neck of an orangey-tan coat in some kind of thick, matted fabric that looks stiff but moulds itself perfectly to her waist and breasts. Brian does not have the fashion vocabulary to know what this fabric is, but it sets off the white beautifully and makes her skin glow. She has pulled off her hat and her hair, sticking up in little spikes, shines like gold under the café lights.

Isn't it funny how the more women cover up, the more you try to imagine what's underneath? This is something he has never got across to Eily. Eily's attitude is always to flaunt whatever you have. Which she does in spades. Even those bloody tents she floats around in at home have plunging necklines.

He becomes aware that Sophie has stopped talking but can't respond because he hasn't been paying attention. Embarrassed, he scrambles around in his mind, trying to remember something she might have said – anything. 'That's a lovely coat,' he says desperately. 'What kind of material is it?'

'It's felted wool. Thank you. It is nice, isn't it?'

'Yeah. It's lovely.'

As though by common consent, both look around at the half-empty café. They take in the huge murals behind the counter, the utilitarian tables and chairs. 'In all the times I've been coming to the Ilac,' he says, 'I've never been up here before.'

' "Of all the bars in all the world, she has to come into mine." '

'*Casablanca* – don't know how many times I've seen it, they seem to roll it out at least twice a year on telly. Remember when the four of us went to the pictures that awful bank holiday in Tramore when it never stopped pouring the whole time?'

'Indeed I do.' Sophie grins. 'That disastrous B and B, that awful salty wind that cut us to pieces. As for that cinema . . .'

'At least the smells are a bit better in here, and the tables are a good bit apart. That's nice.'

'Yeah, and there's plenty of light, thank goodness. I hate dark cafés. And the wooden floor is good too. This could really be a nice place.' She fiddles with the top button of her coat and gazes up at the glazed roof.

Brian is finding this inconsequential chitchat somewhat surreal. They are talking to one another as though they are schoolfriends who have not met since the last day of term many years previously. He casts around for some way to take them in a more natural, normal direction. 'Oh, my God,' he says suddenly, 'I completely forgot – your job! Mick told me this morning. How awful – I'm very sorry.'

She is concentrating on her coffee. 'Don't be,' she says quietly. 'Michael thinks it's the best thing that ever happened to me. That it will shake me up a bit.'

Brian hesitates. Who should he side with? He knows who he wants to side with, but he must be fair. 'I sort of agree with him,' he says slowly, 'not about the shaking up bit, of course, but that you could do so much better, Sophie.'

'Could I?' She continues to stare into her cup.

'Have you thought of what you might like to do?' It is on the tip of his tongue to offer her a job at EconoCar – but he stops himself just in time. That would be disastrous for all of them. Take the Yvonne Leonard situation . . . God, he could throttle Mick Dolan.

She shakes her head, then looks up at him at last. 'Something will turn up. It's not urgent, anyway. It's not as if I'm on the bread line, and I'm going to be paid for the next month.'

For something to do, although he always takes his coffee black and unadorned, he reaches for a packet of sugar. Simultaneously so does she, and their hands touch. Immediately both withdraw, apologising.

'Sorry.'

'Sorry.'

Her eyes slide again to the table as he casts around for the next thing to say and, with relief, remembers that they are here at her instigation. 'So, what was it you wanted to talk to me about, Sophie?'

This brings her up. 'It's Donny, actually.'

'Eh?' He is discombobulated now. 'Donny?'

'He came to see me. Look, Brian, this is difficult for me and I know it's none of my business . . .'

'He came to see you?' Brian is astounded. Then: 'Of course it's your business, Soph, don't ever say that. What's the problem? Is something wrong with Donny?'

'He's up the walls about Zelda, Brian.' Her tone is so vehement he is taken aback. 'I know that we all are,' she leans forward, 'but do you know that he's trawling the Internet on a daily basis following all the latest therapies and theories? That he's offering himself all the time as a guinea-pig for transplants and cell extractions and everything he can come up with, but no one seems to be paying any attention to the poor kid? He asked me to talk to you. As a last-ditch attempt to get you to listen.'

Brian struggles. Somewhere in the back of his mind, he had been dimly aware of Donny's activities on the computer in his bedroom – he can even remember snatches of conversations about blood and bone marrow – but he has been so wrapped up in his own grief and frustration, and in his private war with Eily, that he had paid only a smidgen of attention as his son rattled on, thinking on one level that Donny was just doing what teenagers do and rationalising that it was good therapy for him to believe he was involved at some level. He sees that Sophie is gazing intently at him now, her expression at once tentative and grave. Somehow, he knows he is not going to like what she is going to say. 'What is it, Sophie?' he asks quietly. 'Spit it out, please.'

'He's right that no one is listening to him. He's only fourteen, but his feelings are as deep and strong as ours – more so, probably. Please don't take this wrongly, but I think that with everything that's happening, maybe we're all neglecting Donny a little bit.'

'You mean me and Eily, don't you? He's our son.' Brian's big strong heart breaks. Poor little bastard – of course he's upset. He gazes back at

Sophie. 'Help me with this, please, Sophie. Help me.'

Her reaction to this is instantaneous and stunning. As though she has been threatened, she leaps to her feet and grabs her handbag and woolly hat from the table. 'I can't help you, Brian.' She starts to back away. 'Ask Eily to help you.'

Before he knows what is happening she is clattering down the stairs.

CHAPTER THIRTEEN

'You're joking. You're bleeding joking!' Yvonne stares at the young woman standing in front of her. The files, forms, stationery, pens, boxes of rubber gloves, KY-jelly and all the other junk lining the shelves around them seem unreal. This whole thing seems unreal. 'I want a second bleeding opinion.'

'Certainly.' The young woman, a foreigner with precise but heavily accented English, is not put out. 'By all means. May I suggest you go to your GP? I can assure you that I am not wrong. You are nine, perhaps ten weeks pregnant. You should take one of our diet sheets and make another appointment. You have to take care of yourself. And the baby.'

'Shit!' Yvonne's knees seem to turn to elastic and she sits down on the rickety chair, the only one in the windowless room. She had been feeling off colour lately and had put down her lack of menstruation to a bad diet and too many late nights. She had come here only because Collette, who is a drama queen, wouldn't leave off nagging her. Right up to this moment, she was convinced that all she needed was an iron tonic or something. Whatever they give you when you're run down and burning the candle, *et cetera* . . .

She wouldn't mind but she'd been very careful. Well, pretty careful – you know the way it is, you forget the pill some night and you take it the next morning and then the next night you can't remember whether you took it or not so you take two, and then you leave it a day because you don't want to overdose. It's that bleeding low dosage. She should have insisted on a prescription for the full one.

Well, if anyone thinks she is going to get fat and ugly and ruin her life for Mick Dolan's child, they have another think coming. That's for sure. She's young. She has her whole life ahead of her. He'll have to help her get rid of it. She doesn't have that kind of money. What's more, he's going to have to pay for the best.

She looks at the young woman, hating her. Bitch! This one doesn't have to worry about buns in the oven, quite obviously. Who'd look at her anyway, with her pimples and her greasy hair and her smug expression? Probably gets her rocks off by breaking the bad news. Probably thinks Irish girls like Yvonne are *stupido* – scum of the earth. 'I want counselling,' Yvonne says, 'non-directive, or whatever you call it.'

Having listened to people moaning and going on about the bleeding abortion referendums in this bleeding country – banana republic, that's all it is – she knows she won't get even a shout at the English clinic addresses unless she goes through the full Monty. Yvonne didn't come down with the last shower.

'Certainly.' The young woman does not blink. 'I will make an appointment for you.'

Yvonne folds her arms. 'Now.'

The woman stares at her and Yvonne stares back. Yvonne wins. 'Come with me, please.' The woman exits the stifling little room, leaving her to follow.

By the time Yvonne gets back to the clinic's waiting room and Collette, she is rock.

'God, I thought you were dead – what's the story?' Collette stands up as soon as she comes in.

'I need a drink,' says Yvonne. 'Come on, there's a pub across the road.'

They dodge the lunchtime traffic and make it safely through the door of the pub, one of those revamped jobbies in heavy dark wood, with copper and brass, horrible patterned tiles on the floor and stone jars on display. At this time of the day it is empty except for a few diehards at the bar. They order Bacardi Breezers and crisps, and sit down in a corner. Yvonne takes a deep draught then fumbles with a cigarette and matches that won't light, but Collette, who is almost purple with curiosity at this stage, can wait no longer. 'For God's sake, cough it up. What gives?'

'You were right.' Yvonne's mouth is tight and ugly as she blows out her first lungful of smoke. 'I've got to get to England and pronto.'

'Jesus H. Christ!' Collette's eyes grow like waxing moons with the thrill of it all. 'Are they sure?'

'Ten weeks. By the way, the counselling . . .' Yvonne's mouth grows even uglier as she sneers, mimicking her counsellor, ' "Will the father stand by you, Yvonne? How do you feel about him, Yvonne? How do you feel about the baby, Yvonne? Were you planning a long-term relationship? How do you think he will react?" ' She takes half of the Breezer in one large slug. 'How does she bleeding think he'll bleeding react? How would any fella react? Especially when he's bleeding married.'

'Are you going to tell him?'

'What do you think? Are you thick? Of course I'm going to tell him. Where would I get that kind of money? It's his responsibility. And he needn't think I'm going to go to any bleeding dive down some bleeding Cockney back alley. No way.' She pulls on her cigarette. 'I'm booked in for Tuesday afternoon, they'll do it on Wednesday morning. Apparently it's right in the centre of London.' She taps her handbag. 'I have the address and because I'm not twelve weeks yet it won't be too bad.'

'Right!' Collette is thoroughly enjoying this. 'Ring him. Straight away. Right now – there's no use putting it off, it'll just get harder the longer you wait.' She proffers her telephone, covered in ocelot fun fur: 'Here, use this if you like.'

'I have my own mobile.' Yvonne does not hesitate.

Sophie's mobile rings as she is climbing into the Mini. She checks its little face, no number displayed. 'Hello.'

'Sophie, it's me, Brian,' his voice is low and urgent, 'don't hang up. Please. I'm sorry I frightened you. I'll talk to him tonight. You're absolutely right, he shouldn't have had to come to you.'

Sophie clutches the telephone. She is embarrassed. Her reaction had been adolescent and stupid, but when he exposed how vulnerable he was, it was flee or throw her arms around him.

She swallows hard. Having somehow breached a code with Eily's husband, she is now intent on shoring it up again. 'I'm sorry I ran out like that,' she says, quietly and firmly. 'It's just that I feel as helpless as everyone else and I didn't know what to say to you. I'm very upset too – she is my godchild, after all – but I can't think how I can help. I wish I could.'

He hesitates. 'We're all acting a bit weird these days, for obvious reasons. There is something you can do for us, as it happens.'

She notes his careful use of the word 'us' and is glad. 'Yes?'

'I've been meaning to ask you for ages, but it kept slipping my mind or I just never got the opportunity. Would you take a few photos of Zelda for us? I'd – we'd like to have them in case . . . We've no recent ones.'

Sophie seizes on this. 'Of course I will, Brian,' she says. 'I'll stop in to the hospital over the next few days and fire off a few rolls. Just make sure Zelda agrees. All right?'

EconoCar seems to have managed quite well in Brian's absence, although the constant racket of the interminable construction work, which had not impinged on him all that much before his hospitalisation, now seems louder and more irritating than he remembered.

The work experience kiddie has clearly been grafting her little socks off: he picks up the neat pile of printouts and client invoices, which she has cross-referenced by name, date, and type of car going back over a period of five years. She watches him nervously as he flips through the bundle. 'I hope you don't mind, Mr McMullan,' she says, 'but I took it on myself. I thought your database could do with a bit of updating.'

'Thanks.' Brian smiles at her. He is thinking that this youngster, who is only eighteen or nineteen, is worth three of that pushy little Yvonne. 'Thanks a million,' he repeats genially, 'and it's Brian, by the way. We don't stand on ceremony here. I'm sorry we didn't get to know one another sooner – I was, as you know, otherwise engaged. When are you due back at college?'

'Week after next.'

'Right, how would you like to stay on with us for an extra week? We'll pay you this time. Strictly cash, of course, the government doesn't have to know about one measly week – would a hundred and fifty be acceptable?'

'I'd love it.' The kid's eyes light up and she blushes. 'Thank you very much.'

'Okey-dokey!' Brian, too, is pleased: he has done not only his good deed for the day but a good deal for EconoCar.

His smile vanishes as he pages through the telephone directory then punches out the number of Peter White's agency, where he finds that Eily has beaten him to it and her reservation is history. He decides to double-check – he wouldn't put it past her to try again with another agency. Telling the kid he'll be back in a second, he goes to the ATM and inserts his credit card, asking for an on-screen balance. Fine. The money is back in the account.

His victory gives him no satisfaction, however, and he is gloomy as he mooches back towards the desk. He hates acting the amateur detective but Eily has left him with no choice. He'll just have to keep a better eye on her from now on. This goes against the grain: it is not nice to behave like a head prefect.

He sends the kid to her lunch and, as she is leaving, sees Mick standing aside to let her pass in the entranceway to the desk. Oddly, his heart jumps, startling him. What the hell? Let's get a grip here, he thinks, nothing's happened. Nothing's changed, just because he and Sophie happened to bump into one another. 'Howya, Mick,' he says, watching a fax oozing out of the machine. 'I met Sophie in town. We had a cup of coffee, as a matter of fact.'

'Oh, is that right? Where'd you meet her?'

'The Ilac Centre. She was coming out of One Hour Photo and I was just coming along from . . .' He looks up from the fax, about to embark on a long, detailed and totally unnecessary explanation about the coincidence of their meeting but realises that, for one thing, this is way over the top and, for another, the other man doesn't seem all that interested.

Come to think of it, Mick looks like he's seen a ghost. Brian tears off the fax. 'Is everything all right?'

The other man reacts as though he has been asked to disprove the accusation that his grandmother was a hooker: 'What do you mean?'

'I dunno.' Brian looks hard at him. 'You're not yourself, you look quite peaky, actually. Are you coming down with something? Or,' he grins, teasing, 'could there be some other disaster you want to tell me about? Like another booking lost?' The reference to the débâcle of the previous morning is light-hearted – in Brian's eyes, the lost golf party is spilt milk, he's made mistakes like that himself, no point crying.

Mick certainly doesn't take it as a joke. What is left of the colour in his face drains away.

'That bad? Tell me.' Brian is alarmed now.

'This has nothing to do with cars—' Mick stops talking abruptly as the desk is approached by a customer clutching one of EconoCar's pink reservation confirmation slips and he has to deal with her. By the time the client has left the desk for the car park, Brian is dealing with another, then Mick has to take a long telephone call of complaint from an elderly lady who has found herself stranded somewhere in the Midlands. Then the kid comes back after her lunch break.

With the comings and goings of the next hour, they don't get a chance to talk to one another until eventually, when the desk is temporarily slack, Brian pulls his friend aside. 'What is it, old son? You're in terrible form – what's happened?'

'Nothing! Everything's fine!' but despite him being able to pull the wool over his wife's eyes about his shenanigans, Brian has known Mick Dolan's body language since they were kids. He can see the guy has serious jitters.

'Wait a sec.' Brian glances at the booking schedule: no one is due to come to the desk for at least another forty minutes. 'You're in charge,' he says to the kid, 'but if there's any problem, we'll just be over there in the Green Room – all right?'

The kid nods solemnly and Brian indicates to Mick that he should follow him.

As he follows Brian, Michael is mentally rehearsing how he is going to approach this. He had been in the crapper when his mobile rang but when he checked the number displayed and saw it was Yvonne, he'd thought nothing of it. She was supposed to be off sick but what else was new? 'Hello?' he chirped, all set to have a good laugh – who else would find him with his trousers around his ankles? – but changed his tune as she spat fire at him down the line. Nevertheless, despite the hysterics, it took a few seconds for the penny to drop and as it did, sort of in slow motion, Michael felt his legs, his cheeks, his forehead, even his scalp going cold. Despite the gibberish, the message was unmistakable. She was up the pole. And she was holding him responsible.

The repercussions started to hammer immediately on the top of his head. Sophie for a start. She would find out for sure – this was Dublin, not London or New York, and if Yvonne didn't tell her, some other busybody would.

The money. He would have to pay for the kid's upkeep. How would he do that, on his salary and with Sophie now unemployed? And how would Sophie respond to the regular hiving off of some of their money for – how many years? Eighteen, or is it twenty-one? It's not as if they're all that cushy.

The airport, it'd be all over the airport in jig time. He wasn't the first, of course, and he wouldn't be the last, but still. 'Mick! *Mick!*' Yvonne's screeching cut through his panic. 'Are you friggin' listening to me, Mick?'

'I'm listening – will you give us a break?'

'I won't give you a break. And you needn't think I'm taking the friggin' mail boat either.'

'Mail boat?' It took a moment but then Michael realised what she was talking about. 'You want to get rid of it?'

'No. Of course not. I want to play happy families with it, you and me and it and your wife and the whole friggin' sodality – of course I want to get rid of it.'

Michael's heartrate returned to normal. Thank God.

Yet—

Somewhere deep, very deep, something else had stirred.

When a couple is childless, all the attention is on the woman, as far as Michael can see. All her friends cluster around her and cluck like hens, sympathising and being there and all the rest of that stuff. But what about the man? The man is just wheeled into a corner, like a redundant accessory. All right, men don't talk about that kind of thing – Michael can just imagine himself and Brian cooing over little baby bows in Mothercare (not!) – but that doesn't mean they don't have feelings about it.

'Wait a minute,' he said to Yvonne. 'Can we not have a discussion about this?'

This served only to send her higher: there was nothing to discuss and he needn't think he was going to weasel out of his obligations.

As he listened to her, Michael's heart and head fought a small war.

Thank your lucky stars – a few bob and no one need ever know.

This is your child, your baby . . .

He had brought the conversation to an abrupt close by lying that someone was calling him. He'd call her back on the instant he could find a bit of privacy. That had been nearly two hours previously and still he hadn't called.

Briefly he considers not telling Brian, now shambling towards the table carefully balancing the two pints – he can just imagine the patronising I-told-you-sos and all the rest of it – but he has to bounce this off someone, he just has to, and Brian is the only game in town.

Michael's boss settles himself in the seat opposite and wastes no time. 'All right, what's this about? We've weathered a lot together, how bad can it be?'

Michael takes a swallow of his pint. He attempts to chuckle, which backfires and, in his own ears, comes out as a yelp. 'You're not going to believe this, but I'm up the creek without a paddle and there's a waterfall ahead.' He makes a downward curve with his hand. 'Ker-splash!' He can see that the other man is mystified.

'What do you mean? Is this something personal?'

'You could say that.' He tries again to laugh, can't manage it, yet the ingrained habit of flippancy is hard to shake. He looks deep into his pint. 'After all these years I'm going to be a dad, would you believe? Or not. Or a separated man. Or not. It seems I will have few choices in the matter.'

Sophie pregnant? Having been with her so recently, Brian almost reels with shock. And had Mick mentioned separation? Why on earth – he has to struggle hard to keep his face from betraying his mixed feelings.

But, he thinks, two seconds later, his place now is as a friend. To both of them. 'Surely it's congratulations we should be talking about here,' he says staunchly. 'It's what you both want, surely? I mean, I always thought the two of you were trying. For years, like. So I don't understand the bit about separation.' He trails off as it strikes him that maybe the kid is handicapped or something. That always leads to complications in relationships, or so they say. 'Oh, God.' Impulsively, Brian puts out a hand but, seeing that the other man is frowning incredulously, withdraws it immediately. 'What, Mick? What am I missing?'

'For God's sake,' his friend is still looking at him as though he's an idiot, 'it's not Sophie, it's Yvonne! And she wants to get rid of it. The problem is,

I don't know whether I want her to or not. But whether I do or I don't, I seem to have no say.'

Brian's first reaction is one of high relief. Recognising this, he is instantly ashamed but sees that the other man, his expression lacking the usual, somewhat cocky veneer, is not paying attention to anything other than his own misery as he traces little smily faces in the cream of his pint: 'You see, me oul' flower, this is probably Mick Dolan's one and only stab at immortality.'

His attempt at levity is highly embarrassing. Brian wishes he would knock it off. Then Mick puts his head in his hands. 'What am I going to do? Even if I do persuade her to keep it, which I think is doubtful, given the way she's talking now, there's Sophie – what'll I tell Sophie? There's no way she'd stand for it. She'd leave me and, of course, that'd probably ruin me financially. *Sophie's Choice!* Ha, ha! One way or another, I'm buggered.'

After a moment, Brian overcomes his natural distaste for touchy-feely outbursts and, although wishing like hell he could be anywhere else, inexpertly pats his friend's arm. 'We'll sort something out, Mick. I'll talk to Mizz Leonard if you like.' This has popped out willy-nilly. He has no idea what he might say. It is just one of those consoling offers people like Brian make when faced with overwhelming misery: by nature he is a fixer and cannot bear problems with no solutions. There is always an answer somewhere: all you have to do is to search. Except when it comes to Zelda's illness.

To his dismay, however, Mick takes his suggestion at face value, seizes on it. 'Would you? Will you talk to her today?'

Brian wishes he had kept his big mouth shut. Although he had hired her – because at the time it had been a seller's market and it was impossible to find staff – he had not taken to the girl. However, the pleading in his friend's eyes is impossible to turn down. 'All right,' he says reluctantly. 'I've to go back to the depot for a while but if everything is OK there, I'll make a quick run. You have to tell me what you want me to say to her, though. You're an effin' eejit to get caught like this, you know that, so I won't go on about it, but now that the genie is out of the bottle, what do you want, Mick? Like, how do you want me to handle it?'

'I'm trying to sort that out.' The other man runs his hands through his hair. 'Bear in mind that I only heard about this a couple of hours ago and I'm still trying to take it in. The main thing now is that I don't have much time. She's made it clear she's not going to hang about – and it's difficult to think straight with a gun to my head like this.' As he continues to comb his hair with his fingers, Brian observes that a fleck of Guinness has caught in the stubble developing on his friend's chin. He hasn't the heart to point this out. He waits, sipping his pint. The bar is not called the Green Room for nothing: there is a greenish cast to the lighting, reflected off the many stainless-steel surfaces surrounding them, and Mick Dolan's colour seems wan and unhealthy.

'Stupidly, I suppose,' Michael's head is low now, and he could be talking to the pint in front of him, 'and don't worry about this, I know I can't have it, but I want the best of both worlds.' His voice becomes hesitant. 'Sophie wouldn't believe this because we stopped talking about it years ago, but the idea of having a kid is . . . Well, it's something I've thought about . . . but when Sophie . . . those tests . . .' He stops, lifts the pint and sips. 'At the same time, I don't want to end up like all the other poor miserable sods in bedsits all over Dublin paying through the nose for separations and divorces.' He groans. 'You see? What I want is impossible.'

Brian has noticed something. 'Just one question, Mick,' he says carefully. 'I hear you talking about Sophie leaving you, but only in the context of bedsits. Is it only money?'

Michael looks up at him, quite startled. 'Are you offering me a loan?'

'No – I hadn't thought of it actually, but if you want some money . . .'

His friend seems then to realise what Brian is getting at. 'Oh, yeah, sorry. Of course I don't mean that the way it sounds, of course I don't. For Christ's sake, obviously a break-up would be very upsetting – but you have to know what it'd be like. How many guys do we both know who will be sitting in a poxy bedsit tonight, having tinned sardines or baked beans or a takeaway for their dinner?

Brian keeps his own counsel about what he considers is monumental selfishness. Right now he has to keep his mind on the conversation. 'You still didn't tell me what you want me to say to Yvonne,' he says.

'Try to talk her out of it, I suppose.' If Michael has noticed the chill wafting across the table, he shows no sign of it. 'I know you'll think this is off the wall, Brian, with the way I conduct my life, but somehow I can't face the notion that a kid of mine is going to be destroyed. Weird or what?' Again he tries to laugh and fails. But his voice gets stronger. 'It's all very well being pro-choice when you're talking in the pub and there's a referendum going on, but when it's your own . . .' He grabs Brian's arm. 'Look, tell her I'll support her all the way through if she has it, I'll pay her. She won't even have to work if she doesn't want to.'

'Think, Mick, think! I'm not advocating abortion, it sickens me actually, but I feel I have to put the other side. How can you support two households and a child on your salary? It's a lifetime commitment, Mick.'

'Do you think I don't know that?' Michael lets Brian's arm go and again hangs his head. 'I'll just have to get another job. Or a second job. That's all detail. Or maybe take a loan from you like you offered before. The main thing is stop her getting on that boat. Or on that plane. She made it perfectly clear that she wants to go first class.'

'What about Sophie?' Brian sips his pint to conceal his growing rage at what this man is going to do to her.

'That's something I'll just have to take care of. She could accept it, it's a long shot but she might − if I handle it right. After all, she wouldn't like the disruption of a separation − ' He does not sound confident. The suggestion that Sophie might acquiesce is so outrageously cruel that Brian wants to expostulate, if not physically to clock the guy. But he decides he has said enough about Sophie. 'Did you say any of this stuff to Yvonne?'

'I tried to − at least I think I did. I can't remember clearly − and it was hard to get a word in edgeways. She's not exactly being calm and reasonable about it.'

'So let me get this straight.' Brian speaks very carefully. 'If I can talk Yvonne out of this abortion, you are resigned to the consequences with Sophie?'

'I'll have to deal with that, won't I? Look, the way I see it, it's one step at a time and the most urgent problem is Yvonne. She's even made an appointment at a clinic. As for Sophie, well . . .' He stops to consider, then puts his head in his hands again. 'Oh, sweet Jesus! How did I get myself into this mess?'

Brian fears the unthinkable: his friend, flip Mick, superficial Mick, bragging, pain-in-the-arse Mick and, yes, Mick the mate, might even weep. He glances furtively around the bar but no one is looking at them, thank God. He slugs from his pint and waits for the other man to compose himself. Now and then, friend or no friend, he has allowed himself treacherously to wonder what Sophie, lovely, talented Sophie, had seen in this man and had concluded that, as with him and Eily, opposites attract.

It had all been so simple when they were young.

He remembers so well that first hop at the rugby club when Eily had zeroed in on him. He had not been sure at first, because when he caught her eye across the dance floor and recognised the come-on he had thought her tarty. The women he was used to flaunted it, all right, but not quite so openly and with such celebration of their physicality. Eily's cleavage had been on show half-way down to her knees.

From the first dance with her, however, he had discovered that this overt and unapologetic sexuality was genuine and exciting. At almost twenty, he had already grown tired of the vapid procession of manipulative, underfed girls, who, one after the other, had made it clear they were not interested in a guy if he didn't have looks, a car, cash and prospects in that order. To them, apparently, everything else – personality, even character traits – was secondary.

Eily had been different. As well as making it clear that she was interested in him as a man, she had also been curious about him as a person: he had originally thought of it as a talent for listening – this, of course, was long before the Jay Street nonsense had taken hold. Even still, despite their difficulties, he found the way she lamped you with those big brown eyes to be quite a turn on.

Sophie had been harder to read but, from their first outing as a foursome, he had sensed that, while more reserved by a mile than her exuberant friend, she was ahead of them all in the grey-matter department. Truly a classy woman.

Now as Brian looks at the basket case sitting across the table from him, he cannot help despising him for his vanity and weakness. With such a woman at home, what on earth had Mick Dolan been at with that stupid little cow, Yvonne Leonard? If Brian had Sophie— Instantly, he curbs the thought. 'Where does Yvonne live?'

Michael gives him the address, then has another idea: 'Could you get Eily to talk to her? You know how persuasive she can be.'

'So you don't want me to go, then.' Brian is relieved but finds he is not to be let off the hook.

'Oh, yes,' the other man is alarmed, 'please. As soon as possible – but we should use Eily as back-up. We're going to need all the help we can get, here, Brian.'

Brian does not like the sound of this 'we' that keeps creeping into the conversation but, as something more fundamental occurs to him, lets it pass. 'Is it fair to bring Eily into this? How is she to be expected to keep it from Sophie? They're best friends, Mick.'

'There is that.'

Out of the corner of his eye, Brian now sees that he is being called back to the desk. The work-experience kid, wearing an alarmed expression and with a red-faced, Stetson-wearing wheelchair client beside her, is beckoning from the entrance to the bar. What now? 'Gotta go, Mick,' he says, finishing his pint and standing up quickly. 'We'll talk about this again. In the meantime, try not to worry. I'll talk to Yvonne.'

Although even from here he can see that the client is angry, Brian welcomes the diversion.

CHAPTER FOURTEEN

The meeting with Yvonne, in her tumultuously untidy, bra-on-the-mantelpiece bedsit on the North Circular Road did not go well. It had not been helped by the aggressive interventions of Yvonne's friend Collette who, in Brian's opinion, was acting as though she was delighted to be at the coal face of this predicament. She certainly seemed to relish hyping it up.

Even more trying was the subsequent phone conversation in which Brian had to break the news that Yvonne was going ahead with the termination in England whatever Mick said, promised or threatened. The clinic booking had been made, the Aer Lingus ticket was to be picked up and paid for at the airport on Tuesday at lunchtime and, in that context, she had asked Brian to pass on the message that unless Mick came up with the readies by Monday evening or Tuesday morning ('Early! Tell him it has to be early!' was Collette's contribution), Yvonne will contact Sophie to 'explain' the situation.

'How much is this going to set me back?' Despite a mouldy telephone line and the construction din in the background, Brian could tell that the poor bugger was peppering. Although in general, he had little tolerance for this type of situation – because no one with any sense should get caught like this – he could empathise with his feelings. 'Fifteen hundred,' he said quietly. Then, when the other man didn't answer, 'Look, if you're stuck . . .'

'Of course I'm not stuck.' But through the hammering and drilling, Brian heard what was undoubtedly a defeated sigh. 'Yes, I could do with a dig-out. I won't need it until Monday, though, because I'm still going to try to talk her out of it. I'll go to see her straight away as a matter of fact.'

'I wouldn't, if I were you.' Brian remembered the girl's mood – and Collette's – and injected his voice with as much conviction as he could muster. 'You're not going to get anywhere today, Mick, especially with that friend of hers *in situ*.'

'Collette? Don't get me started on Collette. That little—'

'Just take my advice,' Brian interrupted, 'leave her alone for today. A night's sleep might make her see things differently. Try and get some rest yourself, you sound as though you're going to explode – but I will have that money for you on Monday morning, tomorrow if you like. I could slip it to you at the Pro-Cathedral.'

The other man made a sound somewhere between a yell and a groan. 'Christ, I'd forgotten about that. Although Sophie did remind me of it the other night and I did say I'd go to support her. Not to worry. I'll get out of it somehow – it's a good opportunity to see Yvonne. That other cow won't be there on a Sunday morning – at least I hope not. If there's a chance of a lie-in tomorrow, I can't see that one rolling out of the scratcher to rush to Yvonne's. Is Eily going?'

Brian felt himself slipping deeper and deeper into Mick Dolan's grubby life. 'Yes, I think so, although she's dodgy about it. For once I don't blame her. It's going to be pretty harrowing. I'm not looking forward to it one bit.'

'Good.' Michael hadn't been listening. 'It's good she's going, she'll keep Sophie out of my hair for a few hours.'

They bade one another goodbye. Brian sat for a moment or two, resenting being involved in this situation although he knew he had no one but himself to blame.

Now, as he sits outside Yvonne's flat, he looks at the mobile in his hand. What next? 'All right,' he mutters to himself as, with one hand, he throws the phone on to the seat beside him and, with the other, stabs the key into the ignition, 'let him who is without sin cast the first stone, or however the hell way that thing goes.'

He had never seriously erred. He had been tempted, of course: what man isn't tempted while steering a course through a long marriage – especially in a place like the airport, swarming with young, beautiful and liberated women? In his case, it might even have been understandable, given the headstrong and self-serving way his wife had got herself in so deep with that shyster Street.

In fact, twice within the past three or four years, Brian had walked right up to the edge of the orchard. Each time, he had thought at the last moment of the fallout, not least for Donny and Zelda, and had veered away to safety instead of reaching for the apple.

But now . . .

Like a bright sun rising behind his eyes, Sophie appeared in her sculpted coat – what had she said it was? Woolly mammoth or something?

Although he is alone in his car and neither Sophie's husband nor anyone else can guess what he has been thinking or imagining, Brian drives off too quickly in an effort to shake off the image of the way that orange coat curved in and out on her body.

★ ★ ★

Sunday has dawned bright and clear. A pet day.

The Pro-Cathedral on Marlborough Street has long been a cross to bear for many old-style citizens of the capital. It is all right in its way, of course, does the job, nice few statues, grand bit of a plasterwork above the altar and plenty of pillars, but it is, after all, only a substitute – even the name tells you that.

All over the inner city they sip their pints and contemplate the injustice of it all.

Because across the river, the competition has in its possession not one but *two* magnificent *full* cathedrals – Christchurch and St Patrick's – and can claim at least one world-class celebrity in Dean Swift. Each of those two *real* cathedrals is a splendid medieval edifice filled with atmosphere, historical plaques and really good tombs. The worst thing of all is that they were both originally Catholic until the oppressor snatched them and kept them for himself in *secula seculorum*. This is the legend. Historical accuracy does not count.

What these Dubs refuse to acknowledge is that, wonderful though they are, the Catholic hierarchy would not take back the two Protestant cathedrals now if the Church of Ireland paid them and handed them over block by block in a solid gold wheelbarrow. Those huge roofs with all that flashing and guttering? Those spires, that ancient stonework, all that complicated decorative brass inside that needs constant polishing? Who'd volunteer for that? Who'd pay for the maintenance?

To the Dub bent on grievance, that's just minor detail. The Pro's all right, of course, but for the big do, the full cathedral is your only man.

This certainly is a big do. Large as the cathedral is, space is at a premium. Two-thirds of the seating has been reserved for the near relatives of the dead, representatives of the government and other holders of high office in Church and state, plus the handful of survivors and their relatives. Only the last few pews at the back are available to the general public. As a result, Marlborough Street outside has been closed to traffic and a public-address system is in place for those who wish to pay their respects and hear the ceremony. Ironically, the temperature is almost at a level not usually experienced until late spring, and across the road from the Pro, the birds, assuming falsely that spring has indeed burst upon them, are dashing about in the grounds of the Department of Education and Science.

Sophie is surprised by the size of the crowds as she waits in line to park the Mini in the multistorey car park at Cathal Brugha Street. All the way into town on her way to meet Brian and Eily, she had seethed quietly about Michael having copped out of the service, citing work commitments. If the situation was reversed, she would be down on her knees thanking anyone and everyone – God, Shiva, Gaia – on whom she could pin gratitude for the deliverance of her husband.

Work, my eye, she thinks scornfully now, as she inches ahead towards the ticket barrier behind a battered old Astra. It's not as though January is high season and, in any case, weekend coverage at the airport desk is usually provided by a part-timer and one of the men from the Finglas depot. He was just making excuses, punishing her for the row.

He hadn't told her until the last minute, either.

She had not bothered to argue with him, just slammed out of the house to take out her fury on the car's protesting gears. Yet even as she raged to and fro in her mind, pitting all her arguments against his, she knew at some level that she was overreacting and had been forced once again to conclude that something fundamental had gone wrong within their relationship, maybe even something caused by her. She never used to be as touchy as this. Early menopause, maybe?

Finally she parks the car and then, on foot, turns the corner into Marlborough Street. When she sees the multitudes, she is shocked into putting her own situation in perspective. Normally when an Irish crowd assembles, even for a funeral, the air is pungent with conversation and gossip. Now the people of Dublin are standing quietly, loosely packed on both sides of the street, leaving a respectful corridor for the arrival of dignitaries and the grieving. In the absence of traffic, their silence is creating a sound of itself, a thick, intense hum, across which a cough can travel thirty yards. The street scene is at odds with the gaiety of the sky and sun above it, and Sophie's anger drips away. So what if one husband didn't come? At least she and Michael are not mourning their dead today, unlike hundreds and thousands of others.

As she passes along the temporarily pedestrianised area, a few people, seeing her bruised face, come forward wordlessly to shake her hand. One man's eyes are filled with tears, she sees, and once again the true enormity hits her of what happened the previous Monday.

Shaken, she mounts the dingy steps outside the Pro-Cathedral and immediately sees Brian who, head and shoulders above the crowd around him, is standing a little to the right of the door. Immediately her heart goes out to him: he looks so forlorn, locked uncomfortably into his suit, collar and tie. She glances around, searching for a bright peacock flash in the middle of all the black, brown and grey, but cannot see Eily. She goes up to Brian and touches his arm. 'Hi!'

'Oh – Sophie.'

'Where's Eily?' Sophie looks around her again. 'I can't see her.'

'She pulled out at the last minute,' he runs an index finger under his collar, 'couldn't face it. I don't blame her, I'm dreading this – it's awfully warm, isn't it? I suppose it's the body heat from all these people on top of the sunshine.'

'It is warm—' she agrees, but he interrupts her.

'Yeah,' he says, 'she was all set but then decided, in her own words, that she'd do her own mourning in her own way. She's gone to the hospital – I'm meeting her there after this and we're going to spend the rest of the afternoon with Zelda.' As jumpy as a stray dog, he looks across the heads of the crowd towards the door. 'So, will we go in?'

Before Sophie can respond, an usher, designated as such by the black armband he is wearing on the sleeve of his blazer, comes forward to take them inside and show them where they should sit. As they follow him through the doors, she is still puzzling about why Brian seems to have accepted Michael's absence without enquiry. 'Michael had to work, of course,' she offers.

Instead of apologising – after all, he is her husband's boss – Brian takes her elbow and helps her into the seat. Because it is such a nice day, she has not worn a coat and his hand feels huge on the sleeve of her jacket, a charity-shop buy but tailored in wool so fine she can feel the warmth from his palm. As they sit side by side, she makes an effort to forget about it, about him, herself, even about Michael, to focus on her surroundings and on why they are both here.

The cathedral is filling fast but, again, the silence is uncharacteristic, and just as the weather outside is at odds with the mood, in here the muted pastels of the décor and blaze of candles on the altar seem inappropriate when set against the dark, sober garb of the congregation. Although the TV personnel are ensconced as directly as possible behind pillars, the carnival brightness cast by their lights adds to the incongruity. This is a church for a wedding or a christening, Sophie thinks, not something like this – and although in deference to the circumstances there are no flowers, except a single spray of white lilies in front of the lectern, she cannot help wishing they were mourning somewhere a little darker.

Their pew is about half-way down the main aisle – the worn brass plaque in front of her invites her to pray for one Jas Gavan, interred in 1842 – and the rows and rows of somewhat dazed people in front of them are sitting quietly, displaying no histrionics or open weeping. They are probably in shock, Sophie thinks, then notices one tiny boy, of no more than two and a half, who is having a whale of a time, toddling up and down, saying hello and shaking hands with those in the seats along both sides of the aisle. He stops now and then to show off, spinning like a top until he trips over a trailing TV cable, falls and grazes his knee on the tiles. The woman who scoops him up is tall and slim and not much younger than Sophie.

Sophie, stabbed by familiar loss and envy, gazes at her knees. She will not look at this child and his mother, she will not. Although the mother is sitting amongst the relatives of the dead, and is therefore a mourner, Sophie will not make allowances for her loss. She has such compensatory riches in her arms. What Sophie would not sacrifice to cuddle a pair of chubby little legs . . .

The feelings are corrosive and unworthy and she hates herself for them, especially on such an occasion. She forces herself to think instead of her final *Wild Places* column. Should she substitute the piece about the seal cull in Scotland for the one about vanishing corncrakes? Both are hackneyed perennials but the seal cull is more immediate.

She becomes aware of a heightening in the atmosphere. Everyone stands and she, too, scrambles to her feet.

Dressed in a black suit, the President of Ireland walks up the aisle with her family and aide-de-camp. They make slow progress because she stops many times, stooping to speak to some of the mourners whose eyes she catches as she passes. At last she takes her seat, the altar floods with hierarchy, clergy and servers, and the Mass, concelebrated by two archbishops, seventeen bishops and more than forty priests, begins. Sophie picks up her Mass leaflet to follow it.

She has not attended a High Mass at the Pro-Cathedral since childhood when she was confirmed from a pew near to where she is sitting now. She had forgotten the soothing quality of the repetitive rubric, the communal bowing, the aromatic clouds from the censers, the polyphonic singing of the Palestrina Choir, who instead of offering a requiem by a single composer have chosen to integrate components from requiems and Masses by Mozart, Verdi, O Ríada and Fauré. As she surrenders to the old, rooted ritual, which offers such a secure platform on which to lay memories and a weary psyche, she decides that a sung High Mass is one of the great gifts from the Catholic Church to the world.

But when the stately ceremony moves towards its conclusion, and the army of priests fans out through the cathedral to offer Communion, she is struck by the white faces and dead eyes of those queuing. It is all very well for her to stand apart, to enjoy this Mass as art or comforting tradition; she does not belong in the ranks of the bereaved.

One very old lady, whose movement is too slow even to be described as a shuffle, is being assisted in the line nearest to Sophie by another woman, middle-aged or elderly herself. A daughter?

Who have they lost? How many? Both women, dressed from head to toe in deepest black, are weeping freely. The old woman stumbles a little and, with a hand as bony and thin as a claw, grabs the end of Sophie's pew for support. Automatically, Sophie's arm flies to help her. She catches the woman around her stooped back, and encounters such fragility that she is afraid to support her in case she injures her. The daughter, however, has grasped her from behind and both women look at Sophie to thank her.

For one moment, as their eyes hold hers, Sophie recognises devastation on a scale she could never have imagined and her own tears rise to join theirs.

In the quiet after the communion, all movement stops at the altar and, after a brief hiatus when the only sound in her ears is the barely perceptible whir of the camera nearest their pew, Fauré's 'In Paradisum' floats from the choir loft.

For the old lady, the daughter, and all the other bereft, the exquisite purity of the boy trebles must pierce as keenly as a rapier – all those travellers, a small army, starting down that runway so full of anticipation and high spirits, unaware of what awaited them only yards away:

> *In paradisum deducant te angeli:*
> *in tuo adventu . . .*
> May the Angels lead you into paradise:
> Upon your arrival . . .

All those empty beds; all those articles thrown out of too-full suitcases at the final hectic minute, handled so heedlessly by sons, daughters, wives and grandchildren who were not to know that these shoes and bags and bulky jumpers would be wept into later and embraced as treasured icons. That they would be crushed to so many faces and their scent inhaled as something, at least, of the vanished presence.

From beside her, across this plain of communal grief, Sophie can read Brian's agonised thoughts and knows he is crying as hard as she. He is thinking ahead to Zelda's funeral service.

She does too.

> *. . . suscipiant te martyres,*
> *et perducant te*
> *incivitatem sanctam Jerusalem.*
> . . . may the Martyrs welcome you,
> and lead you
> into the holy city of Jerusalem . . .

She can see Zelda, her beautiful face radiant, her blonde hair restored and shining like water, her body whole and full of youthful health as she strides joyfully towards the glittering, light-filled city:

> . . . *chorus angelorum te suscipiat,*
> *et cum Lazaro quondam paupere,*
> *aeternam habeas requiem.*
> . . . may a choir of angels welcome you,
> and, with poor Lazarus of old,
> may you have eternal rest.

Sophie has always been sensitive to the emotional power of music and when the final note of this sublime piece dissolves like vapour on the silvered air, her tears become virtually uncontrollable. Brian turns to her. She can see his face only dimly through the haze; her instinct is to put out her arms to hold him. It seems to be his instinct, too, but then he turns back and bows his head over his hands, which are clenched on the brass plaque.

Her heart physically hurting, Sophie fumbles in her handbag for a tissue while the television people attend to their business and while, on the pale unyielding marble floor up at the altar, the Archbishop of Dublin raises his hand for the final blessing. Alongside and all around him, a small forest of sacerdotal hands rise in concert, scattering benedictions that are too late for the dead and of dubious comfort at present to those who continue to live.

In Donny's bedroom, the beat is sweet, the lyrics are bitchin', the volume is approaching the threshold of pain for ordinary ears as Eminem, the rebels' friend, raps through 'Stan', laying out the story and the feelings Donny wishes he could have thought up first. What a story! The guy's a genius.

Donny, Trevor and their joint friend-who-is-a-girl-but-who-is-definitely-not-a-girlfriend, Fiona, are hanging out and have finished swigging their individual portions of jungle juice, a lethal mixture of whatever spirits each could filch from their home drinks cabinet, shaken up in litre plastic bottles, then topped up and sweetened to taste with 7-Up. Fiona's mixture is the simplest: her soft drink is strengthened only with whiskey and the remains of the Christmas sherry. Although she was up for it when Donny suggested it, she didn't want to get too smashed because she has to go to her granny's for her tea.

They had started on the session at just after twelve when the house became free and they are sprawled around the room, which is painted in Donny's personal colour choices of purple and black. Carefully separate, they are yet joined in the knowledge that they are doing something daring. Something at which their parents would be satisfactorily appalled.

'What time are we s-safe until?' Of the three, Trevor's small, slight body is least equipped to deal with alcohol, especially not the explosive combination of vodka, gin, brandy and Malibu, which is what he had found in his parents' sideboard.

'Tea-time at least – they'll both be going into the hospital. They said they wouldn't be home until after four.' Donny giggles, astonished to hear his own voice. Laid over the rapper's driving urgency, his words had sounded feeble and far away, as though they had been uttered by someone else, some wet whose voice hadn't broken yet. They have loads of time. Plenty of time to see what it's like and then to recover before adults come back into their lives.

He wants to say something to Trevor, cowardy-custard Trevor, who's been moaning and groaning about his parents killing him if they find out . . . He wants to tell Trevor that because he has been such a pain, he, after all, will not be the Chosen Pal for the second Liverpool ticket. Donny has been dangling the trip to Anfield in front of Trevor, teasing him with it, enjoying his power. Now he wants to use that power again, but he can't get the words out.

It doesn't matter. Others before them who had travelled the route laid out by jungle juice had spoken in awe of their own experiences and, so far, Donny likes what's happening. Other than lack of control over his voice, there have been few surprises. 'We'll just kip here for an hour,' he goes on, making a supreme effort, 'a – an' then w-we'll go to the park.' That came out like p*hark*. Hilarious. Donny feels the giggle rise like gas but it doesn't emerge.

'Bitchin'.' This is Trevor again but it sounded more like *knittin'*.

Trevor's obviously lost it – Donny doesn't look over, though. Too difficult.

They have been warned about tomorrow's hangover. Big deal. Just in case, though, the three have their Solpadeine ready. How bad can it be? Donny tries to hold on to the thought but it slips away.

Anyway, today is today and he is more than happy to go with the pleasurable flow. The blood is pulsing behind his eyes, his lower stomach and groin feel sort of fluid, his knees and wrists are rubbery and his brain feels like a big, expanding sponge, filling in fits and starts with little gushes of warmth and woolly comfort. The main alcoholic quotient of his personal cocktail is, like Trevor's, a mixture of vodka and gin, but with the addition of bourbon and sweet Martini because his mother likes Manhattans.

Overall, he is flooded with great relief. No tension between his parents, no myeloma or death flags flying over Zelda's bed, no trying to screw up the courage to donate bone marrow or stem cells that nobody wants or even wants to hear about. No rejection.

Only his friends and the beat and this woozy, spinning feeling that is quite pleasant as long as you don't fight it. When you relax, it's like being on a colourful wooden horse rising and falling gently on a kids' roundabout, another worry shed with each circuit, myeloma the last to go.

Before getting down to the drinking part of the proceedings, the three had messed around for a while with the Internet on Donny's computer, a cool Indigo iMac his dad had got for him. The myeloma sites are bookmarked, of course, and he had insisted on opening them to show the other two, but it turned out to be a waste of time because his sorrow went beyond their comprehension and he could see they were dumb with sympathy but embarrassed. He had to travel that road alone.

So that he could save face and they could all pretend he was just surfing, they logged on to the E-Bay auction site but found nothing exciting. They couldn't find much else either: they had grown out of the stupid chat rooms and that kind of stuff, and even the so-called porn sites had become predictable and boring. Anyhow, his Mac doesn't have enough wellie properly to sort out the grainy pictures and videos that took for ever to unroll over his screen. He had logged off, and for an hour or so they had contented themselves with playing a few of his games, Unreal Tournament, Klingon Honor Guard, Deus Ex, the kind of shooter stuff that Trevor likes but that Fiona always wins. Until that got boring too.

It was only then that they got down to the serious business of the afternoon.

Things are growing solemnly hazy now, but Donny is not in the least worried to see that the ceiling is far away, very, very far away. From his position on the bed he looks over at the other two on their beanbags to see how far away they are. Funnily enough, not all that far – he tries to make contact, smiling again, or trying to, but the muscles of his face don't seem to be working properly and he gives up.

Anyway, they wouldn't have noticed. Trevor is lying on his side, clutching handfuls of black corduroy as though he is afraid he might fall off; on her beanbag, Fiona is lying asleep or perfectly relaxed, head back, throat exposed. Her hair, a mass of fiery corkscrews and normally scraped into a ponytail as tight as she can make it, is loose and, like an urgent red waterfall, cascades over one shoulder. She has kicked off her boots and socks and from under the hem of her long skirt, like two little dead birds, her bare feet are pointing limply towards Donny. Above the feet, her legs are slightly parted and he can see, like the light at the end of a dim tunnel, a small white triangle.

Fiona's knickers.

Through the fog of alcohol, Donny feels his body come alive. He reaches instinctively for his groin but is too confused to recognise whether or not he has an erection. That little white triangle continues to flash like a beacon, showing him the way he must travel. He eases off the bed and somehow makes his way to the beanbag. He flops on to the floor and puts a hand under Fiona's skirt, moving it up along the warm smooth column of her leg until he touches what he has been seeking all his life. She murmurs, but makes no move to resist him as his fingers, almost independently of hand or even thought, pluck gently at the elastic of the knicker-leg and slide inside. Then, incredibly, they find the moist, secret softness. It feels natural, as if he has done this a million times.

Fiona moves a little: she starts to fumble at his hair as though trying to stroke it. Donny thinks he hears his name. He makes a serious effort to listen to what she is saying and hears it again: 'Poor Donny, poor baby.'

He becomes conscious of movement elsewhere in the room. Trevor is approaching from the other side. Fiona moves again as he, too, reaches her beanbag. Donny almost laughs because of how funny Trevor sounds: 'Wahh, wahh . . .'

He would laugh if he had any voice.

Just before he closes his eyes and floats away, he sees Trevor's head behind Fiona's shoulder and realises that his friend is clinging to her back like a baby koala latched on to its mother. He wants to tell Trevor to back off but it is too late. Like dark feathers, an awesome silence is settling over him.

In the CD player, Eminem gives way to Puff Daddy but, fitted together like a three-dimensional jigsaw, none of the three hears.

CHAPTER FIFTEEN

Riba is pushing along with her plans to spring Zelda. She had arrived at the hospital in a taxi at around the time her husband was walking into the Pro-Cathedral. He had the replacement for the Mustang, a boring Volvo, because the original plan for the day was that he would go home after the ceremony and they would come in together.

She had not gone directly to Zelda's room. Instead, she asked at the reception desk for an urgent totting-up of the bill. This being a Sunday, her request was met with opposition, until Riba, her voice soft, her gaze calm, pointed out that, if necessary, she and Zelda would leave the hospital without paying. This resulted in a little fluttering in the dovecote and, after what seemed like an age, somehow or other, from behind closed doors, a handwritten account was passed out to her. She did not even glance at it but handed over her credit card. There followed yet another delay while the doves behind the door messed around with authorisations and so forth.

At this stage, she is still kicking her heels in one of the armchairs in the reception area, the nodding black Labrador on the Guide Dogs for the Blind collection box has become her friend and she has memorised every detail of the entrance atrium, every blemish on the polished linoleum, every trailing strand of ivy, each religious icon and item on the notice-board. She works to retain her focus. This is going to work out, one step at a time: this minute has to be got through, the next when it arrives and then the next. Faith. Trust.

Finally, although the entire transaction has taken more than forty minutes, her trust is rewarded and she is given her receipts. 'Thank you very much – and please thank all the staff and consultants for us. This is for all of you.' With a sweet smile, she hands over the gigantic box of Cadbury's Milk Tray from a service station, the best she could do at short notice.

To her delight, when she gets to the room she finds that Zelda's drips are gone and she is out of bed. A blanket around her lap, she is sitting in a chair that has been pulled up to the window of the room. As she turns and looks at her mother, the sunlight flashes off the row of silver sequins fringing the gypsy bandanna she wears around her head so it seems, for an instant, that she is surrounded by pulsing light. Riba's heart lightens and lifts like a kite. 'You look so lovely, darling, and isn't it a brilliant day?' She leans down and kisses Zelda's thin, bluish cheek. 'Great news,' she continues. 'As I was coming in, I had a chat with a few of the doctors downstairs and they say you can go home. Today! Now!'

Zelda's face creases. 'But the haematologist isn't here – he's away for the weekend.'

'No, but I had a lovely chat with some of the other doctors and they all said it's OK.' She tightens the blanket around her daughter's knees. 'You sit here, lovey, and enjoy that sunshine, it'll do you a power of good.' She turns away to survey the room so she won't have to look for too long into those huge, alarmed eyes. 'My goodness, look at all this stuff – where will we start?'

'Mum, please, who did you talk to?'

'Now, darling, you just rest, leave everything to me.'

'But—'

'How long have you been here? Less than a week? This is ridiculous.' Riba hums loudly as she bustles around the room, tidying, folding and gathering up Zelda's things. When she is fairly sure there will be no further questions, she utters a quick, silent act of contrition for the white lie. It was in a good cause: even God could not hold it against her. Jay teaches that lies spoken in a good cause are not lies at all. For instance, in Hitler's Germany, if you told the Gestapo you weren't harbouring Jews when you were, did that count as a lie? Pish-tush! Of course it didn't.

In Yvonne's flat, Michael is getting nowhere. If the truth be told, he has shocked himself with his attitude and maybe she is picking up on the mixed vibes. Because if you had asked him, even a week ago, what he would do if he found a popsy of his up the pole, he would have looked at you askance and answered, without hesitation, that he would escort her personally to the boat. ASAP. Yet here he is, pleading with this girl not to destroy his baby.

To his horror, Collette had opened the door to him. Dark, where Yvonne is blonde, rotund where Yvonne is curvaceous, she has always reminded Michael of a baleful, spotty Christmas pudding. It is a nasty image, he knows, but she earned it all over again as she blocked the doorway, hands on hips. 'Well, look who's here!' Then, over her shoulder, 'Hey, Y, we have a visitor!' and before he could stop her, she had taken the flowers he carried and turned on her heel, leaving him to follow her into the bedsit. Then, to make things worse, she had tossed the bouquet on to the bed as if this were any old bunch plucked from a newsagent's bucket.

He couldn't suggest getting rid of her, however, because he didn't want to upset Yvonne straight away – or upset her more. He was quite shocked at the way she looked: the self-confident slapper he knew was nowhere in sight, her face, which until today he had never seen without makeup, was pink and puffy as though she had been crying, and she seemed barely to be paying attention to anything, slumped in the sole armchair and gazing at the floor. Although it is unseasonably warm outside, the flat is stuffy and gloomy, lit only by the central light fitting. The curtains at the window are still drawn.

Michael would have set fire to himself rather than sit beside the pudding, and he had had no choice but to pull out one of the rickety kitchen stools by the shelf that served as a table, turning his back to Collette in an effort to cut her out. He had got little satisfaction in attempting to engage with Yvonne, however: although he had hoped he sounded gentle and considerate, she had answered him, if she answered at all, only with gestures or monosyllables, or stared past him at her friend.

His patience is now running out fast: he has been here for the best part of half an hour and still she hasn't even looked him in the eye. He tries once more: 'Why are you doing this, Yvonne?' A stupid question, of course, but he is seriously frustrated. Anything to jolt her into some sort of response.

Shrug.

'Would you not postpone it at least for a little while until you're thinking clearer?'

Shrug.

'At least try to explain to me how you are feeling right now.'

Shake of the head.

The pudding on the bed can contain herself no longer. 'Listen, Mick, can't you see she's made up her mind? Just hand over the money and leave us alone, willya?'

That does it for Michael. 'This is outrageous.' He gets up from the stool and stands directly in front of Yvonne. 'This is between you and me, Yvonne, it has nothing to do with her – and if she doesn't go, and let us discuss this privately, you can whistle for any support from me, financial or otherwise. I mean it. I don't care what the consequences are.'

This brings Yvonne up. 'Oh, really? What about your wife – eh?'

'Tell Sophie.' Although he knows he isn't thinking straight and doesn't mean this, any development is preferable right now to the stonewalling.

'Tell her if you like,' he repeats. 'I'll probably have to tell her anyway, one way or the other. This is Dublin, not New York, and if you have an abortion, it'll be all over the airport in three weeks.'

Yvonne seems to teeter. Then, she says, 'Collette? Would you – do you mind?' After its brief eruption of energy, her voice is fading again.

Reluctantly, the ovoid one removes herself, but not before issuing a warning that she will be back within the hour and firing one last shot. 'You don't bug her, Mick, do you hear? She has enough to deal with. She's very tired and she's been throwing her guts up.'

After the door slams behind her, Michael decides it would be wise not to make any comment about Collette. He sits on the bed beside his bouquet. 'Do you like the flowers, Yvonne?'

'They're lovely. Thanks.' Her friend's departure seems to have made little difference: Yvonne has relapsed into her state of sullen lethargy.

Nor, over the next ten minutes, will she budge from her decision on the substantive issue. All his arguments and persuasion make no impression. It is almost as though she has been hypnotised for she repeats over and over again that she is going to England.

In the face of this blank, all-encompassing passivity, Michael, who has come armed for an explosive row – or at least a ding-dong argument – fears defeat. He glances at the plastic cuckoo clock on the cluttered mantelpiece. The service at the Pro-Cathedral must be well under way and he can't hang about for too much longer – he has to get out of here and up to the airport to justify his story about pressure of work in case Sophie rings him. He still has a little leeway, however – thank God for mobile phones, and that drillers and hammerers take Sunday off: if he doesn't make it in time, hopefully she won't notice the lack of background racket.

He forces himself to relax a little and changes tack. Although he is reeling, he knows this much, that to make any concrete offers right now would be downright stupid. Suicide. At least until he gets a chance to catch his breath.

Anyway, with someone like Yvonne, it is better to keep things simple. To give himself time to think he gets up and crosses to the window, a matter of just four steps. *All right, Mick. One thing at a time. Just concentrate on preventing her from going to England right now. Stall.* Without looking back at her, he opens the curtains, flooding the room with light. 'It's very warm in here. Do you mind if I let in a little air?' He raises the sash window and stands for a moment, breathing deeply.

Yvonne's bedsit, on the first floor of a tall, red-brick house converted into ten 'units', stands well back from the street and boasts a good-sized front garden, sadly overgrown and strewn with fast-food rubbish, builders' rubble, sawn-off pipes and broken slabs of concrete and brick. Right in the middle, an old lavatory, green with algae, boasts a tonsure of Russian ivy, already well advanced across the open bowl.

Further out, beyond the rusted iron railings, the North Circular Road is virtually deserted, except for a couple of cars driving by at a leisurely pace and a family, young mother, young father, baby in buggy, plus a toddler lagging behind as he sucks an Ice Pop with great concentration. A normal Sunday scene, far from what Michael is thinking about now.

He moves across and kneels beside Yvonne like a suitor, but as he does so, he sees a vial of tablets on the side-table, partially hidden by makeup, used and clean tissues, half-full coffee cups and other debris. He picks up the bottle, relieved to find it is Valium: it presents a rational explanation for the passivity, the blankness. He thinks swiftly – no point in pushing too hard. 'Listen, sweetheart,' he reaches up to stroke her bent head, 'you're so unhappy. I hate seeing you like this. Remember, you don't have to do anything right this minute, or tomorrow even – and you certainly don't have to face anything alone. Because there are three of us in this now, you and me and the little baby. Think of our little baby, sweetheart, it's done nothing to you, has it? Why would you kill our little baby when I'm prepared to look after you both? I love you, Yvonne – and I know I'll love our child. You will, too, if you give him a chance.'

She raises her head incredulously.

It has caught him, too, by surprise. 'I love you' is not a phrase that trips lightly off Michael Dolan's tongue, he has always been careful about that. Except, of course, as an automatic catch cry when he is saying goodnight or good morning to Sophie or rounding off a telephone call with her.

Where playaway women are concerned, you flatter them, tell them what they want to hear, but stop short of the love stuff, even if they push for it, because that way disaster lies. But there's no taking back the phrase now, not with her looking at him with those saucer eyes.

Michael forces himself to meet that gaze. If she believes what he has said, there's a chance she won't go. Since the flush of marriage grew pale, Michael has not put it around excessively, he likes to think, especially given that the travel trade is a great facilitator: unusual, somewhat unpredictable working hours, attractive, footloose young women. A man would want to be a saint – or Brian McMullan – to resist what is on offer all around him. Sometimes, especially in the summer when there is a lot of bare flesh and cleavage on show, it is like swimming through a sea of candy-floss. What man wouldn't open his mouth to take a bite?

Now, as he and Yvonne stare at one another, he is working up a head of steam: his affair with Yvonne – or anyone else for that matter – wasn't all

his doing anyway, was it? Sophie has to take some of the responsibility –
after all, she couldn't keep him interested.

It's the kid business too. Years of dreary tests and treatments for both of
them and here's the living proof that it wasn't him who was the problem.
Despite what the quacks had said, he had always suspected Sophie didn't
quite believe that – but now he can show her and the world that Michael
Dolan's sperm count is A-OK.

The cuckoo erupts from its balsawood chalet and calls the half-hour,
startling both of them. 'Jesus wept! That thing shout like that all night?'
Michael's knees are beginning to hurt and he levers himself up to sit on
the sagging arm of Yvonne's chair.

She is still staring at him. 'You can shut it off – do you really love me?'
She hiccups. Then: 'You never said that before.'

Michael puts an arm around her shoulders and pulls her close to him.
From this angle, the black roots are showing through her uncombed, ratty
hair, its colour turned to egg yolk by the sunshine streaming directly on to
her scalp through the open window; he cannot help comparing it with
Sophie's fair, shining cap.

He rejects the image, knowing it is dangerous. This desire to save his
child has caught him so high on the hop he needs to slow down. He needs
to consider the future, the way he has been running his life. He needs to
think, period. A novel task.

In many ways, he thinks now, Sophie has always thought herself too
good for him. With her trees and her birds and her bobby's job that was
just one step up from a hobby. She never properly appreciated him either,
did she? Leaving him to slog, summer and winter, bringing home the
bacon. It wasn't she who had to worry about the electricity bills, or
whether some stupid government tax or union strike would have an effect
on the tourism industry.

Yvonne is snuggling into the crook of his arm and he dares to hope
that, drugged though she is, her compliance isn't all to do with the Valium.
He may have won a stay of execution for his kid.

Mick loves her. Through the fog around her brain, Yvonne tries to grapple
with the concept. No one has said that to her since the summer she
turned sixteen and was being groped by a fifteen-year-old while he tried
to get his tongue into her throat and her knickers over her knees.

Her career with men has been full of variety, she has to admit.

Having successfully resisted the fifteen-year-old, she had lost her
virginity at the end of that summer to a sophisticated eighteen-year-old
from Blackrock College after a rugby disco. He had his father's Beemer for

the night and she had willingly and happily climbed into the back seat with him somewhere out near Rathfarnham.

Yvonne's home life had been problematic – alcoholic father, desperate, withdrawn mother – and her two older siblings had fled as quickly as their feet would carry them. As soon as she started earning money she, too, had gone – into her bedsit: a resting place from the carnival world full of men, almost all responsive to her. Very quickly, Yvonne had discovered what a little flash of thigh and a Wonderbra can achieve.

She had also found out that, rather than play at her own weight, as it were, she gets on better with older men, especially big men like Mick. She wouldn't even have minded a run around the block with Brian McMullan until he showed what a drip he was. But if Mick loves her, if they could be a family – or is she losing it?

She shifts a little in his arms and tries to think of the right questions to ask him about this new development. Like, it's a very, *very* serious thing for a married man to say he loves you, isn't it? Or is it?

Her bloody brain won't click properly. That's probably because each time she threw up today, afraid the Valium was gone too, she took another tablet. Collette was sure it would be OK and it was. The ball of wound-up anger, worries and fear had – has – shrunk to a little blip off in the distance somewhere.

There is something coming and going, some problem she knows she definitely should consider as a result of what Mick said. On one of its wavery passes, she manages to catch hold of it: just as that first boyfriend told her he loved her so she would get her kit off, is Mick telling her he loves her now only to get his own way?

Yvonne closes her eyes and leans her heavy head into his solid frame. Would it not be lovely, though, to have some man take care of her, love her, mind her and be good to her . . . ?'

It might even be nice to be a mother. To give the baby, whatever it turned out to be – even a little girl, maybe – the kind of love she herself had always missed.

Oh, God, why can't she think straight? She did have a quick burst there, around the time he mentioned the wife.

Or had it been her who had brought it up? It's so hard even to order her thoughts, the way they keep drifting by . . . There is something very important . . .

Yes, here it is. The wife. 'And you'll tell your wife you'll leave her? Like, straight away. If you haven't the guts to tell her, I'll tell her . . . Like . . .' The thought is fading and she grabs for one last bit of it. 'No chance, Mick, unless you leave your wife, I'm not going to be – to be—'

She can't frame the words, she can't get any more words out at all . . . Yvonne is so unbelievably tired. She just wants to sleep, and when she wakes up, maybe this whole fucking nightmare will be over.

Donny's room is as quiet as midnight. Trevor has slipped backwards, away from the other two, and is lying on his back, a string of vomit oozing from his slack mouth on to the floor. The other two are still locked together, Donny's hand is under Fiona's skirt, her uppermost arm is wound around his neck. Both are deeply comatose.

It is a quarter to three and Zelda, having given in as usual to her mother, is fully dressed, ready to leave her refuge. She has finished her lunch, said goodbye to the few nurses who remain on duty today. Her medication has all been catalogued, the instruction sheets have been filled in and her room is in order. Her mother has even stripped the bed: the linen is folded and at its foot, while blankets and slipless pillows are piled neatly at its head. 'Of course I will,' she had insisted, when Zelda had protested she shouldn't take things this far. 'Why wouldn't I? Those poor nurses are always run off their feet, there's only the Sunday staff here today and, anyway, they weren't expecting to lose you so soon.'

There had been no point in fighting. She didn't want to go home yet – seriously didn't want to – but her mum would crumble at a hint of such heresy. Of everyone involved, perhaps only Zelda knew how deeply her mother's awesome and genuine determination was threatened by fear about her illness and how quickly that determination could be undermined. Zelda could not face being responsible for that.

Mum and all of them would have enough to bear soon.

They are now waiting for her dad to pick them up. She hopes that this time they won't fight. She truly hates it when they fight about her and, more than once, has wished that there were two of her, one to go to that blasted island with her mum and the other to stay here so her dad can mind her; the sooner she dies and they all get it over with, the sooner everyone can begin to be happy again.

They have given her a good life, she is grateful for that: in childhood, no one could have asked for more than the toys and outings, the trips to the seaside and the birthday parties. As for the dressing-up boxes! Predictably, Zelda's dressing-up box had been the market leader within her circle, an Aladdin's cave of rich colour and flowing materials, stocked not only with her mother's cast-offs but with sale purchases: remnants of gorgeous bridal or furnishing brocades, chiffons, voile. Zelda even remembers, on one occasion, her mother's triumphant return from town with a substantial length of gold lamé.

She can't answer for Donny, of course, but after her mother got caught up in this Jay Street stuff, Zelda wasn't all that put out because, by the time it had happened, she was already well into the development of her own separate life and friendships and wasn't dependent on all-encompassing maternal attention.

Since the crash, her brain has started to dwell on the earliest images and sense memories: the taste of her banky, a tattered piece of binding she had continued to suck long after the blanket itself had disintegrated; the sharp smell of roses when her mother, who hated the smell of baby powder, showered her with clouds of her own talc after bathing her; the pulsating of the push-mower blades as she sat on her father's shoulders while he patrolled their lawn with it on summer Saturdays. The surprising feel of a daisy, spongy centre and moist petals, the first time her aunt Sophie showed her how to slit the stems to make a chain.

Zelda has wondered if this vivid, sense-o-vision slide show is common to all dying people.

One of the more persistent images is of Pangur, the stray white cat that had wandered one day into the front garden to climb into her go-car and sit on her lap when she was about three. Instead of panicking that the creature would smother or scratch her, as any ordinary mother would have done, Zelda's had been delighted: 'Oh, my goodness! That's Pangur Bán!' So the stray had been named and allowed to stay and, like his namesake, the faithful companion to the early Christian annalist who had immortalised him, had been a great pal until, like herself, he had succumbed to cancer. The difference was his great cat-age – or so the vet had estimated – of about sixteen; unlike her life, his had spanned more than normal.

The sense of Pangur being present has become stronger lately and, although she knows it is fanciful and would never mention it to anyone, Zelda has found herself speculating about whether she is to meet him again in the afterlife, if his spirit has been sent to her as a herald. She refuses to rule out the possibility that a creature so friendly and loyal does not deserve his own reward through eternity.

She looks across at her mother, dozing in the warmth of the room. Her misguided, irritating, exasperating, frustrating, stubborn, self-centred and thoroughly annoying mother.

Zelda's heart floods with love. What will heaven be like without her?

CHAPTER SIXTEEN

The lobby of the Gresham Hotel in Dublin is large and commodious, thickly carpeted, furnished with deep armchairs and couches. Dubliners unconcerned about trends arrange to meet here rather than clump across the bare wooden floors of the more fashionable establishments in the booming city. It is packed on this early Sunday afternoon.

Brian looks down at the plate of biscuits beside his cooling coffee. For more than twenty years, conversation has flowed fluently around the areas common to him and this woman: their families, EconoCar, Donny and Zelda, Sophie's brothers and parents, Brian and Eily's lack of same. They have reminisced about when they were young, laughed at peccadilloes, their own and those of their spouses, dreamed up exotic group holidays, which never materialised.

All of that seems to have dried up since the air crash as the world reversed its motion. Even the short walk down O'Connell Street had been fraught so that, long before they got to the hotel, he was half regretting the impulse to invite her.

He can stand the tension no longer. 'Have you been reading the newspapers about all of this?'

'No, as a matter of fact I haven't. I haven't been able to. I can't listen to the radio either, or watch the news. It's too hard.'

'Me neither.'

He swallows hard as the image of his daughter's funeral, which had visited him during the memorial Mass, assaults him again. He is also watching the delicacy of Sophie's fingers as she replaces her cup on her saucer. As usual, she is wearing little or no makeup but he can smell her perfume. As he sits opposite her, in her dark jacket and silky blouse, Brian accepts at last that he is falling in love.

There. He had allowed the thought to finish without choking it off, and although this is the type of falling-in-love that is splashed in bold headlines across the front pages of tabloid newspapers when it concerns celebrities, the acknowledgement felt easy, natural.

More than natural, it had felt like a beam of light across the darkness of what he has gone through recently. It has also allowed him to admit that this process has not been sudden. He recollects little things he has noticed about Sophie over the years, especially in the last few: the way her hair curves across her cheek, how a little vein rises in her forehead when she smiles and, when she is upset, her habit of hunching her shoulders as if to make herself small. As he watches her fiddle with the little silver spoon on the saucer, Brian hugs to himself the illicit, thrilled feeling as some of the questioning and agonising lifts off his back. Because, in the absence of thought police, there is no ban on falling in love when it remains secret. No harm done. No lines crossed.

If he is careful, none will be. All he has to do is make sure he keeps it to himself, and deals with it like a responsible, mature adult. He smiles at Sophie. 'I suppose we'd better be getting on. I told Eily I'd meet her at the hospital.'

She smiles back and stands up.

Instead of going straight home from the Gresham to the silence of an empty house Sophie, who is emotionally at sixes and sevens, feels she has to keep on the move. It is such a pet day – why not a walk? So she sets out for Dollymount, even though she knows that, since it is a Sunday, half of Dublin will probably have the same idea.

As expected, the Clontarf Road is chock-a-block with families and Sunday drivers, all heading for the nature reserve at the Bull Wall, for St Anne's Park, for Dollymount and the Howth Peninsula. She almost turns back but, driven onwards by the need not to think, persists, stop-starting along the Clontarf Road and passing the time by house-shopping along the shining sea-scrubbed terraces to her left and admiring the industrial symmetry of complexes behind the estuary to her right: the soaring twin chimneys of Poolbeg power station, the brooding cranes, angular warehousing and, beneath the superstructure and funnels of the huge ferries and container vessels, the squat storage tanks humping along the far shore like coils of a massive sea serpent. Sophie has always appreciated the sense of humour of whatever authority or city father had decided years ago to name this muddy stretch of seawater the Blue Lagoon, and who had decided to plant the linear park along its length with palm trees.

The tide is out, and when she parks at Dollymount Strand, the sea exists only as a long sliver of light far out towards the horizon, exposing miles of hard-packed, rippled sand. She climbs out of the car and takes a deep, balmy breath from the little breeze curling towards her face from the

Hill of Howth. At the last moment, she takes her camera bag out of the boot of the Mini: habit dies hard.

She hasn't gone far when she hears music and, on investigation, finds that the musicians belong to a group – obviously Romanian, to judge by their swarthy skin and the colourful, patterned scarves and skirts of the women – ensconced within the hollows of the dunes. Sophie is familiar with some, who are sellers of the *Big Issues* and buskers in various parts of the city, and joins the circle of onlookers who are standing around the group to listen. Like most people, all Sophie has registered of the Romanians on the streets of Dublin is their shuttered expressions and extended, mendicant hands. Here, off-duty as it were, these women, men and children are uninhibited, free, and thoroughly enjoying themselves.

As the accordions, bouzoukis and fiddles skirl up and down the scales, she hunkers down and unobtrusively extricates her camera from the bag, lines it up and starts firing. The sound of the motor drive brings round the heads of two of the violinists to look over their shoulders. On seeing her, they smile widely and directly into her lens. Startlingly, neither has a single tooth in her head but the grins are so delightfully unselfconscious that even as the drive whirs and clicks, Sophie knows she must have at least one winner here.

Nothing comes free, of course, and as she stands up, one of the crones throws down her instrument and, agile as a panther, grabs her arm with one hand and holds out the palm of the other, surprisingly smooth in contrast to the rest of her skin. 'Tell your fortune, Miss?'

Sophie, knowing she is caught in fair exchange, roots in her camera bag for her purse. 'All right.' She drops a few pound coins into the palm as some of the onlookers move closer to watch.

The woman puts the money in a pocket then seizes both of Sophie's hands, surprising her with the strength of the grip. She bends low over them, moving them this way and that, examining them minutely. Then she raises her head suddenly and engages directly, her tone matter-of-fact: 'No children.'

Sophie's stomach turns over. She is a private person and, up to that moment, has treated this side-show as a source of public embarrassment. To get it over with as quickly as possible, although she hadn't been asked a question she answers anyway, 'No. No children.'

Again the fortune-teller examines her hands. 'A big change coming in your life, lady.'

This is easier, standard stuff, and Sophie relaxes a little. *You will be married before the end of the year; you will meet a dark man; you will have three children, two boys and a girl; you will have a broken heart but that is only for a short time, then everything will turn out well* . . . Although she has never had her palm read before, she knows the jargon from listening to Nancy at the office who, waiting in vain for predictions to come true, remains devoted to some sage who operates out of a tiny flat in the city centre. 'Anything else?' She glances at the circle of grinning, cynical onlookers.

With a bony finger, the fortune-teller traces something on the palm of her right hand. 'Two men, one dark, one bright. And,' she pauses for effect, 'a baby!' She thrusts out her hand. 'More money, lady!'

Sophie, who thinks she has detected a flash of pity in those dark eyes, withdraws her hands. 'No. No more. Thank you very much. Thank you.' As she backs away, feeling as if her barren womb is on public display, she stumbles over a tuffet of scutch. As she rights herself, her cheeks on fire, she looks back and sees that the woman is now reading another palm and that a queue has formed.

The encounter has unsettled her further, if that is possible. Not the stuff about big changes coming, because that is grist to all fortune-tellers' mills, not even the stuff about two men in her life, although that was tempting since Brian is fair and Michael dark – but how had the woman guessed she had no children?

There is probably an ordinary explanation for what she had said: these knowing, experienced grannies can probably tell by looking at a woman's body.

A baby, after all these years when she is pushing forty? Herself and Mick? That's laughable.

She is coming out now on to the vast beach, filled with Dubliners whacking tennis balls, kicking footballs between improvised goal-posts and, flouting the city's bylaws, exercising excited dogs off their leashes. For generations, Dollymount has served not only as one of the lungs of the city but as an unofficial instruction track for learner drivers, and these learners – some as young as fourteen – hack, jolt and zoom their way up and down in each other's wheel ruts under the anxious eyes of their self-appointed instructors. With her illustrator's eye, Sophie sees it as an airy watercolour, the type attempted by a lot of amateurs: *Dollymount On a Sunny Day.*

It is all so normal.

She stops dead and looks out to sea, ignoring the pleas of a youngster to kick back the football that has crossed her path. Never again will she allow herself and Eily's husband to be alone to enter together into a twilight zone of romantic adolescent rubbish. They are sensible, middle-aged adults.

The kid whose ball she has ignored gives her the two fingers as he races in front of her to retrieve it but Sophie doesn't see. As she resumes her walk under a wheeling constellation of sea-birds squabbling over titbits, she has to work hard to push away the image of the fortune-teller's pitying gaze.

Riba and her daughter are still waiting for Brian to arrive. 'Will I read to you? Would you like that, Zeldy? Let's see what we have here.' Out of her capacious handbag, she takes a small Bible, a dog-eared paperback about angels and a pocket edition of Gibran's *The Prophet*. Choosing the latter, she skims through the pages and picks out a piece she finds particularly edifying and has read over and over again. 'Listen to this, Zel. When you're a mother yourself, this will really mean something to you.' In a low, thrilling voice, she begins to read:

Your children are not your children.
They are the sons and daughters of Life's longing for itself.
They came through you but not from you,
And though they are with you yet they belong not to you.
You may give them your love but not your thoughts,
For they have their own thoughts. You may house their bodies
but not their souls,
For their souls dwell in the house of to-morrow, which you
cannot visit, not even in your dreams—

She stops as she hears a sound and realises that Zelda is crying. 'What's the matter, darling? What's wrong?'

'What do you think is wrong, Mother? Are you trying to torture me? I'll never be a mother and you know I won't.'

Riba throws aside the little book and moves swiftly to take her daughter into her arms but Zelda reacts violently, throwing her off; weak though she is, the gesture is powerful. 'Don't do this. I'm sick of all this pretending that I have a future.' Eyes blazing like torches in her pale face, she gazes at her mother. 'Why can't you just leave me in peace? I'm dying, Mum. Why don't you just let me? Give me a break — listen to those words you just read! *Listen!* It's my life, not yours. I don't belong to you and I can make my own decisions. I'm struggling to stay alive just for you and Dad and other people,' her voice cracks, 'but what about me? It's so hard. I'm so tired, I want to go, it's just a sleep, Mum, it's just like going asleep.' She puts both hands up to her face and sobs openly.

'You're not going to die, Zelda,' Riba says levelly, although she has to employ all her resources to keep from dissolving along with her daughter.

'Listen to me, Zelda, you're not going to die, but you have to co-operate. You have to stop thinking all these negative thoughts.' She reaches out and this time there is no resistance as she cradles the precious, emaciated body just as she had during Zelda's babyhood, rocking it to and fro. 'There now, get it all out – sh-shhh, there now, you'll feel better, let it all out, my little baby darling.'

'I'm never even going to have a boyfriend.' Zelda continues to sob hard but, little by little, the fit diminishes and she becomes calm. She pulls away. 'I'm sorry, Mum, but you've got to understand that it's very difficult to keep up a brave face a hundred per cent of the time.'

'I do, darling, I really do. I promise, if you do it, you'll feel it. You really will – here, put on a bit of blusher.' Again, she delves into the handbag, this time producing a large cosmetics bag, striped in pink and silver. 'You don't want poor old Dad to find you looking like Little Orphan Annie.'

Through her distress, Zelda actually laughs. 'What are we going to do with you, Mum? You're incorrigible.'

Riba laughs, too, but as her daughter submits to the makeup, seeming to bask in the soothing touch, she has to be ruthless with herself to keep her hands steady while she plies the little wands and brushes.

Ten minutes later, however, they have both achieved what passes for normality within their relationship and are sitting quietly when they hear the familiar, heavy tread in the corridor.

'What's going on?' Astounded, Brian stops in the doorway.

'We're leaving.' Riba beams from him to Zelda and back again. 'We're being released. Isn't it wonderful? We were ready ages ago, weren't we, Zel? We could have taken a taxi but we decided to wait for you to share the surprise!'

'But I thought . . .' Brian is understandably bewildered. 'What did the consultant say?'

'The haematologist is away for the weekend, apparently, but all the other doctors, the ones that are here, say it's all right. What's the problem? Do you not want our daughter to come home?' A guilty conscience is a great aid to sounding indignant.

After a small hesitation, Brian takes her at face value. He turns to Zelda. 'So, you're feeling better, then, Zeldy? I have to say you look great.'

Riba has to agree that Zelda, whose thinness is disguised by an enormous, peach-coloured sweater and baggy tracksuit bottoms, looks healthier than she has for a long time. The gypsy bandanna has helped enormously, not only in offsetting her baldness but in adding sparkle to her face. And of course the makeup helps too. 'I'm grand, Dad. A bit tired. Could probably do with a nap – as though I haven't had enough sleep here! Do you know what I'd also love?' She grins. 'I'm sick of food that's good for me. Would you believe a bag of chips from Burdock's? Is it open on a Sunday?'

Although Riba is struck once again by how unnaturally large Zelda's teeth look in her shrunken face, she cannot credit what she is hearing. She is enchanted. If there was ever any proof that Jay and California Monica and all the rest of the group are as good as their word in extending their protection, this is it. This is the first time in many, many months that Zelda has actually asked for food. Even if this is an act for her father's benefit, isn't it amazing that she has the energy? 'I think the one in Phibsboro might be open,' she replies joyfully, 'and if they're not, we'll bloody well knock until they are, won't we, Brian?'

Brian, too, seems delighted as he picks up Zelda's luggage. 'Sure – sure. Come on, let's get out of this place.' He picks up Zelda's bag. 'Burdock's it is.'

The Sunday-afternoon rush-hour is well under way when they pull away from the hospital. With old folk tucked safely between baby seats, the train of family saloons is trekking to the mountains, to Killiney, or north to Dollymount. The lovely weather has brought out cyclists, too, and joggers and walkers. The whole south side of the city seems to be on the move, as though it is just waking up from a long sleep.

When they finally manage to cross the Liffey it is almost as busy on the north side. Yet all the way across the city Brian, who would normally spend such a trip grumbling about traffic and the idiots who drive motor-cars these days, has been oddly silent. Riba, afraid to begin any conversation lest she inadvertently betray her secret, has let him be, chatting inconsequentially to Zelda for a while then lapsing into silence, quite enjoying the undemanding music from the radio station he has chosen.

She waits for Brian to say something about the service, and when he doesn't, feels she should at least ask. 'How did it go, then? Was it awful? It was very long, wasn't it? Considering it started at twelve? What time was it when you got to the hospital?'

Brian, heading for a parking area beside Mountjoy Prison, turns into the laneway running down to it beside Phibsboro Library. 'Sophie and I went for a cup of coffee at the Gresham afterwards. *Idiot!*' This to the driver of a Discovery, who, under the mistaken impression that two cars could not pass in the narrow space, flashes him with his headlights. Riba lets him concentrate on manoeuvring the Volvo past the other car, smiling indulgently as he mutters about show-offs who drive big ignorant heaps of tin. As he backs into a space between an Almera and a Yaris, she has to restrain herself from pointing out that the late lamented Mustang, as red as a fire engine, is hardly your self-effacing standard saloon and turns round to wink at Zelda, but finds the girl curled up asleep in the back seat.

While disappointing, this is not worrying. Coming out of hospital is always tiring: when that fresh air hits you it's like a drug. 'Let's not disturb her,' she whispers, when Brian turns off the engine. 'You go on up and get the chips. We can eat them here, or if she's still asleep, we can bring them home with us – heat them up in the microwave.' She checks her watch. 'Get some for Donny too, will you? He should be home by now. He said he was going to Trevor's for an hour or so.' She chuckles. 'You know him, we won't be able to get away with it – he'll smell those chips off us a mile away.'

With Brian gone, she settles back into her seat to wait. Through the windscreen, her attention is caught by a lone seagull, coasting effortlessly against the pinkening sky above the gaol. This is amazing – Riba gets excited: the bird is definitely an omen, showing her how it celebrates its own freedom in the faces of the poor, trapped inmates below, showing how she and Zelda will also be free, floating above their own prison of pain and trauma.

As she watches the gull, which is cruising along a wide, figure-of-eight pattern, she spots a graffiti on the wall in front of them where, amongst the more lurid exclamations and exhortations, one artist had joyfully proclaimed, in purple, that: *What can go right, will go right. Think about that.*

Riba smiled. *Thank you, God.* That was meant for her to see at this moment. Once you start being sensitive to connections in this world, you start to realise how so many seemingly unrelated events, objects and people turn out to link in to each other in the most amazing way. Brian will come to understand, she has every confidence that he will, especially when they come home and he sees what wonders have been wrought in his daughter.

When he gets back to the car, trailing that vinegary, irresistible aroma, Zelda wakes and they decide to eat their impromptu meal there and then. Donny's can be reheated.

There's something superb about eating fresh chips straight out of the paper: it's the heat on your fingertips, the sting of salt on your lips, the half-pleasurable, half-guilty feeling that you are doing something smashing which is really bad for you – as Riba takes the first bite into the crisp skin and rediscovers the hot, soft flouriness within, her cup of sensuality runs over. Above them, the deepening blue is now streaked not only with pink but with salmon and gold. 'Look at that,' she breathes. 'Isn't it gorgeous?'

'What?' Following the direction of her gaze, his mouth full of chips,

Brian peers through the windscreen towards the high stone walls of the gaol. 'I can't see anything.'

'Up there, look – the sky.'

'Oh, yeah, nice.' Brian gives it only a cursory glance before delving back into his bag.

Riba looks across at him. 'Honestly! I don't know what I'm going to do with you – and not only you. There are wonders out there, all around you, up there in the sky, but it's amazing how many people never look up from their own boots. Philistine!' She digs him affectionately in the ribs but is taken aback when he jumps as though she has hurt him. 'Oh! Sorry.'

'It was nothing – you just gave me a fright.' He stuffs another handful of chips into his mouth.

'Well, I think it's lovely, Mum,' Zelda, whose mouth is also full, pipes up from the back.

Riba decides not to pursue it further and, for the next few minutes, the windows of the car steam up as they consume their chips. Riba revels in this: the quiet, the peace, the little cocoon where nothing needs to be said and they are all enjoying something together.

She holds on to the feelings and, continuing to chew, lowers the window to watch the sky as the colours fade to streaks of grey. That is what life is all about on this beautiful, God-given earth, and from now on, it can only improve. All she has to do for the next thirty-six hours is be careful, say nothing to Zelda, Sophie, or anyone.

If she stays alert, nothing can go wrong.

Brian balls up his empty bag, transparent with grease. He looks across at his wife who, munching heartily, is carefully scraping one of the stragglers along the bottom of the bag to get every remaining smidgen of salt on to it.

At the beginning of their relationship, he had been fascinated by Eily's sensuous approach to even the simplest food, her habit of smacking and licking her lips, of emitting little grunts and groans of appreciation as she first anticipates then eats whatever is in front of her. To her, food is pleasure. What she puts into her mouth should be luscious, creamy, pleasing to the nose and eye; she even takes two cherries in her favourite tipple, the dark, aromatic Manhattan cocktail.

In the early years he had regarded all of this as an endearing eccentricity, had even found it erotic – the bellwether of other appetites – until, as time ploughed on, the novelty wore off and it got on his nerves. He had teased her about it, 'Aren't you afraid you'll put on too much weight?', to which she had always responded with the tart old saw about physical age advancing in one of only two directions: *widen* or *wizen*. 'And of the two I'd prefer the former, thank you very much!'

Brian's own attitude to food could not be more different, and although he would never say this to her, all the care she lavishes on her cooking is wasted on him. Born of unknown parents, discovered wrapped in a filthy blanket in the doorway of a supermarket when he was less than a day old, he had been taken into care then brought up in a series of crowded foster-homes where the food was plentiful but bland and the rule always seemed to be, 'To the Biggest the Spoils.'

Even the foster-mother in his final and best-loved home, the one from which he had been sent to his rugby-playing secondary school, had been less than proficient with the pots and pans. As a result, food is fuel to Brian. You're hungry, you eat, and so long as it tastes OK and fills the belly, there is no percentage in being picky about what kind of food it is. Certainly no point in spending hours and hours slaving in a kitchen to present something that vanishes in a few minutes so you have nothing to show for it except a pile of washing-up.

He knows that, in this at least, he is an ungrateful git: when he hears the way other guys bitch about the diet of convenience foods and packet soups they get fed, he knows he shouldn't take Eily's kitchen skills for granted and should be grateful she still cares.

How does Sophie feel about food? Funny, he has never asked her that, or even noticed.

'Yum!' Eily runs her tongue around her lips. 'Thanks, Brian, that was great. Better than the Gresham.'

Brian almost jumps out of his skin. Is Eily reading his thoughts now? Then he calms down. It is quite a common expression in Dublin but she had startled him all the same and, quickly, he turns the key in the ignition. 'Hey, since we're out anyway, why don't we go to a movie? There's bound to be something on at around five o'clock at the Omniplex?' He twists to look at his daughter. 'Are you up for it, Zeldy?'

'What about Donny?' Riba looks at the dashboard clock. 'Should we stop by and collect him first?'

'Ah, you know him,' Brian chuckles, 'this should be Zelda's treat and I doubt if she wants to go to something that involves explosions and hanging from the bottom of a helicopter – but I suppose we should at least ask him.' He takes out his mobile. 'Let me give him a buzz.'

Neither Donny's mobile nor the home telephone is answered. 'Huh!' Brian stows his own phone back under the dashboard. 'Bloody head-phones. I don't know how often I have to tell him, I'll kill him!' He turns again to Zelda. 'Ah, well, his loss – so, how about it, Zel?'

'What about his chips?' Zelda smiles at him.

'Good enough for him, the little bugger!' Brian grins back. 'Anyway, the microwave isn't going to run away, is it?'

'All right, Dad.' Zelda settles back into her seat. 'I'm a bit tired but I haven't been to a movie in yonks. Go for it!'

If stillness had a colour, the stillness in Donny's bedroom is now a deep shade of charcoal.

CHAPTER SEVENTEEN

'We're just in time.' Brian peers through his windscreen, scanning the marquee above the multiplex at the Omni shopping centre.

'I've changed my mind, Dad.' From the back seat, Zelda's voice is thin and tired. 'I'd prefer to go home if you don't mind.'

Instantly, Brian feels like a big, selfish oaf. 'Of course, dote,' he says quickly. 'It was just an idea.' He puts the car into gear and swings it round the little roundabout in front of the cinema.

When they get to Marble Gardens, an old Carina is blocking their gateway. The two occupants, a man and a woman, get out as soon as they see Brian pull in across their bonnet. Eily recognises them. 'It's Fiona's parents,' she says, as she opens the door. 'I met them at that awful parent-teacher meeting in October I told you about. Hello, there!' she calls.

As they come forward to meet her, the faces of both the man and the woman are creased with either irritation or anxiety, Brian cannot decipher which. He leaves the greetings to Eily and busies himself with Zelda, her luggage, and with securing the car.

The Prendergasts and Eily are still talking outside the gate as he and Zelda approach and he comes in on the tail end of what the wife is saying: 'So it's not like her, really. She knows she has to go to her granny's in Slane – it's a good hour's drive and we hate arriving after dark. My mother does worry if we're even a couple of minutes late.'

'How do you know she's here?' Brian looks at the dark house. 'There are no lights on. Are you sure she said our house?'

'That's her bicycle.' The wife, plump, in a navy raincoat and plastic rain hat points to the purple bike half concealed under a hydrangea just inside the gate. 'So she's here all right, she said she was coming here when she left.'

'That was at about half past twelve,' the man, totally bald and thin as bamboo, chimes in.

Doubtfully, Eily shakes her head as she opens their gate. 'Perhaps she just left the bike here and they all went off somewhere. Come on inside, anyhow – have you met my husband? Brian, this is Mr and Mrs Prendergast.'

Brian nods as the introductions are made.

Once inside, Eily walks to the foot of the stairs and puts a finger to her lips. 'Ssh!' They all stand still to listen. She turns to the others. 'Nothing. Not a squeak – if they were up there we'd know, believe me! They'd always have their music on.' She smiles brightly. 'Try not to worry, I'm sure they're somewhere about and will be back in a jiffy.'

She introduces Zelda, then insists they all go into the kitchen for a cup of tea, 'and a few home-made scones – and I even have lovely fresh cream and strawberry jam.'

'I won't if you don't mind, Mum – I'm knackered.'

Brian looks sharply at his daughter: under the electric light, he can see streaks of reddish-brown makeup on her cheeks, but underneath, the glow he'd got so excited about in the hospital has vanished and she does indeed look exhausted. 'I'll take your stuff up, Zel.' He excuses himself to the Prendergasts. 'I'll join you in a minute.'

He glances at Donny's closed door as he passes it on the way to Zelda's room. The giant Liverpool FC poster covering almost its entire surface has come unstuck on one corner and is curling downwards, in danger of tearing. Having deposited Zelda's bags, Brian comes back and carefully sticks it back again. To make it adhere fully, he has to push hard and even hammer a little with his fist against the worn Blu-Tack. From downstairs, he can hear Eily's blithe chatter ringing around the quiet house. 'She's a nice girl, Fiona, I'm very fond of her, we all are. We even know how fond she is of her granny in Slane.'

Brian stands back to check that the poster will hold. Donny's been a bit of a brat, lately, but of course he would be, being so close to Zelda. There and then, he decides that in addition to the Anfield trip Donny is to take with one of his mates – presumably that weedy Trevor – he and his son will take another in the near future. First class all the way. Father and son. No women allowed.

He hesitates. From downstairs, he can now hear the clink of cups. Dammit! They're settling in. The last thing he needs in his house is a tea party, but he must be polite. He will stay for the minimum time necessary then escape to the airport and the blessed relief of immersion in paperwork, normally a task he detests. He has a good excuse: EconoCar's monthly VAT returns are due and because of his hospitalisation are almost on the deadline.

Feeling far from hospitable, Brian returns to the kitchen, and after ten minutes of chit-chat with their guests is fit to be tied. He is wondering how much longer he has to put in before he can decently make his excuses when he hears Zelda scream.

He is up from his chair and in the hallway as Zelda screams a second time, a sustained wail, sounding on and on—

Ignoring the protests from his neck and shoulder, Brian takes the stairs three at a time. Behind him, he is aware that the others have crowded from the kitchen into the hall and are looking up at him, but his attention is fixed on his daughter, who is standing in the open doorway of Donny's room. On seeing Brian she cuts off the scream and instead, on a shuddering intake of breath, says, 'Daddy – Daddy, they're all dead! They're all dead! I just came in for a CD and they're all dead.'

Brian pushes past her and, under the harshness of the central electric light, sees three life-sized dolls broken on Donny's bedroom floor. Then the smell assaults him: a stench of vomit, alcohol, and what might be urine. For Zelda's sake, he forces himself to speak calmly: 'Go and tell your mother to call an ambulance, quickly. Tell her to dial 999.' But as he drops to his knees beside his son, Zelda stays where she is, fists ground into her mouth as she gazes at this tableau that might have been arranged for filming: one of Donny's hands is under Fiona's skirt, one of Trevor's is wound through her hair.

'Oh, God, oh, God – what has he done to my daughter?' Wheeling, Brian sees the shocked white face of Fiona's mother. Against the woman's protests, he leaps up and bundles her out of the room again, manhandling her without apology. 'Go back downstairs, I'll handle this.' She doesn't obey, but continues to moan.

He dashes back and, dropping again to the floor, presses an ear to Donny's chest to listen for signs of life. Because of the noise Mrs Prendergast is making, however, it is what seems to be a very long time before he can determine whether the faint sound he hears is the rushing of his own blood or his son's. *Thank God!* He sits back on his heels. His son is alive. He doesn't care who sees the gush of tears.

Quickly, he pulls Donny's unresisting hand from under the girl's skirt, then repeats the listening exercise with the other two, and finds them to be breathing too, albeit slowly and shallowly. He swallows hard. 'They're going to be all right,' he says, to no one in particular.

'Will I call Dr Murray? It'll only be a locum, of course, because it's a Sunday.' From right behind him, Brian hears Eily's voice, quiet but unnaturally high. He heaves himself to his feet, picks up Fiona and carries her to Donny's bed. He has revised his thinking about calling an ambulance. He knows enough about drink and its excesses to guess that the benefit to be gained by calling a GP would be marginal; the advice would be to take the kids to the nearest hospital, where they would be monitored as they slept it off. Probably on mattresses on the floor. They are, all three, hearty and healthy and will survive this. 'The first thing is to get them awake and rehydrated,' he says. He props Donny and Trevor against the two beanbags in such a position that he can be sure that even if they do vomit they won't choke. Then he turns to Eily, forcing himself to sound in charge: 'Listen, we've all done it.' He includes the Prendergasts. 'They're young, they're not going to die – although they're going to be pretty sorry for themselves. The chemist in Phibsboro is open, I'll go down and get a few sachets of Dioralyte. In the meantime,' he turns to Eily, 'have we any 7-Up, lemonade, even Coke?'

'I think there's a couple of bottles of ginger ale.' Eily's voice, although remaining calm, is as thin and tight as a drumskin.

'Right, pour it out and let it go flat for a few minutes, add two tablespoons of sugar and a tablespoon of salt to each glass. OK? I'll be back with the Dioralyte as soon as I can.'

'OK.' Eily turns and makes a gesture that the Prendergasts should go before her down the stairs but Mrs Prendergast objects.

'I want to stay with my daughter.'

'She'll be fine.'

The other woman hesitates and then, after a last look at Fiona, who seems for all the world to be sleeping normally, obeys.

In the midst of this crisis, Brian has to admire Eily's *sangfroid*. He turns to Zelda. 'You OK, darling?'

She nods. 'I'll go to my room – you're sure they're going to be all right?'

'All right? They'll rue this day, mark my words. They'll be as sick as parrots. So sick they won't touch a drop for a long, long time. You go and rest, honey. I'll see you soon.' She, too, leaves and Brian, his knees feeling the shock, opens the window of the stifling room to refresh the air. He stares out into the darkness, breathing deeply. It is so thin, the membrane between life and death.

'You're crying.'

He has not heard Eily come back into the room. 'I'm fine.' He doesn't turn round. 'I'll go to the chemist's in a moment. I'm just trying to catch my breath.'

He senses her hesitation and then, quietly, her departure. With one exception, that of Jay Street, Eily has always known when to push and when to leave well alone. He has always admired her for that.

It is not difficult to discern how Trevor Jameson came by his unprepossessing appearance. Both of his parents are pale, earnest and bespectacled;

his father is a computer scientist in the software research area; his mother works in the accounts division of the government's Department of Enterprise and Employment and they have reacted to this crisis with deep worry and pained expressions, rather than with the shock and anger that continues to reverberate around Riba's sitting room from the Prendergasts. Brian has gone to find an open chemist's shop and the others are waiting for a doctor to arrive: the McMullans had yielded to the strident demands of the other parents. This interim conference has been going on for more than three-quarters of an hour, and Riba is tired of it. Although she is paying lip-service to the fretting, the more that the conversational loop continues to whirl around her head like an infestation of horrible black flies, the more she is tempted to stand up and tell them all to go home.

What's the commotion about? The episode is distasteful and unfortunate, that's for sure, but as Brian said earlier, it is a rite of passage and, thank God, all that will happen to the three young people, at present tucked into various beds upstairs, is that they will have monumental hangovers. She did this herself on one occasion at around the same age, although not in quite such a spectacular fashion. On the other hand, to judge by the demeanour of her four unscheduled guests, she doubts that they did. Given her concerns, they have little to worry them.

Of all of them, Fiona's mother is by far the most exercised, not alone by the drunkenness but by what she continues to refer to as the sexual assault on her daughter's virginity: her tirade contains subtle and not-so-subtle threats of reports to the Gárdaí, the sexual-assault unit at the Rotunda Hospital and the Rape Crisis Centre.

To protect herself, Zelda and the general atmosphere in her home from all this strife, Riba now employs one of her mental ruses: she visually shrinks the other four so that they are no more than two-dimensional stick people. It's a great blessing to be able to do this when something unpleasant is going on around you: in her eyes now these people are perhaps six inches in height, with little waving stick arms and kicking stick legs, their voices little high-pitched mouse-squeaks. She nods as though in agreement with whatever they are twittering about, adding cream to her coffee – isn't it marvellous the way cream always swirls thickly on to the dark surface before sinking?

Riba daydreams a little about what present she should buy for Jay. No point in duty free drink, even the best, rarest brands: he doesn't pollute his body with alcohol.

She realises the little stick people have stopped squeaking and are looking at her. She has no idea what she is expected to say. So she smiles empathetically at Mrs Prendergast, who winds one of her little twig fingers into her badly dyed hair, probably to show how upset she is. 'Brian should be back at any moment now,' she says, still smiling. He was able to get only four sachets of Dioralyte from the first chemist and has gone back out in search of more.

It's just as well he's not here, Riba thinks fondly, as her guests start talking among themselves again, he's absolutely hopeless in this type of situation. He would have no patience with four strangers camping in his sitting room, especially when one of them has been making dreadful allegations about his son. Only another few hours – she hugs the knowledge to herself as though it was a cuddly toy.

Donny is a worry, of course, but he'll be grand. She'll make sure of it.

Another gap in the squeaking.

Riba picks up both of the pots in front of her. 'More tea anyone? Coffee?'

Having dropped her film into One Hour Photo on the way home from Dollymount, Sophie lets herself into the house and finds Michael with his feet up in front of the television watching a football match. Oddly, the sound is low, far lower than the volume at which he normally watches football. 'Hi,' he says, reaching for the remote so that Sophie's answering 'Hi' is swallowed by the sudden increase in decibels.

Wonderful, she thinks, he's still in a snit. He doesn't even care enough about me to ask how the ceremony went, or if I'm upset.

Well, she refuses to get upset. So, instead of engaging him or asking him what is wrong as she would normally do, she kicks off her shoes, showering sand everywhere, and goes straight upstairs to her study to put away the camera equipment. As she brushes her lenses and stows everything carefully in its place, Sophie makes a firm resolution – the firmest yet – that she will organise a darkroom for herself. This decision is made every time she becomes excited about a particular picture, in this case the two Romanian women, but up to now she has always let it slide owing to pure laziness.

Her back, legs and feet ache – she must have walked more than ten miles on that beach. Her stomach is complaining, too, and it is only now that she realises she hasn't eaten all day, except for the single Digestive she ate in the Gresham with Brian. Brian – his unruly hair slathered into submission and his large frame corralled into his good clothes—

Stop. Hold it right there. *No thinking about Brian.*

Think about food. She should go downstairs right now and organise a meal. On the other hand, the last thing she feels like doing is cooking. She will go downstairs right now and suggest to Michael that they go out somewhere to eat.

She listens. The commentator is murmuring: the volume has been lowered again. Its raising was definitely a snub to her. Can she face sitting across a table from him while he sulks?

Maybe his mood has nothing to do with her. Maybe he's had a hard time at work. She should give him the benefit of the doubt. Decisively, Sophie slides off her stool and pads down the stairs to the living room. The top of his head is just visible above the back of his leather swivel chair. 'Michael?'

'Mmm?' She sees his hand flicker towards the remote on the coffee table beside him but this time it arrests itself. 'I'm starving,' she says quickly. 'Do you feel like eating?'

He does not turn round but she sees his elbow bend as he checks his watch. 'It's only just after five. Isn't it a little early?'

'I haven't eaten all day. I need to eat and, to tell you the truth, I couldn't face that cooker this evening.'

'Sure. Whatever you want.' He sighs heavily. Then he stabs the remote and turns off the television. 'Where do you want to go?'

'I couldn't care less, to tell you the truth.' She has surprised herself with her vehemence.

Him too, because he immediately puts the remote aside and stands up. 'All right, all right – keep your hair on.'

As it turns out, he had a point in remarking on how early it was because, one after another, they find that restaurants are not ready to accommodate them. Throughout the search, to Sophie's surprise, Michael has seemed distracted rather than angry. Normally he has little patience with what he derides as her *ad-hockery*, and her lack of organisational ability yet today he goes along with her without complaint.

They eventually have to settle for an Eddie Rocket's in Phibsboro where Sophie orders a giant hamburger.

As it happens, the choice is a good one: the raucous, multicultural ambience all around them helps cover over that they are not talking to each other. So does their positioning: the only seats available are two bar stools at the counter, from which, side by side, they can gloss over their separateness by watching the food being flung on to the hot griddles and dug out of the salad containers right under their noses.

She watches covertly as, lost in his own world, Michael toys with a nacho, dipping it in and out of his bowl of chilli without putting it into his mouth. What single adjective would she choose to characterise Michael? He is almost as tall as Brian but bonier, an Irish wolfhound to a

Newfoundland. *Fleet*. That's it. Michael would be fleet, whereas Brian would be powerful.

He has stopped all pretence at eating now, is staring at a boy scooping coleslaw out of a stainless-steel bin and slopping it on to a plate.

Sophie wonders if Michael is lonely in this marriage, as lonely as she sometimes is. He certainly looks lonely now, in the centre of a sort of exclusion zone, almost visible to her, like a forcefield in a science-fiction comic. Right now in this crowded, noisy place, she is tempted to break through it, to put an arm around him, to hug him close to her and to ask him what is wrong.

He slides off his stool, 'I'm going to the jacks,' and the moment passes.

It is probably just as well: she is tired and has gone through enough psychological mish-mash for one day. She is getting as weird as Eily.

Speaking of whom, she should really give her friend a call.

After their meal, as though he had heard her, it is Michael who suggests they call up to see Eily and Brian – 'We haven't been to see them for ages.'

At first Sophie demurs, citing fatigue. Michael, who seems to have got over what has been bothering him, is having none of it, and although she wants desperately to avoid another encounter with Brian, she cannot come up with any convincing reason not to call on their old friends without sounding uncaring and selfish. 'We won't stay, Michael, all right?' she begs, as they get into the car he is using, a spanking new Astra. 'I'm not joking when I say I'm really on my last legs.'

It is after seven o'clock when they arrive at the McMullans'. All the curtains have been drawn but the porch light is on. 'Remember, not long. Promise?' Sophie lags behind, as they approach the door.

'Oh, give it a rest, Sophie.' Michael is irritated again as he pushes the doorbell.

CHAPTER EIGHTEEN

The house in Marble Gardens has settled. The doctor, with the help of all six parents, had managed to bring the youngsters round, temporarily at least, and had prescribed fluids, a long sleep and a good talking-to. Ten minutes after he left, following a brief, whispered conference, the Prendergasts and Jamesons had half carried, half dragged their respective offspring home, to Brian's intense relief. At present, both Donny and Zelda are asleep upstairs, Eily is in the kitchen making soup for the following day, and all is blessedly quiet.

He is just sitting down in 'his' chair in the sitting room to scan the Sunday papers when the doorbell rings. Knowing Eily won't answer it, he swears, hard, under his breath as he heaves himself up again.

When he pulls open the door, his heart lurches. Their callers are Mick and Sophie, he smiling, she standing outside the light cast by the porch lantern so he cannot read her expression. 'Well, well, look who it is,' he says heartily, hoping they are not mind-readers. 'Come on in – Eily's in the kitchen concocting something.'

'We just popped in, we won't stay long. How's Zelda?' Michael shrugs off his sheepskin jacket and hands it over. 'Any sign of her coming home?'

'Funny you should ask,' avoiding eye-contact with Sophie, Brian takes the sheepskin, and her coat as well, 'she's upstairs, would you believe? It was a bit sudden, but it's lovely to have her back.'

'That's brilliant, Brian. I'll just pop down to the kitchen to Eily.' Sophie heads down the hallway, leaving Brian to take Michael's arm and shepherd him towards the sitting room. 'We'll let them at it, shall we? I'd prefer Eily to tell her about the latest melodrama anyway. I'm in here.'

'What melodrama?'

Michael's frown gives way to a wry smile as Brian fills him in. 'Jesus, that brings me back – poor little guy. Wouldn't like to be him tomorrow morning.'

'Yeah, he'll be OK, but I could kill the little bastard. That's all we need now.' Then Brian lowers his voice. 'Well, what happened? Tell me, quick, before the girls come in.'

What he hears does not please him, as the other man, words tumbling over one another, tells him that he thinks he has persuaded Yvonne to have the baby but that the price is probably going to be that he has to tell Sophie. 'Christ!' Brian is truly horrified – at least he thinks he is, he has to be. 'You can't. It'll kill her – for God's sake, you're going to break up your marriage.' Having said it, Brian instantly realises that his friend has no option but to reveal the truth. A mutual acquaintance of theirs has managed to lead a quasi-bigamous existence, but this has been virtually at the cost of his sanity and Brian, for one, has never been able to look the man's wife in the eye.

Before he can amend his reaction, however, the other man reacts truculently.

'So you think I should just let Yvonne swan off and kill my kid? She's not bad, you know, she's just confused. She's quite nice really, when you get down to it.'

Brian forbears to say the obvious: that Mick got down to it rather too quickly and stupidly. Instead, he urges his friend to sleep on the situation. At least that will give everyone an opportunity to draw breath. 'Certainly don't open your mouth about it now,' he says. 'Wait and see. These things have a way of working themselves out.'

'It's not that simple.' Michael gets up and starts to pace. 'Yvonne won't wait. I'm sure of it. She'll tell Sophie herself.

'Well, actually I'm wrong.' He stops dead. 'It's simple. Frighteningly simple. It's one of these either-ors, Brian. Either I leave Sophie and look after the two of them or Yvonne will kill our baby.' He turns to face Brian and says, in a low tone, 'Actually, I sort of said I would.'

Brian, having noted that 'it' and 'the kid' have been replaced by 'our baby', had initially put down Mick's reaction to the type of panic that any married man would experience when faced with such a situation. He is becoming irrationally angry. 'I see,' he says, holding on to his temper. 'You already told Yvonne Leonard that you would leave your wife?'

'Oh, I can't describe it.' Michael drops into an armchair. 'That's just the way the conversation seemed to go. I think I certainly gave her that impression.'

'Is that what you intend to do?'

Michael's head snaps up. 'I'm not sure I appreciate your tone. I'm not in the dock here. I came to you as a friend. I hoped you'd understand.'

Although the self-righteousness is hard to take, Brian lets it pass. Mick has a point – Brian had sounded like the Grand Inquisitor – but who is battling for Sophie? 'I do understand,' he says quietly, 'and I know you're fighting for your child and how important that would be to you, to anyone. But, Mick, try to think what this will do to Sophie. She is such a good woman.'

'Yeah, yeah.' Michael springs out of his chair again. 'Everyone loves Sophie. Well, I'm sick of being seen as the one with the cloven hoof. You don't know her, Brian, she's an ice queen.' He lashes out at the arm of the sofa. 'It wasn't always like this, especially at the beginning when we used to be at it like rabbits, you know the way it is, but she's changed and now, I tell you, she's an ice queen. I'm a normal man.'

Brian feels his gorge rising. He, too, gets up and comes to stand nose to nose with his friend, trying to resist the urge to knock this guy's block off. 'You're an idiot, Mick Dolan, a complete fucking idiot. This crisis is entirely of your own making. You've been whoring around outside your marriage for years and don't you dare blame your wife for it. You've put me in an impossible position alongside you, you're nothing but a selfish prick – and I mean that literally, you fucker, do you hear me?' He shoves Michael in the chest, hard, so that he falls backwards into the carefully arranged cushions on Eily's sofa. 'Now, sit down there and be quiet, and don't talk about your wife like that.'

As Michael, open-mouthed, stares up at him, Brian's chest constricts. He is acting blindly and instinctively, not his usual way of going about things. The conflict is enormous: on one level he must fight for Sophie's marriage for her sake, on another he recognises he is being pretty two-faced about this, pushing hard for the sake of his own conscience. If the split happens, despite his best efforts, nobody can say that he had anything to do with it or spotted a gap in the scrum and took advantage of it.

Before either of them can say any more, they hear their wives approaching from the kitchen. Brian hurries back to his chair.

'I've been telling Sophie about poor Donny.' Eily is carrying an ice bucket when she and Sophie come in. 'It's not pleasant, but that's the nature of youth. Now,' she says briskly, 'who's for drinks? Or a cup of tea? I've lovely Queen cakes, fresh out of the oven – can I tempt anyone?'

All opt for the alcohol and Eily takes bottles and glasses from the sideboard and starts to pour, clinking and fizzing into the silence. After a few seconds, she turns round, frowning, to find them watching her as though she is performing an intricate surgical operation. 'What's going on in here, you people? Cat got your tongues?'

'It's been a long day.'

'I'm pretty tired actually.'

Michael and Sophie have replied simultaneously.

Eily turns back to her drinks. 'Aren't we all? You're right – it's been quite a day, one way or another. This'll do us all a power of good.' She hands around the drinks, gin and tonic for Michael and Sophie, a whiskey for Brian, and then plumps into the sofa beside Michael, licking her lips in anticipation of the first sip of her Manhattan. 'This is nice. We don't do this often enough, the four of us, do we?' She smiles around at them all. 'Cheers.'

'Cheers,' they all echo faintly, and dive into their glasses.

After a moment or two of further silence, Eily looks askance at them. 'My God, you'd think we were at a wake. What's the matter with you all tonight?'

'I'm actually not surprised about what happened today.' Sophie's tone is challenging. She turns to face Brian. 'Did you mention that he came to see me?'

Brian glances at his wife. 'I didn't get a chance yet, but I will, yeah.'

'What?' Eily looks from one to the other. 'Who came to see you?'

'Donny.' Sophie is still looking at Brian.

'Donny?' Eily is taken aback. 'You never told me about that, Soph. What did he want?'

'He wanted some attention.' It's out before Brian even knows it. 'Listen, Eily, tomorrow is going to be a write-off, obviously – none of them will be able to go to school – but on Tuesday the two of us are going to have to sit down with Donny. The kid is starving for lack of attention – that was the gist, wasn't it, Sophie?'

Eily's expression is grave. 'Tuesday. You're right, Brian, whatever is needed. Poor Donny.' She turns away. 'Anyone for more drinks?'

The response to this is negative and Brian turns to Michael. 'So what did you think of the game?' he asks, too loudly for the distance his voice has to traverse in the small room.

Michael frowns. 'Which game would that be?'

'The Premiership, you pillock – on telly. You said you were going to watch it.'

'Oh, yeah. Well, actually, I didn't. We went out to eat at Eddie Rocket's.' Michael's tone is sarcastic and, out of the corner of his eye, Brian notices Sophie stiffen then relax again, as though she had been about to object but had thought better of it. Despite his earlier refusal of a second drink, he gets up to pour himself another.

Behind him he hears Eily chide, 'Children, children! Let's not be nasty. Whatever is going on here, let's start over. We should all be happy. We've survived a terrible week. Let's drink to life and love and the future.'

Brian, his drink replenished, turns round to find her with her glass raised in the air, her expression determined and her flushed cheeks shining in the golden light cast by a table lamp nearby. He smiles affectionately at her: despite all his reservations, he has to admire her tenacity and spunk. He bows his head a little in her direction and raises his own glass in salute.

What the hell has he been thinking of? He has vowed to love and cherish this glowing woman. All right, she's daft, but she's his wife – their lives have been plaited together indissolubly. Is he going through some kind of a mid-life crisis?

Somehow or other they stumble through the next half-hour until Michael and Sophie, both citing tiredness and saying that they had never intended this to be more than a flying visit, leave.

That night, in bed, Eily broaches the subject of the strange atmosphere. Her view is that they had all been affected – at least, three of them had – not only by the crash but by the grim residue of what had happened earlier with the Prendergasts and Jamesons. 'These bad feelings do hang around, you know.' The sheets rustle as she turns away from him and settles comfortably on her side. 'Isn't it amazing that Donny went to see Sophie? But you're right. Extra special attention. Starting in the morning – whoo,' she yawns, 'he'll certainly need it then – and how!'

'Eily?' Brian touches her back.

'Mmm?'

'Will you sit up again, please? I want to talk seriously.'

She surprises him by turning instantly to face him. 'What is it?'

Is it his imagination or is she wary? Before he can decide, she is plumping up the pillows behind her. 'Look, Brian, I know what Donny did today was unfortunate. Look on the bright side, though – the hangover that poor child is going to suffer means he'll probably never do it again. We'll just have to chalk it up to experience. It's a pity those other people can't do the same. No imagination.' She plops into the centre of her pillows with a sigh.

'It's not the drinking.' Brian raises himself on one elbow to face her directly. 'Our son was desperate enough to go to see Sophie, Eily, because he felt he couldn't talk to us. Think about that, Eily.' As he relays in detail what Sophie told him, she listens intently, or appears to.

When he has finished, she closes her eyes. 'Poor old Donny. My poor darling little son.'

'What are we going to do about it?'

'What can we do? We're all caught up in an extraordinary situation. Needs must. We can do our best with him, but I know he understands that, just at the moment, Zelda comes first.'

'Of course he understands that Zelda comes first, but he's old enough now to be talked to. I'll arrange that he should have a chat with one of the specialists. We have to make more of him, allow him to be part of it. I'm sorry to say this, Eily, but you've shut him out with this Jay Street business.'

'Oh, so that's what this is all about, is it? You can't resist it, can you? Blame Jay for everything.'

'No!' Brian reins in his temper again. 'No, it's not. This is about Donny. I'm appealing to you, Eily, please. He won't know which end of him is up tomorrow so tomorrow's out, but do keep him home from school on Tuesday as well and make a real big fuss of him. I'll ring a couple of times – I'll even see if I can get home a bit early. It's you he needs. Make him feel you care.'

'He knows I care,' she puts a hand on his chest and starts to rub gently, 'I talk to him all the time.'

'No, you don't.' Brian feels the conversation slipping away. He grabs her hand and holds it. 'I'm sorry, I don't want to have a row with you. Communication should be two-way but despite all this caring and sharing you talk about so much, Eily, you're certainly not listening to me. As a matter of fact you don't listen to any of us any more, certainly not in the last few years. You appear to be paying attention, but it's just a trick. Nothing is going in that you don't want to hear. It's like bouncing words off a wall of stainless steel sometimes.'

He sees she is about to protest. 'Listen, for God's sake, listen to me now. Our daughter is dying, Eily, our son is suffocating in misery and desperation. Acknowledge the facts. Please. For all our sakes. Let's get on with real life instead of this – this . . .' He struggles for a word while she stares at him, dark eyes glowing beneath the lashes. 'You're living in Fantasy Land, Eily,' he says, gripping both her shoulders, almost shaking her. 'Come down and join us in the real world. We need you with us in this family. All of us. That drinking bout was a symptom of how much Donny, for one, needs you now.'

Gently, Eily removes his hands from her shoulders. She winds her arms around his neck and kisses him on the mouth, then draws back and softly, gazing into his eyes, says, 'Darling, dearest Brian, I'm not living in a fantasy, as you put it. You are the one who won't listen to us, you and that army of deaf people out there who are caught in those destructive thought patterns. If you would only break free, if you would only listen to us, my love. Life could be wonderful, is wonderful, but you have to accept what it offers.' She cuts off his response by kissing him again, deeply, biting his lip and moving her tongue in his mouth in the way she knows will inflame him. Then she takes one of his unresisting hands and places it on her hip, wriggling a little so that the slithery softness of her nightdress on the warm flesh underneath titillates his palm and sends compelling impulses through his chest and stomach.

Brian's wife is an experienced and talented lover and tonight she throws everything she knows into seducing him. He recognises what she's doing but his treacherous body responds nevertheless. He cannot resist her, and although he knows he is being manipulated in some way, the demands of his blood are too direct and insistent for any more bloody psycho-wars.

Two hours later, in his bed, Michael lies awake beside Sophie, who is breathing deeply and regularly. He had always known, deep down, that it would come to this. He has been too lucky. The women he has bedded had come and gone too easily, with too little fuss, causing hardly a ripple in the way he has chosen to conduct his life.

Now he has pushed his luck just that bit too far and been well and truly stung.

He has never flattered himself that he is imaginative, in the way that his wife is, for instance, but although the practice is foreign to him, he tries now to project ahead to what it would be like to have Yvonne Leonard as a permanent companion. As Eily would have it, he tries to 'visualise' this – yet, try as he might, all he can see is Yvonne's pert little bottom and glorious breasts and even that picture is not turning him on the way it usually does. Oh, it's hopeless. He'll just have to stay super alert and get through this somehow. He turns in the bed, careful not to wake Sophie. One thing's for sure. Life with Yvonne, if that's what it was to come to, would certainly be volatile.

Could he see Yvonne putting up – no questions asked – with telephone calls home to say he'd be late?

He'd be pushing fifty when she'd still be in her late twenties – forty-nine sounds so much older than twenty-nine – and she's such a goer . . . Women have such huge reserves, and Michael has always marvelled at how their energy seems to increase with age rather than the other way round. How does that work out? Would he be able to keep up? For instance, would she expect him to take her to pop concerts and nightclubs? Would she think of him as just an old fart at that stage?

The compensation, though, would be that they would have this kid, a little nipper growing up to call him Dad. A kid he could bring to Glasgow to watch Celtic, or, dressed in a little sheepskin, to Lansdowne Road, or even to Twickers for the rugby internationals.

It wouldn't have to stop there: they could have a second, a girl, that wouldn't be too bad either. She'd climb on his lap and give him soft kisses and she'd think he knew everything. He'd be her hero – at least, until she got to Yvonne's age.

Oh, for fuck's sake – what are you like? Michael tries hard to bin this mushy rubbish but the images persist. They are very attractive, far more so than the picture of what happens over there in those English clinics with their buckets and sponges and whatever else they use . . .

Michael needs urgently to speak to Yvonne. For no particular reason, just to connect. To reassure himself about even thinking this way.

Carefully, he eases himself out of the bed and tiptoes out of the bedroom, closing the door behind him.

Downstairs, he takes the precaution of turning on the television, at low volume, before using his mobile to dial Yvonne's.

Sophie, half woken by Michael's stealthy departure, debates with herself whether or not to open her eyes. She hasn't heard the alarm.

She compromises and opens one eye, squinting at the red digital display on her bedside clock. Still only two twenty – hours and hours to go yet before she has to face another day. Rejoicing, she snuggles drowsily into her warm hollow, waiting for the flush of the cistern to herald her husband's return.

When this does not materialise, she comes further towards the surface of consciousness, hears something odd and wakes up properly. Is it her imagination or, through the quietness of the house and silence of the street outside, can she hear muffled voices downstairs? She sits up to listen. Yes. Voices.

What's going on?

She tumbles out of bed and pulls on her slippers, then descends to the living room. 'Michael?'

She stops. His back is turned to her, and to the television. His mobile is held to his ear. Reflexively, she checks her watch: it is now two twenty-five.

He whirls to face her and his frown is replaced instantly with a bright smile. He waves as he continues to listen and, with a shrug, raises his eyebrows, as though to include her in a conspiracy, then mouths something at her. Who on earth could he be talking to at this hour of the night? Puzzled, she mounts the stairs, sloughs off her slippers and gets back into the warm bed.

Within two minutes, he is beside her, cuddling in to her back. 'Jesus, it's freezing down there. We'll have to do something about the central heating in this house, Soph, it's like Siberia.'

'Who was that you were talking to?'

'Brian.' Michael cuddles closer and puts his arms around her tightly. 'He sent me a text message – he couldn't sleep, apparently, so I rang him back.'

Sophie goes on high alert. 'Brian McMullan?'

'Are there other Brians who would be sending me text messages? How many Brians do we know? Of course Brian McMullan.'

Sophie makes a conscious attempt not to betray her thoughts. 'I'm afraid I still don't understand. Brian sent you a text message at this hour of the night because he couldn't sleep?'

He tightens his grip. 'No, silly, the message was about a booking for the morning – I wasn't meant to get it until I woke up. But I did get it because I was awake, too, and since he was obviously near his phone I decided to ring him back. OK?' He kisses the nape of her neck. 'I was lonely down there all on my own. Now, can we stop talking about Brian McMullan and his obsessive behaviour and talk about something real – like, for instance, what the feel of that warm little bottom is doing to me down there?' He presses against her, then reaches for the hem of her nightdress, pulling it free of her thighs and raising it so that it rumples around her waist.

He grinds himself against her, taking her breasts in his hands. 'Sophie, Sophie . . .'

As he starts to massage and knead her, the depth of his desire surprises Sophie. He seems so desperate, so urgent, that somehow she feels this is sort of unreal.

Ten minutes ago, sex with her husband was the last thing on her mind but it has been so long . . . She owes it to him, to herself.

So Sophie works not only with her body but with her imagination to respond to his increasingly frantic caresses; she forces aside all other considerations and turns to him, coiling herself around him and, reactive desire mounting, grabs his hair.

So fine . . . not like Brian McMullan's thatch.

Sophie makes a supreme effort. She throws the substantial presence of Brian McMullan off her body and away from her bed. 'Michael! Oh, Michael – yes . . .'

She and her husband make love, violently, as though they are strangers finding their way into one another for the first time. Or, drowning, as though they are grabbing at the last chance of rescue.

CHAPTER NINETEEN

M onday morning is blustery and cold and Riba shivers as she raises
the kitchen blinds. At just eight o'clock it is still dark, but she can
see by the peculiarly heavy belly of the sky outside that there may be
another fall of snow. Just like last Monday, *exactly* a week ago. Snow again
today – isn't that fascinating? Could it have been only a week? It feels like
a millennium.

She shivers again and directs her mind to something more pleasant. Like
the life-giving sun that, right this very minute, is getting ready to shower
its warm light on Palm Tree Island. Only twenty-four hours to go . . .

She is bursting with the news: it is against her nature to keep secrets,
from Brian or anyone else, but although she says it herself, this time she
has managed it pretty damned well. She slips a cardigan over her kaftan,
bought in one of the new African markets in Moore Street because she
loved its vibrant primary colours, then warms her hands on the singing
kettle while waiting for the central heating to kick in.

Brian has already left for work, thank God, giving her both peace and
opportunity to make a few more discreet preparations. Mentally, she has
already selected the clothes and other items they are going to take with
them – very little, of course, not only because they won't need much but
because they don't have much since the stuff they originally bought for
the tropics went up with their suitcases in the fiery plane.

Involuntarily, she glances at the kitchen counter where, beside the
bread bin, the stack of letters and forms from the various insurance
companies, the airline and even the airport authority is swelling like a
malign fungus. She hasn't read them in detail. She will, of course,
sometime. Definitely. Some time soon. She has flicked through the
covering letters and forms addressed to her but can't face their tone and
complexity – bringing it all back. Brian can go through them in due
course and he can tell her what to say, where to sign. He has his own
and Zelda's stack upstairs in the filing cabinet on the landing. It's quite
surprising he hasn't dealt with it all yet – he's usually so good with the

practical stuff. Poor baby. Brian has his torments too.

Wasn't he a tiger last night, though?

Why wouldn't he be. With a lover such as herself? Remembering how easy it was to get him going, Riba preens a little as she inserts two slices of bread in the toaster. Sex has always animated and invigorated her, to the extent that even late last night, long after he had dropped off to sleep, she had to resist tumbling out of the bed to do something positive like baking, or polishing, or even whipping around the garden with a torch to see what was pushing up. She had resisted, of course, and while he snored gently had simply relaxed, content to experience the ebb and flow within her body as she lay satiated and comfortable in her lovely bed.

Good sex, of course, is the best therapy of all: here she is this morning, after less than five hours' sleep, feeling, if not exactly rested, energised and fully alert. The last time she remembered checking the time before she drifted off, it had been nearly three o'clock.

So – what will she pack? A few T-shirts and skirts for Zelda, the medication, soon to be surplus to requirements, thank God, a handful of kaftans for herself, a couple of beach towels, a few toiletries, lingerie, her tapes and player, and that's about it. They can buy new sun stuff, swimsuits and flip-flops when they get to the island, although as Zelda is self-conscious about her thinness, maybe she won't want to expose herself.

That's not even a consideration right now, of course: the drive is to get airborne smoothly, without hindrance or detection. It would be lovely to share the excitement of it all. Maybe she could trust Sophie?

The kettle boils and she makes the tea, covers it with a cosy and leaves it to draw. When the toast pops, she butters it thickly, trims off the crusts and cuts both slices diagonally then arranges them on a pretty, scalloped plate in Wedgwood blue. Then, into the centre of each triangle, she adds a dollop of her home-made strawberry and orange jam, pausing briefly to enjoy the way the rosy edges bleed into the luscious yellow ponds of melting butter that surrounds them.

'Are you awake, darling?' As she is carrying the meal on a small tray, Riba pushes open the door of her daughter's room with one foot. It is dark and very warm: because Zelda feels the cold keenly, they had left her oil-filled radiator to burn full on throughout the night.

There is no answer or movement from the bed and, like a dagger, fear cuts through Riba's happy mood. 'Zelda! Zelda!' she cries – yells.

'Wha—?' The bedclothes erupt as Zelda shoots upright. 'What was that?'

Riba staggers under the weight of the tray, light though it is. 'It's only me, darling,' she says, relief thumping against her throat and making it hard for her to breathe. 'Sorry I gave you a fright – I brought your breakfast.' She puts the tray on the bedside table and turns on the lamp.

Her panic recedes like a bad dream, for in the lamp's side-cast beam, she can see pinpricks of gold all over her daughter's skull and realises, to her delight, that the long straggling wisps have been undergrown by a hint of fuzz, bloom on a peach. 'Oh, Zeldy.' Despite her daughter's ducking away, she cannot resist kissing the downy head. Then, faced with Zelda's glowering expression, she beats a strategic retreat, saying she will be back in a little while with the medication. Takes after her father in the mood department, she thinks, tiptoeing towards Donny's door and easing it open an inch or two.

In contrast to the tropical climate in the adjacent room, the temperature in Donny's is glacial. Despite the open window, the smell continues to resemble what Riba remembers from her childhood visits to the monkey house in Dublin Zoo. She whispers Donny's name, asking if he feels well enough to take a drop of tea. 'Or would you prefer to sleep on a little bit, hon?'

Donny's response is to pull his duvet over his head, so she tiptoes out again.

Safely back in the kitchen, she sees that the sky is streaked with grey, so pale as to be almost white – and, yes, those are snowclouds. What matter? Soon they will be far from cold. Everything is going to plan. *What can go right will go right.* That might have been written by Jay himself. Riba smiles as she remembers the first day she met Jay in the flesh, as it were. She remembers every detail, every second.

Shortly after Eily had gone with Sophie to that Mind Body Spirit exhibition Jay had come to Ireland on a well-publicised tour and she had attended one of his public lectures, held in a stuffy little room in a south-side hotel. Given the build-up and the advertising, she was a little surprised to find that the mainly female crowd was small, numbering maybe forty. The young South American woman gave him such an adulatory introduction that Eily, as well disposed to him as she was, had serious doubts about this paragon. All he was short of, apparently, was the ability to walk on water or turn loaves into fishes.

Then he had come in, walking quietly from the back of the room through the crowd and taking his place at the lectern supplied by the hotel. He didn't speak for at least four or five minutes, simply surveyed everyone with a gentle but mesmerising green stare. His hair was neatly and conservatively cut, he was wearing a plain, caramel-coloured polo-neck sweater over slightly darker slacks and, as the minutes ticked by, Eily, as she was then, seemed to see light coming from within him and extending outwards to bathe them all. This glowed brighter and whiter until it acted as a reverse eclipse, swallowing the dank yellow from the tacky electric 'candelabrum' that hung from the centre of the windowless room. She could actually feel its heat on her cheeks and forehead while the atmosphere in the room around her gradually tightened and curled in on itself like the mainspring of a winding clock. No one moved, or even coughed. Eily herself hardly dared to breathe. She felt as if she was being drenched, then sucked under the surface to some other world beneath the stained carpet of the room, to an everlastingly light-filled place where nothing was impossible.

Then Jay broke through, in that deep, musical voice with the Midwestern intonations she grew to know so well. 'What you are feeling now is the opening of your mind. You are discovering your limitless potential and this feeling makes you feel wonderful as you realise you are surrounded by light and love and understanding. This is how you should feel when you wake up every morning, it is how you should continue to feel every moment of every day.' Released from the clenching silence, Eily had taken a breath, which felt like the first breath any human being had ever taken on this earth. She felt as though this was a rehearsal for her entry into the presence of God.

More mundanely, as he continued in the same vein, she felt that listening to Jay Street for the first time was like plunging into your own intelligence. Everything he said sounded and felt so *right*, as though she had known it all along but had been too blind to *see* . . . This prescience was extraordinary and terribly exciting. It was as if she had been born with a caul, and had been waiting for these words to ease it off, lift it away and leave it beside her as a shrivelled reminder of the shadowy half-life she had been living up to now.

Seeking affirmation, she turned to the neighbour on her left and, finding the woman's face wet with tears, reached out and clasped her hand. The woman clasped back before both turned to listen once more.

Eily had closed her eyes then, the better to concentrate on the substance of what Jay was telling them and, over the next half-hour or so, was confirmed in her initial view that, at some level, she had known these fundamental truths all along. He used no fancy philosophical jargon, just everyday words and phrases, backed up by his own extensive research in the United States, yet what he was describing, what he promised them if they followed his instructions, spread the word and inducted others to share with them was so beguiling that there was no possibility of refusing him or these wonderful gifts he was offering.

That day Eily was reborn. She wanted to mount the GPO in O'Connell Street and shout these revelations to the thousands below. Everyone should know what joy awaited them if they threw off the shackles of habit and thought, and allowed their minds and souls to grow to full flower.

As a start, she signed up to the organisation, paid her subscriptions for further lectures and put down her name as a volunteer in the fledgling Irish operation so she could help Jay to further his work. She also opened her diary to give the address of everyone she knew who might benefit, and undertook to try to recruit them. All around her, others were queuing up to do the same.

As it turned out, the training she received was mostly in public relations – with a little in nutrition, reflexology and herbalism – and in how to get other people to join because, as the minders who had flown in with Jay had explained that first day, it wasn't until the Irish operation reached what they had called 'critical mass', that they would be able to run the kind of courses they ran in the States: nutrition, mental health, spirit healing, aura reading, rebirthing, reiki and so on. In the meantime, however, Jay's writings were to be used as a good general guide. She had taken away a thick wodge of photocopied tracts.

During this induction process, Jay himself was passing among them, quietly overseeing what was going on. When he came to Eily, he shook her hand and checked her name badge: 'I feel that Ireland is going to be so fruitful for us. Thank you for coming today. You are entering a new life, Eileen.' Eily almost swooned – and thanked God she was wearing something presentable. Although she was aware he had been thanking everyone similarly, as he spoke she felt that he was being more personal with her than with the others, that she was being singled out; he had looked so deeply into her eyes and held her hand so warmly that it could not have been otherwise.

Of course, when she went home, full of delight and zeal to share the good news, she hit nothing but cynicism. If anything, it had become more pervasive throughout the seven marvellous years since that seminal meeting, but while this was disappointing, the constant rejection had deterred her not one whit. Although she had been forced underground, as it were, she was confident that her family and friends – even those with whom she came casually in contact – were constantly deriving benefit from Jay's teaching just by being in her presence. Truth is unavoidable, and if on the surface it is scorned, miracles are daily wrought just by brushing against it. Along with her membership of the organisation, Eily had been given the gift of patience. Although she had signally failed to recruit anyone from her family, or even Sophie, who might at one time have joined out of kindness, she had been more successful with other friends, some from her schooldays, with whom, luckily, she had kept in sporadic touch over the years.

The big bonus now for Riba is that when Jay visits Ireland, she is always one of his first calls. She had even had dinner with him in his hotel on two occasions, marred only by the spiky presence of California Monica and other henchwomen.

She checks Donny's wristwatch, a Swatch, discarded by him as childish and filched from his room. She is dying to tell Jay that she and Zelda are coming – she has to share this good news or she'll burst. It's still a bit too early to call the island. Although California Monica had said they got up early over there. Probably to watch dawn stealing across the quietly curling turquoise waves. Riba drifts off into a daydream filled with helpful dolphins and pink skies.

Oh, no. Sophie groans as she hears the telephone ringing downstairs. She squints at the red figures on the dial: 8.44. For goodness' sake, who's ringing her at this hour? Unlike most of her contemporaries, Sophie continues stubbornly to subscribe to the now-mythical rule that life in Dublin begins at nine a.m.

She had been having a lovely dream, or half-dream, where some faceless giant had picked her up and was rocking her gently and safely in a boat. Or it might have been the boat that was rocking them both on a gentle sea. She needs to find out which it is but can't hold on to the images, and as the phone shrills a second time, the dream slips away. The caller turns out to be Eily. 'Sorry, darling, I hope it's not too early?'

'Not at all, Eil— Riba!' Sophie is glad that video phones are still not common. She would not like Eily to see her expression. 'What's up?'

'Can I confide in you, Sophie? Can you keep a secret? I'm bursting to tell someone and, anyway, I might need your help.'

It is only then that Sophie comes fully awake and wary. This is her best friend, about whose husband she has now seriously started to fantasise. Guilt prompts irrational anger. She doesn't want any more confidences from Eily, for the moment at least. 'Look, before you say anything, Eily,' she blurts, 'do you mind if we dispense with this Riba business? I'm uncomfortable using that name. I've been uncomfortable with it for a long time.'

There, she has said it.

Hearing the hurt silence at the other end of the line, however, she is instantly sorry for the outburst and has to restrain herself from jumping in to reverse her request. It cannot be unasked, however, and she really has hated using the two names, Riba to Eily's face, Eily to everyone else, including Eily's husband.

Eily recovers. 'That's fine, Sophie.' She is calm as always and, strangely, Sophie feels deflated.

'Sorry, but really . . .'

'No need to explain or apologise, honestly, that's your decision and I respect it.' The voice is matter-of-fact, has regained some of its bounce. 'To get back to the reason I rang, I'm just dying for a chat – we haven't had a proper one for ages. Why don't you come over for a coffee? Donny and Zel will both be here but they'll hang about in their rooms.' Then, as Sophie hesitates, 'Come on, you can afford half an hour, surely? I'll bake – why don't you drop in on the way to the office?'

Sophie grips the telephone receiver tightly. Brian had to have told Eily about the closure of *Wild Places* – or had he? 'I will be going into the office,' she says quietly, 'but it will be to clear my desk.'

'Oh, yes, of course. Poor thing. Yeah, Brian told me. It's all for the best, though, Soph. We don't see these patterns, but they are there. You'll see. A month from now you won't know why you stayed in that place for so long. You are so talented, with so much to offer, the perfect opportunity will arise for you now that the door is open for you – so come on, drop in for a quick cuppa, OK?'

Sophie can see no reasonable way to refuse. 'All right,' she says. 'See you in about an hour and a half. I've to pick up some photographs in town and then I'll call in. Only for a few minutes, though.'

As they hang up, she groans aloud. How has she got herself into all these fixes? She surveys her life: her undemanding, familiar little job taken away from her, her love-life plunged into unfamiliar, even uncharted seas where it is floundering; a lifelong friendship, one she values, hedged about with alarming problems, including deceit.

Oh, give yourself a break! She throws off her nightshirt and bombs up the stairs again, then turns the power shower on full and steps under it, face raised to the hot, therapeutic needles of water. Yet as her body is engulfed in blissful, steamy heat, she cannot escape her thoughts, which pop up for attention in quick succession like those little price flags on an old-fashioned cash-register.

First up is the memory of lovemaking the previous night, so surprising in its vigour and blind passion.

It was too blind, that was the problem. Although she is ashamed to admit it, in retrospect she feels almost as though she and her husband had been rutting like animals. Sophie cannot avoid the notion that, by indulging themselves in this physicality, they were trying not to rekindle old fire but, for a few minutes, to obliterate newer ones. She should discuss this openly with Michael but there is already so much space between them that she would find it difficult to haul the two of them back into a mutually safe, neutral area in which to bring up the subject of their relationship.

Could all of this be her fault? Has she thoroughly fallen out of love with her husband – or has she, by commission or omission, shut him out?

Abruptly, to punish herself – or cut off further ruminations – Sophie turns the shower control to cold, yelling aloud as her shocked flesh protests. She endures the torture for thirty seconds then turns off the water. At least she feels a little better physically as she wraps herself in the relative warmth of a terry-towel dressing-gown.

She dresses in well-worn jeans and a sloppy navy jumper, appropriated from Michael because it is so soft. At the last minute, she tunnels through one of the drawers in her dressing-table and extracts a silk scarf, white, splashed with blue cornflowers. This was Eily's Christmas present to her and will, she hopes, serve as a badge of atonement for her waspish treatment of her friend on the telephone. So what if Eily forgot about her crappy job? She's probably right: something better will come along in due course. If it makes her happy to be called Riba, what's the big deal? If Sophie is a true friend, she should be able to call her Mahatma Gandhi, if that's what she wants.

As she leaves the house, Sophie bangs the front door so hard behind her that a screw falls out of the old brass letterbox.

Michael and Yvonne are sitting in the lounge of the Skylon Hotel on Drumcondra Road. Michael, who is supposed to be delivering one of the hand-controlled cars to a client in a hotel on the opposite side of the city, is nervous. For the umpteenth time, he checks his watch.

He is also terrified that they will be spotted. The lounge is at the front of the hotel and is used frequently as a watering-hole by people he knows from the airport. He can see that Yvonne, no longer drugged but, according to her own account, suffering from a thick, muzzy ache behind her nose and at the back of her eyes, is losing patience with him. 'Look, Mick, you're either here with me or you're not. If you're not, I'm off. Coming here was your idea, not mine, and if you'd rather be somewhere else, well, say so! By the way, I don't appreciate being rung up at two o'clock in the morning. I could have been asleep.'

'Well, you weren't, were you?' Michael manages a wan smile. 'Don't go. I just wanted to make sure that we're both singing from the same hymn sheet – you haven't changed your mind again, have you?' She is looking quite well this morning, he thinks. She has washed her hair and is wearing makeup.

'Stop looking at me as if I've killed your old lady.' She has recovered some of her spirit too. 'You're the one who persuaded me, remember? Who was it came to my flat? Who's ringing me all the time until I'm sick of the sound of the friggin' mobile?'

Michael hesitates: what had seemed achievable and logical, even borderline exciting, twelve hours ago now presents huge difficulties. He dreads the thought of the split with his wife. He has not had time fully to examine his feelings about her. This drama will very soon force him, no doubt, to ask himself seriously whether or not he actually still loves his wife, but right now Michael's focus is wholly on keeping abreast of the current and urgent events personified by the girl sitting here with him, and with his own descent into chaos. What will people say? And how will his sainted boss react? Brian has the height of respect for Sophie, and Michael can just imagine the atmosphere at work, all the sniggering, the pitying looks, the taking sides. Ireland has come a long way since the dark ages, but there is still some residual Puritanism knocking about just below the surface.

So, he will probably have to change jobs too.

Michael is unaccustomed to self-analysis; his life, having run so heedlessly up to now, has hit the buffers. Because whatever the traumas ahead, no matter how bleak the outlook, something precious has been planted inside him and is growing in tandem with the new life within Yvonne. The new feeling is so unusual that he can't put words to it yet because it's as delicate as those spindly little flowers they sell now and then in the airport flower shop, the ones that have this strong peppery scent. 'What do you call those flowers – you know the ones, they're white and yellow and purple, real weak-looking?' He tries to describe the blooms with his hands and fingers. 'You know – they've these kind of hanging bell things and long stems.'

'Freesias?' She is gazing at him as though he has lost it.

'That's it.' He is triumphant. 'Freesias. Sorry, Yvonne, it was just something in my head.' Gently, he takes her hand. 'You're so young, you have no idea what it's like to have been married for so long.'

Yvonne's full mouth reduces to a thin, determined line. 'Listen. I know it's going to be hard to face it, but that's your problem, not mine. Now, are you going to do it? Did you mean all that stuff last night or was it all talk just to get your own way? Are you going to tell her? Because if you don't—'

'I'll tell her.' Michael is quietly fatalistic now. 'I'll tell her tonight.'

She takes a piece of paper out of her pocket and hands it to him. On it is written a series of letters and numbers: the reservation confirmation for tomorrow's flight. 'You mind that. We should keep it as a souvenir. Maybe use it to keep the kid in line if it gets stroppy when it's older.' Her expression briefly floods with fright, replaced by a bright smile as the old cheeky Yvonne cocks her head to one side and links arms with him. 'Willya look at us! Collette'll probably think I'm off me friggin' rocker. I'm beginning to think the same meself.'

Michael keeps his opinions on Collette to himself. 'You won't be sorry,' he says, and, to his own surprise, means it. Whatever happens, he is going to protect that little freesia he has created.

CHAPTER TWENTY

The one-sided telephone conflict between herself and her friend is still doing the rounds in Sophie's head when she pulls in at Eily's gate. Before going in, stalling, she opens the wallet containing the photographs she had collected. Even at the first cursory glance inside the shop, she had been delighted with the sequence featuring the Romanians.

She sorts through the bundle now, stopping to gaze critically at the series. Yes, she was right: these are out of the ordinary. Sophie won't congratulate herself that she might be the next Snowdon but she has more here than simply a set of quirky shots showing two toothless women enjoying themselves on a day out. Her lens has tapped into something behind their expressions, a sort of joyful '*Gotcha*', as though this pair knows some secret they may share sometime but not now. Even the way the light falls on the tough old skin gives a painterly, three-dimensional effect to the photographs. She touches the celluloid face of the fortune-teller. A baby? Could she and Michael have started a baby when they made love last night?

She tries to dismiss this as mere fantasy, yet as she stares into those dark, discomfiting eyes, remembers again the animal abandon of the sex the previous night, she presses her free hand into her stomach, as though by doing so she might find new life there.

She throws the photographs back into their wallet and gets out of the car. At the last minute, she grabs her camera bag. Now is as good a time as any to get those shots of Zelda and it may even prove a welcome distraction.

When Eily pulls open the door, Sophie manages a wide, bright smile and immediately raises her head to sniff. 'Oh, my God – I can smell that baking already. This is what a house should smell like.'

'Thank you.' Eily, her flushed face clashing wildly with the swirling reds of her kaftan, smiles back. 'You're wearing my scarf – and I see you have your camera with you!' Before Sophie can say why this is so, Eily turns and walks ahead of her into the kitchen where, leaving her guest to take her customary place at the table, she immediately starts removing scones from a baking tray and placing them to cool on a wire rack.

It all seems so normal: music, luxuriant with strings, swinging from the tape player, the fridge humming along, a stew bubbling on top of the stove, mixing in the air with the smell of the scones. An outsider coming in would have no idea what cataclysmic situation existed within these walls. 'You're looking very well. I love those colours on you.' For the sake of their long friendship, Sophie continues her attempt to mend fences.

'Yeah!' With dainty movements of red-tipped fingers, Eily has started to arrange the scones in neat lines. 'Bright colours always make you look better when you're a little tired, don't you find that? In fact, that reminds me, I must take a few ginseng caps. Didn't get to sleep until after three last night. Brian, of course, was snoring like a shunting engine. Nothing keeps that fella awake!' She smiles an affectionate, reminiscing smile, and Sophie instantly has to suppress the vision of Eily's husband in bed.

'What's the name of the music?' she asks quickly.

' "The Gold and Silver Waltz" – Franz Lehár. Lovely, isn't it? Everyone thinks it's by Strauss, you know, but it's not. There's one now, for a pub quiz. Did you ever see *The Merry Widow*?'

'We don't go to the theatre that often.' Typical, Sophie thinks. Naturally it would be gold and silver. One child dying, another so distressed that he nearly kills himself with alcohol poisoning, and she swans around in primary colours listening to glittery waltzes; if there was a tune called 'Emeralds and Diamonds' she'd be playing that. She pulls herself up, shocked at her bitchiness. Could she be just plain jealous of her friend's sense of her own self, of Eily's lush view of the world?

Or is she jealous of something else – like the fact that Eily is married to Brian McMullan? Shaken, she concentrates on her friend's deft handling of her baking tray. There seems to be an endless supply of scones. 'Baking is a skill that eludes me, I'm afraid,' she says. 'You're terrific, of course. How's Zelda this morning? Would now be a good time to take those photos Brian asked me about, d'you think?'

She is given a break by the appearance of Zelda herself, stealing like a wraith through the doorway of the kitchen and dressed only in her nightdress. It is the first time in ages that Sophie has seen her walking about in anything other than a thick sweater or dressing-gown and her skeletal appearance is painful to observe.

'How's my favourite goddaughter?' Hoping her shock doesn't show, she crosses the floor to give Zelda a hug, holding her gently in case she might hurt the unprotected bones. As she lets go, the scent of apples rises towards her from Zelda's skull – she has obviously had a shower. 'We were just talking about you, as a matter of fact,' she says. 'How would you feel about me taking a few snaps of you?' Not wanting Zelda to think these photos will be of any particular significance, she chatters on gaily, 'I'm going to be asking everyone I know – I'll need the practice! With no job I'm going to need all the skills I can muster.'

If Zelda thinks this is subterfuge she does not show it. 'No problem, Aunt Sophie.' She shrugs. 'Whatever.'

'How about now? In your room?'

'Sure, no probs. By the way, I'm sorry about your job, Mum told me – that's terrible,' and she wanders over towards the sink, leaving Sophie abashed about her earlier dismissal of Eily's concern in this regard.

'These are fresh out of the oven, darling.' Eily turns to her daughter. 'Will you have one?'

'No thanks, Mum – so, any time you want, Aunt Sophie. I'll just throw on some clothes.' Zelda fills a glass with water and wanders out again. Sophie picks up her camera bag.

Ten minutes later, seen objectively through a viewfinder, Zelda's frail, tenuous grin makes her look strikingly like a brave famine victim on the front of a fund-raising newsletter. Sophie finds she cannot bear it so, as gently as possible, she tells the girl to relax and that there is no need to smile.

Although tactfully eschewing close-ups, through her lenses she can also see objectively what the girl's parents probably can't – that their daughter's co-operation in all things masks an almost total detachment. Zelda knows she is dying, knows well that these photographs will probably end up on her obituary bookmarks, and is no longer fighting. In fact, death seems to glow around her like a translucent aura, and it takes a huge effort of will on Sophie's part to keep snapping.

The session over, she is parcelling up her film and equipment when she realises that her goddaughter, who is watching intently, has something to say. 'What is it, Zel?'

'Will you tell them something, Aunt Sophie?'

'Of course. Anything.' Sophie is suddenly fearful.

'Tell them that this is much harder for them than it is for me. I know that. And I'm sorry they have to go through it.'

'Why don't you say it to them yourself?'

'I can't. There are some things I just can't say to them. They'd disintegrate altogether. I have to keep them going.'

Sophie, too choked up to respond, kisses her quickly. 'I'll tell them. Maybe not now, but I promise I'll tell them. Now, you get some rest.' She hurries out of the room, goes straight into Eily's bathroom and locks the door. She runs both taps. Not daring to look at herself in the mirror above the basin, she swallows repeatedly until she has herself under control. Then, in case anyone is listening, she flushes the toilet, washes her hands, turns off the taps and goes downstairs.

Eily is waiting for her. 'How did it go?'

'Grand.' Sophie swallows again. 'Listen, Eily—'

'I've something to tell you, Sophie,' Eily cuts across her. 'You're the only one I'm going to take into my confidence.' She grants this as though it is a pearl.

Sophie does not want this. She is supporting enough secrets about this family. But she is well and truly caught. 'Good news, I hope?'

'Good? Oh, yes – at least, I hope you'll think so. Guess what.' She pauses for effect, then says, breathlessly, 'Zel and me are going again tomorrow morning. I've it all arranged, the tickets and everything. We're going via Paris this time.'

Instantly, Sophie's mood switches from despair to rage. Every instinct in her body tells her that this trip is wrong. The girl upstairs is so brave, this woman doesn't deserve her. What's more, to be the confidante of both warring parents is extremely unfair. 'I just don't believe this.' Knowing she is overreacting, she is, nevertheless, so angry that she can feel herself starting to shake but plunges ahead anyway. 'This is unbelievably irresponsible. At the best it's misguided but, to be honest, I think you're verging on criminal neglect of your daughter.'

'I beg your pardon?' At first Eily had seemed shocked at this outburst, but now her expression closes as she fires up her defences.

Sophie is not going to give her a chance to argue. 'You heard me – and you know exactly what I'm talking about!' She is trying to prevent her voice rising to a level that may be overheard from upstairs. 'To drag Zelda half-way round the world in her condition – and on what everyone except you believes to be a fool's errand.'

She stops. Eily's eyes have taken on the glassy stare that Sophie knows from experience is impenetrable. She has even seemed to widen the space between them.

Instinctively, Sophie takes a step forward but stops short of making physical contact. She forces herself to calm down because, for Zelda's sake, she has to continue trying. In addition, she is remembering the expression in Brian's eyes as he confided to her his fears about this the day before. 'I'm sorry,' she says, more quietly. 'I'm sorry about the way that came out. I don't mean to be rude, or to intrude where it is not my place, but you're the one who brought up the subject so I have to say what I feel in my heart. Listen, Eily, please *listen*. I've been skirting around it, but the situation is too grave now for any more pussyfooting. I've never confronted you like this before and therefore you must know how seriously I feel about this. Zelda is my goddaughter and I have obligations to her. I sincerely believe in my heart, in her condition, a trip like this will kill her.'

She hesitates. Her friend is standing rigidly and still, eyes closed now, tuned out. Sophie, resisting the urge to shake her, takes a deep breath and the next set of words emerges quickly and strongly. 'What's more, I also believe it is wrong to do this behind Brian's back. He is her father, equally obliged to take care of her, and his wishes should be respected.'

She becomes conscious that the palm of her right hand feels sweaty and unusual and, looking down, sees she is holding a jam pot. She doesn't remember picking it up and stares at it as though it is a piece of moon rock, planted there by an alien courier. 'Open your eyes, Eily, please.'

Eily stays exactly as she is. Carefully, Sophie puts down the jam. 'All right, don't open them. I'm sorry if I've upset you, but I'm not sorry I've said what I've said. Because I mean it, Eily. In the end, of course, it's your decision, and although I feel very badly about it, I will respect your request for confidentiality. I hope you can see, though, that it isn't fair of you to do this to me.'

'Are you finished?'

Eily's eyes are open again and, despite their blankness, Sophie knows she has to be deeply dismayed. While there might be a chink, she goes for broke. 'No, actually, I'm not. There is another aspect to all of this. What about Donny? He's your child too. After what he did yesterday, which in my book was clearly a cry for help, you're just going to jet off and leave him?'

'Brian will be here.'

'He needs both parents, Eily. He needs *you*. Anyway, how do you think Brian is going to cope with this? He's just been through an air crash. He's devastated about Zelda anyway – he is not going to be thrilled to find what you've done with her.'

'He's not the only one who's been through an air crash—'

'I think you need to take a hard look at this,' Sophie interrupts, before her friend can career too far down this path. 'Pause for a minute, Eily. And – I'm sorry to say this – I think you should ask yourself if you're doing this for her or for you.'

Eily turns away to rearrange her baking. 'I think you should go now, Sophie.'

Sophie stares at the broad back and shining flood of black hair. 'Do you want me to be simply a yes-woman, Eily? What kind of friend would I be if that were the case?' She can see this gets a tiny reaction and grabs at it. 'I know you're annoyed, and I'm sorry for sounding so angry, but I am angry. I'm going now, and after I've gone, will you think about what I've said? Please, Eily?'

She waits for a few seconds and then, when there is no further response, loses patience altogether. 'Oh, this is hopeless. I can see I'm just wasting my energy.' The words fly again without hindrance: 'Like I said, I'll respect your confidence and I won't tell anyone what you're doing, although it's against all my instincts, but please, Eily, whatever happens in the future, to you, to Zelda, to anyone in your family or your life, don't involve me ever, ever again. I really resent it and if Brian found out that I knew and didn't tell him, he'd probably never speak to me again – and he'd be right.'

As soon as she hears the front door slam after Sophie's departure, Riba stops arranging and rearranging her scones on their wire cooling tray, leaving them finally lined up in perfect rows like a tiny regiment. She sits at her kitchen table. Some friend! How could she have judged this so wrongly? She had got carried away with the excitement. At least Sophie will keep her word about not telling anyone: in that, she can be trusted.

So, it's finally down to herself and Zelda, two against the world.

Outside her window snow has begun quietly to fall. Her waltz tape, so marvellously insulating, has clicked off long ago and she can hear movement upstairs. She cannot decipher whether it is from Donny or Zelda so she concentrates on the small popping sounds from the stove where her stew continues to simmer.

Beside her, the wall-hung gas boiler whooshes into action, making her jump. Slowly, she stands and stretches, then absently picks up one of the warm scones and stuffs it whole into her mouth. Without butter, it tastes of little except flour; the baking soda is harsh, stinging the soft flesh on the inside of her cheeks. She cannot chew effectively because her mouth is so full and she has to swallow in thick, gagging lumps.

Her throat revolts, and she barely makes it the couple of feet to the sink, where she vomits, retching again and again until there is nothing left to bring up.

Gasping, tears streaming down her face, her body painfully in spasm, she draws back a little, then runs both taps full, pouring washing-up liquid round and round the sink, stopping only when the foam overflows on to the draining board and is about to glop all over the floor. As though there are dogs at her heels, she pulls on rubber gloves and cleans, scours, wrings out, then scrubs again with Domestos until satisfied with the bleachy odour and mirror-like finish of the sink.

When all is pristine, she pulls off the rubber gloves and stands with both hands pressed firmly against her solar plexus, fixing her gaze on the snow, so serenely tufting the air outside her window. Breathing deeply, counting off each breath, she projects herself through the glass and allows herself to fall gently with the crystals, feeling them cool her cheeks and whiten the spaces between the red strands of her muscles.

With the calming comes purpose. She walks to the telephone in the hallway and takes it, trailing its long lead, back into her warm kitchen. She has no need to look up the number, which rings clear and close in her ear as though it is in the next room and not thousands of miles across two oceans. When it is answered, she asks for Jay. 'It's important.'

'Whom shall I say is calling?' The sing-song accent is delightful and her spirits rise: this is definitely the right thing to do. She pictures the girl with hibiscus flowers behind her ears, or frangipani, maybe. 'Tell him Riba. Please tell him I need to speak to him personally.'

'Just one moment, please.' The girl clocks off and her voice is replaced by a jolly version of Elvis' 'The Wonder of You' played by a steel band.

Riba finds herself humming along. Her heart jumps in her chest as the line clears but immediately lies flat again. It is not Jay, it is California Monica. 'Riba, have you news for us? Are you coming on over?'

'Yes, Monica, we are. We're coming tomorrow – I'll give you the times in a moment, but I really need to talk to Jay himself. Is he there?'

'That's great news – you're so brave, Riba, after what you've been through. Why am I not surprised? You're one of our Irish warriors, aren't you? I'll tell him.'

'Is he there, Monica?' Riba makes herself sound assertive.

'Could he call you back? He's meditating at the beach house.'

'I'd really appreciate it if you could get him to the phone.' Riba is galled that she has to beg like this from one of these self-appointed women who form a tight girdle around Jay on his island. 'I don't mind waiting,' she says stiffly. Hang the expense.

California Monica, sounding cross, gives in. 'It may be a while, Riba, but I'll go tell him. Looking forward to seeing you, dear.'

Dear yourself, Riba thinks scornfully, as the steel band again erupts into full jangle.

The snow is really coming down now. It's very pretty, of course, but may pose problems for the flights tomorrow. Wouldn't it be the ultimate irony if, having successfully negotiated all the hurdles, their initial flight from Dublin were to be cancelled? Riba shudders: this doesn't bear thinking about. Of course it is not going to happen.

As the minutes drag on, the row with Sophie creeps back through her pores. Those awful things she said – how dare she? It's all so easy for those without children, of course. What would Sophie know about the fear of losing a daughter?

Yet a worm of unease wriggles deep in her belly. Is it possible there is some truth in what was implied? Is she a bad mother, a bad wife? Because that had been the underlying theme of the row, hadn't it? Is she misguided and criminal and all the rest of it, like Sophie said? Against 'The Wonder Of You', the images she has managed to keep at bay by sheer willpower for eighteen months flicker in and out.

Zelda in her coffin, her cheeks unnaturally rouged, surrounded by a white frill of satin . . .

Zelda's sunken eye sockets . . .

Black, black rain falling on the freshly turned earth over her grave . . .

'No! No! Go away – go away.' Horrified, she springs out of the chair and speaks aloud, flapping at the air in front of her with her free hand, beating away the images as if they were big, terrible birds. To replace them, she focuses on the snow swarming past her window, trying to separate out the individual crystals, so lovely and clean and fresh.

The world rights itself. Jay's deep, lazy voice is in her ear. 'Riba! I believe we're to see you tomorrow?'

The contents of Riba's heart explode upwards like a geyser, form themselves into a choir and burble as gaily as the drums of the steel band. 'Yes, Jay – that's right,' she says. 'We should be knocking on your door at about eight o'clock tomorrow evening, your time. I can't wait. In the meantime, there is something I really want to talk to you about – have you got a moment?'

'For you? Always!' His deep, comforting chuckle thrills her anew and she pours it all out, the row with Sophie, all the hateful things her friend has said. Her worries about Zelda. She does not exaggerate her daughter's condition, of course, although the death-images are still very fresh, merely she says she is very, very ill and that all the drugs, however necessary and beneficial they are, are making her feel dreadful.

Jay listens to the monologue without interrupting and, when she has wound down, tells her she must not worry. In the same compelling tones he used on that day she had first met him, he explains patiently that she must trust the process. That Donny is taken care of and so is Brian, so is Zelda, 'and so are your friend and her husband. Everyone connected with you, Riba, is protected because of you. We can be discouraged seven times a day but we need to look outwards and above ourselves. This life is beautiful, this earth is beautiful, and we must have tolerance in our hearts for those people who don't yet accept this. Don't forget that Jesus Himself was spat at but wiped away the spittle and carried on. You know what the right course is, Riba – what does your heart tell you?'

'To get on that plane with Zelda as quickly as I can,' Riba says happily, all doubts dispersed. 'To bring her to you.'

'Then you're doing the right thing. We look forward to seeing you. Your timing is perfect. Monica told you about our wedding feast next weekend?'

'She didn't, actually, Jay, but that's great.' Although this is the first she has heard of it, and is sure it will be terrific, Riba's thoughts are not on weddings. 'The only problem . . .' she hesitates and, even though there is no one nearby to overhear, lowers her voice almost to a whisper '. . . until we get there, we have to keep this trip quiet, Jay, all right? You know the way my husband thinks and I wouldn't want anyone to call here to check or anything like that. Will you spread the word?'

She can hear the smile in his voice as he agrees. 'You have to take care of your own affairs, Riba, but don't worry. Our lips are sealed. Looking forward to seeing you.'

'Me too – still waiting, Jay?'

'Of course, my dear. All you have to do is raise your beautiful finger.' It is their private little joke. Jay has been married once, in the distant past, but his wife has not been in the picture for many years and he is now celibate, on the basis that, like a Catholic priest, he can better concentrate on his work. He and Riba nevertheless maintain this ongoing thing between them where they pretend that some day they will explode into carnal knowledge of each other. It is deliciously intimate and she adores the deceit.

His voice changes, becomes matter-of-fact. 'Now that I have you, would you mind doing me a small favour?'

'Anything.' At this point Riba would have bundled herself in a carpet and sent herself by air mail to Timbuktu if that's what he wanted.

'I hope it won't be too inconvenient for you, but could I ask you to drop in to my Auntie May in the nursing-home? We have no relatives left over there and today is her ninetieth birthday. I would like her to know that I'm thinking about her. That we all are over here. In fact, I was meditating about her when I got the message that you were on the line. She's a great old lady, the last of my mother's sisters. There were nine of them in that little cottage in County Mayo, Riba, and she was the only one who didn't emigrate. All that's left now is one uncle in Chicago – they were a great generation.'

As Riba accedes to this request and fetches a pen and paper to note the name of the home, Donny, pale and dishevelled, comes into the kitchen, shuffles over to the sink and fills the kettle.

He has plugged it in and is staring morosely out at the snow when Riba finishes writing. She calls out the address again, then, without using his name, says goodbye to Jay and hangs up, replacing the receiver on its cradle as though it is made of the finest, most delicate spun glass. She feels like a girl again. Jay always has that effect on her. All the stress and worry melt away as easily as the snow on the warm panes of her window. Everything becomes so simple when you talk to Jay.

Even as she drives away from the house, Sophie is already regretting her handling of the situation. It was crass, over the top, and she has probably torn irreparable holes in the fabric of a friendship that has survived the wear of decades. As she remembers the suffering rigidity of her friend's back, she hears her own hateful, berating voice running balefully through the Mini as loudly as one of Eily's tapes. While intellectually she knows she was not at fault in that kitchen, emotionally she wants to take it all back, to tell Eily she loves her.

It is a useless exercise, but Sophie longs for the old certainties before that damned plane crash – or for amnesia.

Half-way to the office now, her instinct is to go home and get back into bed. She could not do that to poor old Imelda – although what is the point of being meticulous about a bloody column that doesn't matter a damn to anyone? Michael is right.

Something that has been niggling underneath comes to the surface.

Three. Three o'clock.

Didn't Eily say something about Brian snoring at three o'clock in the morning? But hadn't Michael been talking to him around then? Before he came back to bed? Before the sex?

She concentrates, 'seeing' the digital display on her clock when she woke to find Michael gone from her bed. It was definitely two twenty. She is sure about that because the digits add up to four. As a birthday present, Eily had once dragged her to a numerologist to have her numbers done and, although she was and continues to be sceptical about this so-called science, like the fortune-teller, the woman had seemed very convinced – and therefore impressive. Sophie's personal number of significance, calculated by using her birthday 9 April, ninth day of the fourth month – turned out to be four. Nine plus four equals thirteen which, in turn, adds up to four.

For whatever reasons, the outcome of the numerology sessions stuck and since then she has surreptitiously totted up various numbers she has come across. At the risk of sounding like an ersatz Eily, it is weird how often the number four crops up in a significant manner. Take the registration of the Mini, for instance, which is 5701. This tot returns 13, adding up to four. So does 31, the street number of their house. Maybe all human beings need such cryptic touchstones, even false hope, to make sense out of the random nature of their lives – and maybe she is therefore closer in inclination to Eily than she thinks.

Stopped temporarily in a queue of cars at a red light, she opens her handbag to take out her mobile but then the car in front of her begins to move. If she gets a quiet moment she will ring Michael from her desk at the office. In the meantime, she parks the revelation that he lied to her.

If he did. She must be fair.

When she gets to the office, she turns off the engine and is about to go inside when she pauses. Eily had definitely said three o'clock. She had definitely said he was snoring long before that – it had been only an inconsequential, throwaway remark, so why would she lie?

Michael had said he had received a text message from Brian about some EconoCar booking – because Brian couldn't sleep. Although she is not suspicious by nature, she cannot avoid thinking that something is seriously awry here.

Sophie re-starts the Mini, performs a risky U-turn and heads out of Arbour Hill for the airport. It has started thickly to snow.

CHAPTER TWENTY-ONE

As soon as she hangs up after her conversation with Jay, Riba crosses to her son and puts an arm up and around his shoulder. 'How are you feeling, darling? A bit fragile?'

'What do you think?' For once, Donny does not shrug off her encircling arm. He looks down at her with wary, bloodshot eyes. 'Who was that on the phone?'

'You're afraid it was something to do with you?'

'Wasn't it? The school or something?'

'No,' she smiles at him, 'relax. I was just having a chat with a pal.'

Donny hangs his head. 'On a scale of one to ten, just how pissed off with me is everyone?' He looks so chastened and young, that Riba, who does not in any event feel angry with him, cannot find it in her heart even to pretend. She rubs his back between the shoulder-blades, circling with the palm, the way she used to when he was little and she had to wind him. He covers his eyes with one hand. 'I can't remember anything, Mum, not since we went into my room yesterday. I can sort of remember music, and then it being dark and being made to drink stuff, horrible-tasting stuff, but the only clear thing I can get is putting on Eminem and the next thing I was waking up at about five o'clock this morning feeling sick and horrible. I've never felt as awful before. I can tell you, I'll never drink again – I mean it!' He uncovers his eyes. 'Sorry, Mum. Really. Does Dad know? What did he say? And what happened to the others? Are they in fierce trouble? Fiona's parents – they'll kill her. Did she ring?'

'All in good time. The first thing to do is get you back on your feet.' She is about to pull away from him but he grabs her arm.

'Don't tell Zelda when you go in to see her today, it'll upset her.'

Riba is saved from telling him the truth by the kettle boiling. Dealing with a physically sick Donny is easy, something she can get a handle on, and she bustles into action. 'Sit down, love. I know you don't feel like it but I'll make you a little bit of toast to go with your tea. Dry. No crusts, no butter, all right? Dad thinks you should stay home from school again tomorrow,' she adds, casually. 'What do you think?'

'I dunno. I'll see. I think I'll probably be all right tomorrow.'

'You probably will.' She keeps her voice light and matter-of-fact. 'Stay up now so you'll be able to sleep tonight. Just take it easy for the day, and go to bed early tonight.' She smiles sympathetically at him. 'Sleep is a great doctor, and by tomorrow morning you'll be feeling a lot better, believe me. I've been there at your age.' Her heart goes out to him as she surveys his woebegone posture and pasty skin. 'Don't beat yourself up, hon. We'll have a good chat about it later on, but I'm afraid, in the meantime, I've got to go out for a little while.'

Even as she is talking to him, concerned though she is, Riba's brain is busy performing several sets of calculations. The nursing home is in Dalkey, way over on the other side of the city, practically in the next county. She can't give Brian one iota of cause for suspicion, certainly can't tell him she was on an errand for Jay, so she will have to get to the nursing-home and be back at the usual dinnertime. He has taken the car today, so she'll have to take a taxi to the Dart station.

Then there is Zelda and her medication. Can she trust Donny to oversee it while she's gone? The poor darling. He looks so forlorn.

Briskly, without making a drama of it, she tells Donny about Zelda being home and that it was she who had found the three of them sprawled all over his bedroom. His face shows that he is appalled.

'Don't you worry about it,' she soothes him. 'All's well that ends well, you're OK and she's OK too. She's fine this morning, honestly. You should go up and see her as soon as you've had your tea.

'As a matter of fact,' she says now, as though it has just struck her, 'speaking of Zelda, she'll need her medication in about an hour's time and, as I told you, I have to go out on an errand.' She pauses, then echoes Jay exactly: 'Would you mind doing me a small favour?'

Michael jigs from one foot to the other. 'You rang me in the early hours of the morning. Well, it was a text message, actually, about a booking but I rang you back. About half past two – get it?'

Brian looks askance at this gibbering wreck, a shadow of the man he has known since adolescence. Although it is not hard to guess what is going on, he is supremely irritated at being dragged into it and is not going to make it easy. 'What do you mean?' They are standing in front of the EconoCar desk at the airport and he doesn't care who hears. Leaving aside his disapproval of the tangle these two so-called lovers have got themselves into, he is not well disposed at present towards either of them, especially not to Yvonne. When he got in this morning there was a message on the voicemail from her to say she would not be in today because she had woken up with a bug. Some bug.

'Stop being so thick.' Michael's agitation escalates. 'You know what I mean. You and I were talking on the mobiles, if anyone asks.'

Brian works to control his temper. 'Stop involving me in your messing, Mick. I don't appreciate it – it's not fair.'

'I know it's not fair, I know it's not, but one more day, please. Just bear with me for one more day. I won't ask you to do anything else for us. You won't have to anyway, because it'll all be out in the open.'

Brian reacts with disbelief. 'Out in the open? You meant that about telling Sophie?'

'Tonight, I promised Yvonne.'

'You promised *Yvonne*? What about Sophie? Never mind. Get that, will you?' – this in response to the ringing of the EconoCar telephone nearby. Both the work-experience girl and another employee who is usually out on deliveries are busy with calls. He is having to make a big effort not to say something he will surely regret, so he walks away down the busy concourse and towards the airport information desk where he has to pick up a referral. How dare Mick use him as an ally against Sophie?

On the other hand, what can he do or say about this without betraying something he should not betray, and should not even be feeling? Brian wants to kick the nearest tourist.

As he gets to the information desk, he looks back over his shoulder. Sure enough, through the crowd, he can see the sad bastard still standing where he left him. Dammit. Probably didn't even answer that call. So now he's probably lost them another blooding booking. Damn and blast!

As he is walking back towards his desk Brian, reading the referral, collides with a luggage trolley being wheeled across his path by a stately old lady, causing one of her ancient suitcases to fall to the ground. 'Sorry, ma'am, I hope there's nothing breakable.' As he stoops to pick it up and replace it, he glances towards the EconoCar desk. Mick is still there, but so is Sophie. His stomach clenches. What on earth is she doing here?

Again he apologises to the old woman, who is dressed all in black and who is glaring at him as though he is a particularly odious maggot. When she has hobbled away, he is about to resume his progress towards the desk when he realises by their body language that Sophie and Mick are having a row. Jesus! Is the creep telling her right here in the open? In the middle of Dublin airport?

Instead of continuing to his desk, Brian turns towards the escalators and travels upwards towards the departure bars and restaurants.

★ ★ ★

Until she had spotted Michael standing in front of the EconoCar desk, Sophie had been deliberately concentrating on her future or lack of it at *Wild Places*, not on the forthcoming confrontation with her husband – after all, there might be a perfectly reasonable explanation for his lying to her and she should not pre-judge him.

She had never been all that ambitious for a career in journalism in the first place: although she hated to admit it, Michael was right about that. So maybe something like this had had to happen to her so she could get a grip.

When news got out about the magazine's demise, there would certainly be no rush by other publications to hire its employees. Although Imelda had always insisted that the magazine had to be a union shop, and Sophie was therefore a member of the NUJ, she had never attended any meetings and had no idea if help was available from that quarter. She doubted it. She had never heard of the union finding employment for individual members, so the best she could hope for, probably, was statutory redundancy and other than that she was on her own. This was her wake-up call.

Right. Start at the top. Supposing there was a fairy out there to wave a magic wand and grant her a wish. What skill or profession would she wish for? What did she actually want to do with the rest of her life? What would give her most satisfaction?

This was unrealistic: Sophie trimmed her sails. What *could* she do?

As she piloted the Mini carefully up the airport motorway through the snowflakes, she peered through her windscreen and counted her skills. She could type a little, could do a little word-processing, could draw – or certainly make credible copies – could take pictures, could cut and paste articles from other publications and dummy them up into a sort of narrative, could do captions and maybe even write.

Then there was her passion for wildlife – what Michael referred to disparagingly as tree-hugging. This was life-enhancing but, at her level, hardly a professional skill, and it was difficult to see how it could be talked up sufficiently into a qualification for a job.

In fact, she had no qualifications in anything.

Sophie swerved to avoid the flattened body of a cat – fox cub? – that had been foolhardy enough to attempt a crossing.

She was disgusted with this pathetic little list of half-skills and with her lack of drive. What had Sophie Dolan to show for her nearly-forty years on this earth? Barren as she is, she didn't even have genes to contribute.

On the other hand, she had to admit that this self-flagellation was somewhat over the top. Barrenness aside, she had had a lovely life up to now, at least professionally. Left to wander at will through the dusty columns of *Wild Places*, all she had to do to satisfy her editor was to have a few ideas for items and articles so Imelda could commission them, cut and paste her own quota of pages, string together her own column, present a few decent illustrations and photos and write long captions for them. Any time she was not in the office, it was assumed she was 'in the field', which frequently she had been. Quietly enjoying herself.

In fact, the more Sophie thought about it the more she realised what a unique sinecure she had occupied. She'd never have the like again and the more she visualised the journalistic jungle outside the calm waterhole of their little mag, the more she realised she didn't even like the journalistic profession all that much and had drifted into it like a piece of flotsam, snagging gently on *Wild Places* with neither the will nor the desire to free herself.

All right. So much for the past. Look ahead, Sophie.

The lights at the airport roundabout were showing red and, as she waited in the stalled traffic for them to change, she gazed at the roundabout's centrepiece, a huge sliver of stainless steel. She had always liked it and although she had heard it was meant to represent the finely engineered proportions of an aircraft wing, in her eyes it had never meant anything more than itself. The snow was easing off and the weak, come-and-go light of the sun glanced fitfully off the column, burnishing it so that it soared like the stem of a glittering tornado through the greyish vortex of flakes.

Sophie envied artists, and never more so than at that moment. It must be lovely to conceive an idea or an emotion, paint or sculpt it, then have it there for ever, expressing and communicating your talent and thoughts for the rest of your life and afterwards. Sophie Dolan, artist – she tried it on for size. No, it didn't fit. Like most Dubliners who do not consider themselves part of the arty set, she had been to only a couple of formal art exhibitions in her life and one of those had shown not paintings or sculpture but dim, quite bizarre photographs.

Strolling around the 'real' exhibition in the Hallward, a basement gallery on Merrion Square, she had struck up a conversation with the gallery owner, a friendly woman who had not pressured her in the slightest but who had allowed her, guided by the catalogue, to wander unmolested through the wonderland of the artist's world. When she was handing back the catalogue, Sophie had summoned up the courage to ask about her Charles Lamb and described it as best she could, size and so forth. 'How valuable would it be? I'm not selling it, of course, I'm just curious.'

To her surprise, the woman had told her that maybe her painting might fetch as much as five thousand pounds at auction. 'Depending on who wants it badly enough, of course. Maybe less, maybe a little more, it's hard to be sure, but the market is buoyant. I'd need to see it, of course, but he always sells well. And he's dead. That always helps.'

What Sophie really liked was photography, of course. In her mind, she re-created the celluloid images of the Romanian women. Those were really top class in anyone's book, she could certainly stand over them, also her beech tree. She had managed to catch its intricate, living construction, as timeless as the sculpture she is looking at now.

Then there was the series of shots she had taken last year in the Phoenix Park of two ponies who had thrown their riders and, manes, tails and stirrups flying, were delighting in temporary freedom by dashing through a herd of the park's deer, scattering them to the four winds. Those had been good too.

These aside, though, she was an amateur and there was the world of difference between showing a bit of aptitude – and being lucky with subjects – and developing professional skill. Would it be too late to take it seriously? Had she the guts? There were plenty of courses available. This capital city in modern Europe, stuffed with colleges and institutions of study and learning, spread its wares before her and she should take advantage of the privileges offered. What was to stop her going back to school? Plenty of middle-aged women did it, are doing it. As she had some equipment, she would even start with an advantage.

If she did try to make a go of herself in photography, could they afford it? Would Michael wear it? Since he constantly goaded her about her lack of ambition, he probably would. Sophie's excitement grew as she indulged this fantasy. She would probably have to unlearn a lot, but she was prepared for that. *Change coming. Big change, lady* . . . Had the fortune-teller really seen something? Or was Sophie latching on to something she had secretly wanted to come true? Like that stuff about a baby.

Sophie pulled herself up as the lights changed to green. She had to stop referring to Michael as a touchstone. Michael this, Michael that, Michael says. She had to be her own person now.

Michael. Her heart turned over. In her eagerness to change her life, she had temporarily forgotten why she had been sitting there staring out at the airport roundabout through the slackening snow. She must concentrate.

She had seen him immediately on entering the arrivals concourse, and is now looking up at him, at his confused, red face. He has tried to convince her that she made a mistake about the time of the phone call but she knows he is lying. She knows this as surely as she knows that the screeching just behind a piece of plywood fifteen feet away is the sound of an electric drill. The awful sound has become a metaphor for the screaming inside her head.

There are two people behind the desk, a young man she has met only peripherally at the company's Christmas drinks and a girl she hasn't seen before who is even younger. Both are rigid with curiosity but trying to conceal it by pretending to work. 'Please don't treat me like a fool, or a child, Michael. What's going on?' she asks, calmly enough, although she does not feel in the least calm.

Her husband, obviously embarrassed, glances towards his colleagues, then grabs her arm. 'Come on, let's get out of here, we need to talk. Let's go upstairs for a cup of coffee.'

'Why can't we talk here?' The screeching intensifies and, more importantly, the ground beneath her starts to slope backwards, threatening to topple her. Sophie grips tightly with the soles of her shoes. She wants to stay for ever on this piece of airport ground she has captured and made her own. This is all she knows right now, this feeling of solidity under her feet. 'I don't want coffee,' she says, holding firm on her beachhead, around which successive waves of trolley-pushing raiders divide and re-form. If she moves one inch from this spot, she will dissolve as quickly as the snowflakes, heedless of their destiny as drops of common rainwater, that continue intermittently to land on the window behind the EconoCar desk.

'I'm going for coffee. If you want to join me, you're welcome.' He walks away from her. Sophie is afraid that even a first step will be fatal. Reason takes over and she follows him.

She is not stupid enough to think that the lie was to cover something innocent, like a surprise party, for instance. No, if she had had any doubts that this was sinister, he had dispelled them by being so shifty. No matter what he can concoct between now and the time they start talking – and she starts listening – she will be able to detect any hint of prevarication. It may not be in her own best interests to find out, many women would tell her so, but so be it. The desire to know supersedes all others, even panic. That can come later.

As Sophie weaves her way through the queues and crowds towards the escalator, something awful happens. Just as she did on the night they had their row last week she wonders again if all this is worth it. Does she even like her husband any more, let alone love him? When did this withering begin?

While he is away fetching the coffee in the clattering self-service franchise, she briefly debates the attractions of inertia. She could shrug this off, do nothing, say nothing, accept his version of events and they could limp on. The prospect is beguiling. After all, there is enough upheaval in her life with her job gone. Plus, she does not underestimate the effort it will take to repair the damage done to her major friendship.

Then there is this unexpected and dangerous flare-up that seems to have happened between herself and Brian. She thanks God that both she and Eily's husband are sensible people. They will see this out and sometime, hopefully soon, they will be able to resume a relationship more normal to their station as a pair of spouses to old friends. What has happened between them could be put down logically to the way they have been thrown together by the air crash. After all, this is something that will bind them closely for the rest of their lives; also, although she does not want to think too much about this, there is the insidious partnership with him against Eily in the matter of Zelda.

To deal with all of this, she certainly needs the bulwark of a secure marriage. So what is she doing shaking it up by asking risky questions? People are entitled to their privacy and their own lives.

Inches away at the next table, three girls, their orange, fake-tanned skin bedizened with waterfalls of cheap jewellery, are shrieking at one another in anticipation of a package holiday to the Canaries. Sophie envies them their high spirits and uncomplicated vision of the world because her husband is coming towards the table now, his gait slower than normal, carrying the coffee as though to spill a drop would be to spill his own blood.

CHAPTER TWENTY-TWO

'There's somebody else, isn't there?' Sophie decides to save her husband the trouble of lying. This is not to make it easy for him, but to make it easy for herself. Knowing Michael as well as she does, her suspicion that he has something awful to convey is confirmed before he takes his first mouthful of coffee. He is having too much difficulty opening the little packet of sugar.

She knows she has hit a bullseye because his mouth drops open, like a cod's. 'Wh-what do you mean?'

'You know perfectly well what I mean. Do I have to spell it for you? A.N.Other Woman . . .'

An extraordinary thing happens. He seems to relax. Avoiding her eye, he picks up his cup, takes a long draught from its sugarless contents then puts it back carefully on its saucer.

Sophie is thrown momentarily but recovers. The restaurant is so devoid of privacy, comfort or any hint of class that, like a navvy, she has instinctively grasped her own cup around its belly as though it had no handle. She grips hard and, oddly, finds that it provides a measure of succour and stability. 'I see,' she says. All she needs to know now is the who, why, where, when and how. How often. And – very importantly – who else knows.

The three girls at the next table laugh up a storm at some joke or other, and Michael turns his head to look at them. Sophie's focus is so narrow, though, that although she has noticed it, the eruption and all other noise in the place has shrunk to the level of the faint clicking from a pipistrelle she once heard on a bat detector. It is as though the universe has narrowed to a single point and there is nothing outside it. Nothing important except this one issue to be resolved in the tragi-comedy of their marriage.

She is not prepared just yet for the final act. 'Your timing is terrific,' she says quietly, 'given that I've just become unemployed.'

He whips back towards her, seizing on the opportunity to postpone what cannot be postponed. 'You know I'm sorry about that, Sophie,' he says, his expression earnest. 'I hope you do. Despite what I've said in the past about *Wild Places* being such a shitty little rag, I'm genuinely sorry—'

'Who is she, Michael?' Sophie cuts in. 'What's her name?'

He lowers his eyes, as cowed as a thrashed greyhound. She notices a small scratch just beneath one of his eyes. Not a shaving cut, not there. Raking nails? Bile rises into her throat. 'I asked you a question.'

'Look, Soph, can I say how sorry I am? We didn't mean for it to happen.'

There it is. Straight away. There's that 'we'. Inexperienced as she is in these matters, Sophie's radar has been scanning for it. Once there is a 'we' in the equation, it's all over.

The realisation is something she will deal with later, along with the hurt and the recriminations, the pain and the humiliation. In the meantime, the jealous drive to *know* overrides even her sense of dignity. 'There is no point in hiding it, Michael, this is Dublin, I'll find out anyway – who is she?'

'You met her.' His voice is low and shamed. 'Although you may not remember. At the Christmas party. Her name is Yvonne Leonard.'

This does kick, right where it hurts. Foolishly, even within this instant of betrayal, Sophie had hoped that at least Michael's bimbo had a bit of style. 'Yvonne Leonard? I remember her all right, she's the one with the—'

'Don't,' he says swiftly, seeming to recover. 'Don't insult her, Sophie. I'm very, very sorry. I can't tell you how sorry I am, but it was inevitable.'

'Inevitable?' She is glad of the opportunity to be openly hostile. She realises the three at the next table are all ears but doesn't give a sweet damn.

Michael obviously does because he lowers his tone. 'Yes, inevitable! Keep your voice down, will you? We have an audience here, for Christ's sake!'

'This venue was your choice, not mine.' As she says it she realises that this franchise café is appropriate for the killing of a marriage: exits and entrances, meetings and goodbyes, hopes, dreams and endings, all conducted in the environment of mediocre food and indifferent service. 'I really don't give a fig about who hears me, Michael, I'm not the one who's having an affair – but I do need some answers. You owe me that much after so long.'

'I'd prefer not to go into it. You'll thank me for it later. Look, Soph—' He attempts to take her hands in his but she snatches them away.

'You said inevitable. How was it inevitable? What have I ever done to make this inevitable?'

He examines the surface of the table, littered with other people's crumbs. 'It'd only hurt you more than you are hurt already,' he says quietly.

But Sophie's relentless tongue will not be stilled. 'I'll deal with my own feelings, thank you. Just tell me what I've done.'

'You've done nothing, Sophie. Nothing at all. You are a good, no, a wonderful woman. I don't deserve you.'

'Oh, spare me!' She knows she is losing it but, more than ever, does not give a toss. 'If I'm all that wonderful, why do this? It's just your bloody gonads, isn't it? No wonder you chose that tramp.'

'I warned you.' He shoots to his feet. 'I warned you not to insult her because she's going to be—'

'Your mistress? Your concubine?' She, too, leaps up, to the obvious delectation of the three at the next table. 'Your what, Michael? That little trollop is hardly going to be your wife. What age is she? Seventeen? Eighteen? How long do you think she'll stay with you?' They stare at each other across the table, and because he is no longer remonstrating, Sophie feels her body fill with black slime. 'You're going to marry her?' The slime hits the back of her knees and she sits down abruptly. She is to be replaced by a teenage tart with yellow hair and cleavage.

'Don't, Sophie, I hate to see you like this, don't humiliate yourself.' He puts a hand on her shoulder and, violently, she swipes it off. 'Don't,' he repeats quietly.

The three chrissies at the next table have given up even the pretence of minding their own business and are staring with slack-jawed awe at the pantomime taking place right under their noses. Michael turns away from her and leans threateningly over them, intimidating them with his physical size: 'I would appreciate it, girls, if you would keep your eyes to yourselves.'

The three, raising eyebrows at each other, turn away. Sophie thinks that, given the naff surroundings, it is quite fitting that it was these three who had been chosen to witness the end of a partnership.

She looks up at the face she knows so well. The small scar above his nose as a result of an injury in a rugby scrum, the off-centre cow's lick that has defeated all barbering, the pouches under his eyes that give him a somewhat louche air. It is as though her brain is operating independently of her will and is committing these features to memory before they physically vanish.

She can see his mouth is bursting with something momentous. It is no doubt some other cliché about how he – or 'we' – cannot stand inflicting pain, wants to minimise it, hopes this can be amicable, some nonsense like that. She refuses to hear it and fixes on a partition a few feet away. 'I don't want to listen to any more. Your stuff will be packed by eight o'clock this evening. Please don't arrive before that. I won't be there. I never want to see you again as long as I live.'

Again, there is that sense of dislocation. It is as though another Sophie is speaking through her. Both Sophies now want him to go. 'Please leave your keys behind you. We can talk through solicitors, but not just yet. Give me a few days. I'll contact you via your job.'

'Or the mobile?'

'Yes. The mobile. I need to get used to the idea. Go now, please.' She is afraid that if he says one more word, cracks will start to appear at the tip of her crown and will spread all over her face and body so that within seconds she will resemble a figure in an old, dark painting consigned to a neglected corner of a museum.

He hesitates and, because she is not looking at him, she feels, rather than sees, that his expression has cleared a little. Whatever platitudes he had been going to mouth were now off the agenda.

Her hunch was only partially right because he moves a little closer to her, blocking the view of the three harpies. 'Are you all right, Soph? Will you be all right?'

'The keys. Don't forget to leave the keys.' Sophie feels she is barely holding on.

He hesitates again. 'For what it's worth, Soph, I admire you. Maybe you're too good for me.'

'Will you, for God's sake, go?'

He hangs his head, and then, mumbling again that he is sorry, turns away and hurries out. Sophie does not turn to watch him leave because all sensibility is draining from her heart, soul and mind, leaving them blank. She can think, feel and imagine nothing.

She looks across at the three young ones, but they have already lost interest in her and her problems and have launched into a discussion about whether English fellas or Dutch fellas are the best rides.

It is Sophie's turn to eavesdrop. The first girl goes for the Dutch, the other two for the English because, one of them says, at least the English go through the motions of foreplay. 'Unless they're ossified, of course – and then it doesn't matter anyway because they can't get it up in the first place.'

This sends them all off into mirthful paroxysm. It occurs to Sophie that it has been only a matter of days, hours even, since she was reassuring herself that whatever his other faults, at least her husband had been faithful to her. And as the laughter at the next table continues, absurdly, Sophie smiles too. The choice is to smile or collapse.

Thirty feet away, behind Sophie and these three, Brian McMullan has been a fourth spectator to the conversation, obviously fraught, between the Dolans. He had just settled in with his own coffee and Danish when he saw them arrive.

Both coffee and Danish remain untouched in front of him.

As soon as he saw Michael's abrupt departure, his instinct had been to rush over to Sophie but he knew that that would be unjust and untimely, and that if he did there would be no going back. Whatever might happen in the future, he must not intervene but let matters unroll as they would. For his part, faced now with making a choice between want and duty, duty won.

Now, as she sits rod straight in her chair, he enters a sort of personal lottery. If she turns round and sees him, he will respond. If she doesn't turn round, if she doesn't see him, he will let her depart unmolested.

So, watching her stiff back, he suffers with her as the seconds tick and tick.

She does not move a muscle.

Beside her, three overweight girls, wearing too much makeup and bulging out of short skirts and strappy tops to show false tans, stand up and organise themselves for departure. They are loudly effervescent with the prospect of what is obviously going to be some pretty uninhibited holiday. Brian envies them.

He concentrates on Sophie's straight back. Despite his high-mindedness he now wills her to turn round. Fuck the lottery. *Come on, Sophie, please, please, I'm here.*

She is looking after the three departing holidaymakers. She is standing, picking up her handbag . . .

Over here . . . Just turn round . . .

Without looking right or left, she is following the girls towards the top of the escalator at the exit point of the restaurant. She is nearly there, putting out a hand to grasp the moving handrail . . .

Resolve, lotteries, noble considerations, all are shucked as Sophie steps on to the top step. Brian's knees flex independently of his will. He finds himself on his feet to go after her. He even takes a step – but at the last moment reason reins him in.

As a swimmer in difficulties hangs on to a lifebelt, he clutches tightly to the edge of the table until she has descended out of his sight.

During the time she had been in the airport restaurant, the snow had deteriorated into a murky grey drizzle and Sophie, who is carrying out the normal functions of a human – breathing, walking – nevertheless feels like an automaton as she goes to the car park. She manages to insert the money into its slot in the pay machine without letting any of the coins

spill from her numb fingers. Then she drives to the office, this time giving
the silver wing on the roundabout neither a glance nor a thought as she
swings round it. She grips the steering-wheel tightly, travelling slowly in
the inside lane all the way to Whitehall as the rest of the motorway traffic
swishes contemptuously past her. She turns right at Botanic Avenue, left
up Mobhi Road, right again to pass the old Richmond hospital and
almost causes an accident when crossing Manor Street to enter Arbour
Hill because she doesn't see that the lights are red. From then on, however,
she stops and starts on cue at the yield and stop signs in the little streets as
though everything is still normal in her universe.

As she drives, the practical problems she is now to face are lining up in
phalanx at the back of her brain, preparatory to their march past her
attention. She can identify them all, individually and collectively: cash,
finance, income, a new job – imperative now – the house, solicitors, the
dividing of their joint possessions, cash again. No single socks being lost in
the wash, no toilet seats being left up, no maddening snoring, no key
turning in the lock of the front door.

Loneliness.

At least there are no children in the equation. What heart-stabbing
efficiency!

When she gets to *Wild Places*, Imelda is nowhere to be seen, the door to
her office hangs open, her desk has already taken on the appearance of a
house suddenly empty because its owner has died. In fact, the *Wild Places*
office resembles a funeral home, with Nancy acting as chief steward,
mournfully bagging up back issues, spent faxes, everything that is no
longer of any use to anyone. Even the gospel music issuing quietly from
her ghetto-blaster seems subdued and sad. Being Nancy, however, she tries
to find something positive. Although she doesn't know for sure, of course,
Imelda, she thinks, is out at another meeting, probably engaged in
discussions with new investors.

Sophie, who knows how quickly her colleague will need a replacement
job because of her domestic responsibilities, is also aware that no investor
in his or her right mind would take on this moribund anachronism.
Temporarily roused from her stupor, she casts around for a way to help, or
at least to let Nancy down gently. This is not easy. When set against the
glossy and professional titles, *Wild Ireland*, for instance, and all the imports
jostling for shelf space in every newsagent's shop, *Wild Places* hasn't a
prayer. In fact, it's a miracle it survived as long as it did.

It is time for lateral thinking. 'Look,' she says impulsively, 'I can't
promise anything, but I could probably get you a job at the airport. At
least for the summer – they start taking people on from about February,

that's only a couple of weeks away – and then . . . you never know. At least you'd have a foot in the door. It would take a little while to organise but I'm sure I could get you something. Would you like me to try?' Michael owes her at least this. Not yet, of course, but when she can face him. If he won't help, she'll ask Brian.

'What could I do at the airport? I've no travel experience.'

'Nonsense, Nancy.' Sophie, welcoming this distraction from her own troubles, warms to her theme. 'What we're talking about here is a desk job at EconoCar or one of the other concessions, even the sweet kiosk – something like that. In fact,' her conviction is growing, 'they have some work-experience student in Michael's place who's leaving shortly, and by the way they've been talking she's become an essential part of the team. They could probably do with replacing her straight away. Instead of getting someone free they'll just have to pay. Don't worry, you'll pick it up – you're a brilliant organiser.'

'Really?' Nancy is now seizing on the idea, and although Sophie has conveniently overlooked her little colleague's Mad Hatter ways, she begins nevertheless to believe her own rhetoric.

'You've been wasted here all these years,' she says. 'After all, how difficult can it be to rent cars to people? It's all documentation. Certainly it has to be far less complicated than organising a magazine month after month.'

Sophie's colleague rushes over to her and throws her arms round her neck. 'Oh, Sophie! What would I do without you? You're so good – are you sure your husband won't mind? You won't be putting him under any obligation?' The relief infusing her entire body is so moving that the cotton-wool around Sophie's own heart is in danger of shredding.

'He won't mind,' she says lightly, 'but you'd have to give up that bloody ghetto-blaster.'

Despite the tone, it is just as well that Nancy, who had turned away to mop her eyes, cannot interpret the grim expression on Sophie's face either then or afterwards while she throws her final column together.

This takes an hour and then, not wanting to prolong the agony, she gives Nancy another quick hug, promises to call within a couple of days 'with news one way or the other' then flees the office.

The most effortless emotion is anger. Within minutes of getting home, in its white heat, Sophie is stuffing Michael's jackets, ties, pants, shirts, pyjamas, underwear and toiletries, even his washing from the laundry basket, willy-nilly into suitcases and holdalls, not caring about folding or preserving, hoping that his precious possessions will emerge tumbled and unkempt; when she has run out of suitcases, she shoves the remainder into black plastic rubbish sacks.

When there is no more clothing to pack, she moves on to his collection of *Far Side* cartoon books, his jokey beer mugs, his plaques and medals won for schools' rugby, his trainers and golf clubs and the Waterford glass vase he won in a pub quiz, cramming them in on top of the clothing and hoping some of them will not survive. When she can find nothing more, nothing movable anyway, she stands back to regard the jumbled heap piled against the wall at the front door. Some of the black bags have torn. Good. Appropriate. *A Life in Black Plastic and Suitcases* by Sophie Dolan. Perfect caption. Sophie is on the point of running for her camera to preserve and validate the moment.

Then her rage fizzles out and, with it, her energy, so that from her toes, sleep ascends like a relentless indigo tide. She grabs a magic marker from the box by the telephone and scribbles a note on the message pad, 'KEYS, PLEASE!', and places it on top of the pile. Then, instead of going out as she had planned, she trudges upstairs and climbs fully dressed into bed. Her bed now.

Her last act before she loses consciousness is to remove her wedding ring and fling it into the darkness, not caring where it lands. If she hoovers it up when she finds the energy to clean again, so be it. That would be terrific, actually. That's where it belongs. Lost in the detritus within the darkness of a brown-paper vacuum-cleaner bag—

Incredibly, she falls into dreamless sleep.

She wakes abruptly with the red digits on her bedside clock showing 8.32 p.m. For a moment or two she is disoriented and, then, like a dam-burst, the events of the day come crashing in on her. She scrambles out of bed and runs downstairs.

The pile of Michael's possessions is no longer by the front door. Scribbled on the back of her note are four words: 'I'm very very sorry.' His keys are beside it and he has placed both in the dead centre of their glass-topped coffee table.

Sophie sits in an armchair in front of the television and turns it on, then adjusts the volume so that the sound is barely audible. For the next three hours or so, she does not move, flicking between channels without knowing what she is watching.

She had meant it when she said to him that she never wanted to see him again. She still means it intellectually, but her emotions are tuned to every footstep outside, every shush of every tyre going by through the slush, every creak that might indicate he is creeping quietly towards the front door to beg her forgiveness. He has to call at least. He is a bastard, but why doesn't he call?

With ears geared acutely to catch the first ping of the telephone bell, she notices each household sound against the murmur of the television – the abrupt quiet after the fridge clicks off, the slight hiss from the nearby radiator – and every minute is as slow as a week, each hour interminable. All the while, she continues to dissect the events of the *dies horribilis* since she answered the telephone to Eily fourteen hours ago.

By midnight, although she is not hungry, she feels she should eat and mentally surveys the contents of the fridge in the kitchen. Yet although she hates the feeling of physical inertia, of blood coagulating within her limbs, she finds it impossible to stir.

It's the not knowing where he is or what he is doing that is torturing her, although she is realistic enough to recognise that this is only because she has lost him; in recent years when they have been about their separate daily business, she rarely gave his whereabouts or activities a thought.

She must get up out of this chair. She must. She is growing into it, her hips spreading into the cushions as tenaciously and virulently as Russian ivy.

She will get up. In a minute. She is a big girl now. Marriages break up all the time. She did absolutely the right thing in throwing Michael out immediately and not hanging around to be kicked some more.

Technically, of course, he has left her, but at least in her own eyes she has regained some dignity.

Dear God, how long will it take for these feelings of disorientation, of wild swinging from despair to frenzy, to settle into something more normal?

For the umpteenth time, her eyes fall on his keys where he left them. Loud in the sarcophagus of the sitting room, they tap-dance on the glass of the coffee table with mocking metal feet.

CHAPTER TWENTY-THREE

In Marble Gardens, Riba pulls back the sitting room curtains on the drabness of a wet Tuesday morning. No sign of snow, thank God. The forecast is for this rain to clear up before noon, but of course it will be irrelevant to herself and Zelda because by noon they will be flowing with the human rivers along the glassed-in channels at Charles de Gaulle airport.

Through the ceiling she can hear Brian, God love him, gargling away with that minty mouthwash he uses every morning in the mistaken belief that it will help preserve his teeth. She smiles affectionately: marriages are rarely built on the big things, mostly they coast along on these little familiarities and if Brian and she were ever to split up, not that it was likely, this sound, which signals the start of every day, is one of the domestic intimacies she would miss most.

He is in a strange mood this morning, though – not exactly irritable but not benign either. Sort of absent. That's it, he's sort of absent. In the present circumstances, that's not an unwelcome phenomenon, Riba thinks, going back into the kitchen where Zelda's breakfast of juice, cereal with cream and a thinly sliced banana is already laid out on her tray. As a matter of fact, Brian's mental blankness this morning is quite a gift because he won't notice anything out of the ordinary in her own routine – for instance, her getting back into her dressing-gown after her bath. Alongside Zelda's breakfast, Riba now dispenses medication in little plastic cups, carefully adding an extra caplet of painkiller. The risks are minimal, because now she is almost as knowledgeable as any medic about the interlinking effects on each other of all the drugs her daughter ingests.

She brings the breakfast upstairs, draws the curtains of Zelda's room and wakes her. Then she goes into her and Brian's bedroom and taps on the door of their *en suite*. 'Breakfast in ten minutes, hon!' Without waiting for a response, she glides out again. Luckily Brian has an early start at the airport this morning so he will be rushing and won't quiz her about Donny.

Downstairs again, she goes about the rest of the small kitchen tasks, squeezing Brian's orange juice, spooning the Bewley's coffee he likes into the coffee-maker, putting bread into the toaster. Any pangs of guilt she might feel in deceiving him are easily quelled by the knowledge of *why* she has to lie. As she waits for the coffee to perk, Riba closes her eyes and visualises Zelda sitting at a table laden with tropical fruits and organic vegetables, the type of food Jay urges everyone to eat but which is so expensively exclusive in Dublin; she sees her daughter swallowing the health-giving vitamin and mineral supplements, anti-oxidants and nutrients that Jay will recommend; she projects ahead to the image of herself sitting outside a pristinely white closed door, looking out at the quiet Caribbean Sea and knowing that, inside the room behind her, Jay is working his mental magic on her daughter. She sees Zelda walk out of that room with glowing skin and bright eyes.

The air fills with the scent of citrus aftershave as Brian bustles into the kitchen and she has to jolt herself out of her visualisation. 'How are you feeling this morning, darling?'

'Not too bad – I don't have time for toast, is the coffee ready?' Although hurried, Brian seems to be his usual affable self yet Riba cannot help thinking he is still only half with her. As he gulps his juice then pours coffee into the waiting mug, she decides not to push her luck and turns her back to busy herself at the sink. 'You should eat something.'

'I'll grab a cooked breakfast later.' Half a minute afterwards, behind her, she can hear him clattering the empty mug on to the counter. Then: 'See you, Eily – I shouldn't be too late this evening. Good luck with Donny – will you take him out somewhere for lunch or what?'

'I'll see – I don't like leaving Zel.'

'Well, just remember what we discussed, OK? Lots of attention and TLC – and do try to give him some sort of a treat.'

'Don't worry.' Riba doesn't trust herself to turn round. Instead, she runs the cold tap. 'Have a good day.'

'You too.' He is gone and, despite his strange mood, it has been an ordinary morning in an ordinary marriage. Up to now. Riba waits until the front door slams, then turns off the tap and races for the stairs.

Through the open door of the room adjoining hers, Zelda, her mouth full of banana and sweet cream, can hear her mother harrying and cajoling her brother to get up for school. Can hear Donny moaning and cursing and objecting. His reluctance to get out of bed is not just because of his recent adventures in the drink trade, it is a daily occurrence.

She takes another mouthful, then closes her eyes and while she chews, fits her head into its warm groove on her pillow, revelling in the soft comfort. For some reason, probably because of all the medication, she now needs her food sweetened or salted beyond the norm.

She doesn't know whether or not she would switch places with her brother: on the one hand, he has a life ahead of him. On the other, poor little guy, he still has four long years to go in that jungle of competitiveness and fear of failure called school. It is no wonder schooling is another word for disciplining – i.e. punishing – horses. At least that's all over for her.

Although she had never told either of her parents, Zelda had hated school. Academically successful and popular, she had nevertheless been unhappy and had ploughed on to get her Leaving Cert as a passport to better things. No one had been overtly unkind to her but she hated the regimentation, the uniform, most of all the expectations that were hung around the necks of the brighter pupils. It was as though you had to get the points for the school, not for yourself, so that those who ran it could boast about you and their prestige would be maintained.

The only two subjects she had enjoyed were English and French. As for the rest, it was slog, slog, slog. For instance, what was the point of trigonometry? Or of learning the work of poets who wrote obscurely in the Irish language – a subject Zelda had shaken off her heels for ever on the instant she placed the last full stop on the last Irish examination paper. She had walked out of her secondary school with a light heart. Intending never again to study anything she did not enjoy. Planning to take a year between the Leaving and going to university, to travel in Australia, in Greece, in eastern Europe, even in South America. She would fund her ticket in the first instance with the proceeds of a summer job and then work her passage. Her dad, who was an old softie, would have given her money too, she had been sure of it.

That was until multiple myeloma had reared its ugly head to grin at her.

The daily gavotte is nearing its climax next door. Although Donny's shouted expletives are muffled and largely unintelligible – his head is probably buried under the bedclothes – the gist is clear: their mother is to get out of his room right *this minute* and leave him alone.

Next move will be her mum's. Sure enough, Zelda can now hear her mother's quick footsteps. It is only a matter of time until Donny thumps his size tens on to the carpet.

'All right, darling?' Her mother is hovering in her doorway.

'Fine, Mum, fine.' Zelda takes another spoonful of the cereal.

She expects her mother to leave but, instead, she comes and stands beside the bed, picks up one of the empty plastic cups. 'Oh, good, you took all your medicine.'

From next door, Zelda hears the next move in the gavotte – *thump!*
Donny is out. This seems to galvanise her mother. 'All right, darling, I'll
just sort him out and then I'll be back for the tray.'

The next half-hour or so runs its normal course in Marble Gardens.
Half aware of what is going on – her mother does seem to be running
up and down the stairs a lot, and foostering more than usual in her own
room – Zelda finishes as much as she can of her breakfast. It seems to
be a dreary old day although it is hard to tell because it is still dark. The
weather should be a matter of indifference to her, of course, but for
some reason, even at her sickest, her mood for the day can be seriously
affected by whether the sky outside her window is blue or grey. She
makes herself comfortable again under her duvet: nothing to get up for,
anyway . . .

The air on the landing whooshes as the front door opens and slams,
with Donny finally leaving for school. Instantly, her mother's footsteps
sound yet again on the staircase.

Zelda closes her eyes. She has no desire for conversation, or even a
massage. She just wants to be left in peace to enjoy the absence of pain.
She is feeling quite floaty, actually: whatever painkillers she is being
prescribed at the moment are really the business. She could probably sell
them in a Dublin nightclub.

'Zel?'

'Mmm?' She is aware of the shadow over her bed. Her mother sounds
out of breath. Maybe if she just keeps her eyes closed like this – but she has
to move her legs to accommodate her mother's seating herself on the bed.

There is a short pause. Then: 'Open your eyes, darling, there's
something we have to discuss.'

'Can it wait, Mum? I'm terribly sleepy.' Zelda is not exaggerating.
Sleep, like a blue cloak, is creeping over her. She feels her mother's hand
on her head.

'Well, actually, darling, it can't wait. You see, I have a great, great
surprise in store for you today – for both of us.'

At last Zelda opens her eyes and becomes instantly wary because she is
now being fixed with that intense, brown gaze she knows so well and
which means that this isn't going to be anything run-of-the-mill. 'What?
What is it, Mum?'

'Listen.' Her mother's voice is low and thrilling. 'I know this is short
notice but guess what?'

'For God's sake,' with some difficulty, Zelda raises herself on one elbow,
'stop with all the dramatics.'

However, her mother continues to draw it out. 'How would you like,' she breathes, 'to get up and put on your clothes and come with me to Dublin airport? Right this very minute.'

Zelda frowns. 'I don't understand. Why on earth would I want to go to Dublin airport? Are we going to surprise Dad?'

'No, we are not going to surprise Dad. We will be in Departures, not Arrivals, because what we are going to do, my dearest, darling daughter, is . . . we are going to get on a plane to Paris and then we are going to go on that trip we should have taken eight days ago to the Caribbean.'

For the first time, Zelda notices that her mother is all dressed up and not wearing one of her kaftans. What she has suggested is so shocking that it doesn't make sense. 'You're joking, of course?'

'No. No joke. I have the tickets and the passports, we're packed – not that there's much or that we'll need much – so we're all ready. All you have to do, my darling, is get out of that bed, get washed, and put your clothes on. It's a quarter to eight now. The taxi is coming for us in exactly forty-five minutes – by the way, as a special treat we're going business class this time. Air France. We deserve it, don't you think?'

'But, Mum—'

'So you'd want to put on a bit of a spurt. Is there anything specific you want me to put in the case for you? I think I've thought of everything – but while you're getting ready, I could—'

'*Mum!*' Outrage is too mild a word for what Zelda feels. 'Don't even think about it. We were in a *crash*, Mum, *you* were in a crash, how can you even *think* about getting on a plane again so soon?'

'You know what they say about getting back up on a horse, darling.'

'But—'

'I have to admit I'm a bit nervous too. We can be nervous together.'

Zelda does not believe a word of this assertion: from her mother's excited expression, she can see she is not remotely nervous about flying.

To be truthful, Zelda wouldn't be all that nervous either. What difference would another crash make to her? Shortcut to blessed oblivion, where she would have no more choices to make, would have to face no more painful, lying conversations. That is probably unnatural and absurd, but what is not absurd about this entire situation, about her crackpot mother?

What are you thinking? Don't entertain this even for a second . . . Her agitation has waned, however, and she is now deeply tired. That blue cloak of sleep, which had slipped off her with the impact of the proposal, is creeping back over her again. She flops back into her pillows. 'You are completely bats, Mum,' she says quietly. 'Do you know that?'

'Yes, but I'm nice bats. Please do this, darling. Otherwise . . .' Despite her mother's wide, encouraging smile, alarmingly, her mouth wobbles and those amazing eyes fill with fear.

Zelda cannot stand to see it. 'Don't, Mum, don't look at me like that.'

'I can't help it.'

As her mother takes a tissue from the box beside her bed, Zelda becomes frantic. She has never before seen her other than serenely certain. She starts to rationalise. She had agreed to the first trip not only because her mother had worn down her resistance and it eventually became easier to accede, but because she felt she had nothing to lose. Also, since she wouldn't be able to travel the world as she had planned, mightn't she as well see one exotic island before she died? That still holds, doesn't it? Wouldn't it be nice to feel the sun on her cold bones? Zelda remembers, hazily, what the nice consultant had said to her about vitamins and sunshine: he, for one, would probably approve.

The proposal remains bizarre nevertheless, as bizarre as this Jay Street she has been hearing about since she started taking notice of what adults really say. Yet what harm could he do? Her mother believes in him so wholeheartedly that Zelda, although not convinced he will be able to do anything for her, feels that at least he won't kill her any sooner than she'd die anyway.

If it comes to it, what further harm can the trip itself do? She is being offered a free holiday in the Caribbean. Who in their right mind would say no to a free holiday? Isn't it preferable to lying here looking out at all this grey bloody rain?

While all this is flashing through her mind, her mother is watching her closely with those huge, frightened eyes. Zelda makes one last stand: 'If I agree to this and it doesn't work, will you leave me alone for good?'

Her mother crushes the tissue between both hands as her face flames with hope. 'It will work – oh, thank you, Zel. You'll see, it will work.'

Zelda stares, as hard as her energy will allow, and for once, it is those brown eyes that skid away. 'Of course, Zelda.' Quietly. 'Anything you want.'

'For good. No more interventions. Promise?'

'I promise.'

So what if the journey kills her, Zelda thinks now. Big deal. Wearily, she lifts the duvet, which is seized joyfully by her mother, who then helps her out of bed. 'You go and get ready. I'll just clear away the tray and make sure to leave everything shipshape.'

'I'll regret this – I know I will . . .' But as Zelda walks shakily towards the bathroom, she stops. 'Wait a minute. Donny and Dad didn't come in to say goodbye. All this last-minute stuff – what's going on, Mum, do they know?'

Her mother, who has been drawing up the duvet and neatening the pillows, stops. She turns round. 'No. They don't. Because Dad would have moved heaven and earth to prevent it. I've written letters to both of them.'

There is a moment during which Zelda wants to hit her. She wants no part of this, but then her mother takes a step forward, pleading, 'They'll be fine – I've stocked the freezer.'

Seeing the renewal of the terror, Zelda is cursed once again with her mother's pain, with knowing what it is like helplessly to watch a daughter fading into death. 'This is wrong, Mum. I don't like it.' But she is lost.

Because she couldn't stand the silence of the house, Sophie came in to *Wild Places* early this morning, earlier than she ever did when she was usefully employed there.

It is now almost eleven o'clock and she is regretting the impulse because the atmosphere is tomb-like as she, a poppy-cheeked Imelda and a distraught, dishevelled Nancy continue to fill rubbish bags with yellowing faxes and ancient printouts.

Nancy stops abruptly. 'How did the meeting go yesterday with the investors, Imelda?'

'What investors?' Imelda, hands full of papers, looks over her shoulder. She has continued to dress bizarrely: today's ensemble is a tweed skirt in deep bottle green teamed with a frilly blouse made from some diaphanous synthetic fabric in bilious yellow. Sophie guesses that she has been shopping in the rash of charity outlets that have colonised the area and seems to be multiplying as quickly as measles on a baby.

Nancy is confused. 'Oh, sorry – I thought—'

Suddenly, the editor lashes out and kicks one of the bags so hard that it splits and topples over. As both of her employees watch, fearfully astonished, she goes berserk, flinging and kicking papers, staplers, even a fan, around the small office as though they are mortal enemies. This is not the Imelda they know.

The storm is over as quickly as it blew up and the editor, panting a little, stands in the middle of her domain. 'Sorry about that, folks. Just lost my temper there for a moment.'

'Are you all right, Imelda?' Sophie feels desperately sorry for her, standing there like some bewildered bird decked out in garish mating plumage.

'I'm fine. Sorry about that – it's just . . .'

'Something will turn up. You'll think of something,' Nancy falters.

The editor shrugs, then turns away and starts to tie up one of the black bags.

Sophie, too, turns away. Poor Imelda. Poor Nancy. Dammit, no! Poor Sophie! She drops the bag she has been packing and, for the hundredth time that morning, checks the face of her mobile. No messages.

There is nothing to prevent her telephoning Michael. Except her pride.

Or she could call Brian. Although she is quite sure Michael will already have told him what has happened, she would have every justification in ringing him to tell him her side of the story. For a few moments, Sophie considers the idea.

She even goes outside the office and starts to punch in Brian's number, but half-way through presses the 'No' key. No. Definitely not. Not while she is still so raw. To confide in him would be unfair to both of them. And to Eily.

She goes back inside, puts the mobile back into her handbag and picks up a fresh rubbish bag.

Poor Sophie, how is she coping with unemployment? Although she is still sore about the row between them, Riba's heart goes out to her. With Zelda resting safely in the Air France business-class lounge, she is browsing the glittering, cavernous duty-free shopping area at Charles de Gaulle, searching for a gift for Jay, something really fine but not ostentatious – a Breitling watch?

Too expensive, even here.

She should not dwell on the unpleasantness between herself and Sophie concerning Jay, everything will come good in the end. She shares Jay's views that the wells are always bubbling under the surface and what people like themselves have to do is keep drilling.

She moves away from the jewellery and towards the clothing. Almost immediately, in a glass case in one of the speciality shops, she spots a silk shirt, displayed as only the French can, in soft pearl-grey, a shade of which even Sophie would approve. It costs about £160. That's nothing when you consider what she and Zelda will receive in return. Gladly, Riba pays, using her credit card.

As she replaces the card in her wallet, she smiles on glimpsing the old-fashioned holy picture Auntie May gave her to pass on to Jay, to thank him for his kind thoughts. Christ the Good Shepherd. How appropriate, even if the old lady had snatched it at random from between the pages of her overstuffed missal – 'Here! Give the fecker that with my best wishes.'

Riba smiled indulgently. Old folks and their little ways!

She can already picture Jay in the shirt as she hurries back to where she has left Zelda.

CHAPTER TWENTY-FOUR

This must be what they mean when they talk about the Dark Night of the Soul. It is hellish, the longest night of Brian's life.

Pacing the sitting room, cursing his stupidity and blindness, he stops for a moment, picks up the remote control and flicks through the television channels: nothing but rubbish, cheap, garish sets, talk, talk, talk, stupid comedians, sad sacks pouring sad stories over pretend-earnest hosts, hordes of half-sized, half-dressed people jigging around with spears on a documentary programme about some jungle. He turns off the set and flings the remote into a corner of the couch.

There must have been some sign, she couldn't have been that clever – but she had. He picks up the letter for the umpteenth time: 'My dearest darling Brian, By the time you get this letter . . .' Blah, blah, blah, she hoped he'd understand, he'd be delighted later, blah, blah . . .

Reasoning that Eily might have taken Donny out for the entire day, he had not been unduly put out to have got no response when, as promised, he telephoned at intervals throughout the day to find out how things were going. In retrospect, he should, of course, have listened to the little voice inside him saying that she wouldn't have left Zelda for that long – and even if she had, Zelda would have picked up at least one of the calls.

At the time, however, he had told himself his daughter was zonked on her medication or listening to music on headphones in her room.

So, supremely unaware that his house was empty, he had immersed himself obsessively in bloody EconoCar. He had had to work doubly hard anyway. Thank God for the disabled: as well as being loyal customers, they had lots and lots of equally loyal relatives who took the ordinary cars and, considering it was January, EconoCar had had an unexpectedly cracking business day.

Dammit – he should have followed up, should have come home. If he had, he might have been in time to intercept the connection to Paris. Or at least he could have made a telephone call.

Thank God for travel-industry contacts. Although jobs would be put at risk if this activity were discovered, a pal of his had managed to find the reservation through various computer systems, so at least he was able to follow their progress, even if he couldn't stop it. Anyway, Zelda is of age. She has her own passport and must have co-operated. Even he, furious as he is, could not believe that his wife would put a gun to their daughter's head and force her to Palm Tree Island against her will.

At one level, he has a sneaking admiration for his wife's tenacity. She had planned everything to the minutest detail. To save him detective work, she had even come clean in her letter about the way she had finagled the finance to turn the original tickets into new ones. In fact, she had told him everything bar their route and timings.

There is a further dilemma: What is he going to do about Mick and Yvonne? Mick deserves censure at least. Boy, does he deserve it. Haunted by the vision of Sophie being demolished by her husband in full public view, Brian's respect for his old friend is in tatters. Imagine telling your wife such an awful thing in that place.

All right, he can understand the man's confusion because of the baby. Brian had never thought of himself as a family man until Eily first got pregnant with Zelda. Then – oh, God – those astonishing, overwhelming feelings . . .

Quickly, he rummages through the cushions, finds the remote and turns on the television again. Where the hell is Donny? It is nearly midnight now and there is still no sign of him. He'll kill him when he gets his hands on him.

No, he won't. Donny, let's face it, has every reason to be pissed off.

Sophie has spent an aimless, fraught day. She again went in to *Wild Places* for an hour or so but found there was little point in her staying: the final issue had gone to press, most of the clean-up had been done and the remaining weeks of their employment would suffice for herself and Nancy to leave the place shining. She had left and gone into town where, after wandering around for a bit through the post-Christmas sales crowds, she had decided to see *102 Dalmatians*. Unable to concentrate, she had left half-way through. Then, unwilling to go home to sit by a silent telephone, she had tried a little clothes shopping but this activity had never interested her, didn't interest her now and she had abandoned that, too.

It is now nearly midnight, she is again curled in her armchair, listening to the silence, and has been for hours. When the doorbell rings, it sounds so loud that she jumps with fright.

This has to be Michael.

Now that he is here, despite all her waiting for him to ring, she is suddenly afraid. Should she answer or shouldn't she? He will know she is in the house because the lamp is on beside her. There is a fanlight over the front door.

While she hesitates, the bell rings again and, stiffly, she uncoils from the chair.

It is not Michael, it is Donny. Sophie's reaction is mixed: disappointment on one level, relief on another. 'Come in, Donny, what on earth are you doing here? What's happened?'

As though she didn't know.

She forgets her own troubles temporarily as Donny erupts all over her living room. He is not going back to that poxy house, he is never going back. Nobody gives a shite about him so he doesn't give a shite about them . . .

After she has settled him down a little and he is cradling a mug of tea, he shows her the letter from his mother: 'My dearest darling son . . .'

Sophie scans it only superficially because, after the first few words, the platitudinous ease with which her friend justifies leaving the boy enrages her and she knows that if she concentrates too hard she will despise Eily for the rest of her life. She will also be no good to Donny.

She has to keep things in perspective. She has to ask herself – again – how she would behave if Zelda was her flesh and blood, her precious only daughter, instead of just a goddaughter. If she firmly believed that Jay Street's mumbo-jumbo was the girl's only chance of survival, would she, too, not ignore all other considerations?

Yet she has to struggle to remain neutral and balanced about this, doubly so because she can sense Donny's alertness for her reaction as she reads. 'I have to be honest with you,' she says gently, as she hands back the letter, 'I can see why your mum did this. Zelda is very ill, gravely so, and I can't say with my hand on my heart that I wouldn't do something like this if she was my daughter and I thought that this was the only chance.'

'But, Aunt Sophie—'

He stops. His woebegone expression would have dissolved the flintiest heart, but for his sake, and for Brian's, Sophie steadies herself. 'I know how bad you must feel, I really do. Sometimes there is nothing we can do but accept. You poor thing, you've been trying so hard, with the Internet and everything.'

This pierces Donny's armour and tears spill down his face, dripping off his chin. He weeps, not like a baby but like the confused, frightened and betrayed teenager he is, making no effort to hide his distress or check it.

Since the onset of adolescence, his big body has become so awkwardly uncoordinated that his presence in this house has been an anachronism at the best of times. Now it is horrifying, his sobbing shattering the fabric of the room into millions of jangling pieces. 'She'll die. I'll never see her again – I didn't even get to say goodbye – I'll never forgive Mummy for that. She never even let me say goodbye—'

Sophie, who had been sitting opposite him, moves across to sit beside him on the couch. She puts one arm around him and removes the tea from his hands to the safety of the coffee table, then holds his ungainly, convulsing body tightly to her own. The rough thatch of hair, so like Brian's, abrades the soft skin under her chin as she waits. She wants desperately to weep in sympathy for him and for them all, for the whole world, but if she gives in to this impulse, they are both lost.

The storm calms little by little, and when she feels it is near its end, she leaves him and goes to fetch tissues from the kitchen. 'Here.' She hands him the box then moves away again, knowing that his grief will be replaced pretty soon with embarrassment. 'You'll want more tea? That first lot has to be cold by now.'

She takes her time making the fresh brew and when she carries it back to him he is red-faced but controlled. 'I'm sorry, Aunt Sophie,' he mutters, as he takes the mug from her. 'I shouldn't have come here.'

'Of course you should. Where else would you go?'

'I'm not a baby any more and I shouldn't have—'

'Don't be a goose – think nothing of it. These are tough times for us all.' She sits down again, gazing at the contents of her own mug. 'Now I think I have to call your father. He'll be going out of his mind with worry.' She goes across to the telephone table, picks up the instrument and holds it out to him. 'Why don't you do it?'

'No, please, Aunt Sophie—' He takes fright.

'All right. You agree we have to tell him?'

Miserably, he nods.

Standing in the centre of the sitting room, Brian tries to concentrate on the Sky News headlines. Nothing of any interest, really. The usual mayhem in the usual trouble spots around the world. The royals in a tizz yet again.

Is there anyone else he could ring? He has already telephoned everybody he could think of, the Jamesons, the Prendergasts – receiving short shrift from Fiona's mother who said she would never again let Donny cross her front doorstep – then trying every other name that looked vaguely familiar in Eily's address book.

Maybe by this time he should have called in the Gárdaí – he had held
off so far because his son would never forgive him. Chances are that
Donny is in some bolthole that teenagers use. Probably the house of some
second-rank pal who will not automatically be in the line of telephone fire
from his parents. Brian had done stuff like this when he was young and
wanted to hide.

He'll hold off on calling in the Guards for another couple of hours. He
tries to concentrate on the news. Angola now. No, thank you.

He clicks off the TV set and looks at his watch. Eily and Zelda will be
arriving on that goddamned island pretty soon, within the next hour
anyway. According to his *ABC*, they should have left Antigua by now,
unless they've been delayed. He has wasted a fortune trying to reach them
with repeated but fruitless calls to the paging service at Antigua airport.
Either they weren't there or she was deliberately not answering.

Needless to remark, he had had no satisfaction from Street's people. Yes,
they were expecting his wife, they'd get his wife to call, they'd give her the
message, they were sorry but that was all they could do. Brian's rage,
fuelled by impotence, centres now on Jay fucking Street, but in the man's
absence he has to find another target so he kicks one of Eily's flowery
chairs. He hates this frigging furniture, always has. Chintz has no place in
a modern semi-detached house.

As soon as he has Donny fixed up, Brian is going to go out there
himself and sort out that shyster. The hell with work. Let Mick Dolan see
what it's like to be really in charge. Being boss for a few days while Brian
was in hospital – but available for consultation – was one thing. It will be
quite another to take full responsibility for the company when the boss is
thousands of miles away. That'll put a spanner in the building works of his
little love nest – after what he's done to Sophie.

For something to do, Brian plucks his *ABC* from the coffee table, sits
down with it and starts to plan his own route to Palm Tree Island. Via
Gatwick and St Lucia looks handy. He flips pages. Maybe he should try
Continental, who fly directly to the island via New York. After trying a
few more combinations, all of which involve multiple connecting and
even stopovers, he throws the tome aside. There is too much choice. What
he needs is access to Galileo or one of the other computerised reservations
systems. As the minutes tick by, his brain locks itself into a frantic, circular
rat-race around worry and rage: worry about Donny, rage at Jay Street, at
the world, at his wife's actions. He stands up and begins again to pace.
Should he ring Sophie? She would understand—

No. Better not.

He becomes so distressed and frustrated that he breaks one of his own rules – that a man should never drink alone – and is pouring himself a large whiskey when the telephone rings.

He looks at it, suddenly afraid. Eily? Hardly. His Bible of schedules says they wouldn't have landed yet and, if he knows her, she won't make contact until she is safely where she wants to be. No. This has to be something about Donny. Please, please, dear God, please, let it not be bad news about Donny . . .

The Liat hostess pulls aside the door of her little white plane and, although Riba had thought she was blissfully warm up to that moment, the gale of moist heat that blasts directly into her face from the apron outside feels as though it is blowing directly from a barbecue. She loves it. Basks in it. This is an additional bonus resulting from the fuss she had had to make to secure these front seats when they had changed planes at Antigua.

They're a bit early too. These little inter-island planes seem to operate like buses: when they're full they take off – they don't hang around.

While the stewardess is organising the aircraft steps, she leans forward into the warmth to take her first look at Palm Tree Island. Nothing much to see at present on the ground, just patched Tarmac and a ramshackle hut, obviously the terminal. In front of this a pair of baggage-handlers shoot the breeze as they wait for something or other to begin.

Look at that sky! Riba marvels. The books were right: darkness does fall like a sword in the Caribbean. Only a short while ago, maybe ten minutes, she was looking across Zelda through their porthole at the blue, blue ocean and seeing all the little whitecaps glowing in the sun. Yet now the sun has gone altogether, its light bleeding away into the edges of the ground on either side of the hut.

Hey! Over there on the sparse, sandy grass – her first genuinely tropical palm tree! Really and truly, outlined against the gathering darkness, just like in the movies, or those silhouettes you see in the brochures advertising sun holidays! 'Some Enchanted Evening', *South Pacific*. All right, this is the Caribbean but it's terribly exciting: Riba feels that the opening of the aircraft door is like the curtain going up on an exotic show.

She turns to Zelda. 'Wake up, Zel! We're here.' She sees that the bandanna has slipped a little and readjusts it before she snaps open the buckle of her daughter's seat-belt, sunk into the concave stomach.

Zelda opens her eyes, milky with sleep, but she doesn't move. For a second, she looks at her mother, then says, 'I can't. I don't want to.'

'You don't want to what, darling? You're awake now, come on, I'll help you.'

Zelda groans and closes her eyes again.

Riba strokes the damp forehead. 'Open your eyes, Zel, come on, now. The hostess is waiting for us to get out.' She realises she is speaking as though her daughter is still a baby, but the hostess is indeed looking expectantly at them. Riba gives the girl the full benefit of her best smile. 'We'll be a minute or two, please don't mind us, let the others go ahead.'

'Do you require a wheelchair?' The sing-song intonation is beautiful in Riba's ears. 'I don't have notification, but if you wait I'll get one for you.'

Riba widens her smile. 'You're very kind. Don't worry. She'll wake up, it just takes a little while. We'll be able to manage perfectly. It's been a very long day and she's a little tired. You see, we've come all the way from Ireland.'

The hostess smiles professionally and signals to the other passengers to come forward. Riba, who had been prepared to field exclamations about Ireland, is a little disappointed at the girl's indifference to their epic journey. She strokes Zelda's forehead again, soothing her into wakefulness, then leans over and kisses her cheek: 'Hey, Sleeping Beauty! Wakey-wakey! Seriously, darling, you've got to wake up now.'

At last Zelda opens her eyes and looks around her at the interior of the aircraft, now empty. 'Mother, where the hell are we?'

'Remember, darling? We're here. Welcome to Palm Tree Island. More than a week late but we got here! Aren't we great?'

Zelda sits up quickly, looking around her, then, with a hand to her head, 'Oh, God, I feel like shit.'

'Don't worry. We'll be in the compound in no time. It's only about ten minutes away, I believe, and then we'll have all the time in the world to sort you out. Just keep thinking of all that lovely peace and sunshine, sweetheart.'

As she assists Zelda down the short flight of steps, Riba has to suppress a quiver of debilitating guilt. By now Brian and Donny will be well aware of where they are. In fact, she knows they are: while she and Zelda were in Antigua, waiting for their final flight connection, she heard their names over the Tannoy. That had to be Brian. Luckily Zelda, who had slept through most of the trip, had been too dozy to notice and Riba had not reacted to the call so that no busybody would poke a nose in.

He has probably rung the resort too, threatening God knows what.

Let him. She must stay focused and remain resolutely positive. As she steps on to the sacred Tarmac, she feels so happy. Her reunion with Jay is imminent and as soon as they meet, she can hand over to him. Jay will take care of everything.

★   ★   ★

Brian does not answer until the fourth ring. Briefly, keeping her voice level and matter-of-fact, Sophie tells him Donny is with her. 'Would you like me to drive him home?'

'No.' Brian's voice is dizzy with relief. 'Keep him there, Sophie, I'm coming over.'

'He'll murder me.' Donny's eyes are wide when she hangs up. 'He'll ground me for weeks.'

'Not at all, he won't. I'll make sure he doesn't. Look, Donny, I'm sure your dad is even more upset than you are. The two of you will just have to be there for each other while your mum and Zelda are away. You're not a baby, you said it yourself, but this is where you're going to have to grow up fast – too fast in one way. He's going to need you – in many ways even more than you need him.'

It was the right thing to say because she can see that the proposition has worked. He even brightens a little. 'Yeah, you're right. I suppose I have to be charitable about Mum. She's only doing her best.'

'We all are.'

He takes a slug of his tea and looks around the room. 'What time is Uncle Michael coming home? I saw him in Bewley's earlier.'

'Did you?' Sophie's heart, so sorely tried, leaps to attention.

'Yeah.' The crying jag has relaxed Donny to the extent that his tongue loosens. 'I was going to go over but I just didn't feel like it. Anyway, he seemed to be waiting for someone, he kept looking at the door. I thought it must be you. I'm glad he wasn't here to see me like this, though.'

If he was waiting for her, he couldn't have moved in with her yet. 'Did the person arrive?' Sophie hopes she sounds conversational.

'No, not by the time we left anyway.'

She has to stop this. 'So, who were you with, Donny?'

'Just a friend.' He becomes guarded.

'Oh dear!' Sophie manages to smile. 'Have I put my foot in it? A girlfriend?'

He looks at his big hands. 'Not exactly. She's just a girl I know. Fiona Prendergast. I'm not supposed to be seeing her at all, her parents think I'm a perv or something, Aunt Sophie.' His face lights with indignation and Sophie, while welcoming the change, decides it might be tactful not to pursue this line of discussion: this Fiona is undoubtedly the same Fiona with whom her young friend had been caught drunk and in a compromising position. She picks up the remote control. 'Let's watch television while we're waiting for your dad, shall we?'

They find a documentary about the pygmies of the Amazon basin.

Sophie settles in, concentrating fiercely on the earnest, soothing voiceover and the verdant landscape.

'Oh, my goodness! Look, Zel – over there.' Is it Riba's imagination or had she seen a pair of bright yellow eyes caught in their headlights? What could it have been? Some rare animal, no doubt. She is determined not to let a single moment of this great experience pass without due regard.

She had been a tad disappointed that Jay himself hadn't come to meet them at the airport but is not going to let it ruin her excitement and delight. She can have her reunion with Jay in private. They have a lot to discuss. While she was looking around for him, she had spotted California Monica's platinum head riding high above all the darker ones in the crowd and, forewarned, had been able genuinely to fall on the woman's neck in greeting.

They are in an open-topped safari Jeep, driving along what is obviously the main route out of the airport, but in reality is a narrow, rutted track. 'There aren't many vehicles on the island,' California Monica explains, in her lazy, lofty drawl, 'so I'm afraid there aren't any good roads either. I hope Zelda isn't getting bumped around too much.' This is addressed directly to Riba's daughter, who is occupying the front passenger seat beside her.

'I'm fine.' But Zelda, who has been fully awake since they came off the plane, is holding both edges of her light jacket tightly around her neck as though she is feeling cold.

Riba leans forward. 'Would you like my jacket as well, darling? I'm roasting.' Zelda declines it.

Riba sheds the jacket anyway. Even though their movement is creating a breeze in her face, the clinging humidity feels quite uncomfortable and she has started to sweat. Must be the clothes she is wearing, she decides. She can't wait to have a shower and get into something loose and cottony. 'Is it always this hot?' she shouts at California Monica, over the whine of the Jeep's engine.

'It's the humidity – you get used to it,' the American shouts back. 'I hardly feel it any more. The States feels like the Arctic to me now.'

Riba settles back against the vinyl seat and continues to peer around through the velvety darkness. To her left lies a festive, twinkling cruise liner at anchor, to her right a dense forest. No moon, but above her head and as far as she can see, stars are piled higgledy-piggledy.

She is so happy, her heart could sing. When Zelda gets a little stronger, they might even take a little boat trip to some of the other islands in this archipelago she has looked up – so many times! – in one of Brian's atlases.

Such lovely names. White Island, Moonrise Island, Sandy Atoll, Flora's Beach – she knows them off by heart. Unlike Palm Tree, which is the largest in the group and serves as a sort of unofficial capital, some of the smaller ones are private, but others, uninhabited, are accessible. It must be the most glorious experience to sail across to one and, like the books say, leave nothing but footprints behind.

It takes less than ten minutes to reach the compound, which proves to be a collection of white bungalows loosely spaced along a wide horseshoe facing a beach. Between the rim of the horseshoe and the beach is a grassy quadrangle, around three sides of which is ranged a selection of wooden benches, chairs and loungers, leaving open the side fronting the sea. 'That's the grand assembly,' explain California Monica, 'where we're going to have the wedding ceremonies.' She points to a corner in which is stacked a heap of curved planking. 'You can see the arches over there. They're strong enough, they have to be reusable of course. We'll be putting them up tomorrow, but the flowers won't go on 'em until Friday morning. You'd be good at that, Riba, you can help.' She turns off the engine and, expertly, allows the Jeep to roll into a space marked 'JEEP' between an old Beetle and a Rolls-Royce convertible.

Riba's excitement reaches fever pitch. This is Jay's – he has referred to it almost as another man would speak of the woman he loved. 'Who's getting married on Saturday?' she asks, in the quiet after the engine has stopped.

'It's what Jay calls a mixum gatherum.' California Monica chuckles fondly. 'No Irish, alas, not on this occasion, but they're from all over the world, four couples from the States, two locals, one English, one German, an Australian and – would you believe? – a pair from Hong Kong.

'It's a new venture for us, Riba, as you know, but we're all very excited about it. The response was amazing. We had to turn people away in the end because, for this first one, we wanted to keep it to ten couples to see how it works in practice. Really, the sky's the limit. Everyone, it seems, wants to get married in Paradise. They'll be consummating in the forest in the most beautiful little thatched rondavels. Jay had them copied from a book about South Africa. So,' the American reaches into the back and picks up one of the bags, 'are we ready, kids?'

Riba is not going to admit ignorance about the nature of the rondavels. 'Wonderful! They're not staying here?'

'Goodness, no. We've leased accommodation for them in town for before the weddings and afterwards, but we're allowing them to stay for up to two weeks in their little forest Eden, should they wish. This compound is strictly for ourselves in the organisation, Riba. Let's go!' Like a gazelle, she leaps gracefully from the Jeep to the ground.

'This is marvellous.' Riba, not to be outdone, jumps out on the other side, landing heavily on an ankle. She ignores the brief, wrenching pain and cocks her head to listen. She had thought the Caribbean sea would be like a lagoon, but no. Even though there is not a breath of wind, she can hear the soft, insistent sound of waves breaking on shingle. She takes her daughter's hand to help her alight. 'Tired, hon?'

'I'm exhausted. I need to sleep, Mum.' Indeed, in the starlight, Zelda's face seems ashen and Riba takes extra special care as she helps her down off the high running-board of the Jeep.

'Let's get you checked in and into your room, you guys.' California Monica swings ahead of them, her long legs covering the distance between the Jeep and what is obviously the reception area in about two seconds. Her ankle throbbing ominously, Riba follows, supporting Zelda. She is not overly concerned about her daughter's fatigue. It had, after all, been a gruelling trip. As they move slowly along the sandy path – Riba forcing herself not to limp – she continues to look around, nodding and smiling at two women who are chatting quietly on a bench seat, obviously fellow residents. They smile and wave in return. This is going to be brilliant, just brilliant – although there should be more people about surely? Where is Jay? Which house is his?

Following the Californian, she leads Zelda through a sort of gazebo, twined with ivy and huge flowers, their petals contracted for the night so she can't see what colour they are. Maybe, she thinks happily, loving the music of the syllables, they are frangipani or jacaranda.

The gazebo leads into a one-roomed building in which a computer terminal rests on a desk. Now this *is* disappointing. The intrusion of modern technology into this paradise is quite a blow: Riba had thought that, in this place above all others, Jay's place, everything would have a more informal, natural ambience.

On the other hand, why should a computer bother her? It's just a more modern extension of phones and faxes and she doesn't object to those. As she helps Zelda into a peacock chair, Riba resolutely refuses to be cast down. Of course they would need communication tools. 'Where is everyone?' she asks.

'They're all in town with Jay.' The Californian is busy with keyboard and screen.

'So, ten couples are getting married?' Riba is getting a little worried that Zelda cannot take much more. Her eyes are closed and her head is lolling on her neck. Gently, she takes her daughter's head in her hand and supports it against herself. Zelda's eyes don't open.

'Yup.' California Monica reads whatever it is she has been keying in. 'It's going to be awesome, Riba, your timing couldn't have been better. I'm sure Zelda will enjoy it too. Now, how will you guys be paying?'

The question is shocking in its simplicity. Riba had not considered anything but that she and her daughter would be honoured guests on Jay's island. She gapes at the china-doll face behind the computer screen. 'Pardon?'

The Californian smiles helpfully.

'Cash or charge?'

CHAPTER TWENTY-FIVE

Because the documentary is interesting, Sophie's troubled mind has stilled by the time the doorbell rings for the second time that evening. No hesitation this time: she stamps firmly on the butterflies that emerge from their cocoons in her stomach and passes the remote to Donny, who immediately increases the volume. She gives him an encouraging pat. 'No, don't worry, he won't eat you. I told you I won't let him.'

'Hello.' In the yellowish glow cast by the sodium street-lamps outside, the lines of worry and fatigue are etched deeply on Brian's face and, despite his robust size, he looks unhealthy, as though he could do with a square meal.

Sophie is ruthless with herself. She is the wife of this man's best friend. 'Come in,' she says, as though he's a latecomer to a gathering of other friends. 'We've been watching a terrific documentary.' That sounded perfectly reasonable. She glances over her shoulder to where Donny sits hunched and apprehensive, gaze fixed on the screen. 'Go easy on him, Brian, he's having a hard time. Anyway, I promised him he wouldn't get into trouble.'

'Thank God he came here.' Brushing raindrops off the shoulders of his overcoat, Brian ducks through the doorway. 'And don't worry, all I want to do is get him home. I'm sorry you were dragged into this, Sophie, but he's the least of my worries as it turns out. I suppose you've heard?'

Sophie closes the door behind him. 'Yes.'

'I'm going to follow them,' he says quietly, glancing at Donny to make sure he can't overhear against the film's soundtrack, 'just as soon as I can make the arrangements.' He jerks his head towards his son.

'Can I come?' Sophie asks, with feeling, then realises she is only half joking. It would be so nice to leave everything behind and fly off to the sun for a week. Even to bloody Palm Tree Island.

'Do you mean it?'

'No, of course I don't.' She smiles. 'I couldn't afford it anyway, not now.'

He hesitates. Then, looking towards Donny, who has lowered the volume again but is pretending to be fascinated by what he is watching, 'I know it's none of my business, but I don't know what to say about you and Mick—'

'No, it's not your problem,' Sophie interrupts him swiftly. 'Sorry, Brian, I didn't mean to be sharp but I don't want to discuss it. Not now, anyway.' Of course Michael would have told him. Or Yvonne. The whole world now knows that Sophie Dolan has been discarded by her husband like a used tissue. Then she can't help herself: 'How long have you known?'

'Not long truly—' He is about to say more but she cuts him off. His response is so quick and heartfelt she knows he is telling the truth and, in any event, what is to be gained by dredging through this? Anyhow, she has no intention of humiliating herself in front of Brian by showing how upset she is. She hears herself chattering, the hostess with the mostest: 'Would anyone like a cup of anything? Tea? Coffee?'

Brian takes the hint. 'No, thanks, Soph, we've got to get home, I'm knackered.' He crosses the room to look down at his son. 'And this idiot has to get up for school tomorrow morning. For Christ's sake, Donny, don't ever do this again. Ever. I nearly had the Guards out. I would have in another half an hour.' He cuffs his son on the side of the head, but gently.

Donny looks as though he might burst into tears again but the moment passes. 'Sorry, Dad.' He turns off the TV and stands up.

For the first time, Sophie realises he is virtually as tall as his father. It is unsettling. She chatters on, wanting both of them gone, telling them that now *Wild Places* has bitten the dust she might start taking photography seriously.

'That's a great idea, Sophie, you're far better than you think you are – it's actually a good thing that your magazine has folded,' Brian says.

Had she been the only one on the planet who hadn't thought herself too good for her little job? She remembers her promise to Nancy, about an opening at EconoCar for her. 'You remember Nancy? You met her at our Christmas party last year.'

'The small woman with the hair? Yeah.' He is doubtful about hiring her. 'At her age, Soph?' Sophie stares at him, and he has the grace to yield. 'All right. I'll talk to her.'

Somehow she gets them out and, after waving a cheery goodbye, leans against the solidity of her closed front door, listening to their retreating footsteps as they hurry to get in out of the rain, to the opening of their car doors, to the slams, to the engine starting, to its rumble shrinking towards renewed silence and loneliness.

She is very, very tired, but since there is little possibility of sleep she crawls back to the seat she had vacated on Brian's arrival and switches on the Open University. Mathematics. Just the obscurity she needs.

Some time later she is half-way between dozing and wakefulness when she hears light tapping on the front door. She thinks at first that it is coming from the television set, then that it is an aural fantasy, but then she hears it again.

She jumps up and, like a missile armed for combat, takes off for the door. If Michael thinks he can come crawling back now—

It is Brian.

He is leaning against the door-jamb with an arm higher than his head, staring straight at her. He seems perfectly composed, as though to come to her door at a minute past three in the morning is a normal event in both their lives. Even the lines on his face have softened. 'It's no use, Sophie. May I come in?' His collar is turned up, rain glistens in his bright hair.

She plays for time. 'What about Donny? You've left him on his own.'

'Donny is tucked up safely in bed. He's fourteen years old, you know, old enough to baby-sit other kids, so he can baby-sit himself for a while.' He smiles ironically. 'And I checked the batteries in the smoke alarms only last week. All over the house. There's one outside his room on the landing.'

'Smoke alarms? Brian, I said nothing about—'

'So can I come in?'

Sophie has a decision to make. She can invite him in or she can dismiss him, each choice is irrevocable. She and Brian are both supremely vulnerable. It would be a disaster. It makes no sense. Someone is going to be very hurt. Maybe everyone is going to be very hurt.

'Come in,' she says simply.

He passes her in the doorway, careful not to brush against her. Sophie continues to hold the door open, to watch the ragged waves of rain blowing through the cones of yellow light outside as if they, too, are tardy guests dragging their heels before entering her house. 'You know what this means?'

'I know only too well.' With one motion, he kicks the door shut, reaches for her and takes her in his arms. The sound of the beating rain vanishes – all outside considerations vanish – as his kiss bruises her. Sophie feels as light as bog cotton, as though the wisps of her physical self are floating away on the surface of the wind.

They tumble towards the couch, and when they finally come together, she is unashamed about this treachery. This is not sex, not making love, but wholeness. She was born for this.

She cries out, and in her ears that long uninhibited wail belongs not to her, but to some mermaid or siren.

He cries out too, a male roar of ecstasy that in another arena might have been mistaken for agony.

The rat-tat of the rain outside is augmented by the sound of a tap dripping into the sink in the corner of Yvonne's untidy flat. Michael sits at the window staring at the street outside. Behind him, Yvonne sleeps loudly, mouth open.

She is under notice to quit – the landlady has spied him coming in – so, with nothing to lose, they made love earlier, rather perfunctorily, because his mind continued to beat around his problems. She had been cranky, hard to please and demanding. Afterwards, when he had asked her what was wrong, she had given him a dig. 'What do you think is wrong? Thanks to you I'm not only up the pole but I now have to find somewhere to live.'

'Well, you shouldn't be sorry about that at least – this is a dump.' Michael had thought sorrowfully of the cool, clean spaces created by Sophie in their house.

'Ah, for God's sake, Mick, stop looking like that. It's only my hormones.' She had laughed lightly. 'Better get used to it! If you're sticking around, that is.'

Instead of answering, he had cuddled her close so that she couldn't see his expression.

Behind him, she gives a little snort and turns heavily in the narrow bed. Michael glances over his shoulder: with her mouth open and her hair spread out like that on the pillow, she looks even younger than she is, and not so tarty. Turning back to his contemplation of the street and the rain, he drags on his cigarette. He gave up smoking more than ten years ago and the first one today had almost choked him but he had persisted and had since consumed fifteen, each more easily than the one before.

Maybe it will work out. Who knows? All *he* knows is that the surge of protective love for his sprog had taken the feet from under him. That had felt real, still feels real in a way nothing else has ever felt in his whole life. Real enough to screw up his home, his finances, everything. Only time will tell if this surprising emotion will last, but for once in his life Mick Dolan is going to follow his instincts.

All right, he will have to live for ever with the deep silt of self-loathing for his betrayal of Sophie, who, despite his surface rationalisations about her being too uppity and all the rest of it, is a good, kind person who longs for a child. This news will devastate her even more than his desertion, and telling her will be the hardest thing he will ever do, harder even than that horrible scene in the airport yesterday. How can he face it?

'Hey! Where are you? Come back to bed.' Yvonne's voice is hoarse with sleep.

Michael laughs. He has made his bed and now he's going to lie in it. Literally.

'What's so funny?' She is coming awake. He raises the sash, flips the cigarette butt into the rubbish-strewn grass outside, and closes the window again.

'Nothing. You wouldn't understand.'

'Try me.'

'I'll try you all right.' Michael walks across to the sagging bed, gets in and pulls her to him, hard, trying to feel through his belly what is happening in hers.

'Ow! I'm still half asleep.' She wriggles in an effort to break his hold.

Michael laughs again but something is wrong: the laugh feels heavy, wobbly. As he kisses her, he realises his eyes are wet. This has not happened to him since childhood. 'Come here, you.' He inserts his tongue in her ear to get her going, then buries himself in her, not as roughly as he might have because, fleetingly, he wonders how a baby responds in the womb to such proximity to its father.

'Jesus, what time is it? You're some piece of work, you . . .' but Yvonne responds.

As she writhes and groans under him, Michael thinks he should go out to buy another pack of twenty: he'll need them for the morning.

Riba stares disbelievingly at California Monica who, fingers poised over her keyboard, continues to beam her perma-smile. 'I – I'm sorry,' she stammers, then manages to gather up the rags of her self-respect. Cash or charge? Who does this woman think she's talking to? 'Let's leave it until the morning, shall we, Monica? I'll sort it out with Jay.'

'Good luck with that, dear.' The American, unfazed, laughs gaily. 'You know what he's like, Riba, mind on higher things, hates all the lousy paperwork as he calls it.' She taps a few keys. 'Of course we can leave it till the morning, that's no problem at all.' She comes out from behind the desk. 'Poor Zelda's beat, isn't she? I guess after all that travelling what you both wanna do now is have a shower. Come on, follow me. We've put you in the end bungalow where it's real quiet and all you'll hear tomorrow morning is the ocean.' She laughs again as she picks up both bags, 'Sleep well tonight, Riba, it's gonna get pretty hectic around here for the next few days.'

She sets off at a brisk pace, leaving Riba to help Zelda to her feet and with a strong desire to score those flawless porcelain cheeks with a teeny tiny pin. She is now nearly as tired as her suffering daughter. 'Almost there now, darling. Then beddy-byes. Won't that be lovely?'

'Mum, I can't walk another step. I mean it—' Zelda's bodyweight, insubstantial though it is, increases abruptly because she can no longer contribute to her own support. She unfolds from her mother's grasp and drops to the ground where she keels over to lie on her side in the sand, knees drawn up.

'Monica!' Riba yells, to be heard against the waves.

The American drops the bags and sprints back towards them. 'My God, this is awful. Want me to call the paramedics, Riba? Should she go to the hospital? Or, better yet, we have a good relationship with the American clinic here.'

'No, she'll be all right. She's very weak, that's all. If you could just help me get her inside, I have all her medication with me and I know what she needs. Maybe if we could have some ice and drinking water?'

'No problem, Riba. You'll find coffee, crackers, fruit, the usual welcome pack in your refrigerator. Oh, by the way, unfortunately we've been having problems getting cleaning staff on PTI so we'd appreciate it if you'd be aware that official cleaning will not take place until the day of your departure. Let's get her into the house.' She assists Riba in lifting the impervious Zelda to her feet.

When Riba had pictured their arrival in paradise, she had seen Zelda transfigured, full of light and joy, not like this—

She suppresses this defeatist attitude as, between them, they carry her daughter, feet dragging, towards the end bungalow. This is just a temporary setback. Zelda will sleep well and will wake to imminent healing. That's what's going to happen.

As they enter the bungalow, the American snaps on the overhead light. The room is simply furnished with a double bed and two singles, a kitchenette in one corner and a small bathroom off. Together, they ease Zelda on to the double bed, and when they are sure she is secure, California Monica lowers her voice to a whisper: 'You need anything else, Riba, you just holler. I'm the first house to the right of Reception. I'll come down later, make sure you're both OK.'

'Thanks, Monica.' Riba looks around. 'Where's the phone?' When she had got Zelda settled, she would have to face the music with Brian. 'No phones here, Riba,' Monica chides. 'At Reception, of course, but not in the rooms. We're all here to escape our pressures, not add to them, aren't we? You want I should call someone for you? Or you're welcome to come and use the phone yourself, of course.'

'No, don't worry about it. Thanks. Tomorrow will do fine.' Brian will just have to wait. He knows where they are.

After she leaves, Riba undresses Zelda, slips the nightdress she had packed in the carry-on bag over the bony, fragile body, then holds her daughter's head while, one by one, she dispenses the pills. She has kicked off her own shoes and the terracotta tiles feel cool under her sore, swollen feet. The throbbing ankle is distracting, however, and despite the fan that had begun silently to rotate above their heads as soon as the light was switched on, it is humid in the room.

As soon as all the pills are gone, Riba breaks open the ice-cube tray from the freezer compartment of the fridge and cools some water with it. She wrings out the corner of a towel and sponges the clammy forehead, face, neck and chest, as she did when Zelda and Donny were babies and running a fever. Then she pulls up the sheet and kisses her goodnight. 'Sleep well and dream of tomorrow, darling,' she whispers. 'Tomorrow will be wonderful.' Zelda does not respond and very soon she is breathing regularly in deep sleep.

Tenderly, Riba strokes her cheek. This love of children is so stunning, so unexpected when first it comes; it is a love filled with fear, because from the moment they emerge from your womb, they are already lost to you, to potential accidents, to other people, to their own desire for separation from you as though you are the enemy. Although you try to trust and to remain in the flow, your imagination betrays you by showing them crushed under the wheels of cars, staring with hollow, unseeing eyes as they float under the surface of a river, a canal or the sea, blue and lifeless from an overdose of heroin. Never, however, had Riba's imagination risen to the horror of slow decline from disease. It refuses to do so now. Tomorrow, tomorrow, tomorrow, she repeats slowly, like a mantra, in an effort to convince herself that she has not made a huge mistake.

She heaves herself to her feet, cracks the rest of the ice into the towel. Too tired now to unpack, she throws off her travel-weary clothes, winds the ice around her ankle and stuffs the lot into a plastic bag. Then she slips naked under the sheet of one of the single beds and stares upwards at the three wooden blades of the ceiling fan, mounted in brass. The relief they dispense from heat is minimal, but at least the thick, heavy air is being moved around a little. She should really go over to the door and turn off the light, but would that mean the fan would go off too?

An unfamiliar feeling of depression continues to grow in her belly and, although she hates to give it recognition and thereby feed it, she has reluctantly to acknowledge that she feels not only disappointed but a little humiliated at her treatment.

Where is Jay? All right, maybe he couldn't get to the airport, but why wasn't he here in the compound to greet them? Riba tries to convince herself that Jay's business with the notary was too urgent to postpone – but she knows he had all day to go to town. He knew what time she was arriving and none of the flights was delayed.

Then there is this 'cash or charge' business. Is she to be treated as an ordinary paying guest to the compound?

She refuses to believe it. Not given *her* special relationship with Jay. No, no, no, no, *no*! There has to have been a misunderstanding. Miss Perfect Pins just misunderstood, that's all: Jay, featherheaded about material details as always, hadn't got round to telling her. When Riba gets to talk to him, he'll have a quiet word and everything will be cleared up. She should probably wait up for him, sort it out as quickly as possible.

Even as she manages to subdue her misgivings, Riba cannot suppress an overriding feeling of letdown. This is not how it is supposed to be. She and Zelda are not supposed to be stuck at the end of a row of identical bungalows between four white walls that, although freshly painted, support nothing except a single picture of Jay and a list of printed instructions about what to do in case of fire. Where even the furniture, the veneered headboards, cheap wardrobes, white plastic chairs and round white table in the sand outside, could have come straight from a package-holiday apartment on some overcrowded European *costa*.

It is supposed to be flowers in her hair and in Zelda's as they walk barefooted along the virgin sand to a joyful welcome from Jay. It is supposed to be a beautiful, colourful room, decorated with fascinating native artefacts and with a railed veranda for viewing the sunsets over a spectacular amethyst sea.

It is supposed to be Jay looking into her eyes, and through them into her soul, and making everything better.

Riba works stoutly to crank up her original vision. She is just tired, that's all. What she has promised Zelda still holds true and everything will look wonderful in the sunshine tomorrow when Jay is back.

In the seconds before full sleep descends, she half remembers, half dreams of Auntie May, of the nursing-home reached after two hours of tortuous travel across the clogged city, of the semicircle of winged chairs occupied by shrivelled and hopeless geriatrics who had perked up when she arrived. Of Auntie May's bird-like face out of which stared two suspicious little eyes, black as currants, from under a lopsided paper hat placed on her head by well-meaning staff. Of her contemptuous dismissal of Jay's good wishes and messages of love: 'Where's his birthday card, then, if he's that interested?' Auntie May had been a teacher and retained the stentorian tones of her profession.

In this half-dream, Riba, conscious of the parliament of old ears straining to hear, explains, as she did in reality, that Jay has no need to send cards. That his powers of meditation and thought are far more beneficial to the recipient than any piece of colourful cardboard sold for profit by some multinational corporation, but Auntie May will have none of it. She claws at Riba's arm with fingers as bent and sharp as talons and her quavery voice rises with vitriolic energy: 'Poppycock and balderdash. Meditating my eye! Palm Tree Island! Did you ever hear such nonsense? His poor mother – thank God she's not alive to see what she's reared. He had a good trade too, there's always work for a tradesman in America.' She flops back against her chair with a malevolent snort.

Reality begins to sink into full dream as, from far away, Riba hears the slamming of car doors, laughter, quiet voices. Jay must be back. She wants to get out from under the sheet, to run to greet him, but something is holding her back. Auntie May's twisted claws are stuck deep into her ankle, so she cannot move.

Now the walls of her bungalow fall away and she sees him coming towards her, dressed in a robe of yellow and white. His arms are stretched out and, in one hand, he holds a hammer. She struggles to get away from Auntie May but those claws are remorseless and the more she struggles, the deeper and more painfully they sink into her ankle bone.

She is so weary that sleep finally overcomes every image and sensation.

Lying with her head pillowed on Brian's chest, Sophie waits for a pincer attack from remorse and guilt for what she has just done, but so far neither has arrived. Instead, she feels light, warm, comfortable, as though to have made love with your best friend's husband and to lie there afterwards like this is of consequence only to yourself and him. 'I know it's impossible, especially now, but I wish this was simple. I wish you could come with me.' His voice, amplified in his chest, rumbles against her ear.

She kisses him. 'Try not to worry. You never know, we might all be doing Street an injustice. In any case, she might improve with warmth and a different regime.' Sophie, who had never had sex with anyone except Michael before now, traces a line of sweat across Brian's chest, which is so much wider than her husband's. She kisses the golden hairs around one of his nipples.

'I should go,' he is whispering, although there is no one there to hear.

'Yes, you should.'

Neither moves, and except for the gentle movement of Sophie's finger, they remain curved together on the couch, like a pair of entwined sculptures. 'Is it because of the crash, do you think?' She must remember every detail of his body, because they may not do this again.

Or they may. 'Because we went through something so traumatic together, are we just in a state of heightened awareness?' *Good God*, she thinks, *now I'm even beginning to sound like Eily*.

'You mean post-traumatic stress disorder?' He laughs dryly. 'If that's what leads to such great sex, give me another crash quickly.'

'You don't mean that.'

'No, of course I don't. Look, Sophie, I know this is crazy, we both know it's crazy, but let's not discuss it or over-analyse it, let's just enjoy it for the moment.' He kisses her with surprising delicacy, his lips just touching hers.

'You're right,' she says. Then, lazily, 'Since neither of us smokes, do you fancy a post-coital drink? I think I have whiskey, brandy or gin. Or a beer?'

'Whiskey, please.'

'Coming up.' She pecks him on the cheek and, disentangling herself, rolls off the couch and pads towards the kitchen. Strangely, although she knows he is watching, she is unselfconscious about being naked, even enjoying the sense of his gaze roaming appreciatively over her body. While she and Donny had been waiting for Brian's arrival, she had overridden the timer clock on the central heating and had not bothered to turn it off again so the house is toasty warm. In addition, the rain outside acts as an insulator between the two of them and the world, cutting it off and consigning their problems to temporary purdah.

She fetches a pair of rugs from the hot press in the kitchen and as she brings them back with the whiskey, she is struck by his unconscious pose. Sprawled on her couch with one foot on an armrest, the other dangling on to the floor over the side, he is gazing pensively into the depths of the empty fireplace. With his massive proportions, he might be a sitter for one of those sentimental Victorian artists who loved to interpret myths; he has been arranged so that someone can paint him as Jupiter. All right, Sophie pulls herself up a little, that was over the top, but she doesn't care as she commits every line of this picture, too, to memory.

Hearing her come, he gathers himself up, makes space for her beside him and at once becomes big, ordinary Brian. Her lover. Sophie can't get over it.

For the next fifteen minutes, neither feels the need to speak as they sit wrapped up together, sipping their drinks. Then Sophie finds herself looking absently at the Audi calendar, forgotten in the heat of packing Michael's belongings. She'll take it down tomorrow – or later today. Then she notices that the carriage clock beneath it is showing five minutes to four. 'My God.' She sits up and digs Brian in the ribs. 'Do you know what time it is? We're a disgrace.'

'Yeah, aren't we just?' He smiles and, for a moment, he looks as though he is going to kiss her and start the whole thing again.

'No, you don't,' she says firmly, sitting up straighter and putting her empty glass on the floor. 'You have to be there when poor Donny wakes up.'

They do kiss then, but quietly, familiar now with each other's lips. Then, snuggled up in her rug, it is her turn to watch his nakedness as, trailing his clothes behind him, he mounts the stairs to the bathroom. She loves the sturdiness of his legs, the broadness of his back, not yet run to fat but fleshy none the less. What will he be like at fifty? Sixty? Even though he and Michael are approximately the same height, Brian seems to fill this house, dominating the spaces far more completely than Michael ever did.

She indulges in a fantasy. She is in her darkroom, formerly known as her study, developing a set of prints for her forthcoming exhibition. She hears his key in the lock and, leaving the emerging images temporarily to their own devices, caring not at all whether they ruin themselves, runs downstairs to welcome his huge presence home.

Good God Almighty – she gives herself a mental shake as she hears him emerge from the bathroom: she's really losing the run of herself.

He is fully dressed, except for his shoes, when he comes down into the living room, and she feels that, as he bends to lace the first, he is already slipping away from her. By the time he is tying the second, he is nearly gone. It is on the tip of her tongue to ask him when they will see each other again but she accepts the inevitable when he straightens and she sees that his expression is no longer open and unguarded but troubled. 'Drive carefully, Brian.' She bundles herself up more tightly in her rug although she is not cold.

'I will.' He hesitates, then says quietly, 'I'm going to get rid of Yvonne, you know, come hell or high water, labour laws or no labour laws. That's for you.'

Sophie quashes her automatic concern for the girl, for anyone losing a job. 'Thank you.' She may retract a little later but, for the moment, vengeance feels good.

'I know it might be bizarre to make excuses for him and I don't even know why I'm saying this because, believe me, I think he's a prick, but he's not thinking straight. He's up in a heap. I suppose the thought of having a baby after all this time—'

'A baby?' The warmth in the room seems to vacuum itself out through the walls, leaving Sophie's fingers and throat to fill with frost.

Stricken, Brian stares at her. 'You didn't know? He didn't tell you?'

CHAPTER TWENTY-SIX

After Brian has left, Sophie finds herself staring at her husband's tricksy calendar above the mantelpiece; it invites her to play 'Find the Audi' – a yellow marque hidden among a fleet of identically hued taxis in a New York canyon. Of course, she has spotted the target car long ago, so there is no use playing the game any longer. Yet she continues to stare at the closely packed ranks of mustard-coloured vehicles. How did they do that? They must have used some computerised procedure to multiply the images, adding in the New York streetscape later. It is techniques like this that she will have to learn in her new life as a photography student.

The numbness in her limbs and throat has spread to other parts of her body. She visualises her barren womb as a dark, empty cave, filled with frozen lichen and shrunken, half-dead fungi.

Her first reaction when Brian told her about Michael's child had been one of horror that he knew and she didn't. That was off the point, of course – she had recognised it at once. Nevertheless, when he had raced to take her in his arms again she had rebuffed him: 'No, go home, Brian, please go home – I'll be all right. I just want to go to bed now.'

Upset, full of remorse and guilt, he had left her, but not until she had promised to telephone him first thing in the morning. 'I'll want to know you're all right, please, Sophie. Will you forgive me?'

'What's there to forgive?' She had moved deliberately out of range of any further caress or embrace. 'You're not the one who got her pregnant.'

Irrationally, however, she had blamed the messenger and, as he continued trying to repair the damage between them, had remained adamant that she wanted him to leave. Eventually, still apologising, he had gone home.

She reaches up and rips the Audi calendar off the wall so violently that its hook comes away and, with it, a little shower of plaster and whitewash.

Sophie's sense of order is such that she knows she could not for long abide living with abrasions on her wall so she takes her beloved Charles Lamb landscape from the wall opposite and, using a small brass bowl as a hammer, replaces the hook and hangs the painting where the calendar had been.

This leaves a gap on the Lamb wall. She takes one of her own watercolours and is about to lift it to the place previously occupied by the Lamb when she stops herself. It is nearly five o'clock in the morning and she is a naked woman arranging pictures. She is a naked, adulterous, unemployed, deserted, childless woman arranging pictures.

Sophie drops the watercolour on to the floor. It is of no value anyway. She doubles up into her sofa and pulling her rug, still faintly warm, around herself, curls into the smallest space possible.

From his bed, Brian hears Donny's door open as the boy goes into the bathroom. He looks at the luminous dial of the alarm clock. Nearly seven o'clock: time he was getting up for work and to face the unbearable.

He delays climbing out into this dark day, feeling weary to the marrow. His brain continues to hop incessantly between visions of his daughter lying on some Robinson Crusoe beach surrounded by flotsam and Sophie's shocked face when he let the cat out of the bag.

She had blamed him. Of course she had. It was only natural that she resented him knowing before she did. Him and his big mouth – why couldn't he have let well enough alone? It is no use rationalising that she would have found out in any event. He had been a clot, a dimwit, and he wouldn't blame her if she holds it against him for the rest of their lives.

Maybe, in the scheme of things, this is just as well. The complications raised by a love affair with Sophie Dolan do not bear thinking about. Yet he can still feel her silky contours, so different from Eily's voluptuous curves, can smell her faint, lemony scent, worlds apart from the musky Oriental perfumes with which his wife drenches herself.

Is this a male thing? He cannot imagine that Eily – or indeed any woman he knows – would relive a sexual encounter when so much personal drama and trauma was happening around her.

His attraction to Sophie is more than physical – or is it? In the state he's in, how can he tell? For instance, if he were sitting legless in a gutter in Calcutta would he be able to make such a fine distinction? Love affairs are matters deluxe, afforded only by those who are already emotionally, even corporally wealthy.

Look at him: he has a nice house with every modern convenience, access to as much food, goods and services as he needs, a decent, if somewhat batty, wife, and two beautiful children; if one of those children is destined to die prematurely, she will die with dignity and in comfort, not in destitution and pain, and he and Eily will be left with another who is robustly healthy.

Yet it is of little use scolding himself that, given the difficulties faced by the poor of the Third World, his own situation is peanuts. It doesn't *feel* like peanuts. 'Oh God,' he groans, turning over in bed and burying his head between his own pillow and his wife's in an effort to shut off his relentless brain. Yet as he listens for Donny to emerge from the bathroom, it continues to flip through its Rolodex of problems, solutions and choices. Too many problems, no solutions, difficult choices.

'Shit!' The bedsprings protest as Brian sits upright and swings his aching legs over the side of the bed. This rubbish has to stop. 'Just get up and get on with it, McMullan.' He taps on the bathroom door as he passes. 'Morning, sport! I'm making coffee, want some?'

There is no reply from inside and Brian shrugs. He is too tired and preoccupied to persist. He will make the coffee anyway and Donny can have it or not. Would those fuckers on that island have the decency to answer a telephone at this hour of the morning?

While the percolator is chatting to itself, he peruses his *ABC*, partly as a soothing distraction, partly for practical reasons, resuming the process of figuring out a set of flights to get him to Palm Tree Island as smoothly as possible. He is deep within Schiphol Airport – KLM is frequently the best option for hassle-reduced connections – when, above the popping of the coffee machine, he hears a crash from upstairs. 'Donny!' He flings down the *ABC*, rushes out of the kitchen and takes the stairs two at a time.

When the kids were little, he and Eily were agreed that the worst thing for a parent to hear was a crash or a thump, followed by silence rather than wailing. At least this isn't the case now: the bedlam within Donny's bedroom indicates that its occupant is alive and furiously energetic. He is smashing things. Brian pushes the door. It is locked from the inside. 'Donny!' He hammers on it with his fist. 'Open this door immediately.'

A brief hiatus is followed by a shout: 'Go away. Leave me alone.'

'Donny, come on.' Brian hammers again through the resumed commotion. 'Come on, son, open up.'

Silence again. Then he hears heavy footsteps, the turning of the key. The door opens a crack. 'What? I told you to leave me alone.' Donny's expression indicates that he is teetering on the borderline between truculence and distress.

Brian's tired brain snaps to attention. If he comes the heavy now, he might do irreparable damage. 'I just want to make sure you're all right. That was a lot of noise you were making in there – can I come in?'

'No. Go away, I'm fine, this is none of your business.'

It is on the tip of Brian's tongue to retort that it is his damn business since he had paid for every item in the room, but he cuts this off and steps back a little, putting a few feet between them. 'Come on, Donny, open up, you'll have to let me in at some stage.'

'No, I won't. This is *my* room.'

'Whatever you've done, I won't ground you. Or do anything to you. This is a very difficult time for us all.'

Although the door remains stubbornly in place, Donny is clearly thrown by such a conciliatory approach. 'You'll freak.'

'I won't freak, I promise.' Slowly, he reaches into the gap between the jamb and the door, touching the side of Donny's shoulder, which, except for his head, is all that is visible of him. Then, rubbing his eyes, he says, 'This is no bull, Donny, honest, but to tell you the truth, I don't know how you haven't cracked before now. I really admire how you've coped because I'm not coping very well myself.' Brian looks frankly at his son. 'I'm going mad actually.'

Donny opens his mouth but then, fighting tears, closes it again. Seeing him, this lumbering, lost lunk of his, so scared he has to hide most of himself, Brian is so moved he could cry. 'We have to play on the same team,' he says softly. 'Please, son.'

After another small hesitation, Donny, head low, pulls open the door.

The reality is worse than Brian had expected. In the space of less than a minute, his son has demolished or disarrayed everything breakable or movable in the room so that only the bed, desk and fitted wardrobe remain intact. Books, bedclothes, papers, clothing, boots and shoes are tumbled over what remains of Donny's beloved stereo; he has smashed his work chair and, although his computer terminal and printer are undamaged, the keyboard, obviously hurled upwards with great force, hangs at a crazy angle from the central light fitting, its cable caught on the shade. He has pulled flexes from lamps and has even ripped the corduroy cover of one of his beanbags so that the entire mess is covered in small white spheres. 'Oh, Donny, your stereo . . .' Brian picks up a fragment of the casing and, despite his promise not to freak out, has to try hard to curb a more forthright reaction. How would Eily behave in this situation? Calmly, that's how.

Conscious that he is being watched closely, he turns round. 'Look, it's bad, but it's probably not as bad as it looks. Come on downstairs. I'll help you clear up later.'

'You have to go to work.'

'To hell with work. Some things are more important. Come on and have your breakfast. We need to talk, you and me.' He passes out of the room and goes back downstairs.

It is ten minutes later and they are seated at the kitchen table in front of their breakfast of coffee and toast. 'Is she really going to die?' The boy's voice is carefully flat.

Brian knows there is no point in prevaricating. 'Yes, Donny. I think she is.'

'How soon?' Donny keeps his gaze on his plate. 'Will I ever see her again?'

'You'll see her, Donny,' Brian says quietly, making up his mind there and then to fulfil this promise, 'or I'll kill someone.'

'I'm going with you.'

Brian is so startled he has no time to dissemble. 'How did you know I was planning to go?'

'Easy.' Donny shrugs. 'I know you. Plus the fact that I heard you telling Aunt Sophie last night.'

Brian sits back. In his mind – ridiculously, given the boy's size – his son is still four years old and not fourteen. Although he expects eavesdropping, as all offspring eavesdrop, it is still a surprise to find him capable of making adult-style deductions. 'You can't come with me,' he says faintly. 'It's not practical.'

'Why can't I? If I don't go, am I supposed to stay here by myself? Aren't you afraid I'll smash up the house like I just smashed up my room?' Donny is getting worked up again.

'Of course I'm not – and you wouldn't be on your own. I wouldn't do that to you. I'd make arrangements for you to stay with someone, maybe Aunt Sophie? Or the Jamesons.'

'And nobody's even *mentioned* that Trev and me are supposed to be going to Anfield on Saturday.'

'Oh, my God.' Brian, who had genuinely forgotten about the Liverpool match, hits his forehead with the palm of his hand. 'Donny, I'm so sorry!'

But his son is not interested in apologies. 'Nobody *ever* thinks of *me.*'

Brian can only guess at the depth of the kid's suffering by reference to his own but genuinely feels a trip to Palm Tree Island would not be beneficial for Donny. Not yet, anyway. He wants to find out how the land lies before putting him through something so traumatic – he can fly him out later if the worst comes to the worst. Nevertheless, Donny has entitlements in this. 'All right,' he says quietly. 'You can come with me, no problem, I'm only going for a few days anyway, to bring them back. This is Wednesday, we should all be back by next Tuesday, this day week at the latest.'

He is improvising. Other than maybe socking Jay Street and plucking his family out of the man's clutches, he has not yet formulated any specific plan of action for when he gets to the island – or even, despite what he has just said to Donny, how long he is going to stay. 'On the other hand it would be a real pity to miss Anfield,' he says slowly, as though he is thinking this through. 'In any event, although I know how hard this will be, try not to worry,' he adds, hoping he sounds convincing. 'If I've anything at all to do with it, she's not going to die for a while – at least, not today, tomorrow or even this week or this month. Trust me and listen – who knows? Maybe Mum has a point. We've tried everything else, and this might just work. For one thing, getting into the heat and sunshine couldn't be all bad – certainly can't do any harm.'

'But we haven't tried everything.' Donny's eyes blaze. 'Wait.' He dashes away from the table and thirty seconds later is back in the kitchen with a handful of torn and crumpled computer printouts. 'I've been looking up all about multiple myeloma. Dad, we *haven't* done everything we could have. Ask Aunt Sophie. I told her all about it. There's all kinds of new therapies.'

'But the doctors say—'

'That's the trouble.' Donny's voice is shaking with passion. 'You're not researching, Dad, you're just leaving everything to the doctors. Irish doctors. This is all the very latest stuff from the States. Will you at least *read* it? Please, Dad – *please*.'

'All right. Of course I'll read it.' Dismayed, Brian looks at the ragged heap of paper in front of him. 'If I can piece it together.'

Donny is not letting him off the hook. 'The pages are numbered.'

'I promise I'll read it. Now. Decision time. First things first. Do you feel up to going to school today? As regards the other thing, we'd better decide quickly which it's to be. Anfield or bloody Palm Tree Island?'

'Can I think about it?' Now that he is being treated like an adult, Donny is trying to act like one. 'I'll take a few minutes. I'll get dressed and then I'll tell you.' He pauses. 'Sorry about the room, Dad. You don't have to help me, I'll clean it up myself, and I'll pay for the damage out of my pocket money.'

'Let's see how much it costs first, shall we?' Brian smiles wryly. 'You'll probably be as old as me by the time you've made a dent in it.'

This raises an answering smile but as Donny turns to go, he blushes violently. 'Do you really admire me or was that just bullshit?'

'No bullshit.'

The boy vacillates and then with a repeated exhortation, 'Read that stuff!' flees the kitchen, leaving Brian exhausted – and examining his conscience. Is his son right? Has he done enough for his daughter? Has he gone to the ends of the earth to save her?

Or has he – see no evil, hear no evil – been so emotionally incapable that he has left all the dirty work to his wife and unfortunate young son?

He picks the top sheet off the pile of computer paper and smoothes out the creases: '. . . potent aminobisphosphonates . . . Proteosome inhibitors . . . One such factor is vascular endothelial growth factor . . . drugs are now available which inhibit this new blood vessel formation, such as angiogenesis inhibitors . . . These designer drugs are undergoing laboratory testing and should be available for clinical evaluation soon . . . area of great promise . . .' Page after page, concerning 'advances in research', vaccines and treatments, which will be 'available soon for clinical trials' . . .

Then he sees, vigorously highlighted with shocking pink, 'It is now possible to remove immune T-cells from patients or their siblings and educate them in the laboratory to recognize and kill myeloma cells. These educated T-cells can then be transfused to patients as another way to generate an immune response against myeloma cells . . .'

At the end is the contact address for a myeloma hotline.

Brian riffles through the pages again, stopping here and there to decipher some of the more unfamiliar terms, but finds nothing more than 'encouraging' trial results, aspirations and hope; certainly nothing more than he knows already from Zelda's doctors.

Poor Donny. The relevant words in all of this are *will*, *could*, and *areas of great promise*. No mention of a cure, of course, just quality of life and longer survival times.

Guiltily, Brian prays. He is not a pious or even religious man, and knows he is on feeble ground, yet the prayer, although selfish, is heartfelt and childish: Please, God, I know it's too much to ask that you save Zeldy, but please let Donny not choose to come with me to the Caribbean because I'll have enough on my plate out there without having to cope with a severely troubled teenager on top of everything else – and one more favour, God, please. I promise if you give me this one too I'll never ask you anything else as long as I live. If the kid does decide to stay for the match, don't let him choose to stay with Sophie. How could she, in her situation, handle him? I shouldn't have offered that, it was just a stupid slip of the tongue . . .

He stands up from the table. Praying now? This is all too much: too much thinking, too much emotion. Before he goes out of his mind altogether, he has to get himself organised for this crucial day ahead. He gathers up the mashed printouts and folds them as neatly as possible, then, roughly, throws the used plates and cups into the sink and turns on both taps full, making blessed noise, so much noise that he does not hear Donny behind him. Consequently, he jumps when he feels a light tap on the shoulder. Donny, still in his boxers and T-shirt, is standing behind him. 'I've decided, Dad.'

'That was quick.' Brian turns off the taps.

'I'm going to stay, if you don't mind. Like, if you don't think you'll need me out there? And if you're sure I'll see Zelda again if I don't come.'

'I'll manage, son.' *Thank you, God.* 'It's not that I wouldn't like to have you with me, of course I'd like us all to be together, but the two of us'd be only arriving there and we'd be coming back. It wouldn't be much of an outing. So, have you decided where you'd like to stay?'

Donny pretends to consider: 'It'd be handy to stay with Trevor, wouldn't it, Dad? With both of us going to the match.'

'Good thinking.' *Thank you, thank you, thank you.*

Then Donny sees the folded printouts. 'You read them already?'

'Yes. I did.' Brian dries his hands on a tea-towel. 'We'll discuss them again, but you do realise that these are all trials and developments, there's nothing out there yet.' He forbears to mention that nothing is said anywhere in the documents about a cure.

'I know that,' Donny is impatient, 'but did you see the stuff about siblings being able to give their T-cells? They do have that technology, Dad.'

'I know they do, son, and I promise I'll look into it. OK?' Brian is desperately casting around for some way to tell Donny that Zelda's haematologist had told him she wasn't a suitable candidate. Even if these therapies were available. Which they are not. Not yet.

'Promise?' The hope and relief in the kid's face is grievous. 'I'm available any time, Dad.'

'I know you are.' This is heartbreaking. Although he does not regret keeping Donny in the dark about some aspects of Zelda's illness and treatment – after all, he had had to make parentally protective decisions about how much the kid could handle – faced with the stack of printouts Brian is overwhelmed. His son is more mature than he had believed. He hesitates. Then: 'Sit down, son.'

As Donny complies, Brian, hating the task, sits opposite and gently outlines what he himself has accepted: that, at this moment, the research by which the boy puts so much store is theoretical. And while a lot of it gives cause for confidence – 'it's very promising, you're right about that, Donny' – none of the trial results have as yet resulted in licensing by any health or drugs authority anywhere.

There is no need to continue, this is too distressing for both of them; the boy's lips are tightly clamped, his entire body is shaking, and Brian himself is having great difficulty in keeping emotion under control. It is clear Donny has grasped the concept that, whatever happens in the future, it will probably be too late for his sister. The last thing he needs is a weeping father, so Brian stands up and turns his back, moving again to the sink.

'But that's as far as I know,' he says over his shoulder, struggling to steady his voice as he resumes the washing up. 'There may well be other stuff I don't know. From now on, I promise I'll keep you in the loop. All right?'

From behind he hears nothing so he steels himself to turn around. 'All right?'

Donny is sitting rigidly, staring at the surface of the table. Brian longs to sweep him into his arms and make everything all right as he used to do when Donny was little. But instinctively he knows he should not do it, not only because, at this awkward age, his son would undoubtedly react against such a babying gesture, but because Donny has to go through this. This is pain against which he cannot be insulated. To give the lad something concrete against which to react, Brian now forces his tone to change. 'There is something else, son,' he says flatly. 'Can we talk about the other night?'

The ruse works. Donny's head comes up as he reddens. 'It was awful, Dad, I know that, but I swear it was a once-off.'

'I sincerely hope so.' Brian continues to sound acerbic. 'I have to ask you, did anything happen that night between yourself and Fiona? Her parents seem very exercised about it.'

'What?' Donny's blush intensifies. 'What are they saying?'

'I'm not attacking you, I'm just asking, man to man – and don't pretend you don't know what I'm talking about.'

'Nothing happened, Dad, but—'

'But if it did, you don't remember?' Scarlet now, Donny nods. 'Well, I'm not going to lecture you, son,' privately, Brian appreciates the irony of his own position, 'and I believe you when you say that nothing happened, but you've got to be careful with that bloody alcohol. It's brought good men very low.'

'I know that, Dad.'

Donny's high colour is fading and his father decides to let well enough alone. He can see, however, that the kid isn't finished. 'What is it? Say it.'

'I went into your room and you weren't there.'

'I – I went for a walk.'

Oh, God, the lies have started.

What's more, Donny doesn't seem to buy in: 'At half three in the morning?'

'Is that so strange?' Brian folds the tea-towel, concentrating on lining up the edges exactly while forcing himself to speak normally. 'With everything that's been going on, I couldn't sleep after I brought you home – I'm upset too, you know.'

'Your car was gone.'

'I drove to Dollymount. Walked along the beach.'

'All right, Dad.' Donny does not raise his eyes. Seeing him struggle to believe, Brian holds his breath. Then Donny looks him straight in the face. 'Right! Will you ring Trevor's parents this morning?'

Brian throws his arms around his son and hugs him hard. Donny, embarrassed, does not hug back. 'What's this for?'

'I'm sorry you've felt so alone. We shouldn't have let that happen.'

Donny struggles, his face screwed up. 'Dad, for God's sake,' he is mortally flustered now, 'let me go, Dad, I've to get ready for school now.' He breaks away and hurries out of the kitchen, leaving Brian stricken and not only because he is moved. If prayers are to be answered that quickly, maybe he should have asked for a cure for Zelda.

Sophie, sleeping deeply in her rug like a conch in its shell, wakes to the sound of the telephone. The carriage clock says it is just after twenty past seven. Puzzled, she looks at its small golden face: something is wrong. Then she notices that instead of the Audi calendar, her Charles Lamb landscape is hanging above it. She comes awake as thoroughly as though she has just stepped into a freezing shower. The telephone is still ringing.

She stumbles out of her wrappings, and crosses to it. 'Hello?'

'Sophie? It's Michael.' He sounds rushed and muffled, as though he has a hand over the mouthpiece.

Sophie is jolted, but still too muzzy with sleep to react as aggressively as she might. 'What do you want?'

'Could we meet? We need to talk.'

'We have nothing to talk about.' She is now fully awake.

'Please, Soph, we owe each other at least a chat. There is something we have to discuss.'

Sophie is silent. Despite her telephone vigils of the past couple of days and nights, now that it is offered she can think of no way appropriately to confront this man especially after the discovery she made last night about the baby, yet some visceral and primitive urge requires that she does so.

'Sophie? Sophie? Are you there?' He sounds frantic.

The conflict, huge already, continues to grow. She hates Michael with a deep and serious passion. She also loves him. At least, she thinks she loves him, or used to – if a simple mix of familiarity, affection and habit can constitute love. On the other hand, with the imprint of Brian McMullan fresh on her body, how can she tell?'

'Sophie?'

'What time?'

'Lunchtime? Can you come to the airport?'

'Under no circumstances.' Her anger is kicking in. How dare he even think of asking her to go to the airport so that his colleagues can snigger and laugh behind their hands or, even worse, pity her? And Brian will be there.

'Well, where, then?'

She can hear the sound of running water. Is he in a bathroom? 'Where are you?'

'That doesn't matter,' he says quickly. 'Where will we meet? I'll probably only be able to get away for an hour or so – I've a lot of ground to make up because I didn't show up yesterday, took a sick day. I can't really swing the lead today.'

'The Regency.' Sophie has plucked this at random. The hotel is on the main road to the airport. She must be mad. She forces herself to stay calm as they arrange to meet at one o'clock.

After they break the connection, she walks back to the sofa and wraps herself up again. Her pulse is racing, throbbing high in her chest. No, she doesn't love him or hate him. He is small-fry.

She hates the world. She hates the universe that has made her barren, lost her both her job and her man, in the same week that she herself betrayed her marriage vows.

She is also furiously jealous. All those years and years of painful, expensive tests and treatments, and what happens? Nothing. Meanwhile, Mizz Leonard carelessly opens her legs and gets pregnant.

Sophie bitterly regrets giving money to that fortune-teller. To think that, however briefly, she had even entertained the notion that it might be she who was pregnant.

She draws her knees up to her chin. She will not cry or give in. More than anyone on earth, certainly more than Yvonne Leonard, she has a right to that baby.

CHAPTER TWENTY-SEVEN

Riba wakes and, like Sophie half a world away, is disoriented. Although the clammy sheet covering her is light, she is uncomfortably sweaty, her scalp itches and a regular, hushing sound permeates the air. Abruptly, she realises where she is. She is on the island and that is the sound of waves a few feet away outside her bungalow.

Donny's Swatch shows that it is almost twenty past six in the morning – twenty past two, Irish time? Or twenty past ten? Timing is crucial in the dispensing of Zelda's medicine, but she is so tired it takes her a minute or so to work it out. The island is four hours behind. It's twenty past ten in Ireland.

It is an effort to drag herself out of bed. As she checks on Zelda, sleeping, mouth slightly open, it occurs to her that this is how her daughter will look after death, before they do her up . . .

What brought that on? Riba shakes off the macabre vision. What is wrong with her this morning? She has pulled it off, she is here, in Paradise, Jay is within reach and she will soon see him. He will work his magic and everything will be wonderful. So why is she feeling so down in herself?

Quickly, she walks into the bathroom and steps into the shower, turning it on full, intending to stand under the water for a while. Unfortunately, all that comes out of the rose is a thick brown dribble.

Right. No point in being dismayed. The sea is on her doorstep and five minutes won't make any difference to the dispensing of Zelda's medicine. Don't even bother to open the suitcase – Riba pulls on a cotton nightdress and steps out of the bungalow on to the sand outside.

Immediately she feels better. The air against her damp skin feels fresh and cool, and with its fringe of quiet, creamy surf, the velvety blue of the Caribbean echoes the paler hue of the sky overhead. Broken only by the white of the liner at anchor about half a mile offshore, it stretches like a looking-glass to the horizon where a thin line of pink and salmon clouds heralds the imminent return of the sun. Who could feel miserable on a morning like this? She walks in without hesitation and finds that the beach shelves steeply so that within two seconds she has immersed herself fully, revelling in the cleansing billows under the nightdress and the lifting of her hair off her scalp.

After a few moments, she surfaces, then turns and floats on her back. This is glorious. Glorious. The huge bowl of the sky overhead draws her upwards and into itself and nothing exists now except this feeling of freedom and lightness. No wonder Jay has settled for this instead of the weather extremes of the American Midwest. Even if she'd never met him, Riba would be quick to replace the winter drizzle and misery of Ireland with this, if she had half a chance. This is Eden. This is what God intended for us.

Lazily, she turns her head to survey her new domain. She can see tiny white figures moving on the decks of the liner as the crew prepare for another day at their guests' pleasure. An islet, high and deeply forested, is the only other land within sight on this side and, although she searches, she can see no sign of human habitation anywhere on its vivid green slopes. Turning the other way now, she can see that the crescent of their own beach is backed by similarly dense forests climbing to the hump of a bare mountain.

She has to ring Brian. Very soon. As soon as she has taken care of Zelda.

How is she going to handle it? She has not planned anything. All she can say, truthfully, is that she is doing the best she can for their daughter. That *is* the truth, isn't it? Despite what Sophie said to her . . .

Riba's feeling of luscious relaxation is ebbing, but as she continues to procrastinate, putting off the moment when she has to leave the sea, she sees a woman, dressed in bright green and carrying a bucket and mop, ambling towards the first of the bungalows at the far end of the beach. Two or three people are moving about now and one, wearing what seems to be boxer shorts, is stretching and twisting his torso, reaching for the sky then bending first right and then left; California Monica was right when she had said business starts early here.

Then she sees another person walking purposefully towards the water. She would know that stride anywhere. It is Jay.

Riba, never a strong swimmer at the best of times, almost goes under in her excitement. She wants to call out to him, but not in front of the others. So she simply watches as he walks without pausing into the sea then sets out, barely breaking the surface of the water as he slides through it with quiet, rhythmic strokes. As if on cue, a demi-circle of sun slips above the horizon, and from beneath its thin canopy of cloud a parabola of silver and gold shoots along the water, catching the liner in its path so it glows like a vessel newly arrived from heaven. An enthralled Riba holds up her face to receive its benediction. Then she looks again towards Jay: in her fevered imagination, he seems now to be moving along a pathway of shimmering light.

The illusion lasts for only thirty seconds or so and then the brilliance is dispersed through the lines of cloud and along the ocean. The liner fades to become an ordinary ship again and the sea's gloss is the Technicolor enhancement of a brochure extolling the attractions of a sunshine holiday, while Jay is just a privileged swimmer taking a dip at dawn.

Except he is not just any old privileged swimmer. He is still heading in the direction of the sun and probably out of reach of recognition but Riba is tempted nevertheless to call out, to have him turn in surprise and delight as he recognises her voice, to have him swim towards her.

Well, he has to turn back sometime, and she will be ready for him when he does.

She heads for the shore, having to pluck and peel the sodden nightdress off her thighs and stomach so as not to make a show of herself in front of any onlookers. She hurries back into the bungalow, where, after drying herself, she quietly opens her suitcase and extracts the least creased of her kaftans, throws it on, wrings out her hair and runs a comb through it. Then she checks to see that Zelda is still sleeping and slips out again to settle on the shingle at the fringes of the waves to wait and watch. He is already coming back, the long lazy strokes as regular as a turning wheel.

Riba knows what a picture she will present to him, with her wet dark hair stirring in the little breeze and her knees drawn up to her chin under the bright green garment, large enough to hide her legs or any other little imperfections in her body.

He doesn't see her until his feet touch the bottom in the shallows a few feet away and he stands up. 'Well, well!' Torso glistening, he smiles widely. 'Look what the sun brought today!' Shaking water from his ears and eyes, he comes ashore and pulls her to her feet with one strong hand. 'Riba, what a pleasure!' Smelling of salt and sun and disregarding the fact that he is wetting her all over again, he enfolds her in his arms.

'Hello, Jay. Long time no see.' As Riba happily hugs him back, the rest of the world falls away into nothingness.

'Are you all right? You promised you'd ring and when you didn't . . .' Brian's voice is urgent. 'I was just about to hang up, actually – are you sure you're all right?'

Since Michael's call, Sophie had sat rigid on the couch, her mind and imagination churning. She had debated whether or not to answer this time but it had continued to shrill, getting under her skin. 'I'm fine, Brian. Don't worry about me. This is something I just have to face and that's all there is to it.'

'Can I see you later? Could we meet for lunch or something?'

'I'm sorry – I'm meeting Michael.' Unusually, she now has quite the social diary, Sophie thinks, appreciating the irony.

'Oh,' he is disconcerted, 'sorry, I didn't think.'

'I could meet you afterwards, sometime during the afternoon, maybe?' Was that *her* voice making that offer?

Obviously it was, because he grabs at the suggestion. 'Grand, grand. How about the Half-Way House – no, not there.' He attempts to laugh lightly, but his voice cracks. He clears his throat. 'Do you know the Brian Boru?'

The Half-Way House, near the Phoenix Park, is – was – a pub frequented by them as a foursome; the Brian Boru, on the boundary between Phibsboro and Glasnevin, is a pub Sophie knows only peripherally. She shouldn't meet Eily's husband there or anywhere else, especially now. Yet she hears herself arranging the details. She hears them both being carefully casual as though they meet spontaneously in the Brian Boru all the time, as though their activities of just a few hours previously are of no consequence.

After she hangs up, Sophie stands for a while looking at the silent telephone. Underneath the table on which it rests is one of her shoes. How had it got there? She looks around for its fellow and sees it, on its side, right in the middle of the floor, alongside the blouse she had been wearing the previous night. She wraps herself in her rug again and goes about the room, picking things up. As she straightens the sofa cushions she finds one of Brian's shirt buttons and it all comes back.

Sophie blushes to the roots of her hair, not knowing whether this is from shame, desire, or chagrin that what she and Brian did together can never happen again. The latter is one of the decisions she has made in the cold hour spent fulminating on her couch.

Who knows what will happen in the future? Right now, however, Brian's and her responsibilities to Eily, Zelda and Donny far outweigh any carnal or romantic aspirations they might have together. It is, will be, a good memory for both of them – and, for her, will be locked away in a box in a private part of her brain. The pain, too, will be private.

Perhaps it is just as well that she has agreed to meet him because she will tell him what she has decided. They owe it to one another to be honest.

It had not been the only resolution Sophie had made during that hour. In a way, the experience had shown her something she had been trying to avoid for years – that at the heart of her marriage were ashes. She cannot blame Michael completely, for what has she contributed lately? Did she have any idea how he felt about things any more? After the disappointment surrounding her childlessness, she had jogged along blindly, seeing and hearing little, feeling even less.

From these ashes, where the old, vague Sophie had wallowed, a newer, more focused and determined Sophie had risen. This Sophie had plans.

At least, that is the way she feels now.

She has an interesting day ahead.

'You're not serious? Tell me you're codding me!' Collette's eyes are round and sceptical.

Yvonne, who has called in sick again today, takes an irritated little puff from her cigarette. 'I'm not looking for your advice, Collette, I just wanted to talk to you. Will you bloody shut your trap and just listen? That's the friggin' nth time you've asked me if I'm joking. He says he's left her and he's with me now. He says he loves me, but I'm sure it's just for the sake of the kid. That's why I wanted to talk to you about it. He's definitely left her. I'm not joking – will you get that through your thick skull?'

Collette, who is between jobs at the moment so has time to dance attendance, takes offence and picks up her handbag. 'If that's the way you feel, I've better things to do.'

'I'm sorry!' Instantly Yvonne is contrite. 'It's these hormones. They're doing my head in. Honestly, Collette, half the time I'm excited – that has to be the hormones, right? The other half of the time I want to get to that clinic as fast as I can. I tell you, you wouldn't want to be in my shoes. I wouldn't want my worst enemy to go through this.' She has another go at her cigarette, a deep, consoling drag. 'So I'm sorry. No offence?'

Mollified, Collette stuffs crisps into her mouth. 'None taken. 'S all right.'

They are in the Flowing Tide pub with the lunchtime trade cranking up all around them. Although she is contributing to it, Yvonne wishes it wasn't so smoky. That must be the hormones too. She hates feeling like this, all these unusual and up-and-down feelings, with the decision about the abortion still up in the air too. It's like she's on a bloody seesaw or standing in a rowing-boat with no oars.

All right, she has let Tuesday's appointment in London go, but this is only Wednesday and it's still not too late. 'So, what do you think, Collette?' She blows smoke high in the air as though by doing so she will not add to the fug. 'Am I mad or what?'

'I know this is geeky, and don't bite the head off of me, but do you love him?'

Yvonne snorts. 'How do I know? I thought I was in love with that looper from Killiney – remember him?' They both smile reminiscently about her brief but intense fling with a Trinity student who thought he was a Trotskyist until he failed his first-year exams, leading to withdrawal of Saab privileges. 'How do you really know, Collette?' She sobers up. 'He says he loves me but, like I say, I have the feeling that it's not really me he wants, it's the kid. We get on all right, I suppose, but there's a helluva difference between shagging in the Furry Glen a couple of times a week and living together. Like, I'm being evicted at the end of the week.'

'Friggin' landlords.'

'Yeah. They have all the rights and nobody cares.'

'Yeah.'

Yvonne remembers the odd times, not so long ago, when she would lie awake at night and wonder about Mick and the wife, even telephone him. That had to count for something, surely. If she didn't have real feelings for him, would she have been wondering those kind of things?

'You OK, Y? Want another?' Collette indicates the empty glasses in front of them.

'In a minute.' Yvonne is continuing with her train of thought. 'He's not a bad bloke and he's good-looking for his age – but that's another thing, Collette. I mean, look at the age of me and look at the age of him. Like, he's nearly forty! People will think he's the kid's grandfather. Would you want to be seen with a grandfather?'

They consider this. The pub is filling up now and Collette has to move up on the banquette seat to accommodate two scruffy-looking actor types, obviously from the Abbey Theatre across the road. She gives them a quick once-over then turns back to her friend. 'Well, forty's not that old these days, I suppose. It's more important, probably, that you think you can make a go of it. You know what I think of him, Y, but we won't go there. This is you we're talking about. For instance, here's a thought, how will he react to all the nappies and stuff? I mean, he's been round the block, is he going to stop all that now? Take you to Mothercare instead of cruising Temple Bar or the nightclubs in Leeson Street?' She shakes her head slowly. 'To tell you the truth, Y, I'm gob-smacked about this kid business. I wouldn't have put him down as the type.'

'Me neither. You never know, do you?'

'What about your folks? Did you tell them yet?'

'Huh!' Yvonne snorts again. 'In a pig's eye. What's it got to do with them, might I ask? I can just imagine what they'd say – *if* he was sober and she could take her head out of her arse. Don't even mention them. But wait a second,' she says reflectively, 'we'd be our own family, right? I'd be running my own show – so I could be in charge, showing off the kid and so on. It'd be the first grandchild, that's supposed to be a real big deal, right? I mean, they'd have to like that, wouldn't they?'

'Yeah.' Collette nods vigorously. 'There's Christmas and stuff – and I'm sure you'd want to ask them to the christening and the kid's birthday parties and that?'

'Yeah, I probably would. But, dammit, what about *my* parties? If I go along with this, there goes my fairy-tale wedding!'

'And *my* bridesmaid's outfit. Look, Y, whatever you decide, you'd better decide fast. You're running out of time. He thinks it's all settled, does he?'

'I suppose so. He's certainly begun to treat me differently in the sack. Gentler, as though he doesn't want to hurt the kid.' Wearily, Yvonne stubs out her cigarette in the ashtray in front of her. 'Ah shite! Up, down, in, out, yes, no, maybe – I just don't know what to do. Like I said, in my head one minute I'm the mom in the Daz ad and the next, nothing's changed. I'm fancy free like always.'

'Which way are you now? Right now? Say it quick without thinking.'

'Right now it's Ibiza Uncovered.'

They look at one another in dismay. 'You've a bit of thinking to do, Y.' Collette balls up her empty crisp bag.

Yvonne grasps her arm: 'Thanks for listening. You're a pal.'

'You're welcome. Let's have a refill?'

As Collette orders two more Bacardi Breezers from the lounge-boy, Yvonne knows that no one can help her with this decision. It's all very well mouthing off but inside it's still all shite, round and round in her head until it's driving her crazy. Temporarily or permanently, she has allowed herself to be snowed by a man who is obviously desperate for a child.

And not only by him: the awful thing is that the longer the kid is in there, the more she thinks about it as a kid and less as a problem. Already, in just a few days, it is getting more and more difficult to see it as something that can be flushed away. She's sure she'll be upset if her decision goes against it – those damned hormones again. So if she's going to do it, she'd better do it soon.

She glances across at Collette, who is openly ogling a familiar-looking guy at the counter. Yvonne recognises him: he's a character from a TV soap and he's a ride, all right.

Shit! Nothing to do with her. Her style is well and truly cramped, no matter what. For a while anyway. Then something strikes her. 'Hey, Collette?'

'M-mm?' Collette returns from her ogling.

'Do you think it's my biological clock?'

'What do you mean?'

'You know – that's making me even think about this?'

'For God's sake.' Collette snorts. 'At our age? Give us a breeze, Y.'

'Yeah. Sorry.' Yvonne smiles. 'It was just a thought. You're dead right, it couldn't be.'

'So what are you going to do?'

'Stop pushing me, willya?' But as their drinks arrive and they lift their glasses, the pendulum over the head of the baby in Yvonne's belly is still swinging.

The lounge bar of the Regency Hotel in Whitehall is also full. It is a dark place – perfect, Sophie thinks, for what is about to transpire between herself and her husband.

Alone at the moment – because when he arrived he ordered their drinks then went to the gents' – she picks up her glass of mineral water but puts it down again untouched. Her newly hatched mood of determination has survived at least this far. She does not even feel angry at present, although there was a brief flare-up when he came in, followed by an unseemly surge of satisfaction when she saw the circles under his eyes and his shaken expression. Good, she had thought, savagely. *Suffer, suffer!* However, she greeted him with civility.

He is returning to their table now and she assesses him as though for the first time. Tall, well built but not fleshy, looks his age but no older. Walks with confidence.

Confidence trickster, more like – look at the way his eyes keep darting about. *Would you buy a used car from this man?* Her anger is showing its head. Good, she thinks again, it will keep her on course. She must keep it on a tight rein, though. 'You've started smoking again, I see?'

'Mmm.' As he sits, he drops a disposable lighter and two packets of cigarettes on to the table beside the drinks. One packet is fresh and he busies himself for a moment with unwrapping the Cellophane. 'Look, Sophie,' he says hesitantly, 'I know how you must feel, but will you let me talk for a minute? I want to explain—'

'No explanations necessary. Or wanted. Everything is perfectly clear.' She feels the muscles at the base of her spine twisting in on themselves but sits more upright, forcing the back of the chair to take the strain. She mustn't let him see how upset she is but must keep her cool to have any possibility of success with her plan. 'If you must try to justify the unjustifiable, however, please feel free.' She can see he is intimidated by

her freezing tone. 'Go ahead,' she says, hoping she sounds more conciliatory. 'I'm listening.'

'I know this is weird, Sophie, and completely the wrong time to say
this, and I wouldn't blame you if you got up and walked out right now,
but I know now, now that it's too late, that I'll never love anyone the way
I've loved you.'

'Don't make me laugh.'

'I said I knew it was inappropriate in the present circumstances but
there's a reason for what I'm doing. I know you're going to take what I'm
going to tell you very hard, Soph, but there's no easy way to say this.'

Their armchairs are at right angles to one another and Sophie, aware
that he is staring at her, gazes away from him, towards a brass light fitting
on the wall above a nearby couch. She refuses to make this bit easy for
him: that would be a concession too far. Silence in the midst of hubbub
sounds loud, and as their silence stretches, it begins to jangle. 'So tell me.'

'There's a baby. Yvonne is pregnant.' By hearing it, she is shocked afresh,
but holds on. She is watching him peripherally and sees that now he has
blurted it out he seems to sag, become smaller. Thank God she was
prepared. If her plan is to succeed . . . 'I see,' she says, turning to look him
in the eye. 'You're sure it's yours, I take it? From what I've seen of that
little trollop, I can tell she puts it about a bit.'

'That's lovely, that is.'

She can see she has scored, but the jibe was cheap and she regrets it. She
is appalled by the way she is behaving, but she is being driven by anger so
pure now that it feels coldly exhilarating, like ice-skating along the edge of
a sharp knife while knowing the trajectory is safe and true. She lets him
splutter and expostulate for a bit, but is further appalled when he lets slip
that the reason he has left to live with his lady love is because if he doesn't
the baby will be aborted. 'I can't let that happen, Soph, not to my baby.'

'That's blackmail, of course,' she cuts in, 'but I don't need to tell you
that. You needn't go on about it in any case because I know about the
baby already. I've known since yesterday.'

Speechless, he gapes at her while she calmly picks up her drink. 'I have
to say I don't appreciate that you told everyone else before me.'

'Who told you?'

'Never mind. It doesn't matter.'

'It does matter—'

'It's beside the point.' She stares hard at him. 'Why don't you ask
Yvonne?'

Sophie has never behaved like this in her life, but like foam, recklessness
is filling her mouth and she must let it spill.

His hands are shaking now as he picks up his pint and she would almost feel sorry for him if she didn't have to push on. 'I haven't thought this through completely, of course, there hasn't been enough time for that, but I have a proposition to make to you.'

'What?' Still shocked, he looks at her.

'Yes. Have you a moment?' she asks, although she knows she has his undivided attention. 'I have a strong hunch that Mizz Leonard does not share your newly discovered devotion to parenthood. In fact, given her age and her lifestyle, I suspect that after the shiny new paintwork on the child's Lolita buggy gets a few scratches, she will take off and leave you holding the baby, no pun intended.'

She takes a deep breath. 'So here is what I propose. Our marriage is over in any case, no matter what happens. I can see that. But this isn't England or America, Michael, and you cannot divorce me for four years under Irish law, as I'm sure you know already. If I contest it I can drag it out for longer, make it very messy for you. After all, I am now a totally dependent spouse, am I not? Qualified for nothing. As far as I am aware, the level of maintenance goes hand in hand with the length of the marriage. In four years' time we will have been married for twenty-four years. That's a lot of entitlement, Michael.' She has Nancy to thank for the detail in all of this. She has been listening to the older woman's stories more closely than she realised. She has embroidered a little, but not much and certainly not in essence. Divorce Irish-style, if it comes to it, will be to her advantage.

Michael's eyes are widening satisfactorily.

'I won't screw you,' she says quietly. 'I'll co-operate fully. I'll keep the house, of course, but since I intend to get a job quickly, I won't dun you for maintenance – at least not in the long term. Provided . . .' Her nerve fails her and she takes a sip of her water.

Michael's eyes are virtually bulging now as he tries to recover. 'I didn't say anything about a divorce, who's talking about divorce?'

'I am.' Her nerve restored, Sophie takes a few more sips. Being a bitch can be satisfying, everyone should try it at least once. She knows that blackness and grief lie in wait for her but, for this moment, she is enjoying watching his horror. 'You honestly don't think this marriage is still alive, do you? What did you expect of today's meeting, Michael? That I would beg and weep and implore you to come home to wifey?'

He shakes his head, eyes still on stalks. 'No, not that.'

'No, I suppose you didn't, in all fairness. I suppose you thought you'd "explain" and I'd understand, like the good old Sophie I've always been – but that's no matter. Here's what I propose.' Sophie holds her glass tightly.

'After this baby is born, she signs it over to us for adoption – in fact, since you're the biological father, I'm the only one who will legally have to adopt. We will still be husband and wife and, if this is her express wish, there is no way the authorities can refuse.'

Nancy again.

'After that,' she goes on, 'as soon as the baby is safely ours, you will be free of further obligations to me – except I am assuming, of course, that since you are now so hell-bent on fatherhood you will want to support your child. We can sort out joint custody and you can have as much access as you want.'

'And if she won't do it?'

'I think she'll do it, if you offer her money.'

'What money?'

'My compensation from the air crash. All of it. I'll sign a legal document to that effect.'

Michael sinks back in his chair.

Sophie turns away from him to let him digest it. She is not as calm as she is presenting. At one level, her entire body is screaming at her to kick the hell out of him and his tart. At another, she is terrified that even if they accede to what she is proposing, she would not be able to love and care for a baby conceived so hurtfully. Nevertheless, the desire for a child is so deep and fundamental that it towers above all other considerations. To have this chance, she would build a love nest for her husband and Yvonne, she would give both of them the clothes off her back, even her house.

She has no intention of revealing her desperation. 'Well?' she demands coolly. 'I know that on the surface what I am proposing seems strange, but it would not be the first time this has happened – I've read about arrangements a lot stranger in those tabloids you bring home. Used to bring home.'

'Suppose she goes ahead with the abortion?'

At least she has shocked him into considering it: his voice then was barely audible. 'It's up to you, isn't it, to make sure she doesn't? You can tell her that the sum involved will probably be substantial.' She is improvising now. She has not contacted a solicitor yet, so she has no idea how much compensation she will be due.

'Suppose she wants to keep the kid? If she won't sign it over?'

'I haven't thought that through fully, Michael. But I think she will.' She looks at him from under her eyebrows. 'You do too.'

CHAPTER TWENTY-EIGHT

'Good trip?' Jay, obviously delighted to see her, releases Riba from the wet bear-hug on the edge of the glittering sea.

Fondly, Riba notes how the green of his eyes seems almost transparent in the rapidly increasing glare. 'Great. Thanks for asking. You still have that awful Mormon haircut, I see?'

'What can I say? I'm the height of respectability, these days.' He is already moving up the beach and she has to hurry to keep pace with his long stride.

'I went to see your Auntie May like you asked. She was delighted to receive your good wishes, Jay – I have a little holy picture for you from her. She is doing really well, marvellous for her age, isn't she?'

'Yes, she certainly is. And how's the little girl?'

'To tell you the truth, Jay,' Riba is finding it difficult to keep up in the soft, thick sand and is panting a little, 'she's exhausted. It was a long day yesterday, but now that she's here I'm sure everything is going to be just perfect.'

'Bring her along to breakfast, best meal of the day. We eat communally here – you'll love it, Riba! See you in a few minutes.' He sprints off, sand spurting from under his feet, leaving Riba to catch her breath.

Back in the bungalow, Zelda is slow to wake and equally slow to take her medication. Then she delays them further by insisting on trying to disguise her pitiful thinness by wearing one of Riba's kaftans, discarding one after another until she finds one she thinks suits her. Although Riba forbears to point out that it is far too large, hanging off her like a tent from a coat-hanger, she is able to offer stout reassurances that the colour, a nice bright coral, suits Zelda and tones well with the soft-brimmed khaki sun-hat she had had the foresight to pack as a substitute for the give-away bandannas.

At last she is ready and as they come out together into the sunshine, Zelda looks around her, shading her eyes. 'Oh, look, Mum!' She points towards the liner that, like a sleek narcissus, basks in its own reflection in the glassy green water. 'Isn't that a beautiful ship?'

'Yes.' Riba, who is carrying the shirt she has bought for Jay at Charles de Gaulle, has to work to prevent the tears rising so she looks down at the package, checks the silver ribbon. Zelda's excitement, so long in abeyance, is worth all the hassle of the trip. She tucks her daughter's hand under her arm. 'Some day, darling, we'll take a cruise, all of us.'

'What's all that over there?' Zelda indicates the large pile of lumber in the grassy compound.

'Didn't I tell you? We're in for a real treat. On Saturday there's going to be this big multiple wedding with feasts before and after it. We'll be invited, Zel, it's going to be some great event – maybe you'll be next. Maybe you'll catch someone's bouquet!'

'Yeah, right!' Zelda grimaces, but good-humouredly. 'I'll look forward to it.'

She definitely seems to have a little more energy this morning, Riba thinks, as, slowly, they traipse through the sand towards where she can hear a low buzz of voices. She is absolutely convinced now, if any convincing was necessary, of the rightness in coming here.

They take a little path between two bungalows and find that the buzz is coming from inside a large wooden stockade, circular and about ten feet high, constructed from what might have been shortened telephone poles. They enter through a door wide and high enough to let in an elephant, and arrive in a sort of earthen paddock. In the centre is a long trestle table, occupied along both sides by perhaps twenty people of various skin tones, mostly bronzed Caucasian. Mostly women.

But Riba's gaze is drawn to Jay – changed now into a dazzling white singlet and slacks – seated at the top, deep in conversation with a beautiful Oriental girl to his left. He doesn't seem to have seen them come in.

She is starting to lead Zelda towards him when bloody California Monica jumps up from her place and bounds towards them. 'Riba! Zelda! Welcome to our boma. Gracious, Zelda, you look *soooo* much better this morning. Isn't it a glorious day? What did I tell you, Riba?' She takes Riba firmly by the arm and leads them towards her own place at the table, midway along, while those on both sides move to create space.

'Yes, it's lovely.' Riba, annoyed but determined not to show it, smiles at the gathering and, while she assists Zelda to climb over the bench, manages to slip her conspicuous package under the table. 'What did you call it, Monica? Bo-something?'

'Bo-ma.' California Monica exaggerates the syllables with movements of her full, luscious lips. 'It's a South African term. It's where they have their open-air game roasts or something, but it really works for PTI, don't you think? It's where we'll be having our feast on Saturday after the ceremonies.' She pushes a bowl of fruit salad and another containing mini-packets of Kellogg's cereals towards Riba and her daughter. 'Enjoy! Now, let me introduce you to these folks.'

But as the introductions are made to people up, down and across the table, as she smiles and nods, Riba has to own up to a little feeling of disappointment that, so far, Jay hasn't acknowledged her. She stifles it, however: why should she be put out? Of course he can't show favouritism.

She admonishes herself not to be so self-centred. That is one thing about Jay: he is always scrupulously fair and at present he is doing what he does best, giving the girl to whom he is talking his undivided attention. This is one of Jay's characteristics, shared by only a few in this world – like the Pope, apparently, Bill Clinton and the Dalai Lama. He makes you feel you are the only person that matters in that moment. She'll just have to be patient.

So she chats to all these new friends, most of whom, she discovers, are from California. Carmen, immediately to her left, is a virtual clone of Monica, down to the blondeness, plumped lips and giraffe legs, although her hair, instead of being smooth and straight, is twisted into long falls of curls. She, too, is jealously protective of her special status with Jay, it seems. 'You're a wonderful height. How tall are you?' Riba asks, in an attempt to be friendly.

'Oh, about six one.' Carmen flashes her double row of perfectly capped teeth. 'Jay likes tall women.'

'I know.' Riba smiles back. 'Dark hair too. His mother was very dark, you see.'

Carmen turns to talk to the neighbour on her other side, and Riba, contrite, nevertheless feels that the woman asked for that. She doesn't believe those curls are natural. They couldn't be, bouncing around like that with every move of her head – the woman is a walking commercial for shampoo. 'Taste that blessed sun, darling.' She adjusts the brim of Zelda's hat so that the beams can reach her face. 'Isn't it marvellous?'

Riba's chance with Jay comes a little later that morning, just as she has settled Zelda for a nap. She is on a high. Already, she sees an improvement in Zelda's condition. Definitely. She ate quite a good breakfast and Riba thinks that even after such a few minutes' exposure to the sun – limited by the hat brim as it was – those pale cheeks have developed a little colour.

She comes out of the bungalow, intending to slip off somewhere quiet to put in a bit of sunbathing. Blinking in the brightness, she sees that construction of the circlet of wedding arches is well under way although – having assumed that this is some sort of commune or kibbutz – she is surprised to notice that the workers hammering and sawing are not her companions from the boma but locals. She forgets about them, however, when she sees Jay come out of the reception bungalow. 'Jay – hang on a minute.' She starts to run, then, hampered by the sand and the protest of her 'bad' ankle, not wanting him to see her clumsy gait, slows to a walk.

'Riba!' He smiles at her as she comes level with him. 'I should come and see Zelda, shouldn't I?'

'Yes, would you, Jay? She's sleeping now, but it's only forty winks and she'll be easy to rouse. Oh, Jay, I'm so happy that we're going to be under your protection – everything is going to be all right! But listen,' she lowers her voice, despite construction noises behind them, 'there's something else I want to talk to you about, if you don't mind. It's a bit personal.'

'Of course. Let's go into my office.'

He takes her into a small room off the reception area, furnished with extreme simplicity: a table, bare of everything except a neatly squared-off desk diary, two chairs and a plump floor cushion in white silk. In front of this is a book stand. Two volumes lie on it, both closed; the Bible and a leather-bound edition of *The Tibetan Book of Living and Dying*. There is no glass in the windows and – unlike in her bungalow – the air feels fresh and cool. 'This is lovely, Jay. Is this where you do your meditation?'

'Sometimes, but more usually at the beach house.'

'Oh I'd love to see it! A beach house!' She waits for the invitation, but when none is forthcoming, carries on, 'I hope there isn't a misunderstanding, Jay, but it's this money thing. Monica seems to think we're just – oh, I don't know what she thinks! Like, Jay, she asked how we'd be paying – cash or charge!' Riba laughs uproariously, sharing the joke, deflecting any embarrassment he might feel about one of his employees making such a *faux pas*.

But soon the laughter trickles away. Something is wrong. Jay is not laughing with her but is looking at her as though he does not understand. 'I leave all that kind of thing to the girls,' he says quietly. 'I don't get involved.' He hesitates for a moment or two. 'Since we're such old friends, Riba, I'll tell you what I'll do, but don't tell any of the others because they'd kill me. How about half price, rock bottom, twelve thousand Irish for the two of you? I'll sort out their commission – I'll think of something. Of course you don't have to stick to the exact fortnight – a few days more, no problem.' Then he does laugh. 'No refunds, mind, if you leave early!'

She has always loved Jay's easy, deep laugh. He taught her to laugh too, to allow God's gift of mirth to well up from deep inside her. But just as he did not get her joke, she doesn't get his and stares in consternation. 'I thought we were your guests. You invited us – seemed to . . .' She trails off as she sees that she is the one who has made the *faux pas*.

'Of course I did, but you're right, there has been some kind of a misunderstanding. I thought you knew how we worked it here on the island. I'm not operating a charity.' His mesmerising, musical voice with its gentle, Midwestern consonants, is soothing. 'You have no idea what the expenses are in a place like this, Riba. I won't bore you with it, private water, sewage – oh, God,' he sighs gently, 'I hate talking about money but I'll tell Monica and Carmen that since we're such old friends our arrangement is private, all right? That way, they won't know the details. A personal cheque made out to me would probably be the best way.'

Riba can only nod. Then, desperately, she starts to rationalise. After all, the error has been hers, she had jumped to silly conclusions. Of course he has bills to pay. Look at all those locals working out there. He has to pay them.

It was crazy to expect to come here as a freeloader – two freeloaders – and he is doing her a great deal after all. Fifty per cent isn't bad. Not bad. Pretty damned good, actually, whatever way you look at it.

It is to be their secret, theirs alone, to be kept from that Gorgon and her Medusa-like sidekick. 'Thank you, Jay.' She manages a wide smile, her lips at their fullest stretch. 'I haven't my cheque book with me, unfortunately.' She thanks God that at least Jay has this American directness about money. If this were Ireland, they would be slip-sliding around the subject.

'Riba,' he leans forward across the desk, drawing her into the green depths of his eyes, 'how long have we known each other?'

'A long time.' Riba is already approaching full recovery. If it makes Zelda better, no price is too high. 'Thank you, Jay,' she says simply.

He leans back and grimaces with slight distaste. 'Now that's out of the way – ugh!' He gets to his feet and, with fluid grace, bends to pluck the books off the lectern. 'Shall we go visit Zelda?'

Outside again, in the balm and light, Riba, good humour restored, has to trot to keep up with him as they go past the construction gangs and head towards her bungalow. 'How're things in Ireland?' he asks.

'You'd see some changes there now, Jay – although things aren't bad, I have to admit. If we're to believe what everyone is saying, we have full employment, the economy is booming, all the rest of it.'

'I really must make the effort and go visit there again some day soon. But I'm a sun bunny, Riba. You wouldn't believe those Chicago winters –

I couldn't wait to get away from *that*! Now I find it so hard to leave all this.' He gestures lazily, sweeping an arm around his little kingdom of sun, sea and sand.

'I can believe it, Jay!' Riba, killed by the pace, almost trips on a concealed rock and he puts out a hand to steady her. 'Thanks, Jay.'

'You're welcome. Yeah,' he picks up the pace again, 'I've to do a series of lectures for our organisation in Canada next month. My God, Riba – it's the Arctic!' He pulls a comical face and she laughs.

They are almost at her bungalow. 'Which house along here is yours?' she asks.

In response, he waves in the direction of a high bluff sheltering the beach on its western rim. 'Oh, I don't live down here, I live at the beach house – it's nice and private.' He doesn't elaborate, and just as she had felt excluded from an invitation to visit, Riba feels warned not to ask any more nosy questions.

They have reached her bungalow, but instead of entering straight away, he stops just outside the door. 'One thing,' he says quietly. 'I have to say that we did get a bit of a shock this morning when we saw Zelda – although Monica had prepared me somewhat. You see, Riba, you were giving us such positive reports of her progress.'

Riba frowns. 'But she is doing well. Especially this morning. I thought she was really a step up—'

'Well, let's see, shall we?' His expression is unreadable as he turns to go in.

Zelda's presence in the dim room, which smells faintly of lavender because of Riba's oils and potions, is betrayed under her sheet only by a low mound, like a freshly covered grave. She is breathing shallowly and quickly. 'Wake up, darling,' Riba hunkers down beside her, 'Jay's here. He wants a word with you.'

Slowly, Zelda opens her eyes, and for a moment or two, seeing the effort required, Riba almost panics. Jay unsettled her out there with what he said. 'Can you sit up, sweetheart?'

'I think it would be better if I spoke to Zelda alone, Riba,' Jay says, from behind her. 'Would you mind?'

Riba does mind, of course, but after helping Zelda into a sitting position against the headboard of the bed, leaves the two of them to it. Jay knows best. Before leaving, however, she picks up the gift she has brought for him and takes it with her. She wants to be alone with him to share his delight when he opens it.

She closes the door quietly, sits in one of the plastic chairs with the package on her lap and occupies herself by watching the busy little tenders zipping to and fro between the liner and what must be the port further along the coast. From this distance, she can see the double rows of heads in the shore-bound boats and tries to imagine these tourists' expectations. Such a simple life some people have. They pay money to a travel agent, who books them on a holiday for two weeks and then they go off to enjoy themselves, end of story. How long had it been since things had been so simple for her?

She shakes off this maudlin rubbish and, closing her eyes, raises her face to receive the sun's kiss on her starved Irish skin. This is exactly as she had envisaged it: Jay inside with Zelda, she sitting outside, while a few feet away, the whispering, blue-green water stretches its lazy back to meet the sky.

She doesn't hear him come out and is only roused when he touches her shoulder. 'Well?' Searching his face for clues, she pulls out one of the other chairs. 'What do you think?'

He sits beside her, lining up his Bible and *The Tibetan Book of Living and Dying* on his lap so the books have a precise, geometric relationship to one another. 'We've had a good chat and she's sleeping again.' Suddenly he reaches out and takes her face in both his hands, delighting her with his warm, strong touch to the extent that she is unprepared for what comes next. 'Riba, listen to me,' he says gently. 'I think she should be moved to the American clinic. It's a very good modern facility and they'll take good care of her there.'

As she stares at him, he broadens his tone to the rich, almost hypnotic timbre he uses in his lectures and courses while his fingers seem to dig in to her skin, like worms into clay. 'She's very ill and it would be irresponsible to keep her here. We are equipped to deal with emergencies, of course, but we have no round-the-clock medical personnel.'

On Zelda's behalf and on her own, Riba finds strength and pushes away his hands. 'No! We've come all this way, and we've only just arrived. You invited us to come, Jay. We spoke on the telephone and you made it clear that you would try to help her.'

Even as she speaks so resolutely, the panic is rising because here, facing her, is their bourne, their destination of last resort. She changes her tone, begs: 'Of course she's tired. Just give her a few days, please, Jay.'

'She's your daughter,' he says gently, 'and you know her better than any of us, so we'll leave it for a day or so, shall we? Of course we'll all use our best endeavours. I will give over all my meditation today to her. But, Riba, you must understand this.' He takes her hand now. 'We can't have her around during the wedding feast.'

'But she was so looking forward to it, Jay — we both were.'

'Try to see it from our point of view, my dear. She's sick, very sick. What if something were to happen to her? Can you imagine the chaos? These couples have come a very long way, too, and it's their big day. Just think how you would have felt, Riba, if your lovely wedding to Brian had been ruined by something happening to someone in the congregation. These people are relying on us and we wouldn't want to spoil it for them, would we? After all, we need their good reports of us to spread around the world so that others will come and join us. No,' he relinquishes her hand and pats it firmly. 'I think it would be better all round if she were to go to the hospital. You have insurance, of course?'

Unfazed by her jaw-dropping disbelief, he gazes back, his wonderful green eyes tender with what, up to that moment, she had considered to be solicitude for herself and her daughter. 'What did you expect me to do, Riba?' he asks softly. 'She's very ill. She needs specialist care.'

'Jay, I thought you would take her on. We spoke about this. Work your healing on her, at least improve her. All those articles – all those miracles that happen . . .'

He shrugs. 'Riba, you and I both know that I can't be responsible for what people write about me.'

'But your wonderful lectures, those interviews you gave, what you said when we worked together so intensely that time, what you did for me, Jay! The power of the mind, the limitless power of the mind—' Riba fights desperately to hold on as bricks tumble off the walls of her faith, exposing a shoddy surface on which it is impossible to find a firm handhold.

'Limitless, yes,' he says. 'The potential of the trained mind is limitless. Maybe, after all, we will be able to help – we will certainly try. I told you I will dedicate every moment of meditation today to poor little Zelda.'

'Nutrition. Isn't there new research, Jay? Your own work in that area.'

'There is always new research, always new developments. And, yes, there is important work being done in various universities and institutions about disease and nutrition – we're very aware of that, particularly in light of the new discoveries being made every day now.' He is warming to his subject. 'This is a wonderful planet, Riba. Everything we need is growing right here under our noses and in not too many years' time, who knows, immortality might even be achievable. Certainly we will all be living a lot longer and much more healthily.'

'We'll try anything, Jay, anything. Please. Don't put her away. I took her *out* of a hospital to bring her here to you.'

He stands up, and looks down at her. 'You have my full support and sympathy, Riba, as does Zelda, of course. We will do the best we can. We're very busy, as you can see,' he indicates the work gangs further down the complex, 'but we will pull out all the stops today and tomorrow. I will personally organise a regime of supplements for her and she can start on them later today. On Friday, Riba, she has to go to the clinic. I'm sorry. I just can't take the risk.'

With that, he bends to kiss her cheek. Blindly, barely knowing what she is doing, she holds out the shirt. 'This is for you.'

'What is it?' He takes it.

'It's nothing, just a small gift, Jay. To thank you.'

He hesitates a little, then tucks it under his elbow. 'You're very good. Thank you very much. I'll leave you now. Try not to worry, Riba, Zelda is in my thoughts and prayers. We will all pray.'

Riba's mind plays tricks, postponing its search of her soul. She admires the crispness of the crease in his beautifully ironed slacks, their icy whiteness, wondering who did his laundry, his ironing. Hardly himself because, if she remembers rightly, he used to admit in their lighter moments together how he was all thumbs, domestically. He must be in his mid-sixties by now, she thinks as she notices, not for the first time, that his body is perfectly proportioned as a result of a stringent physical workout regime and his carefully managed nutrition and supplement intake. Yes, Jay is a walking advertisement for their organisation: a body balanced, a mind in control – how often had he said it, taught it, tried to make people understand?

As soon as he is out of sight, however, she succumbs to a wave of horror, which carries with it lurid stories relating to the cost of American medical care. She has no insurance. She hadn't even paid for her ticket with the credit card which might have given some cover—

Of course, Riba had known that no insurance company would touch Zelda. For the previous trip she had pretended to Brian that they had cover from some specialist company in England and he had been so mad at her he hadn't queried her about it in detail. This time she hadn't even tried.

Financial considerations count for nothing, however, when set against the way she has been set adrift in a universe filled with dust, the knowledge that she and her daughter have been rejected, swept under the carpet by the person she trusts most in the world – she has placed more faith in him than she has even in her husband. The sun above her head is ready to burn and wither; instead of leaves, the palm trees along the beach sprout monstrous tentacles, reaching out to strangle her.

Riba, fighting hard to repel despair, heaves herself painfully out of her chair. She is conscious of a dull, background ache in her ankle and she limps a little as she goes back into the bungalow to check on Zelda, who is asleep again. She makes heavy weather of lowering herself to her knees by the side of the bed to stroke the girl's damp cheek. 'Don't worry, love,' she whispers. 'We'll do it ourselves.'

The slackest day of the week for EconoCar is usually Wednesday – Brian has figured that it is a sort of a valley day between the starts and finishes of 'long weekends' even in January. He was grateful today for the lull as he hit the phones, first contacting Trevor's mother – who was delighted to accommodate Donny – and then the airlines. By eleven, he was confirmed to Palm Tree Island via Atlanta and Caracas on Delta.

Alone at the desk, he struggles to complete paperwork and accounts before he goes away. If the situation had been anything other than it was, he would have been thrilled to embark on such an exotic trip; but visited by the image of that grotesquely huge Frisbee with the Arda logo slicing towards himself and Sophie, and not knowing what condition Zelda is in now, the prospect of the next few days fills him with dread. He has tried to get through to the island but failed. The operator told him there was a temporary fault on the line but that it is expected to be restored 'some time today'.

'Hi! I'm back. Do you want to go now?' He looks up and sees Mick standing in front of him. He looks wretched, worse, if that is possible, than before he left and Brian, whose conscience is bothering him, feels he has to ask what is wrong.

'What's not wrong?' The other man shrugs miserably. 'I had lunch with Sophie.'

Brian's stomach lurches. 'Oh? How is she?' Then, just in case, 'I rang her actually.'

To his relief, the other man's reaction is relatively normal. 'Did you? When? She never told me. What did she say?'

'What do you think she said?' he parries. *Please, God, let her not have told him that I was the one who told her about the baby.* 'She's very upset about the whole situation,' he goes on. 'I offered to go and have a cup of coffee with her.' Unable to meet the other man's eyes, he turns away, pretending to scrutinise a printout: 'I don't want to get caught in the middle of this, Mick. You are both our friends, after all.'

'Would you go and meet her? I'd really appreciate that. You don't have to tell me how upset she is – it'd be great if she had you to talk to, Brian. She has this idea . . .' He hesitates. 'Oh, I'll let her tell you herself. I'm sure she will.' His voice is eager now. 'I'd value your advice. If she doesn't bring it up, will you ask her? Just ask her what she wants to do with her compensation money from the crash – all right?'

'All right.' Brian, still studying the printout, is glad the other man can't see his expression. Once you have started, it is too bloody easy to continue down the trail of lies.

CHAPTER TWENTY-NINE

Rain batters the glass roof of the conservatory built on to the rear of the Brian Boru, where Brian and Sophie have been sitting for the past half-hour. The pub is very quiet and they have this part of it to themselves.

They have had two drinks each, have debated whether or not to order a third but have decided, as two mature adults, that they shouldn't prolong this, either the drinking or the meeting. They are silent at present, as though they have run out of things to say. Yet Brian feels he has left so much unsaid he will burst.

Over his many, many apologies for his indiscretion in telling her, they have briefly discussed Sophie's hurt about Yvonne Leonard's baby but she has clammed up about it so, after telling her to call him if she wishes to talk more about it, Brian has subsided.

He hates this. They have agreed, again like two mature adults, that what happened between them was a once-off and that even to contemplate its repetition would be not only immoral and dangerous but downright stupid.

Brian hates that agreement. He hates that they have agreed to close the book on it: to accept that once in a lifetime two people, if they're lucky, may be granted a single golden moment, that they had had theirs and they should be happy they had grabbed it – but that now it is time to face real life.

All that stuff. He agrees with it yet the air between them remains thick with regret and intense physical desire.

He doesn't know what he expected – or even what he really wants because his head and heart are at odds. The latter wants him to fling it all away, take Sophie in his arms right now and fly with her to some place where there is no EconoCar, no Mick Dolan, no bloody marital or friendship ethics. It wants him to take Sophie to bed. Now. Immediately.

The former wants him to button up, to accept that this, whatever *this* is, was too traumatically born, developed too quickly, is too fraught to last and that the odds against anything good coming of it in the long run are hopelessly high. His head tells him to grow up.

Head and heart together want to start over, for himself, Eily, Michael and Sophie to be allowed back to the carefree days when none of them had ever heard of multiple myeloma, never mind Jay Street, and where a weekly card school, or a fund-raising dinner-dance was the height of sophistication and enjoyment for them. Where none of them would have dreamed of compromising any of the others; where they had knocked huge entertainment out of the simplest things, such as when they had viewed the grid of half-built houses and had thought 'Marble Gardens' the funniest, most stupid name ever dreamed up by a wily developer to attract young couples to a 'good' address. They had outdone themselves in the pub trying to come up with a more stupid name – because who but an eejit would try to lure people to an estate with connotations of graveyards and headstones and gardens of remembrance?

Typically Eily had been the one to find the positive side. 'I dunno. When you think about it, marble is so beautiful and so *permanent*, and gardens are always growing. Maybe the name's to make people think of living and growing with beauty, even of heaven.'

'Would you ever shut up, Eily?' The other three, roaring, would not let her finish.

Brian no longer thinks the name is funny. Zelda, who will have spent all of her short life there, probably doesn't either.

Zelda. Brian's heart jolts. What will he find when he gets there? Should he have been so definite in his assurances to Donny about his sister that her death wasn't imminent and that he would fetch her home? All that confident talk about doctors – these days he finds himself blurting, saying things he has not properly thought out . . .

He is aware Sophie is watching him and afraid of what he might betray if he returns her gaze. He looks at his watch, does not see what its face tells him, and breaks into the heavy silence by telling her he had better be off, he has to make arrangements.

Sophie says she has to go too.

Neither makes a move.

'I know it's not going to be easy,' Sophie says next, gazing out at the rain, 'but I envy you in a way. It would be lovely to get away from this misery and to lie on a beach, even for a few days.'

'You could always come, you know.' Brian laughs, and thinks he sounds crazy. 'I could certainly do with the company – and I'm sure Eily wouldn't mind a bit of support either. I'm mad as hell at her, but however sunny it is, it's probably no picnic for her, having sole responsibility for Zeldy.'

★ ★ ★

Leaving aside the sunshine and the Caribbean, the prospect of travelling all that way with this man is almost irresistible to Sophie: sitting shoulder to shoulder beside him for so many hours in aeroplanes, having drinks in transit lounges, talking intimately together for hours . . .

And then there is her distress about Zelda – she can truly sympathise with Donny in this because, on top of everything else, she is seriously upset at the notion that she may not see her goddaughter again. She toys with the slice of lemon in her glass – Brian is right, Eily would welcome her with open arms. 'Do you really think she'd like me to come?' She is on the point of considering it seriously – after all, she is a free agent now – when into her mind pops a vision of herself with Eily: the Judas kiss on Eily's cheek, the too-enthusiastic hug. She reminds herself fiercely that there is also the little matter of the proposition she has put to Michael. She can't just throw in that little grenade and not watch where it lands. 'Better not,' she says quickly, avoiding Brian's eyes in case she is tempted to take this back.

'No matter. If you change your mind, the flights aren't until tomorrow morning. Just turn up with your passport at about half past seven. I'll be there, waiting. There'll be no problem with seats because you won't be looking for deals or packages. I had no difficulty anyway. And in case you're worried about the cost, don't be. The way I feel now, I don't give a shite about money. I'd re-mortgage the house, sell the business – it's all balls anyway—' His voice cracks.

'Don't.' Sophie looks at the tiled floor. Fancy. Black and white and red, pastiche Victorian. 'Please.'

'All right. I won't.'

They lapse again into silence.

'All right there, folks?' The barman pops his head through the entrance. 'Need anything else?'

'No, thank you.' They say it simultaneously, and although they are sitting decorously, four feet apart, they had jumped guiltily, as though they had been caught doing something illegal. The barman vanishes and, once again, Brian looks at his watch. 'I really should go.'

'Me too.'

Still neither gets up.

The longer this goes on, the more the air between them curdles with sexual tension. She has to take the focus off it or she will choke – or do something she will seriously regret. 'Listen, Brian,' she says quietly, 'there is something I have to say to you. Zelda asked me to. It's hard.'

'What?' The diversion has worked. His alarm is almost palpable. 'She asked me to say that she knows her situation is more difficult for you than it is for her.' She looks frankly at him. 'She knows she's dying, and she's accepted it. I think she wants the rest of us to accept it too.' Now that the spotlight is off, Sophie feels she can talk normally. 'I can see it, Brian. I saw it when I was photographing her.'

Brian, who has started to slosh the remains of the ice round in the bottom of his glass, lowers his head and she can't read his expression. 'I know it too,' he whispers, 'but I don't want her to die out there. Maybe that's selfish of me.'

'Are you going to bring Donny with you?'

Almost imperceptibly, he shakes his head. 'Again, maybe that's selfish.'

'Have you talked to him about it?'

'Yes.'

'Do you want me to look after him while you're away?'

This brings him up. 'That's really decent of you, and I did think of asking, but you have enough on your plate. He's going to stay with Trevor. There is one thing you can do, though.'

'Anything.'

Brian puts down his glass and takes out a small notebook from his inside pocket. Having flipped through it, he notes two telephone numbers from it on a beer mat on the table in front of him then hands it to her: 'That top one is Trevor's, and the second is the private number of the haematologist. Would you make an appointment and take him to see the guy? He's a decent bloke. You were right, Sophie. I've promised to get Donny up to speed. Better late than never. I suppose he showed you his printouts?'

Sophie nods and puts the beer mat into her handbag. 'I don't know what else to say, Brian. This whole thing is tragic.'

'There's nothing left to say, is there?'

Sophie knows she must get away now, but she still has some unfinished business. 'Listen.' She's unsure whether or not a change of subject would be crass but, given that she doesn't know when she will see him again, goes ahead anyway. 'Did you get a chance to talk to Nancy – or have you changed your mind? Since you're going away, the others should know.'

'Nancy?' For a moment, he looks blankly at her, then remembers. 'Oh, my God, Nancy – yes. Sorry. It slipped my mind. Tell her it'll be OK.'

'Are you sure? With you not there – she'll have to be trained . . .' Sophie, thinking of Nancy's unique approach to office routines, suffers a quick pang of conscience.

'I don't give a sugar.' Brian shrugs. 'She can start on Monday when the kid goes back to college – let Mick train her in. I'll tell him before I go.'

Then, in a different, more careful tone, 'I told him I was meeting you, by the way, and he said I should ask you something pretty peculiar.'

Brian was discussing her with Michael? The tension winds up again so Sophie's back feels as though it has been stretched in a vice. He misinterprets her reaction. 'Don't worry,' he says quickly, 'it was nothing compromising. I'm to ask you how you're going to spend your compensation money when you get it. I didn't understand.'

She had managed to maintain severe control in the airport yesterday, in the Regency, and right up to this moment, but now her restraint, stressed beyond its limits, threatens to explode under the pressure of pain and outrage. How dare her husband discuss this, make a messenger out of Brian, get him to do his dirty work? She can just imagine him, mealy-mouthed, pathetic, creepy-crawly, cradle-snatcher that he is . . .

She covers her eyes, calling on all her reserves of will to contain the storm. 'You go on, Brian, you've a lot to do. But Michael Dolan is a shite. A complete shite.'

'Yeah, he is – that's the only word for him, he's a shite.'

For some reason, distraught as she is, the schoolboyish fervour of this response strikes Sophie as incredibly funny and she starts to laugh through the tight veil of her hands. She uncovers her eyes, and sees Brian's stricken expression. 'Oh, Brian,' she says, not sure for which of them she has more sympathy, 'I know – you think I'm losing it. I did there, for a bit. It won't happen again.'

'I've never heard you use language like that before.' He is stunned and she reaches up briefly to stroke his face.

'Well, I've never in my life been through a series of events such as this before. You've got to admit it's been quite some week and a half!' She laughs again and when this new laughter threatens to turn into crying, manages to fend it off. 'Thank God we're on our own in here,' she says ruefully. 'If we weren't, someone'd be sending for the men in white coats by now.'

'Sophie . . .'

This time she allows him to take her into his arms and hold her. It's a chaste, loving hug but Sophie closes her eyes, breathing deeply to memorise the scent of his jacket, of the area behind his ears.

Sophie finally admits to herself that the lovemaking had been a long time coming. Over the years, she had frequently imagined how it would feel to be this close to him, but, until this last whirlwind period, had always ruthlessly suppressed each untoward thought about Brian McMullan as it arose. She will have to suppress them again, but soon. Not now. She inhales once more. He hugs tighter, presumably because, like her, he knows that they will never again hold each other like this, with the memory of sex still clinging to their skin. She breaks away before that recollection can act, turning the hug into something more urgent. Without looking at him, she gathers up her handbag and mobile, checking the time on its little face. 'A quarter past three. Whatever about you, I really am going now.' She stands up. 'Don't worry, I'll watch over Donny from afar and I will make that appointment.'

'I'll walk you to your car.'

'*No!*' She has almost shouted it. In a calmer voice, she amends this: 'Thanks. I'd really rather not.'

'All right.' He stands up too. 'Have you an umbrella?'

'I don't need one.'

'But you'll get soaked.'

'Brian.' She puts out a hand and touches his sleeve. 'I'll be all right. A few drops of rain won't hurt me.' She turns and hurries across the tiles, pushing the glass door violently and walking out without a backward glance.

Outside, she welcomes the cold shock as the rain unleashes on to her unprotected head. As she gets into the Mini, whose bonnet is facing the conservatory, she cannot avoid seeing him again. He is still standing where she left him but his huge outline is now doubly blurred by the water streaming down the glass and by the tears springing into her eyes.

At home, without hesitation, without even closing the front door, she marches straight to the mantelpiece and, after its brief sojourn, removes her Charles Lamb from the wall above it, replacing it with her own despised and discarded watercolour. The Lamb had been a wedding present anyway, so it is appropriate that it should pay for a firebreak between the raging end of the marriage and her own new life. So what if it is half Michael's? Let him sue her for it. As she checks its frame and glass for dust and superficial marks, it occurs to Sophie that she is pathetic. Another crisis, another rearrangement of her pictures.

Quickly, before she can descend into a morass of self-pity and recrimination, she goes outside again and throws the painting into the back of the Mini.

The woman in the Hallward Gallery remembers her and admires the landscape, scrutinising it closely under one of the picture lights. 'I can't give you the full whack until I've sold it, OK? That may take some time – and you know about our commission system? You won't get what the buyer pays.'

Sophie cannot care less about commissions or anything else. 'Would you give me two thousand for it? End of story?'

The woman, taken aback, examines the painting again. 'All right – if you're sure?'

Sophie is sure and, within minutes, is climbing the steps leading from the gallery to the street above with a receipt and a cheque for two thousand pounds safely in her handbag. She turns left and walks quickly towards Merrion Street, then left again into Nassau Street. She is out of breath when she reaches the Dublin Camera Exchange on Trinity Street.

'Can I help you?' The kid who approaches her can't be more than twenty or twenty-one. Yvonne Leonard's age. Sophie swallows hard to repel the fresh wave of jealousy at the thought of Yvonne Leonard and of what is nestling under her breastbone. Quickly, she takes out her credit card. 'How much darkroom equipment could I get for two thousand pounds?'

After Sophie left, Brian could not face going back to the airport. For one thing, he did not want to talk to Mick Dolan, but it was more than that. He had felt that, in his state of mind, he couldn't face anyone.

He ordered a third drink, a serious one this time: double whiskey and a pint of Heineken. He had downed the pint quickly, then sat over the whiskey for almost an hour, sipping absently without tasting it while he had tried to sort out what he should do, or if he should do anything at all. He had even switched off his mobile because he didn't care whether EconoCar, his baby for so long, lived or died.

The impact of what Sophie had said about Zelda had hit him only after she had gone. He had not only failed to keep his daughter safe from her awful disease, he had not even managed adequately to conceal his distress about it so that his poor, overburdened girl had felt she had to take on his grief – and Eily's and Donny's – as well as her own.

Now he is so sunk in misery he doesn't notice the time passing and comes to only when four young women of about Yvonne Leonard's vintage come in. In Brian's present mood, their bawdy enjoyment feels almost sacrilegious. He quickly slugs back the remainder of his drink and leaves.

But when he gets into the car park, woozy from lack of sleep and alcohol poured into an empty stomach, he decides he isn't fit to drive so, in an effort to clear his head, decides to take a walk. He turns left from the pub with his back to the city centre, and, moving as briskly as the weakness in his legs will allow, follows the recently refurbished stone wall along the perimeter of Glasnevin cemetery. Within minutes he is soaked to the skin, welcoming the cold discomfort because it serves as a distraction from his torment. It should also help with the sobering-up process.

When he finds himself at the gates of the graveyard, on impulse he goes inside.

On this day of rain and wind, the cemetery, usually busy with people visiting graves or even taking quiet exercise along its paths, is virtually empty.

As he walks along slowly in the undemanding company of the dead, Brian finds himself wondering if his parents are here somewhere. If they are dead, the odds are good that they are, Glasnevin being by far the biggest graveyard in the country. He has no idea, of course, where to start looking. The name McMullan was of his own choosing: at a time when everything was possible, he thought 'Brian McMullan' would look good on the roster of Ireland's international rugby squad.

He had lost contact with everyone who had had a hand in his rearing, even his last foster-parents, and he had carved out his own life as contentedly as any man, or thought he had, until the diagnosis of Zelda's illness and her subsequent decline took every stone from under his feet. Compared with having to watch that the trauma of the air crash was piffling.

He has reached the end of one pathway and is hesitating as to which way to turn when something bright, shining even through the murk of this day, catches his eye. A balloon?

Shaken momentarily out of his black mood, Brian, curious, goes towards it. It is indeed a metallic helium balloon, bearing the legend *Happy Birthday, Coley!*, its string tethered to a set of painted stones decorating a tiny grave. There are more balloons flying from other graves nearby, and toys and teddy bears, even a little ride-on tractor in vivid red, and a tattered pink blanket fastened with string to a small wooden cross. He is in the Holy Angels plot, the part of the cemetery reserved for babies and children.

Brian collapses on to the edge of a grave behind him. He is at the lowest ebb of his life. He has failed abysmally, not only as a father but as a husband, betraying his wife carnally – and in other ways, too, so that she has felt obliged to run to the protection of another man.

He is supposed to be the protector of his family. He is supposed to be the man.

Riba has spent the rest of that day tending Zelda, and, except for being slowed somewhat by the injured ankle, has carried on as though nothing untoward has happened. She has even managed to put in a bit of sun-bathing on the beach directly in front of their own bungalow, pretending to be asleep or reading when approached by any of the others.

When California Monica had come to enquire what time they would need the private ambulance on Friday, Riba had been able to discuss it calmly.

Pleading jet-lag and fatigue, she had not joined the long table in the boma for lunch but had taken plates of food to the bungalow and had settled Zelda after they had eaten.

All the time, however, Jay's words tolled in her head like a funeral bell and he seemed to dance in front of her, taunting her with the perfection of his green eyes, his marvellous physique. This 'island Jay' was not the Jay she had known. Or the Jay she had thought she knew.

For the first time since she had encountered the organisation, Riba has entertained doubts about her own naïveté. Would it *actually* cost twelve thousand pounds to feed and house one person for a couple of weeks in a third-world country, even assuming, as Jay had implied, that the essential services here were astronomically expensive?

And he had thrown Zelda off his property. To be fair, he had said he wouldn't charge her at all, given the circumstances and that she was going to be moving into the clinic after such a short stay. At least they were down to six thousand.

Even that . . .

As for his meditating – her brain had raced busily away on its ferrety little errands. Riba had never before questioned this, believing implicitly in Jay's powers to transcend time and distance – but now she was not so sure.

All the old defence mechanisms kicked in: it wasn't Jay. Here on the island, for instance, those two women seemed to think they owned him. They were the commercially minded ones. After all, he had said he left all that kind of material rubbish to them. The girls, he had called them. And he had referred to their commission.

Some girls. Riba would like to know what their cut was.

Back in Ireland, were the foodstores and health franchises run in his name operating a scam? Were they passing on to Jay all the money they got from the punters? Could Jay be the real victim here? Yet the insistent little voice within her had continued to pipe. Jay is no child: he is not to be manipulated, or even influenced, by anyone.

She had then remembered her mystification during one of California Monica's telephone calls when she had wondered about the big push to get herself and Zelda out here. It was clear now: this place was a business for them and they were all creaming it.

Dunce, idiot, moron. *Fool.* She had made such a clown of herself. Riba's tortured imagination pictured Jay with California Monica and that

Carmen, all three mimicking her desperate, unavailing pleadings, her fat unfitness, her stupid kaftans. Her craven gift-giving, even as he had kicked her in the teeth.

No. That wasn't fair. He wouldn't do that. Nevertheless, she felt like bashing in her skull with one of her shoes.

She has mixed feelings, therefore, when, on returning from a solitary walk along the dark beach that evening, she finds Jay sitting in one of the chairs outside her bungalow. He greets her with a cheery wave. 'I just called down to say goodnight.'

Overhead, there is a new moon and by its light reflecting off the sea, she sees, glistening like water on his shoulders, the shirt she gave him. 'Like it on me?' He stands up and preens a little, turning this way and that so she can admire it. 'I love it, Riba. You always had great taste. Thank you.'

Riba manages to smile. She accepts his kiss on her cheek as she used to back in Ireland years ago when everything was less confused and confusing. Then, pleading continuing fatigue, she tells him she'd love to chat but she is out on her feet and is going inside to bed.

'Goodnight, my dear, see you in the morning.'

'See you, Jay.' Riba enters the bungalow and closes the door behind her with a soft click.

In the shadowy room, lit only by a single bedside lamp, she leans against the PVC door. All her adult life, certainly since she had embraced Jay's organisation, she has never spoken of death using that word, but has maintained an arsenal of euphemisms for it: going to a better place, leaving us, passing on, moving to a higher plane, being called when God decides He wants us for Himself. Now, however, in light of Jay's comprehensive rejection, everything she has learned from him about how to fend off Destructive Thought has deserted her and the naked precision of the original has come crashing in. Death. *Death*. Black and vanishing death.

She walks over to her sleeping daughter.

In sleep Zelda's expression is serene and her eyelids flutter with dreaming as her mother strokes her head. 'What do you see, darling?'

CHAPTER THIRTY

Over and over again, Michael has rehearsed how he will introduce the subject of Sophie's offer, but now that it's crunch time, he is finding it difficult. It's not that he is afraid of Yvonne, it's just that the stakes are so high. Also, his 'love 'em and leave 'em' credo has been in operation for so long that to have to treat a doxie with kid gloves is a new and quite frightening experience.

So far it is not going well.

At his suggestion, they are eating out. 'A nice meal, Yvonne – what do you say? I've booked Chapter One for eight o'clock,' this as they left the office together, Michael thinking that it presents the additional advantage of putting off a return to her claustrophobic bedsit. That is another awful task in prospect: he is not relishing the notion of flat-hunting with his new mate. Although the basement restaurant, in Parnell Square, is an upmarket one, he is playing safe: he and Sophie have frequently eaten there and never been disappointed. Yvonne's tastes and attitude to food are unknown to him – it hasn't been that kind of relationship.

At present they remain unknown. She had ordered salmon but most of it is still in front of her, although Michael has polished off every morsel of his duck. The conversation is not going well either and he is getting desperate – not only because he hasn't yet found an opening, but the prospect of this social mis-match facing him now, possibly for years, certainly until the baby is born, fills him with something close to terror. Apart from meeting for sex, almost all of their outings to date have been to pubs and fast-food joints.

He looks around: the candlelit room, decorated in soft pastels, is filled with people laughing, eating, staring lovingly into each other's eyes, having a great time. Everywhere, except at his table, the buzz is good.

She has never been all that forthcoming about her background, so he has tried to interest her in his: Sophie is off limits, for the moment at least – the whole situation is too raw. He has just confided in her the reason why he has been left in charge of the office, telling her of how Eily has spirited Zelda away. 'Poor guy. I'm sure that's why he didn't come back to the office that afternoon.' Michael did not share with her that their boss had been with Sophie. Or that Brian had told him he had nothing of any significance to report about that meeting, except that Sophie seemed fine. 'You'd have to feel sorry for them, wouldn't you? Poor girl. Imagine, she's only nineteen, such a short life.'

Yvonne's reaction to that is, yes, it's very sad, but that's life. 'Isn't it weird the way these things go? It might sound hard, Mick, but it's the truth. It's always the same, isn't it? One's born, one dies. It never fails.'

There is no answer to that.

Michael is beginning to question whether all of this is worth it – he has left his wife, the home she has created, for this? And what about Sophie? In his panic, he has barely considered his feelings for her. Had it been that bad during all those years? Especially at the beginning. No. He must not go there. His focus has to remain clear. Grimly, Michael reminds himself of the reason he has left his wife. To save his child from being killed. Instantly, that extraordinary, inextinguishable little flame starts to burn in him again. 'Do you not like the salmon? Would you like something else instead?'

'It's all right.'

Everything has been 'all right' this evening – the wine, the weather, the little bunch of flowers he had bought her in an effort to cheer her up. 'OK,' he says, as light-heartedly as he can, 'let's see what we'll have for dessert.' He signals to the waiter hovering near the doorway to the reception area.

'I've had enough. I don't want any.'

Michael, rapidly losing patience with what he considers to be deliberate bolshiness, sits back in his chair but manages – just – to keep himself from yelling at her. 'What's wrong, Yvonne?' he asks. 'You're in terrible form this evening.'

'Don't be bleedin' stupid! What do you think is wrong?' She throws her knife and fork on top of the salmon and glares at him.

Although he feels like strangling her, Michael counts to ten mentally. 'Are you not feeling well? I thought you'd like this place.' She opens her mouth but he pre-empts her. 'I know, I know! It's all right!'

At least this raises a reluctant smile. The waiter clears away the plates and leaves the dessert menu. Michael builds on the opportunity: 'Look, as we're out, why don't we enjoy ourselves? Let's play a little fantasy game, eh? What would you do with, say, a hundred grand, Yvonne? Suppose you won it in the Prize Bonds, or shared the Lotto? Something like that.' He had picked the figure at random, calculating that Sophie's money certainly would not be any less, after the solicitors had hyped up the level of her pain and stress and so forth. He makes a mental note to advise Sophie to develop a phobia about flying, even about seeing an aircraft. That should bump things up.

'That's stupid.' Yvonne's lips turn down with contempt. 'I'm never going to have that kind of money – I don't even own a bleedin' Prize Bond. It's stupid to even talk about it.'

'Come on, be a sport. No point in coming out for the evening to a place like this and sitting there like a gargoyle! Life isn't worth living if you don't dream. I'll tell you what, I'll go first, because I've thought about it, believe me, I've thought about it! For instance, a hundred thou is not enough to buy a house or even a Lamborghini, but it's certainly enough to go round the world on a luxury cruise in a big suite for three months. Twice if you still had a nose on and wouldn't come with me!'

'Yeah, I'd like that,' he says dreamily, 'six months of being waited on hand and foot, a different exotic port every day.' Watching her out of the corner of his eye, he picks up the menu. 'Hey! They have rhubarb tart! I love that with ice cream. So, come on,' he says casually. 'What would you do with the money?'

'I dunno.' But, almost despite herself, Yvonne is getting involved. 'I'd buy a car, for starters, maybe even a Merc. And I'd buy about a million pairs of shoes. I'd certainly give up that poxy job, take a decent break. I've only ever been on two holidays in my life, to Lloret del Mar and Santa Ponsa, but I'd like to go to Ibiza, to a villa, not a poxy apartment. Collette says Ibiza is brilliant. Or maybe Greece, even, or Disney World.'

Then she remembers. 'Of course I can't, can I? I'm not going to be going anywhere on a holiday for at least fifteen years!' She glances at her still flat stomach then holds out her wine glass for a refill.

Encouraged, Michael takes the bottle from the ice bucket and pours. 'I never knew you liked shoes.'

'You never asked, thicko!' Yvonne slugs the wine.

It's now or never. Michael takes a mouthful from his glass. 'It is possible, you know . . .'

'What?' She frowns.

'It is possible to lay your hands on a hundred thousand pounds. Even more, maybe.'

She raises a cynical eyebrow. 'Oh, yeah? What'll we do? Rob a train?'

He stares at her, hoping he can compel her to listen.

It works, because her eyes widen. 'That wasn't a game, was it? You're not joking me, are you?'

'No, I'm not, Yvonne, I'm deadly serious.'

She puts down her glass. 'So, go on, then. I'm all ears.'

'I'll tell you how you can get that kind of money and have as many holidays in Ibiza as you like. Buy as many pairs of shoes as you can fit into your wardrobe. You have to promise me one thing, Yvonne. You won't make a scene in this restaurant when you hear what the story is. All right?' He makes his voice sound teasing. 'I like this place. I want to be able to come back here.' He sees he now has her full attention. 'Are you going to promise?' he asks quietly.

'I promise.'

He lets the silence develop until she can stand it no longer. 'Is this something to do with the IRA? Because if it is, I'm having nothing to do with it.'

'It's nothing to do with the IRA. It's to do with our baby.'

Yvonne's reaction is extraordinary: she blushes – a phenomenon he has never seen before – then pales. 'What about our baby?' Her voice has lost all its street noises. It sounds very young.

Michael reaches across the table and takes her hand. 'Now, you promised you wouldn't make a scene—'

'Get to the point, willya?' She withdraws her hand and stares at him. 'Jeez, it's like bloody *EastEnders*.' The blushing had obviously been a temporary glitch. She has bounced back. Way back.

'All right,' he says, 'give us a break – I'm as surprised as you about this—'

'*Mick!*'

'I'm getting there, I'm getting there.' Michael is very nervous. His entire life depends on how she reacts now. 'It's to do with Sophie,' he says quickly, in case she interrupts again. 'She has always wanted a baby. She says if you have this one and sign it over to her, she will give you every penny of what she gets in compensation for the air crash.'

There. It's said. Michael's breath is coming in quick little gasps. He watches Yvonne closely. Her face is working as she takes it in.

He has said nothing about his own part in this, considering that it is best left for another day. One step at a time. If she agrees to this proposal, he can deal with their relationship later.

He has reckoned without Yvonne. 'What do you get out of all of this? What's in it for you, Mick? Is this your idea?'

'On my sacred word of honour, Yvonne, I had nothing to do with it. She came up with this herself and I was as gob-smacked as you are. Now that I've had a few hours to think about it, it makes sense. She has wanted to have a baby since we got married – she'll do anything for one, we had years of tests.'

'So why didn't youse adopt?' At least she is not jumping up and down.

'Look, Yvonne, can I be honest with you?'

'Feel free.'

'Until you made your surprise announcement, I had no idea in the world that I would even be remotely interested in having a child. I went through all those bloody tests for her sake. But now—'

'I get it. But now you want one. Your wife wants one. Youse both want one and I'm to be bought off. I'll give you *my* baby and youse can both ride off into the sunset and play happy families. What about all that malarkey about us being together? That was all bullshit, wasn't it?'

'I didn't think you were all that keen anyway. I had to persuade you if you remember. Calm down, Yvonne, you promised you wouldn't make a scene.'

'Yeah, right. Well, promises are made to be broken, and that's why they put rubbers on pencils.' All conversation in the restaurant dies as she springs to her feet, her voice rising. 'Fuck off, Mick Dolan! Fuck you and your friggin' baby and your friggin' wife. Fuck the lot of you. I'm out of here and I'm on that plane tomorrow morning.' She picks up her handbag and, head high, flounces out of the restaurant through the dumbfounded diners. As she goes into the reception area, Michael is upset rather than embarrassed. Despite what he said about wanting to come back, he need never see any of these people again. As he watches her go, he thinks that with her lush body and too-tight clothes, she looks as out of place here as a whore at a hockey match. The hell with political correctness.

Quickly, as the buzz, low and shocked now, rises again around him, he calls for the bill. 'Everything all right, sir?' The eyes of the waiter do not flicker.

'Fine, fine!' Michael glances at the slip of paper then throws a few twenties on to the tablecloth. 'That should cover it, keep the change – I don't need a receipt.' Before the man can react, he hurries out after her.

On a kitchen chair, in his dressing-gown, Brian is sitting at Donny's computer, blasting a series of e-mails to EconoCar. Under different headings, VAT, weekly and monthly spreadsheets, repair, maintenance and general personnel rosters, he is leaving instructions as to how the company should run in his absence. He has included an instruction to Mick Dolan that he is to contact Nancy and have her turn up the following Monday. At least he can do something to please Sophie.

It is after nine o'clock and he has been at it for almost an hour with his tortuous, two-fingered pecking at the keyboard, now restored to its proper place. Although Donny's room still looks as though a hurricane has been through it, everything irreparable has been thrown out and, superficially at least, order has been restored. Donny himself is safely installed with the Jamesons.

Brian had not gone back to the office at all that afternoon. After the cemetery gates closed at half past four, he had walked slowly back to his car in the pub's car park, and had sat in it for a long time, pretending to be going through papers on his lap, just in case anyone thought he was casing the joint. In reality, he was trying to face up to his real life, to letting Sophie go, to letting his daughter go permanently. The Holy Angels plot in the cemetery had been the last straw, the sight of those gay, brave little icons had destroyed whatever defences he had left against his feelings of total loss.

It had been half past five before he could rouse himself to drive out into the rush-hour traffic. At least that was action, and the drink-induced stupor had lifted somewhat. His mobile had a hands-free set-up and he took advantage of the crawling pace to telephone Donny – telling him he was on his way home – and the office. Mick, of course, had peppered him with questions about Sophie, but Brian hoped he had been able satisfactorily to head them off at the pass.

Driving Donny to Trevor's house had been difficult. The boy was still on about coming to the island – and Brian was on the point of turning the car round, when his son finally decided to stick with the arrangements already made. Brian will never forget his white, anxious face, his too-careful tone: 'You will telephone me, Dad, the minute you get there?'

'I will. You have the number of the place if you want to call us?'

Donny had nodded. 'I can ring Aunt Sophie too, any time I want? Like, she knows the score, Dad?'

'Everything. She'll be expecting you to ring, she'll be ringing you too.' They were pulling up outside the Jamesons' house but before Brian turned off the engine he put a hand on Donny's shoulder. 'I can think of nothing to say that can make this any easier, son. I'm sorry. If you change your mind again, all you have to do is call us, or Aunt Sophie, or Uncle Michael, and you can be out there with us in twenty-four hours.'

'It's all right, Dad. I understand.' Donny, not flinching from his father's touch as he would normally, was gamely trying to be twenty years older than he is.

As soon as he got back to Marble Gardens, Brian, too tired even to make himself a snack, collapsed on the sofa in the sitting room. Even though his physique was usually robust enough to absorb quite an amount of alcohol without too much damage, the combination that afternoon of drink, emotional turmoil, fatigue and hunger had been lethal and, within minutes, he had fallen into a deep dark sleep.

He had woken a couple of hours later with a thundering headache and a queasy stomach.

Now, having attempted to subdue his hangover with a hair of the dog – hesitating between gin and more whiskey and plumping for the latter – teamed with what Eily calls a Dagwood sandwich, a monumental concoction of everything edible in the fridge squashed between two thick slices of bread, he feels slightly better. He finishes the last e-mail, presses the send button and, having waited for the outbox to clear, turns off the computer.

He stumbles into his bedroom, sets the alarm for six o'clock and crawls into bed.

Meanwhile, on their third last night in her flat – they have to be out by Saturday – Michael is slowly getting somewhere with Yvonne.

She is sulky but intrigued too. 'She'd really give me all that money?'

'Apparently so. She offered, Yvonne, I keep telling you.'

'I'll think about it.'

'Well, don't think about it too long, eh? She might change her mind. In the meantime, just come to work tomorrow as normal.' They are on her bed, she lying on her front with her face turned towards him, he sitting beside her. He risks giving her a playful slap on the bottom. 'I'm your boss now and I'll overlook your recent absences. No more leeway, no getting on any planes, OK?'

She doesn't respond to the slap. 'Not tomorrow anyway,' she says flatly. Then, tossing her head, she raises herself to a sitting position and looks him straight in the eye. 'I think I should meet her to hear this for myself. If I'm to consider giving her my baby, I'll have to see if she'll make a suitable mother. It's my decision, nobody else's.'

Inwardly, Michael quails, but outwardly remains cheery. 'Of course it's your decision. I'll set it up.'

On Palm Tree Island, Riba is desolate. She has had a message from Reception that Brian is coming tomorrow. She should call him, but what is the point? What can she say to him now? How can she tell him how badly she has screwed up?

She has to acknowledge, for the first time ever, that now he has every reason to be upset.

When she was admitted to the inner circle surrounding Jay, she had, as a matter of course, volunteered to help with the nuts and bolts essential to the work, giving up her evenings to deliver explanatory flyers house-to-house, in shopping centres and in the streets, becoming a recruiter when Jay came to Ireland to deliver lectures. She even took her turn to answer the constantly ringing telephone at his new headquarters at Portobello Harbour, which meant an inconvenient hike to the south side of the city. She saw this service as a privilege but Brian, whom she knew was barely tolerating this 'phase', as he called it, never made a secret of his resentment of her absences and constantly complained that she was being exploited.

Apart altogether from the substantive issue of Zelda being thrown off the property, she is dreading his I-told-you-so triumph, now so glaringly justified.

'I have news for you,' Michael is talking very quickly. 'She wants to meet you to discuss it.'

Sophie can hear traffic noises but this time she won't ask him where he is.

'Really?' The telephone receiver slips out of her hands because they are wet. She is also out of breath. She has been scrubbing out a corner of the bathroom, preparatory to fitting it out with her new darkroom equipment. A long length of thick black velvet is draped across the couch behind her, and Handyman Tony's business card is in the pocket of her jeans. She has already left a message on the fellow's mobile voicemail, asking him to telephone her with regard to a bit of plumbing and carpentry.

She scrabbles for the receiver on the floor. 'Sorry about that,' she says to Michael. 'I dropped the phone. So, tell me.'

'I'd prefer not to talk over the telephone. Can we meet to set it up? I could call in.'

'Certainly not, Michael. It's a quarter to ten and I was on my way to bed.' Sophie is damned if she is going to let her eagerness show. 'I'll meet you tomorrow somewhere,' she says coolly, 'you, or you and her together, it doesn't matter to me.'

'Can I call you again in the morning? I can't give you a time now until I know how busy we're going to be.'

'Fine.'

There is a brief silence on the line then: 'Sophie?'

Sophie hangs up quickly.

Her heart is thumping. He had sounded positive about the news. To curb her leap of excitement, she tests herself. *Be realistic, Sophie. Try to be honest. Would you be able to look into this baby's face without constantly seeking resemblances to Mizz Leonard, without remembering your own pain?*

The response to this is like looking into a crystal. Sophie can see the soft hair, the clean Baby-gro, the faint, sleeping smile, her own smile as she watches over the baby's cradle. This baby is its own person. Any baby is its own person.

Of course she will be able to look in this baby's face.

Please, dear God, make it possible.

A baby!

CHAPTER THIRTY-ONE

M ichael telephones at lunchtime and this time, although still urgent, the level of his voice is normal, the ambience that of the airport. 'Would tonight suit you?'

Again Sophie is breathless when she answers the phone. Frustrated by lack of contact from Handyman Tony, despite a second call to his voicemail, she had bought herself an electric drill that morning and has been trying to drill holes in the bathroom tiles so she could at least install a decent-sized shelf to hold the developing bath. 'What time?' she asks shortly.

'Seven o'clock. We could come there straight from work.'

That 'we' again – Sophie tenses but she stays calm. 'Make it seven thirty,' she says. 'There are a few things I have to do.' Not! she thinks, throwing the drill with great force on to the couch.

'Seven thirty it is.' Then his tone changes, becomes cautious: 'There's just one thing, Soph. When I told her about your offer I said the compensation would be about a hundred K. That's the figure she has in her mind.'

'That's not what I said. I mightn't get that much.'

'Of course you will. It'll be at least that. I'll talk to you about how to make that happen when the time comes. The reason I'm mentioning it is that you shouldn't leave her in any doubt. She has that figure in her mind, and if you say it's going to be any less, I have a feeling she mightn't buy it. Believe it or not, I'm on your side in this, Soph.'

'Goodbye, Michael.' Sophie slams down the receiver. How dare he coach her? Then the realisation of what might be agreed this very night hits her.

She picks up the discarded drill but her hands are shaking. Who would have thought it was so difficult to drill a few bloody holes? She had had ambitions to develop Zelda's photographs herself, but it looks like it's going to be good old One Hour Photo again.

In any case she is far too nervous to stay in the house so she puts away the drill and runs upstairs to change out of the old jeans she uses for grunt work, as Michael calls it. Used to call it. She must get accustomed to speaking and thinking of him in the past tense.

Once in the Mini, she finds it turns itself towards *Wild Places* as though on auto-pilot, but there is a shock in store: when she gets there, the premises are barred and bolted.

She has no keys – her work pattern had meant she never needed them because Imelda always held to rigid office hours. Where's Nancy? More than any other aspect of her new status, the fact that nobody thought fit to telephone her to tell her the clean-up was finished hits hard. This is the reality of unemployment. The 'guess what' factor – the glue of many marriages – kicks in and, reflexively, she reaches for her mobile to call Michael, but then remembers.

Eily is away and Brian is well on his way too – she pulls herself up for even thinking his name: he is strictly out of bounds.

It is hardly the kind of thing she can burble over the wires to her parents or brothers in the Antipodes because she will have to be in the whole of her health to ride out the inevitable reaction. Her mother and father are of the old school: a job should be pensionable and for life, and they had always worried about her *laissez-faire* attitude to hers. They will fret themselves sick about this – particularly as it will come on top of what she will have to tell them about her marriage. They will wonder what evil genie has been released over their daughter's head, since her last call had been to reassure them in the immediate aftermath of an air crash.

No, she won't bother them – or make things even more difficult for herself. She is due to call them again in a fortnight. Time enough then.

Her brothers? No, she doesn't have that kind of relationship with either of them.

The realisation that, actually, she has no one to call, or no one close enough, is upsetting. As Sophie stands there, she is lonelier than she has ever been in her life.

The day's post has been tucked neatly behind one of the ornamental security bars at eye-level and she extracts it. There are only five pieces, three for Imelda, one bearing the ominous Harp symbol of government – no doubt from the Revenue Commissioners – a flyer for Four Star Pizza and a circular to herself bearing the logo of the Whale and Dolphin Conservation Society. This group, based in Bath and often mentioned in her column, has kept her on its mailing list since its foundation in 1987, the year she joined *Wild Places*. She replaces Imelda's three letters, scrunches up the pizza flyer and puts it into a litter bin a few paces away, then gets back into the Mini.

She sits for a moment, staring through the windscreen. Where to now? On the spur of the moment, she calls Directory Enquiries, gets the number of her local V.E.C. office then telephones to ask if she is too late to sign up to one of the photography modules currently on offer. 'Well, you've missed two sessions.' The receptionist is helpful. 'But it's a beginner's course. Have you any experience?'

'Lots.' Sophie thinks of her Romanian women. 'I don't really need to know the basics. I'm more interested in learning how to develop and print.'

'Oh, that's brilliant – provided you don't mind paying for the two nights you didn't attend. Come along next Tuesday night. Seven o'clock, Coláiste Íde in Finglas. Do you know where that is?'

'I have a fair idea.' She gives the woman her name, address and telephone number then hangs up. Well, at least she's done something positive. And although she hardly dares think about this, freelance photography would dovetail perfectly with minding a baby.

No. No more wimpishness. She *will* dare to think about this from now on. She will expect it and plan for it. She races home and, with new resolve, cleans camera lenses and clears up the mess she had made earlier with the drill in the bathroom. This house will have to be baby-proofed: she makes a start by casting a critical eye over the electrical sockets in the living room, which will have to be covered. She moves elsewhere in the house, trying to see it from baby level, and finds that, except for the sockets, there are very few hazards; the rooms are clear of clutter and the floors, clean already, will be easily kept germ-free.

There is still quite a lot of time to fill before Yvonne is due, so she makes yet another trek into the city to leave the film of Zelda for developing. Throughout, she has maintained her clear sense of purpose.

By seven forty-five that evening, however, when there is still no sign of Yvonne and Michael, she is fit to be tried for manslaughter. Just as she is about to call his mobile, she hears footsteps approach the door and stop outside.

Sophie makes a conscious effort to stand very straight, and when the bell rings, she is composed as she walks to open the door.

The two of them, side by side. Very hard to bear. 'Come in,' she says. 'How are you, Yvonne?'

'Fine, thank you, Sophie.'

If Michael's ladyfriend is nervous, she is not showing it. Michael, on the other hand, is grey-faced, which feeds Sophie's courage. 'Would either of you like a drink, or a cup of coffee?' she asks, closing the door behind them.

In response, Yvonne turns and glares at her consort, who says that there is a match he wants to hear on Five Live on the car radio and, anyhow, it would probably be better if Sophie talked to Yvonne alone. This had obviously been pre-arranged between them but Sophie doesn't care one way or the other: his presence would give her one set of headaches, his absence another – there is no escaping the difficulties of this encounter. 'Whatever you say.' She walks directly to the sofa.

Reminded of how it was recently occupied by herself and Brian McMullan, she suffers a momentary twinge of conscience – she sure has some neck in taking the high moral ground at present – but it passes quickly because Yvonne crosses to sit in the chair beside the fireplace. She didn't even wait for the door to close behind him, Sophie thinks. In fact the girl seems as relaxed as though she owns the place.

Or does she? As they look at one another, each waiting for the other to speak, sizing each other up, Sophie thinks she can detect a flicker of uneasiness behind those heavily made-up eyes. This is borne out, because Yvonne is the one to crack first. 'Mick tells me you want our baby.'

Sophie is glad that at least there is to be no pussyfooting. 'From what I gather, it won't be that much of a hardship – you're not all that pushed about it – but, yes, I do. I've wanted a baby for years.'

'And you're prepared to give me a hundred thousand pounds. Is that right?'

'What I told Michael to offer you was everything I get in compensation.'

'But that'll be a hundred, right?'

'I'm sure it will. Maybe even more. We can draw up a legal agreement to that effect.'

Yvonne frowns. 'Do you not trust me?'

'I trust you. But do you trust me? I could back off, you know. It's always been my ambition to travel, especially to go whale-watching. Now is my chance. I might be having such a good time that I mightn't come back.' Wildly, Sophie chooses the most exotic holidays she can think of. 'Patagonia, for instance, is supposed to be a terrific place to see whales. And have you ever heard about the river dolphins in Nepal?'

The girl, who has probably never heard of Nepal, let alone Patagonia, is looking at her as though she is talking gibberish. Sophie pulls back. What has got into her? That was mean. She had not prepared what she was going to say to the girl and is pulling this red herring out of the air. She knows, from Nancy's breathless reading of the tabloids, that no matter what agreements have been made, birth mothers have all the rights, but is hoping that if at least there is a piece of paper between them it will make it more difficult for Yvonne to renege.

Michael's doxie gets up and walks around the living room, touching surfaces, examining the watercolour over the mantelpiece. Then she turns round, her expression challenging. 'I want the money now.' The nervousness, if it was ever there, is nowhere in evidence.

'But—' Sophie gazes back at the girl, whose mouth is now set in a tight, straight line. 'I don't know when I'll get it, Yvonne,' she says. 'These things take time and I haven't even put in a claim yet.'

'Not my problem. Get a loan.'

'I couldn't possibly get a loan for that much money – I've just lost my job.'

'But if you're so sure it's coming,' Yvonne shrugs, 'mortgage this house. With the way prices are going in Dublin, even a telephone box could be worth twice that. My friend, Collette, who knows a lot about property, says a house like this, so near to the city centre, has to be worth two twenty, at least.'

'When the baby is born—' It's out before Sophie knows it.

'No!' Yvonne stares, provoking her. 'Now.'

'Sorry. I'm not an idiot.'

'All right.' Yvonne tightens her lips. 'No skin off my nose.' She starts to walk towards the front door.

Panicked, Sophie stands up and addresses her back. 'Half the money now, half when the baby is born.'

This brings Yvonne round again and they stare at each other. Sophie, hating herself, is nevertheless driven by the goal in sight. 'We will definitely have to have a legal agreement if we do it that way, because what guarantee will I have that you won't just walk away with the first half of the money and keep the baby anyway?'

She pulls herself up short before she can say any more. What is she doing? She has descended to the level of a trader, bargaining over a tiny, defenceless *human*.

Then, albeit reluctantly, she has to admire the girl's spunk: Michael has probably bitten off more than he can chew. If his relationship with this girl has even the remotest possibility of surviving, there is no doubt in Sophie's mind as to who will be in charge.

She pulls herself up again. How patronising of her. 'I'm sorry,' she says sincerely. 'I really mean that. I'm not going to haggle like this. No good will come of it. It's a clean, clear offer, but it's your baby, yours and Michael's. And you hold all the cards, Yvonne. I want a baby, desperately, but no matter how badly I want this one, it's wrong to treat her as a commodity.'

'You think it's a girl?' This seems to get under Yvonne's skin. For the first time, her composure cracks a little. 'How do you know?'

'Slip of the tongue.' It had been far more: a careless betrayal of Sophie's own most secret wish. She had always wanted a daughter, a girl as gentle and intelligent as Zelda. She looks at the floor, then back at this odd young girl who seems to have nerves of steel. 'Michael would have to agree to this mortgaging,' she says quietly. 'We have joint ownership. And of course he'll be paying the mortgage until I get my money and can pay it off. Do you want to think about it, Yvonne?'

Even as she is saying it, there is a part of Sophie's brain that is amazed at her own behaviour. This is Yvonne Leonard, her husband's tart, yet here she is, talking to her in relatively polite tones instead of taking an axe to her over-bleached head. Although Sophie has always known that her childlessness cut deep, to discover quite how deep is a revelation. She would be prepared to yield everything she owns, her photographic equipment, her beloved Mini, her clothes; she would even sign over the house she loves, although caution dictates she should hold this option in reserve in case she needs it later. At the present moment, if Yvonne asked her to become her body slave, she would accede; she would sprinkle broken glass on the ground between herself and Yvonne Leonard and crawl across it on her belly if it would guarantee the delivery of this baby as her own.

'He'll agree all right.' Yvonne laughs. 'All right,' she says, 'it's a deal. Half now, half when it's born.' As she looks at Sophie, a peculiar expression darkens her light blue eyes. 'You know what this means, Sophie? This means you and me are going to have to get to know each other better.'

'I beg your pardon?' Sophie's breath gets caught somewhere in her throat.

Yvonne looks levelly at her. 'For instance, the kid might want to get to know me at some stage. Or I might even want to get to know it. Her. Him.' For a moment her eyes hood, then resume their determined cast. 'So you'll have to keep in touch with me. I've made up my mind now and that's definite – a kid is not on the agenda for me. Not now at any rate. But when I'm older, who knows what I'll feel? I have to protect my rights.'

All Sophie can think about is the baby. So near now. 'Whatever you say, Yvonne.' In these circumstances, she would be happy to make closer acquaintance with Madame Defarge.

But then a peculiar thing happens. Yvonne smiles, and this time she is relaxed. 'I've never had a tosser in my life,' she says now. 'I've never even won a bleedin' box of chocolates in a raffle. I can't believe this is happening to me. Did you say something about a drink? Will I go out and get him or will I leave him out there to stew in his own juice?'

Sophie tests for pain. This, after all, is the woman for whom her husband has abandoned her. But the excitement bubbling in her belly is threatening to erupt and although she is longing to be alone so she can allow it egress, as she looks at Michael's new woman something even more weird happens. She begins to think that the girl is not too bad. If they were closer in age and in different circumstances, they might even like each other. 'Your call, Yvonne,' she says evenly, trying to remain severe, or censuring, but she knows she has failed.

The loss of a marriage is not a light matter and there are many painful days ahead but, right here and now, Sophie feels she is floating and those bubbles will not be denied for much longer.

'Why don't we leave him out there?' she says, managing, just, not to sound girly. 'For a little while anyway. We have a lot to settle.'

Brian's plane is jumping around a little and with a *ping*! the captain comes on to reassure his passengers. Like all captains' voices, this one, rich with lazy, good-ole-boy inflections, exudes soothing bonhomie as it oozes through the PA: 'Ladies and gentlemen, we have – aah – some weather up ahead. We knew about it before we took off, of course, and as you probably know there's a series of systems coming in over the next few days, but this one changed direction quicker'n a polecat and we won't be able to get around it. We're still well within the envelope, but we may be bumped around a bit. So, buckle up tight now. I reckon we'll be on it in about five minutes. Ten minutes to landing, ladies and gentlemen.'

'Very droll!' Brian's seat companion's posture belies his words. As he tightens his belt, his knuckles whiten.

'They'd turn back or divert if it was really dangerous.' So profoundly tired that he is dizzy, Brian, in an inside window seat, turns his head to cut off further conversation.

'I suppose you're right.' His worried seatmate takes the hint and subsides.

Despite the captain's announcement, through the porthole the weather below seems blissful, the sun sinking over a calm sea gleaming from horizon to horizon beneath a sky that is just beginning to blush. For most people of his background, a trip to the Caribbean would have been the opportunity of a lifetime.

How will Eily react to his arrival? Although he has left messages, Brian has not spoken to her to say he is coming. She is unlikely to cause a scene, especially in front of Jay Street – not that he cares about *that* – but he feels as if his adultery is written large on his forehead. With her self-professed intuition, will Eily be able to read it?

'Hey, buddy, you're a little grey about the face. You feeling OK?'

'I'm fine.' Brian attempts to open his eyes but can't. He is feeling far from fine. He is swallowing repeatedly in an effort to keep his stomach from rising.

'Five minutes, folks.' The captain comes on again to repeat his instructions to 'buckle up tight now' and to give them the cheery news that this broken weather is to last for a few days before settling down again early the following week. 'So get out that sun-tan oil and have a good holiday. Thank you for choosing to fly with us. Appreciate the business.'

Brian grips his armrests as the aircraft begins its final descent, in long, stomach-churning swoops, swinging and bouncing simultaneously like a cork in white water. Over his head, the lockers creak and groan, as does the frame around the window beside his ear. He is afraid to open his eyes. All the terror of the crash is revisiting him as vividly as if it was happening. Lightning does strike twice. He sees that Arda logo spinning towards him . . . He was mad to do this.

Outside their bungalow, rain heavier than Riba has ever experienced is bouncing so hard off the sand that the whole beach seems alive, hopping and undulating like a swarm of dun-coloured jumping beans. She tries to fall back on habit, to tell herself to find something positive to enjoy in this, it is another new experience, something to tell her grandchildren. She is finding it difficult at the moment to raise enthusiasm for anything.

For one thing, their lovely Palm Tree sun, which announced itself so spectacularly on their first morning, had deserted the island sometime during the previous night and was replaced by this unrelenting rainstorm. Where is it all coming from? Riba had been led to believe that rain in the tropics was intermittent: you got your downpours but they didn't last long and were, in reality, your friends, serving to freshen and revivify the whole atmosphere.

Well, today, the friendship is strained. It hasn't stopped once, but has connected sky and earth with endless vertical strings that haven't even bent a little since there is no wind. Sometimes the torrent eases off to drizzle and the softer falls she is more used to – but since early morning, she hasn't caught even a glimpse of the offshore islet. And as for the liner out there, bigger and higher than the one from the day before, its size and splendour are irrelevant as it heaves in and out of the murk like a wistful ghost.

To add to her emotional woes, she is physically fed up and uncomfortable in the humid bungalow, with little to do except watch the restless grey sky and the streaming palm trees. 'You OK there, Zel?' She stands up and crosses to where her daughter is lying on her bed, face down, head turned away from the light. 'Need anything, a little drink, maybe?'

'No, thank you.' Zelda's voice is expressionless.

'I know.' Riba injects as much cheer into her tone as she can muster. 'I'll rub your back. Would you like that, darling?'

'I don't care . . .'

Taking this as acceptance, Riba bustles into the bathroom and gathers up her store of unguents. While she is helping her daughter out of her nightshirt, she cannot avoid reacting to the knobbed spine, the double row of ribs like broken piano keys. She has seen all of this before, of course, and it is always a shock, but something about the unrelenting rain and general gloom and greyness of the atmosphere is getting to her.

As are other things . . .

She switches on a lamp in the untidy bungalow, strewn with clothes, towels and redundant sun-protection potions. The yellowish glow helps a little, although not much because the wattage of the bulb is so low. Yet she is determined not to pass on her negative feelings and searches for her Strauss waltz tape, the most upbeat music she has brought. 'Are you comfortable, darling?' Again there is little response, but Riba allows herself to lift upwards with the music and begins gently to spread the fragrant oil over her daughter's emaciated back, being careful with the flesh, so translucently stretched over the bones that it feels as though it may tear at any moment.

Usually when she does something physical like this for Zelda, Riba benefits too, as her mind flows into the rhythm of her fingers. This time, as she begins gently to rub and to stroke, her consciousness refuses to move or to let go of its most recent images. All it wants to do is conduct endless, frightfully clear replays of yesterday's awful events. And rehearsals of how she is going to deal with Brian.

Thank God, this awful day of rain and disillusion is nearly over. But she knows that worse is still to come.

CHAPTER THIRTY-TWO

S ick, sore and sorry for himself, Brian is standing by a large hole in the filthy, unpainted wall through which the bags are falling piece by sodden piece. The hole is so big that, through the cloudburst deluging the Tarmac outside, he can observe the leisurely pace at which the plane is being unloaded. He and his fellow passengers had to race unprotected through the downpour, and in here the air is gagging, full of steam from their wet clothes and belongings. Normal conversation is impossible as above their heads the corrugated roof booms, warning like a Greek chorus of further disasters to come.

He turns to scan the small crowd waiting behind a rope at the far end of the arrivals shed. No sign of Eily, as far as he can see. However, even at this distance, he can read the bold black lettering on the placard being held high by one of two thin blonde Amazons towering over everyone around them.

WELCOME TO YOUR WEDDING FEAST, INGE AND RUDI,
MARGARET AND JOHN, SYLVIA AND JOHN

They could be twins, each wearing a skimpy halter top and skin-tight micro-shorts. They obviously speak English − Brian has forgotten to ascertain what the language is here − and it will certainly be easy to keep them in sight. If all else fails, he can ask them to help with a taxi or whatever.

Zelda, who had fallen asleep again minutes into the massage, whimpers a little and Riba rests her forehead in the rumpled space between her daughter's emaciated body and the edge of her bed. She takes the thin, limp hand and places it on her own neck as though to transfer a shaving of her own rude health. 'Dream well,' she whispers. 'See wide green fields and blue skies and angel's wings. I hope you see freedom from all this pain.' Something rises into her throat to choke her. 'And from me.'

She lets Zelda's hand fall, then replaces it on the back of her neck with both her own, and presses down so that her face digs into the sheets. 'But not too soon. Please, darling. Not yet – I'm not ready yet, I'll miss you so very much.' Although she is no longer whispering, her muffled voice is barely audible. 'I'm so sorry, Zeldy darling, I'm so sorry, please forgive me – I'm sorry.'

This is how Brian finds them when he pushes open the door of the bungalow.

He had been directed to it by the Bobbsey Twins, who, on being approached in the airport, had offered him a lift to the complex alongside their bemused but happy charges.

When he was let out at the entrance to the compound, Brian was so tired he had been beyond caring about the rain as he squelched along the walkway towards the bungalow with no thought or desire to seek shelter. He was even beyond apprehension. At least the bloody stair rods bouncing off his skull felt warm.

He stands for a moment on the threshold. Eily's face is turned towards him in bewilderment as though she has just woken up. She is kneeling beside one of the three beds in what seems to be the only room, and although the light from the single lamp wouldn't illuminate a rabbit hutch, he can tell she has been crying. In the bed, Zelda is lying on her back, her mouth slack. Her colour seems even more unhealthily waxen than it had been when he last saw her.

That open mouth, Eily kneeling, crying – Brian's suitcase thumps on the tiles. Is he too late?

He is not prepared for what happens next. Eily launches herself at him, throwing herself into his arms, sobbing like a wild thing. Although he can't understand her babbling, he thinks she is saying something about a carpet.

He can't bear it. Convinced that his daughter is dead, he shoves Eily away and rushes to Zelda's bed.

When he finds she is breathing, relief unmans him, spreading nauseously through his stomach and chest and draining what remains of his strength. He sits heavily on the bed, waking her. 'Dad! What are you doing here?'

'Didn't Mum tell you? No, I don't suppose she did. I've come to take you home, sweetheart.' He cannot let her see how upset he is so he drags himself to his feet again and crosses to Eily's position near the door where he has spotted a light switch and reaches around her to activate it. 'This dump is like an underground cave, for Christ's sake, let's get some light in here.'

When he throws the switch, a fan starts up in the ceiling, pushing the wet air around, but as the general level of illumination in the room increases – although not very much – he is shocked to see the lines and wrinkles on Eily's grief-ravaged face. He has not noticed before that she has become old. Or older than he customarily sees her. As he looks at her his anger ebbs away. He takes her into his arms and hugs her. 'For Christ's sake, quit with the waterworks, will you, Eily? You know I can't hack it.'

He releases her and steps back a little. 'Is it always like this in this bloody place? There's enough water here inside and out to provide electricity for a small town.'

'It's not always like this.' Zelda has struggled into a sitting position. 'Yesterday was a peach of a day here, Dad. It was nice, really. It did us both good, didn't it, Mum? I think I even got a little bit of a tan.'

Her loyalty further enfeebles Brian, draining from him the last of his anger. 'What was that about a carpet, Eily? You were trying to say something to me there about a carpet?'

'We've been swept under the carpet.' Eily hiccups, then says, in a rush, 'We're being sent away, they don't want us here because they're having a wedding feast. Zel has to go into a hospital tomorrow. It's awful, Brian, I'm so sorry.' She leans against the wall and starts to weep again.

'Mum, please don't cry.' Zelda, distressed, stumbles out of bed and goes across to her mother.

'Let's all calm down, shall we?' Brian, feeling as stiff as a tree, sits in the nearest chair. How can he rescue this? What can he do? His plan was to descend on this place, sort out Jay Street and bear his wife and child home on the first available flight.

His tired brain wrestles with itself. It is split many ways, with affection for his wife, guilt for what he and Sophie have done, continuing confusion about his feelings for her, and debilitating terror about the days to come with Zelda.

It is against Brian's nature, however, not to take some action.

'Don't worry. We'll see you soon.' Sophie hangs up. She glances at the carriage clock: five past seven. Five past three o'clock in the morning over there. He had sounded calm as he had asked her to take Donny out to the island. Today, or as soon as possible. Zelda, he had said, wasn't up to coming home just now and he had promised his son that he would do this if he thought it appropriate.

At least she doesn't have to break the news to Donny herself. He'd said he'd do that. He had given her a name and the home number of a friend of his in Aer Lingus: 'Aer Lingus is good at pulling out the stops in this kind of family emergency. Don't worry about the cost, ask him to invoice EconoCar. Roger'll know what to do and he'll organise that too.'

'Are you all right, Brian? How are you coping?'

'I'm fine. I'm so tired I can't think, of course, but I'm really fine.' His tone had told Sophie he didn't want to discuss himself any further. 'Sorry to have left you so little time, but I didn't want to wake you too early and then I couldn't find anyone to open this blasted reception desk.'

'We've plenty of time,' she says quietly. 'Don't worry.'

He had then given her the number of the complex, asking her to leave a message detailing the flight arrival time. 'His passport is in the drawer of the table beside my bed, in case he forgets.'

'I'll remember.'

'And you'll need US dollars. I'll ring Mick, ask him to meet you in Departures with them.'

'Fine, Brian. It'll be fine. I'll get us there.'

'I'm sorry. I'm just knackered, that's all.' Then he had hesitated. 'I'm sorry about asking you to do this, Sophie, but it would be too much for Donny on his own. I know there are all kinds of reasons you wouldn't want to come here.'

'Don't, Brian.'

'Thank you.'

Sophie is firm: it is not appropriate now to dwell on such things. She said goodbye – in that sense – to Brian McMullan in the pub. Her relationship with him now is as a friend. That is more important than any aberrant flight of fancy. It always is.

In any event, she has the most important relationship of her life to look forward to and to plan for now. Despite her fear that something may go wrong and that plans may derail, last night's incredulous joy still fills her, overcoming all other feelings, even foreboding about the trip to Palm Tree Island in such circumstances – she had not been able to sleep because of its bubbling.

It is still pitch dark but at least it is still and quiet outside. The weather forecast is for a bright, sunny day and she had planned meticulously how she was going to spend it. Her first port of call was to have been her bank, to get the mortgage application forms; her second was to have been a secret treat – a visit to the layette department at Arnott's in Henry Street.

She will have to trust Michael to keep Yvonne quiet and to begin the necessary processes with the bank. Although as joint owner, she will have to sign, he is the one who will have to get the mortgage. He will do it, she has no doubt about that – although she would love to have been a witness to the scene in his car as they drove away from the house when Yvonne broke the news to him. She can imagine his shocked reaction – but also Yvonne's steely gaze. Given what her husband has done to her, she should be feeling triumphant at this comeuppance, but, oddly, for a moment or two, Sophie even feels sorry for Michael. It will put him to the pin of his collar to make repayments on a mortgage of a hundred thousand pounds, even if it is only temporary.

How will she feel if Yvonne, who is in ultimate control of this situation, changes her mind or has a miscarriage, or even an abortion The worst thing of all would be if, having handed the baby over, the girl took it back before the adoption was finalised.

She mustn't think about that. She has manoeuvred all she can and from now on the task will be to move as calmly as possible from day to day. It is probably a good thing that she has the distraction of the trip to the Caribbean.

She picks up the telephone again to call this Roger.

Only a few hours to go before the ambulance calls to take them to the hospital. It is well past dawn now and bars of sunlight have crept through the slatted shutters on to the end of Riba's sheet. Quietly, she turns her head to look across from her own bed to Brian's and sees nothing but the top of his head above his mounded back. It is impossible to tell whether or not he is asleep. He has been in and out of bed all night; she has watched him go across several times to check on their sleeping daughter and at one stage he had even left the bungalow altogether, returning half an hour later and getting back into bed without a word.

They will have it out sooner or later, but how is she going to confess, to humiliate herself so thoroughly? How will he react? And wouldn't he have a right to be furious? Guilt at what she has inflicted on their daughter gnaws at Riba's soul.

Dear God, please, please let it not be too bad. She casts around for something with which to barter. *I'll go to Lough Derg, I'll go to Lourdes, I'll go to Knock, Fatima, Medjugorje, anywhere, anything, God. Anything. Just don't make it too upsetting – I know I don't deserve it, but please don't make it too upsetting.*

She is sitting on one of the plastic chairs outside the bungalow, watching the activity around the complex, the stretching, the jogging on the spot, the swimming – it's not Jay this time, thank God – when Brian, wearing only boxer shorts, emerges. 'Good morning.' Curtly.

'Good morning.'

He strides down to the sea and, the sun lighting fires in his hair, thrashes like a huge, wounded fish through the water. That's her Brian. Bull in a china sea.

Then the realisations start trickling in. Is he her Brian any more? Does he want to be her Brian? She wouldn't blame him if he threw her away.

When, blowing and panting, he comes out of the water, he stops in front of her chair. 'Are there any proper towels? I didn't bring any.'

'I'll get one.'

Having checked in passing on Zelda – who is still peacefully asleep – she returns with one of the beach towels and moves to dry off his back with it, but he grabs it from her and moves out of her range, scrubbing furiously at his chest as Riba, chastened, watches. By any standards he is still a fine-looking man, with good buttocks and firm skin; his legs and arms are muscular, his paunch small, even endearing, and his twenty-four hour beard, which he always shaves very closely, shows itself in the sunshine to be a bright, Viking red.

'Can we talk?' she asks tentatively.

'What about?' His expression is inscrutable. 'What's left to say? We're not together any more, Eily, as a couple should be. We haven't been for years. It's serious.'

'I know, you're right,' Riba's tone is humble, 'but please?'

After a brief hesitation, he sits, thumping so awkwardly on to the flimsy plastic chair that she fears it may break under his weight. He gets his bearings, looking up and down the crescent of houses then out to sea where this morning's anchored cruise ship, a small one this time, is flowering into unhurried life. 'What happened to your ankle?'

Riba looks down at it. She has wound a bandage round it. 'Nothing much. I just stepped heavily on it.'

He looks back out to sea.

'Always wanted to do that.'

'What?' She is thrown by another change of subject.

'Go on a cruise. Maybe some day.'

Although she has noticed the absence of herself in his wish, she takes his calm tone as a sort of olive branch. 'I've been watching them,' she says eagerly. 'A new one comes every morning. Very early, I think, when it's still dark. Wouldn't you love to know what that other little boat is bringing out to it?' They both watch as a cargo-heavy dinghy makes slow, whining progress towards the gleaming sides of the liner, at whose rail stand two tiny figures, clad in white.

'Yes,' he says quietly, 'that must be the life, where everything, even the holiday, comes to you, so!'

He turns to her and she blanches under the coldness of his stare. 'What gives, Eily? And no bullshit, please.'

She knows better than to try to elicit any sympathy so, as candidly as she can, leaving nothing out, she flays herself with the sequence of events since she and Zelda first arrived on Palm Tree Island. Oddly, during the telling – of Jay's rejection, of her tardy acceptance that she had erred in stubbornly dragging Zelda out there – she begins to feel a little better. 'However,' she says, at the end, 'with the exception of this time, you've got to admit that the organisation has been very good for me in general.'

'No, it hasn't!' His tone brooks no further argument. Throughout her sorry narrative he has not looked at her once, but has stared at the cruise ship, now lowering a net to take up the supplies from the dinghy that has pulled alongside. He turns to look at her and his expression is pitiless. 'It's over, Eily. You'll have nothing more to do with this shyster and his gang, or you won't have me.'

He leans towards her with a penetrating, angry gaze, ticking off what is going to happen. 'One: there's no point in me going on about Zelda and the damage you've done to her. I accept that, at some Neanderthal level, you thought you were doing the right thing. It's done now and there's nothing for it but to move her to this American clinic you've talked about. She's certainly too weak at the moment to face a return trip to Ireland, although I'll see about that in consultation with whatever doctors are there. I assume that, like me, you would prefer for her to die in Ireland than in this godforsaken place?'

She gasps. The starkness of it acts like a pile-driver against her chest but Brian, ignoring her reaction, continues without pity.

'Two: if you refuse to sever your ties with this organisation, I'll see you in court, where I'll fight you for custody of Donny, also on maintenance or alimony or whatever they're calling it these days. I believe I will have good grounds to do so, despite what normally happens.'

'Three: you will not interfere when I tell Mr Street that he is not getting a penny from us for his so-called services and accommodation. Not one penny.'

As she gasps again he leans even further forward, in danger of toppling off the flimsy chair. His voice shakes with passion as he asks, 'Do you agree to all of this?'

'Yes.' Riba does not hesitate. She couldn't fight him if she tried.

He has not finished. 'One more thing. Do you want to be married to me, Eily? To me – a flesh and blood person?'

'What kind of question is that?' She is astounded at the change in direction.

'It's the kind of question I should have asked you years ago.' He sits back into his chair and his expression covers over. 'I repeat, Eily, do you want to be married to me? Not just to be a married woman with all that implies, but to have me as your husband. That implies equality, not sameness, of course, or compromise and bargaining, but real partnership. You don't seem to take my views into account in the slightest.' Riba opens her mouth to deny this but he holds up a hand. 'Think, please, before you answer, because what you say could be crucial.' He pauses for a moment, watching her. 'Take your time. What does marriage to me mean to you?'

'I – I suppose it means strength and security, and knowing where I am in the world, in society.'

'Good answer. But it's still about you and your status. It doesn't say anything specific about me, about who I am or where I fit into your life, as a particular Brian McMullan not just as a generic husband. I notice you don't say anything about love.'

'That's taken for granted, surely.'

'Is it? Why should it be taken for granted? Why should you, for instance, assume that I still love you?'

Riba's sky, for so many years so blithe and sheltering, crazes over her head. It will soon start to disintegrate, to shower her with sharp, lethal triangles that will cut her into millions of tiny pieces. 'You don't love me any more?'

'I didn't say that. What I am saying is that maybe it's time you thought a little about me, about us, about our marriage. Do you love me, for instance?'

'Of course I do.'

'Why "of course"? What have you – or I for that matter – done lately to prove or to show that, for each of us, the other is all that matters? If I did leave you, Eily – for instance, for another woman – would you care? I know you'd be upset initially, and there would be financial considerations, but deep down, where it should matter, in the long run, would it have much of an impact on the way you conduct your life day to day?'

The pieces are beginning to slash. 'Another woman? What's all this about, Brian?'

He stands up. 'You know exactly what it's about.' He looks down at her and, compassionately at last, puts a hand on her shoulder. 'I would like you to think honestly about these things, Eily. Please. We could both have died in that plane crash and it's made me think, so it's probably made you think too. Let's at least be straight with each other. I meant it when I said you should take your time. I'm not going to push you for an answer, but when I get one, it had better be the truth.'

CHAPTER THIRTY-THREE

The ambulance, staffed by crisply uniformed, relaxed paramedics, is a converted Lincoln Continental saloon with heavily tinted windows; the rear seats have been replaced by a bench seat and a gurney that face each other across a narrow aisle. The vehicle bristles with equipment and monitors, cunningly fitted to maximise the limited space.

As Zelda, too weak to be anything but compliant, is helped into it out of the harsh noonday sunlight, Riba is shocked. Her conscience reels. The improvement she had seen, or thought she had seen, has relapsed – if it had ever taken place.

At the same time she is secretly relieved that the burden is now spread, as she recognises the immensity of the hardships involved in fighting the world as a lone gladiator. Even this morning she had continued to rationalise, telling herself that Brian, for instance, as Zelda's father, had not been properly engaged until now, and neither had anyone else. But her beleaguered heart, having suffered so many blows since arriving on the island, could take no more and had cried, 'Stop!'

As always, Riba gives full measure and her capitulation is virtually total in that now she has swung to co-operating fully with Brian, with California Monica, with the medics, with everyone and anyone who has decided to put in twopenceworth.

She daren't analyse her feelings about Jay – her disillusion and hurt are still too new and raw – and she has no idea how she is going to react when she sees him again, especially in front of Brian.

As for Brian, who knows what he will do?

'Room for one more inside.' With Zelda settled under a blanket on the padded gurney, one of the paramedics smiles at her charge's parents. 'So, who's coming with us?' Her accent is pure honey, southern United States.

'You go, Eily,' Brian says immediately. 'I'll sort things out here. I'll get a taxi, catch up with you at the clinic.'

'Fine.' Riba forbears to enquire what 'sorting out' he has in mind and in many ways she would rather not know. As the paramedic closes the door of the Lincoln, she sees him turn and go back into the bungalow very quickly, without waiting for their departure and as though he is in a tearing hurry. What does the future hold for her with this husband?

Although he is trying not to jolt his passengers, taking his vehicle slowly over the ruts and potholes, the ambulance driver cannot avoid them altogether and his vehicle sways and rollicks on its luxurious springs. Clutching Zelda's bag of medication with one hand, Riba holds on to the edge of her seat with the other.

'Are you comfortable, darling?' She leans across the narrow aisle to whisper softly into Zelda's ear.

'I'm fine, Mum.' Zelda's lips, bluish in the glare of the neon striplight above her head, barely move.

Riba leans across to one of the paramedics, who is trying to note something on a form clipped to a board. 'How long before we're there?'

'Less than ten minutes, ma'am – you're from Ireland? I always wanted to go to Ireland. I hear it's real green – do you know the Corrs?'

'Your daughter OK?' One of the Bobbsey Twins was on duty behind the reception desk when Brian went there to organise a taxi.

'She'll be grand, thank you.' He had no desire to continue talking, and went outside to wait. It seemed to take a century, however, before the taxi, decrepit, tooting the opening bars of the march from *The Bridge Over the River Kwai*, pulled into the compound. By the time it came, he was in rag order and sweating hard. The air outside the air-conditioned reception bungalow was as moist as the mist over an Irish bog.

Fifteen minutes after climbing into the taxi, Brian is wishing he had walked. He is clutching his stomach as the vehicle, chassis cracking off the uneven ground and *Kwai* blaring repeatedly, finally makes it to the straggling, unpaved street of what is obviously 'town'.

He cannot stand to be in the vehicle a moment longer and tells the driver he will walk the rest of the way. 'Whatever you say, man.' The cab squeals to a halt on the crown of the road. 'You can't miss it, it's the big round building, all pink.' Having accepted the five-dollar bill Brian offered him, the driver chugs away, dust swirling after him.

Brian bats at the swarm of flies that dive-bombs his head and face. Squinting into the debilitating glare and taking in the streetscape, he is shocked at the contrast between here and the sanitised – if jerry-built – complex he has just left. Although he can see a few proper concrete buildings, most of the open-fronted shops and houses have been constructed of wood or corrugated tin; some even look suspiciously like cut-up cargo containers. Almost all are raised on flimsy-looking wooden stilts, bark still attached. The confrontation with Eily is still rumbling around in his brain, but for some reason is causing him little pain. Throughout their marriage, Brian has always felt anxious after rows, so much so that within hours Eily could expect to see him arriving home with a bunch of roses, eager to fix things between them. He would be worried about her upset. Yet now he feels nothing.

Similarly, in the aftermath of the conflict in the hospital corridor in Dublin it had not even crossed his mind to make amends for the rotten things he had said.

He had meant every word both then and this morning, and she thoroughly deserved a tongue-lashing, but that isn't the problem. Although he hates himself for this, he doesn't give a toss any longer how Eily feels.

Could his marriage have died without him noticing?

Unbidden, the memory of Sophie's scent under his chin as he embraced her for the last time in the conservatory of the Glasnevin lounge bar puffs against his cheek. *Stop this immediately.*

He looks up as the sky darkens. It is going to piss again. Great. God bless the Caribbean.

'He'll be here shortly, I'm sure of it – we could ring the compound if you like, but I'm sure he'll have already left.' Riba smiles at the girl behind the admissions desk, made of pale, polished wood.

The girl, as blonde as California Monica but about half her height, smiles back. 'Not to worry, Mrs McMullan, there's no rush. I'm sure Zelda would like to get into bed, though.'

'She would.' Riba, who is supporting Zelda on the chair beside hers, tightens her grip.

The clinic girl smiles and goes back to her keyboard.

Riba's smile fades. They have been waiting for the best part of three-quarters of an hour in this large, cool space, filled with glossy plants in matching pots, and despite her outward calm, she is increasingly desperate about their plight. She has no idea how Brian is going to sort things out and her confidence that he will is wavering. She should have mentioned the insurance situation in that note to him so at least he knew about it and wouldn't come into it cold.

She is also on the back foot because the admissions girl had asked for Zelda's charts and medical notes – which, of course, she does not have. But the girl had been soothing: 'Don't worry, ma'am, we can get them on e-mail.'

Where *is* Brian? She hopes nothing has happened to him, like a taxi accident, because outside the weather has changed with extraordinary speed. One minute it was bright, the next the world had darkened and, like sets of relentless little hammers, rain was pounding at the manicured lawn. Through the double – or triple – glazing the cloudburst is eerily silent, however, giving the impression that the climate outside has little or nothing to do with anyone or anything in here where the tick of the girl's keyboard, the chuckle of the water feature and the whisper of the air-conditioning speak of ease and airy comfort.

Riba is far from comfortable. Of immediate concern is that Zelda, whose antibiotic regime is crucial, is due another set of tablets about now. 'Would it be all right if I took her out to the lobby and let her rest on one of the couches out there?' she asks. 'I need to get some water for her medication.'

The blonde girl hesitates. 'I don't know, Mrs McMullan, I'll have to check. We do like the patients to be admitted and go to their rooms – I'm sure your husband won't be much longer – I can get the water from the cooler for you if you like.'

'I'll just take her out anyway.' The subtext of the receptionist's words is clear, *We don't want grubby people cluttering up our nice ambience*, but Riba has had enough, and before the girl can further respond, she is helping Zelda gently to her feet. 'I'll leave all this here with you, all right?' She indicates the sheaf of forms to be filled in, on top of which is an invoice for the hundred dollars they have already run up in ambulance charges.

She is settling Zelda into one of the couches in the wide, plush lobby when she hears the automatic entrance doors swish open behind her, letting in the drumming of the rain. She looks over her shoulder. Thank God. It is Brian at last, as wet as though he has swum here.

Forty-five difficult minutes later, Zelda is at last in her room. The powers that be in the American clinic, PTI, had been unimpressed by appeals, arguments, anger, or long-distance telephone conversations with the international helpline of the Voluntary Health Insurance Board of Ireland. The CEO had been polite but firm: 'We're a small facility, Mr McMullan, self-financing. Our medical staff and equipment are of the highest calibre. Unfortunately your Irish health insurance is far below what we can accommodate. But if you have a major credit card . . .' Brian had no option but to hand over his company American Express card. Only then did a wheelchair materialise for Zelda and the smooth mechanisms of the clinic click into action.

Now, while their daughter is being connected to a saline drip, Riba and her husband sit in armchairs outside her room as an elderly man in a silk dressing-gown makes painful progress past them along the carpet with the aid of a Zimmer frame and a gently cheerleading nurse. Brian makes no effort to keep his voice down. 'Have you any idea how much this will cost, Eily? How could you have been so stupid?'

'There is nowhere else to move her to.' Riba's feelings of guilt are overridden by alarm. 'This is probably the only decent hospital on the island.'

'You're Irish?' The nurse accompanying the elderly man stops beside them.

'Yes, we are.'

'I thought so.' The nurse, in her thirties, allows her patient to rest for a moment. 'I'm from Liverpool, I did my training in Beaumont and I still have a lot of friends in Dublin. I'm sorry, but I couldn't help overhearing – are you in trouble here? Can I help?'

Miracles do happen, Riba thinks, half an hour later, although this time, she doesn't attribute this one to Jay Street or to her erstwhile colleagues in the organisation.

'I'll keep an eye,' the nurse had said. Having shepherded her charge back to his room, and then gone into Zelda's for a little while, she had come back to Brian and Eily saying that what Zelda seemed to need was monitoring and nursing care rather than the high-tech wizardry of the clinic. 'I understand that her stats are good. So, at this stage, anyway, she seems to be stable. She could stay here for the night, then I would suggest that tomorrow she could be moved.'

'To where?' Brian had asked cautiously.

'There is a smaller facility on the outskirts of town, an old folks' home.'

'An old folks' home?' Riba had been incredulous. 'Never!'

'It's not what you think, honestly, nothing like what you'd get in the British Isles. It's more of a convalescent home. The ratio of staff to patients is one and a half to one. We routinely send people of all ages there and it's a nice cheerful place, run by an ex-pat colleague of mine from Scotland. I can recommend the care there. It has wonderful gardens and great views, right beside the sea. It's the kind of place I'd go to myself! Even for a holiday.' She had lowered her voice. 'You probably don't want to think about money at such a stressful time but the bills do mount up and the accommodation charges at St Rita's are less than a third of what they are here.

'Think about it.'

This latter day Florence Nightingale had then offered to drop in regularly on 'home' visits until—

'Well, until she's stronger,' she had said tactfully, refusing point-blank to accept payment. 'My mum died in a hospice and I always said I'd pay back some day.'

After she had left, Brian and Eily had argued. Brian had won. And when they had broached the subject with Zelda herself, she had raised no objections.

Donny and Sophie are racing for their flight to Caracas. Brian's friend, Roger, had come up trumps and the crew of their Aer Lingus flight had been told of their situation: although their flight was delayed, they have been plucked off the 767 at Kennedy in New York by another member of the airline's staff, who is now driving them on an electric buggy through a labyrinth of byways directly to the gate. 'Don't worry,' she shouts over her shoulder, 'we'll make it all right. They're expecting us – they're still boarding.'

'You OK, Donny?' Sophie, holding tight to the armrest of her seat, glances at him.

'I'm fine, thank you, Aunt Sophie.'

He had been very quiet throughout the transatlantic flight and she had let him alone. When she had first spoken to him this morning, she had brought up his disappointment about Anfield but he had interrupted her: 'It's nothing, Aunt Sophie. Anfield will still be there.'

It had been such a prematurely adult thing to say. God alone knows what faces the poor kid when they get to the island. Brian had been calm, of course, but having ascertained that Zelda was still alive, she hadn't questioned him about why he was flying them out there so urgently. Bizarrely, what pops into her head now is the old Irish *piseóg* she had not heard since she was a child: *One dies, one is born . . .*

Michael had bitten the bullet when she had telephoned him, immediately after she had talked to the Aer Lingus guy. Although, knowing him so well, she could tell that he was still in shock about the re-mortgaging, he had not gone on about it, and had met them in the departures area to give her the US dollars. 'It's the least I can do. Let me know what happens, Soph.'

'I will. Would you do a few things for me, Michael? Would you mind ringing Imelda to tell her what's happened? She's been on my conscience and I promised her lunch. Would you also ring this number,' she passed over a page hastily torn out of a notebook, 'and tell the secretary that Donny won't be able to keep his appointment with the consultant. On the other thing,' she had glanced at Donny but he didn't appear to be listening, 'you'll go to the bank as soon as possible? And will you ring a solicitor for me? Any of them, it shouldn't be hard, they're advertising this no-foal-no-fee thing all over the place.' She had handed over the bundle of forms and letters that had been piling up on the telephone table.

'Sure thing,' he took the whole lot, 'and if there's anything else I can do . . .'

'Good luck with your own life. Sorry for burdening you with all of this.' Sophie, glad he was being so co-operative but sensing he was a little too eager, wanted to head off any false expectations he might have. 'Thank you, Michael,' she said then, meaning it.

He had seemed to take the hint and backed off, wishing them a good trip, despite the circumstances. Then he had left them to the care of the Aer Lingus supervisor, who had been hovering nearby to take them into a lounge.

It had felt odd to be dealing with him in such a rational, almost formal manner after what they had been through. A crisis put everything else into perspective for everyone, of course; in her own case, the significance of her short-lived affair had shrunk a little more with each half-hour as the miles between Dublin and New York ticked over.

She might have a few sticky moments when she sees Brian, she thinks now, but that is unavoidable and she no longer dreads meeting Eily as much as she did. Sophie is hoping now to be of some help.

They make the gate just as the check-in clerk is counting the boarding cards. There is a brief kerfuffle between herself and the Aer Lingus staffer, who shakes hands with both of them, wishes them a good journey and drives away in her buggy. For some reason, Sophie is unnerved by the sight of the familiar green uniform retreating into the distance. 'Well,' she says to Donny, as the clerk clicks busily on her computer, 'so far so good.'

'Mmm.' He is shuffling his feet and she can sense his fear and loneliness. In one of her bags, Sophie carries the photographs she has taken of Zelda; even with the rush, she had managed to detour into town, getting the taxi to wait for her then take her directly to the airport. The girl is beautiful in some but in the couple of close-ups taken at the beginning of the session the lens has been cruel. She will keep these, but will not show them either to Zelda's parents or to Donny. She had planned to show the 'good' ones to Donny at some stage during the trip but had changed her mind because even they might upset him.

Looking at him now, shifting and mooching around, Sophie is at a loss. It is one thing to baby-sit or to offer a listening ear, quite another to be in sole charge of a child at such a crucial time. Well she had better get used to it – in her diary is the name and telephone number of a social worker attached to the Adoption Board. This too she had managed to secure during her dash, although she hadn't actually had time to make the call for an appointment. She could telephone from her room on the island.

At the thought of the baby, a thrill, keen as an icicle, shoots through Sophie's body. The sensation is so physical she feels everyone around her must have noticed something happen. She must have jumped, surely? But no. The clerk is still busy. Donny is still shuffling. Everything is just the same.

Both she and Donny sleep on the five-hour flight from New York to Caracas. Despite this, Sophie feels as though she has been through a mangle as their island-hopper takes off for the second and final leg of its round of the archipelago. She has lost track of the time.

She sees Brian on the instant they come into the arrivals hall, which is a sort of shed, really. It would be impossible to miss him, since he is considerably larger and blonder than anyone else in the small crowd corralled behind a rope at the far end of the room.

Since she and Donny have only hand baggage, they could go straight through Immigration and Customs, but suddenly unsure she will be able to handle this coolly, she lets Donny go ahead while pretending to be rooting for her passport. She apologises to the Immigration official who, wreathed in cheerful smiles, tells her to take her time. All the while she is conscious that Brian, hugging his son, is standing only yards away. When she is sure she has relaxed sufficiently, she 'finds' the passport and walks through.

Brian lets Donny go. 'Hello, Sophie, thank you very much for this,' and then, to Donny, 'before you ask, she's in a hospital here. It's a good place, they're taking care of her. She knows you're coming and she's very happy about that. Mum is with her and says she's sorry she can't be here to meet you.'

'OK, Dad. Thanks for bringing me.' Donny's face is white. 'Are we going there straight away?'

'No need, son. Unless you really want to?' He includes Sophie in this. 'She'll be sleeping – she spends a lot of her time sleeping. You people need some rest too. We'll go up there tomorrow at the crack of dawn.'

'OK, Dad. Whatever you say.'

'Come on,' Brian takes Sophie's bags, overnight and camera, out of her hand, 'we've managed to get you a room on your own. I hope you'll be comfortable, although the humidity is devilish. I'll never give out about Irish weather again. Thanks again, Sophie – how was the journey?'

'Long!' Sophie attempts to smile as they start for the exit, but she is so tired it seems that her face muscles are not working properly. Her fatigue is working to her advantage, however, in that Brian's proximity is causing her little stress.

'Sorry about Anfield,' Brian says now to Donny. 'I'll make it up to you.'

'Anfield is *nothing*.' Donny pulls ahead as they go through the doors.

Outside, he asks if he can sit in the front seat of the taxi. There seems no reasonable way to refuse this so Sophie and Brian find themselves bumping along together in the back. Both sit well tucked into their respective corners and pass the first five minutes of the trip in silence. Determined to behave as normally as possible, Sophie concentrates on the terrain, although there is little to see at present, just water glistening under the moon to her left and to her right, behind the roadside trees picked up in the taxi's headlights, nothing at all. Probably a forest. She realises Brian is looking at her and turns her head. 'Listen,' he says quietly, with an eye on Donny, 'I'm sorry, but I never got to tell Eily about your situation at home.'

'You mean Michael and Yvonne?' It stings to couple the names yet to Sophie it feels strangely therapeutic too, as though the more the situation is acknowledged and bruited, the more real it will become and the quicker the hurt will ease.

He is watching her carefully. 'The whole thing,' he says, 'the whole thing . . .'

Meaning you and me, she thinks. Aloud, she reassures him, tells him that it's a good thing he hasn't burdened Eily with it, that Eily has enough on her plate. In the darkness she cannot decipher what is behind his expression. Is it relief that she is not going to create a scene with his wife? Regret for what might have been? *Stop it, Sophie. You are behaving like a bloody schoolgirl.* 'So,' she says as calmly as she can manage, 'tell me about Zelda.'

When the taxi pulls up at the compound, which seems to be right on the sea, the place is ablaze with festive light and activity. 'What's going on?' As Sophie gets out, her nostrils are assaulted with a strong, exotic combination of scents: smoke from tar and wood, roasted meat, unfamiliar spices and heavy perfumes, maybe incense. Perhaps even something that Sophie remembers from her days going to parties where joints were being passed round.

The tar component is coming from dozens of blazing torches, set into the sand in groups of three all along the water's edge, providing most of the light and also a fatal attraction for hundreds of moths and other insects whirligigging around the flames. There are two steel bands, one at each side of an open area in front of the cottages; these are playing – probably – the same repetitive but noisy tune, the enjoyment and enthusiasm of the musicians making up for any lack of musicality.

In the grassy space between the bands and a massive buffet table, laden with meat, fruit, jugs and bottles, there are perhaps a dozen young and

not-so-young couples wildly jigging and gyrating around a set of decorated arches. And a number of women, mostly blonde, thin and very fit,
are dancing with each other.

'It's this wedding-feast thing.' Brian is getting out the other side. 'He's
marrying a bunch of loonies like himself tomorrow. Tonight is the
pre-nuptial feast, apparently.'

Sophie remembers the advertisement from the *Inner Door*. In other
circumstances this would have been a wonderful opportunity to test her
photographic skills. 'Have you met him yet?'

'No. I asked for him earlier this afternoon but I was told he was away
for the day. I'll get to him tomorrow, never fear.'

CHAPTER THIRTY-FOUR

During the night, Sophie wakes, heart thumping, to the sound of huge roaring outside her bungalow. Once she has worked out that it is just a tremendous downpour, she slips back into sleep.

When, some time later, she wakes again, it is to an absence of noise: no rain, no traffic, no Michael snoring, nothing but a quiet static that swells and recedes at frequent, regular intervals. It takes her a few moments to recognise that this is the sound of waves breaking. She feels as though she is suffocating in the shuttered, dark room – the ceiling fan seems entirely ineffectual.

Five minutes later, wearing a sleeveless cotton shift, she slips out of the house to get some air.

Her bare arms and legs rejoice instantly in the pre-dawn cool. In the gunmetal light, the only evidence of last night's rainfall is the pools in the craters of a large rock nearby and the deeply pocked sand. Although cloud blooms along the horizon, the rest of the oyster-coloured sky is clear over a flat sea, the single breaker at its edge opening like a long, lazy hand to offer its translucent foam to her feet as a gift. She steps into it and closes her eyes to enjoy the surging, fizzing sensations between her toes. She is tempted to keel over and submerge herself, give herself to it so that it can wash away all the hurt and dirt and guilt. Wouldn't it be wonderful just to lie face down in this quiet, clean water, to close her eyes and invite it to take her where it will?

Whatever is ahead today, she should take advantage of this wonderful morning. A person cannot feel sad for one hundred per cent of the time after all. She fetches her camera bag from the bungalow, pulling open the lens caps as she emerges. If she's going to be a snapper, she might as well start with the unusual, even surreal scene that faces her right now: the line of used torches like a fence broken by the sea, the semicircle of trellised arches, with their drowned, drooping foliage. Although the light is still low, it registers sufficiently for slower speeds so she snaps open her foldaway tripod and starts right away. Through her lens, the arches seem almost prehistoric, as though erected for a ritual of human sacrifice then abandoned. She concentrates on promulgating this illusion, photographing from unusual angles. Dawn is breaking quickly now and, in the increasing light, she is having to adjust speed and aperture between each set of shots to maintain the fantasy.

For the last series on this roll, she eschews the tripod and, feeling faintly ridiculous – as though she is playing the role of photographer rather than fulfilling it – lies flat on her belly in the damp sand, balancing the camera on a stone. She is focused on the skewed, sinister way the arches rear above her when her careful composition is ruined by the two statuesque blondes she remembers from the dancing of the night before. Clad in Lycra jogging gear, they begin to perform a set of callisthenics smack in the middle of the shot. Sophie scrambles to her feet and repacks her gear.

The thought of going back into that stuffy room is repugnant. It would be nice to walk along the beach, but if she does that she risks running into Brian or Eily who are in one of the bungalows down there. Sophie wants and needs to be alone, so she hefts the camera bag on to her shoulder and walks past the car park and along the rutted, muddy road by which they had come in last night. Within a few yards, just as the sun breaks through, she spots a crude, handmade sign in the shape of an arrow, tacked to one of the trees and pointing directly into the thick forest. Intrigued, she turns off to follow it and finds herself on a pathway about five feet wide. It is fresh – the wounds on the trees are still visible – and so irregular that it has obviously been hacked out by hand.

The atmosphere is immediately darker, cooler and, except for the symphony of raindrops falling from the overhead canopy, densely quiet, so much so that when the silence is cut by a shriek somewhere to one side of her, she jumps in fright. That was a sound she had never heard before, even in the zoo, and she has no idea whether it was the call of an animal or a bird. She stops moving and listens for it to come again. It does not recur but as she stands as still as she can, barely even breathing, she begins slowly to sense a world of secretive foragings, scamperings and rustlings, of scents foreign to her – resins, gums, scat – layered in the stillness like smoke from an altarful of candles. These unfamiliar trees and undergrowths are busy with a multiplicity of creatures yet, try as she might, she can discern nothing except mosses, leaves, closed-up flowers, tree-trunks and, to right and left, this tightly packed floor of moist greenery intent on reproducing itself on the margins of the path cut through it.

Out of the corner of her eye, she sees movement on the trunk of a tree about three feet to the side of her and, turning her head slowly, finds herself looking directly into the bright eye of a lizard, or a chameleon –

some sort of exotic reptile – so perfectly camouflaged against the bark that unless it had moved she would never have noticed it. Should she risk taking out her camera? She decides against this: there will be other opportunities for snapping and this eye-to-eye moment in this wild place is something she should treasure for herself.

The lizard, about ten inches long, seems not in the least frightened, merely curious as, its tongue flicking through its partially open mouth, it continues to stare at her with its protuberant, perfectly round eye. Moving smoothly, Sophie takes a tiny step towards it, and when it doesn't take off, a second. Now she is so close to the animal she can see the individual scales, the pinkish underbelly. She can even smell its yeasty, pungent odour. Slowly, very slowly, she raises her hand to touch it but just as she is about to make contact the creature flicks its tail and scampers upwards.

'Hey! Hey, come back here!' She has spoken aloud, provoking a chorus of consternation and fluttering above her head.

'Good morning!'

Sophie, still craning upwards in an effort to spot what she has disturbed, jumps for the second time since entering the forest. Jay Street – she'd recognise him anywhere – has come up behind her. How he has done so without her hearing him in this quiet place is a mystery. 'I'm Jay,' he holds out a hand to shake hers, 'and you are?'

When she tells him, a smile of recognition lights up his undoubtedly handsome face. Sophie, far from being well disposed towards him, resents the familiarity and arrogance of the single name. Like *I'm Madonna*. Or *I'm Prince*. So she grants him no answering smile, neither does she take his outstretched hand. He seems to take no offence, simply letting his hand fall back against his immaculately pressed white slacks and, annoyingly, she finds herself apologising stiffly for her presence. 'I just followed the sign, I don't know if this is private or not.'

'Not at all, it's all part of our complex – we have ten hectares. I watched you using your equipment earlier on the beach. I know about you, of course, from Riba. I'm on my way to check the rondavels we've built for our wedding couples, to make sure they've survived yesterday's biblical downpours. Why don't you come along, Sophie? You can bring your cameras, if you like.' Without waiting for her answer, he passes her and sets off down the trail, on to which light is now showering through the greenery.

The sheer cheek of him – spying like that on her. He can photograph his own stupid rondavels – it would be so disloyal of her to accompany him. Sophie hesitates.

Then her curiosity gets the better of her and she sets off after him.

A few hundred yards further along the trail, they come across the first round hut, set in a little clearing planted with creeping nasturtium-like flowers. 'Isn't it lovely?' Street, smug enough to know she has followed him, speaks to her without turning round. 'What could be more wonderful than consummating your new marriage in the forest, surrounded by all this?' He gestures widely then thumps one of the hut's doorposts. 'Well this one seems to have survived, anyway.' He sighs. 'El Niño, La Niña, global warming, the rainy season here – all the weather, in fact – used to be so predictable and now we never know where we are. It's dreadful what we're doing to our earth, Sophie, and no one's really listening to those of us who care. Come on, the next one's over here.'

Sheepishly, glad that no one can see her capitulation, Sophie follows him for the next ten minutes as he leads her around the huts, one by one. The unusual softness of his American accent is not unpleasing—

Stop it, Sophie! Remember who you're dealing with and why you're here.

Yet, although grudging it to him, her admiration grows as she sees how each little house is cunningly concealed not only from intruders but from its fellows. If you were a couple in one of these, you would probably feel you were alone in a virgin forest. 'Want to see inside?' Again, without waiting, he throws open a door which swings easily on hinges made from strips of thick leather.

The warming air is buzzing with insect life and she brushes off something big and bumbly: it is persistently investigating her hair. 'What about mosquitoes and other nasties?'

'Hey! She speaks!' He grins, dimpling, and traitorously Sophie finds herself tempted to grin back. Instead, she passes him and goes inside, expecting the heat to be as stifling as it had been in her own bungalow.

On the contrary, it is cool, deliciously so. He tells her why – pointing to the foot-high gap between the rough clay wall and the roof, which is supported at intervals by short wooden staves. 'We have a lot to learn from other cultures, Sophie. As for mosquitoes and such,' he adds, 'the local staff here have taught us how to deal with them. But it's a secret. We might even get round to patenting it if we can find the energy. Life operates at a different pace here. We're all a bit laid back.' Again he dimples at her.

Sophie deliberately summons up the image of the Amazons in their jogging gear and refuses to buy in to his routine. Laid back, my foot! she thinks, while at the same time taking in the sparse furnishings: a large platform bed hewn from wood, the effect somewhat spoiled by the commercial inner-sprung mattress on it, a simple, rectangular wooden table and a small chest of drawers. 'Where do you hang your clothes?'

He points to four wooden pegs in the wall, two on each side of the entrance. 'His and hers.'

'Bathroom?'

He smiles and gestures again with both arms, taking in the entire forest. 'What could be better than the great ocean? They know what they're getting, it's all spelled out in the brochure. It's a Robinson Crusoe experience, Sophie – although I can see you're not impressed by the mattress. By the time we're finished with it, however, they'll think it's made of straw and feathers.

'Anyway,' he grins again, this time wickedly, 'if my hunch is correct, their minds won't be on décor or the instant availability of hot and cold. Would you like to take some photographs?'

'No, thank you.' Sophie can only guess at how much this Crusoe experience is to cost the honeymooners and will not give him the satisfaction of seeming to endorse it. 'Do they pay a lot? How long do they get to stay?'

'As long as they like – within reason, of course, up to two weeks. That's the beauty of it, they get to decide. The girls tell me we won't recoup the cost of all this until we've had at least three groups. You've no idea how much everything costs on an island, Sophie. Just think of it – it's not only food and drink, everything has to be brought in. But it'll be worth it. They'll love it – we will too, doing our bit to add to the gaiety of nations. Are you married, Sophie?'

'Yes.' Incredibly, such is this guy's skill in getting under other people's skins that it is on the tip of her tongue to confide in him but she stops herself just in time. 'So, do they like them? I saw some of the couples last night.'

'Oh, we're not allowing them to see these until tonight, after the weddings. They're going to be escorted here in torchlight procession, Sophie, flower petals strewn before them on the path, the whole shmear, and then when they're all inside their individual huts, we will ceremoniously close the doors on each couple, one by one. Thump! Thump! Thump! Sexy, eh? It's all worked out. They'll never forget this experience. Of course,' he grins impishly, 'we hope they'll all tell their friends.'

All right, Sophie thinks, pulling back hard. 'Thank you for showing me around,' she says stiffly. 'It's a fascinating concept.'

He gazes at her, his expression still humorous. 'You don't like me, do you? And yet we've only just met.'

She is flabbergasted. Yet why should she be surprised, either at his directness or his confidence? The guy has had decades to perfect his charm offensive. As she struggles to find a response, he shrugs. 'Don't worry about it, it's no big deal. Shall we go?' He stands back to allow her to go outside and closes the door behind them. 'By the way, Sophie, you're invited to the wedding feast tonight, if you like.' His voice is soft as he turns away from the door and issues the invitation with a direct, eye-to-eye look. 'It's in the boma – you've seen our boma?' He caresses the syllables of the word and, for an instant, Sophie believes he might even be hitting on her. Before she can decide he moves off and, annoyed with herself for even contemplating such a thing, she follows again.

Yet as they walk back through the forest, she feels she has to make amends for her rudeness. 'What does Jay stand for? Joseph?'

'No.' He pads along at her shoulder, as relaxed as a cat. 'Did you ever read *The Great Gatsby*, Sophie? I read it when I was a kid and I have never admired a character so much.'

'You've called yourself after Jay Gatsby? What about the Street part? Is that your real name?'

'I'll let you into a secret, Sophie.' He twinkles at her. 'It's not generally known but my real name is Stritch. The other kids used to call me Stritch the Snitch. Now, what would you have done?' Unselfconsciously, he stoops to remove a small twig that has caught between the sole of his right foot and his flip-flop, then moves off again. 'Such a writer, F. Scott Fitzgerald, such wonderful words I'd never heard of – well, you don't in grade school, do you? Or you didn't then. Words like *echolalia* . . . Isn't that a lovely word, Sophie? To a working-class kid like me, it promised a different world, full of good and glamorous experiences.'

Nonplussed at the turn this conversation is taking, she can only nod. 'What does it mean?'

'I had to look it up, of course, but what it actually means is not the way he used it. He used it to describe a party, and you can see why, because it's a medical term for a brain disorder where the sufferer robotically repeats what you say to him. To me, though, the word is musical, embracing all of Creation. It could actually be this forest – the way the birds and animals call out to each other, the way the trees respond. Listen, Sophie,' he puts a hand on her arm to stop her, 'listen carefully.'

Obediently, she stands to listen to the clacking, calling forest, although, except for a brief glimpse of blue feathers flashing between the trees ten feet away, she can still see no bird or animal life. She is becoming physically uncomfortable, super-aware of Jay Street's skin against her own and afraid to move in case she draws attention to herself. Although he is not holding her tightly, merely resting his hand on her forearm, the forest's busy clamour rises to the level of a roar in her head while she strains to keep her own arm steady. She notices that the skin on the back of his hand is smooth, certainly not the skin of a man in his sixties . . .

How long have they been standing here, very close but not touching except for that excruciating – or exquisite – contact? Surely he has to be aware of it? Is he playing some kind of mind game with her?

Because she can now see for herself what has attracted Eily to this man. It is his ability to pull the boundaries of the world close around you so that nothing exists on the planet except you and him. Maybe it's the compelling voice, the soft repetition of your name, but however he does it she can now see how effortlessly he can ensnare you. His presence beside yours is not only flattering, it is irresistible.

Again not noticing her discomfort, or seeming not to, he breaks the contact and moves off easily, leaving her to follow. 'Would you agree with me, Sophie, when I say that, to me, this magical place is echolalia? Benign echolalia.'

Shaken, trawling furiously for reason, Sophie follows.

When she gets back to the complex, it is swarming with activity: workers are trimming the torches, replacing any damaged or withered foliage and flowers on the arches, sweeping, putting a fresh cloth on the buffet table. The air rings with their shouts and teasing. By contrast, some of the wedding couples are spaced out in a straggling line, trying to imitate the slow, graceful movements of one of the Amazons she has seen earlier who is instructing them in Tai Chi. Beyond them, the aquamarine surface of the Caribbean is broken with splashing and bobbing heads. Sophie longs to join them, but in the rush of leaving, hadn't packed a swimsuit. She hasn't even brought a pair of shorts she could wear.

So, for the next hour or so, she simply watches.

At eight o'clock, as they had arranged the previous night, Brian and Donny come to collect her to take her to the hospital. 'That's if you want to do this, Sophie.'

'Of course I do! Is Eily not coming?'

'She's sleeping. She didn't come back from the hospital until the small hours. Are you hungry?'

'Can we go now, Dad?' Donny is jigging impatiently from one foot to the other.

'I'm fine, Brian.' Sophie is not remotely hungry. Not knowing what the water situation would be on the island, she had carried with her a two-litre bottle of Tipperary mineral water and had breakfasted on that with a mango from the fruit basket in her room.

'Come *on*.' Donny's tension is expressed in every line of his body.

'Oh, sorry.' Brian backs out of Zelda's room. 'They seem to be hooking her up to a blood transfusion,' he says to Donny and Sophie. The three wait in silence until the door opens again and a nurse comes out.

'You can go in now. We're giving her blood to build her up. Don't worry about all the tubes –' she smiles directly at Donny – 'she's very comfortable.'

'Can I go in first? By myself?' Donny can see that the other two are surprised.

'Of course.' His dad frowns. 'Are you sure?'

'I'm sure.' Donny nods, nervously determined. Since his dad's first call yesterday morning, he has been screwing himself up for this moment, dreading what he is going to see but dreading even more what he will feel about himself if he doesn't face it.

Might as well get it over with. He pushes too hard at the heavy door of the room so that it crashes open against the wall inside and then rebounds. 'Sorry.' He glances automatically at his dad, who doesn't look cross.

When he gets into the room, Donny almost dies with relief, because it is not half as bad as he expected. He has been anticipating a skeleton or something like that, but she hasn't changed much at all: the Zelda he has got used to is propped up on the same kind of pillows as in an Irish hospital, even in the same kind of bed, except this one is bright pink instead of cream. He can handle the drips, bloods and tubes because he has seen them before, many times. 'Howya!'

'Well, look what the cat dragged in. Jeez, is it my birthday or something?' Zelda's smile is peaceful and unforced. She is very relaxed.

So relieved now he is almost dizzy, Donny pulls up a chair and sits beside the bed. 'I didn't bring you anything, Zel, sorry – Aunt Sophie and me didn't have time.'

'Go right back out there and get me a present – don't be such an oaf, Donny! I'm just so glad you're here. Although I don't know what all the panic is. I feel great.'

Donny feels she is lying, but goes along with it. 'Well, you're looking great anyhow,' which is the kind of thing he has heard adults say to one another when they, too, are lying.

'So, tell us about the trip. I can't remember half of mine. This is a howl, isn't it?' Zelda smiles again. 'Here she is, spiriting me away in secret, and here's the whole shooting match galloping over after us. All we need now is Trevor and Uncle Michael.'

'There's something going on there, Zel.' Donny is glad of the opportunity to be first with this adult news. 'I don't know what it is, but he came out to see us at the airport and they didn't think I was listening, but there was definitely something. She told him good luck with his new life. What do you think that means?'

'Haven't a clue. But Aunt Sophie and Uncle Michael? Nah! Rock of Gibraltar there.'

Donny looks at the sister he adores, and believes her. 'What's it like here?'

'American! There's a nurse from Liverpool who knows Dublin and she's great, and another local one, but the rest of them are all Americans. All cheery teeth. You know the way? A bit like Mum, really – but I gather I'm not to be staying here for all that long.'

'Why?' Alarm bells begin to ring in Donny's heart.

'Oh, not that – stupid! I'm being moved to an old folks' home apparently. This place is too expensive and we have no insurance. Or not enough. The VHI we have doesn't even come close.'

'An old folks' home? But, Zel, that's terrible.'

'Oh, it's not like those places you read about at home, with everyone staring into space. This one is medically good and I'll have my own room and the nice Liverpool nurse is going to be keeping an eye on me. It has lovely gardens, specially designed for sitting out in. Really, Donny, I'm looking forward to it. I've had enough of hospitals and I can't wait to get a bit more of this warm air. I feel the cold so much, these days, and it's so lovely and warm out here I don't even mind all the rain. It's quite soothing, actually, and to tell you the truth – don't tell Dad, for God's sake – I'm even kind of glad Mum brought me, especially since we're all here now.' Her voice weakens but she clears her throat and carries on. 'Anyway, this old folks' place will only be until I get strong enough again to get home to Marble Gardens. How're things there?'

'You haven't been gone that long.'

'Feels like it.'

Her voice fades and she closes her eyes, alarming Donny. He stands up: 'Zel – Zelda!'

'What?' She opens her eyes again. 'Oh, sorry. Narcolepsy. Like River Phoenix in that film. It was River Phoenix, wasn't it? Or was it Johnny Depp?'

'I don't know,' Donny mutters. He is uneasy now. 'Are you tired, Zelda? Do you want me to go?'

'No. Stay, please.' But Zelda's eyes again start to droop.

'Lookit,' he says desperately, 'will I get a nurse or something? Would you like a drink of water?' He is reaching for the carafe on the locker beside her bed when he realises she has opened her eyes again and is looking straight at him.

'Listen, Donny,' she says softly, 'I know this is upsetting, but they're all over me all the time and we mightn't get another chance for me to say this.' She hesitates. 'I'm going to tell them you're to get everything, all right?'

'What are you on about, Zel?' Donny's panic catches him hard by the throat.

'You know what. My Puffa jacket, all my CDs—'

'I don't want your poxy CDs, stop this, Zelda—' But as she continues to look at him, with huge pity, the words choke him.

'I'm sorry, little bro,' she says, reaching for his hand. 'I've tried. I've tried so hard.'

CHAPTER THIRTY-FIVE

It is just after noon now, the complex is quiet as everyone involved primps, ablutes or takes naps prior to the main event of the day, due to kick off at six o'clock when the sun begins to set. Sophie and Donny are with Zelda at the clinic in town but Brian, determined to have it out with Jay Street and equally determined that his wife should come with him, has returned to the complex. 'This is all your doing, Eily. You have no choice. You'll come.' She had objected, of course, but only feebly, knowing she was cornered.

She is at sixes and sevens now, standing a little behind him in the reception area as he insists politely but firmly that Carmen tell him where to find Jay. Riba is dreading this. It is one thing to have your illusions stripped from within yourself, it is another to be forced to face it in public confrontation. She is still clinging to the remnants of hope that, somehow, Jay could – even at this late stage – create another miracle and live up to the image of him she has created, but knows in her heart that this is not to be.

Carmen, although reluctant, proves no match for Brian's dogged persistence and eventually reveals that Jay is at the beach house. She quibbles, on grounds of 'security', about telling him and Riba how to get to it but seeing that it may be dangerous to push this big man too far, she gives in and directs them to leave the complex. 'Then, after about two hundred yards, you turn off the main road where you'll see two large stones painted white. That's the start of the track to the house. It's uphill all the way. You can't miss it.'

Ten minutes later, after a tough walk uphill in single file, Brian leading, they reach a post-and-rail perimeter fence. Riba, breathing hard, is taken aback at her first sight of the so called beach house.

Far from the simple cottage she had envisaged – some cobbled-together combination of Brighton bathing hut and informal shack – Street's home is a mini-mansion. Single-storeyed and perfectly square, constructed of pinkish stone and surrounded by lawns, it is set on the clifftop ahead of them above a small rocky cove. Each side of the square, or at least the three they can see from the fence, is bordered by a formal, gravelled semicircle in paler pink, as though the house has been designed to be the heart of an open flower. Its many full-length bevelled windows wink at the sun and, like lighthouses, flash quietly at the rainbows arching in all directions from an array of lawn sprinklers. It's a Mabel Lucie Atwell house, Riba thinks, reminded of the books she has read to Zelda and Donny when they were little.

Brian, of course, has a different perspective as, hands on hips, he surveys the scene. 'I see – well, well well! Everything becomes clear. Come on.' He climbs over the rail. After a moment's hesitation, Riba ducks under it and plods after him. He is waiting for her on the gravel. 'Leave all the talking to me,' he says, in a low voice.

'Sure.' Riba nods, resigned now to follow the script presented to her.

As she follows Brian through one of the open French windows, she finds herself in a pale, mirror-filled room that would not be out of place in Versailles. If the delicate spindly furniture is reproduction it has been cunningly made: there is even a spinet in one corner. So much for everything being so expensive on an island, so much for everything having to be imported. This is the kind of place she has seen heretofore only in glossy magazines in her dentist's waiting room. She can detect a low murmur coming from behind one of the many doors leading off the hall. Brian hears it too. He seizes her hand and, pulling her towards this door, throws it open.

There are five people in the huge room, which is flooded with sea-light from several sets of open windows and furnished for the most part like an ordinary living room, with couches, chairs, bookcases, occasional tables, knick-knacks – and a huge television screen showing Grand Prix racing. California Monica is standing over Jay Street, who, partially covered with a towel and glistening with oil, is lying on his belly on a massage table placed directly in one of the window openings; an Oriental girl is standing at an ironing board, on which is spread a pair of white trousers, and a young black man Riba has not seen before is lounging on one of the couches, sharing a set of double headphones with another girl who is lying in his arms. Riba doesn't notice his face because, to her horror, he is wearing the shirt she had bought for Jay with such care at Charles de Gaulle. All five are gazing in surprise towards the door and Brian, who had been about to charge in, is so discombobulated that he teeters on the threshold.

'Good afternoon.' Street is the first to recover. Pulling the towel around him, he slides gracefully off the plinth. 'We weren't expecting you, I have to say. Good day, Riba.' Had his bow been performed by any other man dressed only in a towel and oiled like a wrestler, it would have looked ridiculous, but somehow he has pulled it off.

Beside her, however, Riba feels Brian tense and she moves quickly in front of him. 'Hello, Jay,' she says quietly. 'I'm sorry we're intruding like this but we needed to talk to you urgently.'

'Any time, Riba.' He leans past her and sticks out a hand towards Brian. 'You must be Brian?'

Brian ignores the hand and Street's tone changes, becomes more businesslike. 'Sorry you caught us in such an informal mode, as it were. We're just making the most of the calm before the storm.' He looks away towards the glittering sea. 'Let's pray God doesn't take me literally. His weather has not favoured us lately.'

Brian's voice shakes as he struggles to contain years of pent-up fury. 'My wife informs me that, according to you, we owe you six thousand pounds for the privilege of setting foot on your little Disneyland here. May I inform you that you will not be getting a single penny, from us, from our daughter, from our son or from our friend. And, pal,' he thrusts his face close to Street's, 'if you object, I look forward to meeting you in court. Any court. If you dare. As it happens, I might see you anyway. I might sue you for deliberate and undue influence over my wife, leading to endangerment of my daughter's health.'

Street, four or five inches shorter but a lot fitter, remains calm: he has not moved a muscle throughout this harangue. Apparently unruffled, he turns his back and walks away, cat-like, from Brian to the window. This enrages Brian and, before anyone can stop him, he has erupted with a flying rugby tackle, knocking Street to the floor. Raising a long-thwarted fist, he brings it down hard – and yells in pain and surprise when it connects with the polished floorboards. Street, slippery with oil, has rolled out from under the punch and sprung lightly to his feet. He is now calmly readjusting his towel while Brian, nursing his injured hand, scrambles up clumsily. 'We are pacifists here, Brian,' he says quietly. 'We follow many prophets, including the one who teaches us that evil is but good tortured by its own hunger and thirst. You are in need of help, my friend.'

'Bullshit!' The physical encounter, humiliating though it was, seems to have deflated Brian's rage and now he is simply contemptuous. 'You're a charlatan, Street – a go-boy. I know your type.' He waves his uninjured arm in a derisive arc, taking in the pair on the couch, the Amazon, the whole house. 'Celibate, my arse!'

Riba gasps, the two on the couch spring to their feet and California

Monica steps forward angrily. 'You bastard.'

Only the girl at the ironing-board remains impassive.

Jay holds up a hand to warn Monica to stay where she is and fixes Riba's husband with his hypnotic green eyes. 'No one is coerced into our organisation, Mr McMullan,' his voice is very soft but it can be heard even above the Grand Prix commentator on the TV, 'and no one is kept with us in chains. If you care to check with your wife, you will find that she came to us of her own free will. I am truly sorry about the plight of your daughter but, again, if you check with Riba, she will, if she is truthful, explain to you that she misrepresented the facts about Zelda's illness. We knew she was gravely ill, but your wife did give us the distinct impression that we could help. If you have a problem with us, it is not of our making. As for the money,' it is his turn to be contemptuous, 'please, Brian, we can manage without your money. You may stay here as long as you wish, all of you. Keep your money. Now I would ask you both to leave my house.' He inclines his head towards Riba. 'Good day to you, Riba – I'm sorry it has come to this.'

Beside her, Riba can sense that Brian is getting himself ready for a fresh assault. She gathers around her what is left of her dignity. 'Brian!' she says, and admonishes him with a look. There is a moment when he might ignore her but then, abruptly, he turns and leaves the room.

As she follows him, Riba looks over her shoulder. Her last sight of Jay is as he climbs again on to the massage table. The contretemps seems not to have upset him.

Riba is careful while closing the door behind her. She doesn't want Jay to think she has slammed it.

Actually, she doesn't know what to think. The really painful thing for her is that Jay himself had blamed her for misrepresenting Zelda's condition. That wasn't fair. All she had been doing was following his training, being positive.

It is even more upsetting to think that she will never again be one of his trusted lieutenants. Will she even see him again? She has loved him so much, platonically, to be sure. He has been good for her, he has.

Even as she hurries after her husband, Riba cannot subdue the resurgent glimmerings of hope that, after a suitable period of repentance, as it were, she will be able quietly to re-join the organisation. She may have to keep a low profile, of course, certainly for a while.

One thing for sure, though, Brian had no right to attack him like that.

When she catches up with her husband, he is sitting on a white-painted bench seat, one of many placed strategically in the emerald-coloured grass in the grounds of the house. She reaches him just as he lowers his head to his knees. 'I'll be all right in a minute. I'm probably jet-lagged.'

Riba decides that now is not the time to talk about what happened inside that house. Instead she rubs his back while he breathes deeply, gulping air as though he has surfaced from a dive. 'I'm sorry I wasn't enough for you, Eily.'

She stops rubbing. 'What?'

'You heard me.'

'Yes, but what did you mean?'

He takes a long time but then he brings up his head and stares out at the horizon. Riba, not knowing what else to do, follows the direction of his gaze. For now, at least, the sun is still shining over the sea and Jay Street's house is still bathed in light but the island is L-shaped and, landward to their left, those ominous, green-tinged clouds have started to billow again. 'Brian?'

He examines the knuckles with which he had missed Jay's jaw. 'I couldn't even hit him a decent box. I'm glad, actually, as it turns out. If I'd connected, I'd probably be feeling sorry for the bastard now.

'The really weird thing,' he looks out to sea again, 'is that, having seen for myself the kind of tricks he can pull on women, half of me doesn't blame you. He's a powerful and charismatic guy and I can see how, if you're vulnerable at all, you could be attracted to someone like him who seems to offer answers. It's so practised, so – so . . .' he searches for the correct word '. . . so *acquired*. That's what I mean when I say that I haven't been enough for you, because the other half of me is appalled that you couldn't see through all that bullshit, Eily. Even that celibacy stuff – it's a fucking harem he has up there. But you couldn't see any of it because you're in love with him.'

'No, I'm not – for God's sake, Brian, don't even give that house room. We never even kissed – he never laid a finger on me.'

'Don't,' he says quietly. 'It's not necessary to touch.' There is something behind this statement that Riba does not care to analyse so she does not. The habit of self-protection, at least, she will take away with her from Jay's organisation. If, of course, she has to go.

After a moment, he turns to look directly at her. 'Have you thought about what I said to you yesterday morning? Have you an answer for me?'

'You mean about being married to you, as opposed to just being married?'

'Yes.'

Riba hesitates. 'You said something about not being sure about loving me any more.'

'Not quite. I asked why you should take my love for granted – that's very different.'

Riba looks at Brian, at whom she has not seriously looked for many years. Then her face is splattered with huge, warm drops. At first she thinks these have come from the lawn sprinklers, but then they come faster: the island is in for another drenching. She does not move, however, and neither does he. 'You're right,' she says quietly. 'I have been guilty of not paying attention. I do love you, I do want to be married to you.'

They are sitting under a serious cloudburst now but neither is making the slightest effort to wipe away the streams running from their hair and down their faces. He has found something of tremendous interest on the front of his T-shirt. 'I'm not going to pretend it's going to be easy,' he says, 'for either of us. And I don't know what I feel at the moment. I know I asked you to tell me the truth, but now that I'm faced with it myself, I can't say what the truth is. At least not now. I'm sorry.'

He looks up again from his contemplation of his T-shirt, so wet she can see the matted hair beneath it. As though sucked up into the sky, the rain pouring over them stops as abruptly as it had started; she can see the shower in its entirety as, compacted into a black box reaching from earth to cloud, it sweeps away to their right, obscuring the port. Her instincts advise her to wait. 'I'm sorry too,' she says simply.

He pats her shoulder briefly, then stands up. 'Come on, kiddo. We have to change out of these clothes to go and see Zel. Got to keep up appearances.'

When she left this morning with Brian and Donny, the wedding arches were still naked. Now, just after one o'clock, Sophie is surprised by how quickly the place has been transformed in her absence. The brief, fierce rainstorm has obviously not deterred the work here and the wedding arches, newly wreathed in dark green vines and laced with brilliant flowers are like something from a Burne-Jones painting, the grass between them has been carpeted with petals and, like an open-sided temple, a silk-canopied pergola erected on the sea-side of the open circle. Just to the side of the reception bungalow, there is a steady trade at a temporary beauty parlour, installed under another canopy, where the brides-to-be are having their nails painted and their hair twisted and braided. Seeing them in daylight for the first time, Sophie thinks that some are rather endearingly long in the tooth. Elsewhere, the complex is busy with workers, augmented by what are obviously members of the organisation, chatting, sweeping, ferrying supplies at a leisurely Caribbean pace to the boma. As though it had never abandoned the island, the sun shines bright and hot over the beach, and the bone-dry bungalows gleam picture-postcard white, showing no signs of their recent dousing.

Now would be as good a time as any to call the Adoption Board at home. Sophie hurries into the reception area but finds that the international circuits are not available at present. Telling the girl she will try again at another time, she goes back out into the sunshine.

Less then ten yards away, Brian and Eily are coming towards her along the walkway.

'Sophie!' Before she has time to compose herself, Sophie is grabbed by Eily and crushed in a bear hug. 'Oh, it's so good to see you, you're so good to do this—'

'Not at all. It was the least I could do.' As she extricates herself, Sophie sees that her friend is in tears.

'Is Donny with you?' Eily is wiping her eyes with the butterfly sleeves of her kaftan.

'No, he stayed in the clinic.' Sophie is conscious that Brian has turned away and, having muttered something about organising a taxi, is on his way into reception. She swallows. 'I came home to take a bit of a break but I'll go back with you. I'll just change my clothes. OK? This heat is murder.' Then, quietly: 'It's probably a stupid thing to say, but try not to worry. She's doing OK, Eily. I'm not a medic, of course, but to me she seems very relaxed and cheerful. Sleepy, of course, but that's to be expected. She's actually looking forward to the move this afternoon, says she's sick of hospitals.'

Eily hesitates. Then, 'Can you understand why I did it? I'm not excusing myself, honestly, but I was so upset and I really thought—'

She stops. Then, quietly, with head bowed, 'I shouldn't have done it like this behind his back. Oh, Soph, can you forgive me? I so much wanted to give her a good childhood, the kind of childhood I didn't have myself.' Her bright yellow kaftan, reflecting the sunshine, is at odds with her demeanour. She could be a bewildered little girl who has been scolded by a beloved teacher.

Accustomed to Eily's certainties, it is devastating for Sophie to see her laid low like this – to the extent that her mixed-up feelings are dramatically intensified. 'Don't, Eily,' she begs, 'please don't beat yourself up like this. You have Zelda, and Donny too, a wonderful life. They're marvellous kids, a credit to you – come on, sit down. The taxi won't be here for a few minutes.'

She sits on one of the plastic beach chairs and pulls Eily on to the one beside it. 'Whatever about anyone else, there is no need to apologise to me,' she says fervently. 'Of course I understand why you would be blind to everything except Zelda's illness – and I shouldn't have been so damned self-important with my own views. I'm sorry too.' Close to weeping too, she puts a hand out to clasp Eily's and squeezes tightly.

Eily squeezes back. 'Oh, Soph! You're such a great pal.'

If only you knew. But at the last moment Sophie manages to morph the confession that was rising in her throat to the story of her own woes. She makes the narrative as quick and matter-of-fact as possible, yet holds back on her most recent transaction with Yvonne and Michael about the baby. It would be too tactless to talk about her hopes on that score with Zelda's life in the balance.

At the end of the recital Eily, who had listened with her hand to her mouth in sympathy, again throws her arms around Sophie's neck. 'I had no idea. The shite. The stinking bloody shite. Her too, and the magazine – all of them. You don't deserve any of this, Sophie, you're too good. I'm so, so sorry, that's so awful – poor, poor Sophie! Why didn't Brian tell me any of this?'

'He had other things on his mind, Eily.'

Something in her tone has betrayed her, she fears, because Eily glances penetratingly at her but then, to Sophie's relief, she does not pursue whatever it was that flashed through her mind. 'Do you want to hear about what happened with Jay?' she asks.

'Sure – if you want to tell me.'

Gradually, while she relates the tale of the episode in the beach house, haltingly at first, Eily's tone picks up as the funny side of it strikes her. Sophie has always found Eily's laugh infectious and, within a short time is laughing along. 'Imagine, Sophie!' Eily's kaftan is rippling as its owner's glee reaches new heights. 'Half a foot taller, probably twice the weight and he clocked him and missed. At a distance of about three inches. My hero!' She laughs again, hard, but this time the laugh changes and just barely survives on the right side of mirth. Sobering, she looks at Sophie. 'Would you look at the two of us. What are we like? We're a right pair, aren't we?'

At the risk of overdoing it, Sophie reaches out to grasp her hand. 'Old friends are best.'

CHAPTER THIRTY-SIX

T he taxi does not arrive at the compound for almost forty minutes and when they get to the clinic they find Donny is frantic. 'Where *were* you? There's a doctor or someone who wants to talk to you. I think he's American. I didn't know what to do.'

The three adults exchange glances. Brian reaches out as though to touch his son but Donny moves away. Brian drops his hand. 'We're here now. Where is this doctor? What's his name?'

'I can't remember. It was some kind of foreign name. That was *ages* ago – where *were* you?'

'Don't worry, we'll find him.' Brian turns for assent to the other two but Sophie starts to move away.

'If you don't mind, I'll leave you a bit of peace and quiet to go in to Zelda. Anyway, I need to make a call from the pay phone.' On her previous visit, she had noticed the booth just inside the door of the coffee shop, which is tucked into a corner of the lobby. They make arrangements to meet later and Sophie hurries off.

She goes immediately to the phone and, *mirabile dictu*, the international lines are working. Praying that Michael will be there, she places the reverse charge call to EconoCar.

Yvonne answers.

Sophie panics and almost drops the receiver. For some stupid reason, she had not anticipated this; she should have made the call person-to-person. Luckily, the line clicks off while the operator asks if charges will be accepted, so she doesn't actually have to speak to the girl. Despite the truce they seemed to arrange on the night Yvonne had been in her house, Sophie is not yet ready to be Yvonne's pal.

She tries to distract her thoughts by perusing the décor of the restaurant, which is prettily decked out in farmer's-kitchen style. As the seconds tick by, a suspicion grows that Michael's lover is refusing to take the call. How dare she? Just when she is about to hang up in anger, the line clears, and Michael is on. 'Sophie! Is everything all right?'

'I'm just ringing—' Off-balance, she scrambles for the best way to handle this. She should have rehearsed. 'In case you might be wondering. We got here safely.'

'How's everything? And I did cancel that appointment as you asked.' His voice is carefully matter-of-fact.

Yes – Yvonne must be nearby.

'Nothing dramatic to report,' Sophie says. 'Zelda is being moved out of the clinic this afternoon.'

'Things can't be that bad, so.'

'No. That doesn't mean it's not serious, Michael. We wouldn't all be here—'

'I know that. Of course.'

This is torture. And now Sophie realises that the reason for making this call was not to check in. It was because she had wanted to reassure herself. 'Listen, Michael,' she says quickly, 'I know you can't talk now and I'm sorry to do this to you. Just say "yes" or "no" – is everything still going ahead? Did you go in to the bank?'

'That's two questions, Sophie.' He has lowered his voice.

So Yvonne *is* listening.

Sophie forces herself to sound cool. 'She hasn't changed her mind?'

'No.'

'And you will go into the bank to talk about the re-mortgaging?'

'Certainly, I will do that for you, Sophie.' He sounds cheery now, as though she is asking him to buy her a head of cabbage. It rankles that this man, to whom she has been married for so long, is having to veil his conversation with her, but she makes a supreme effort not to betray her irritation. She roots in her wallet for the social worker's card. 'And would you do one more thing for me, Michael, please? I wouldn't ask you, but the telephone situation here can sometimes be dodgy and on the other side, I could be put on hold for ages, you know what state institutions are like. Have you got a pen?'

'Shoot.'

She reads out the name and number from the card and asks him to make an appointment for her. 'There will be a waiting list, I'm sure, so there's no danger she'll see me this week or next.'

There is a long pause, during which she hears the mouthpiece being covered. What's he saying? 'Michael, *Michael*! Are you still there?'

The line clears and he asks her to repeat the name and number.

She does so. 'And I'll ring again in a couple of days.'

'Fine.' His tone has resumed its formality. 'And please tell Brian not to worry. The place is ticking over, no problems.'

After Sophie hangs up, she is angry about the obvious eavesdropping, but she is uneasy too. Ringing Michael at work was a mistake. She will have to ring his mobile in future because she must not under any circumstances alienate Yvonne. One flick of that girl's mind and the baby – *Sophie's* baby – is a goner.

But there is another reason for her discomfiture: by talking to Michael in what was, in effect, coded language, she had entered into a conspiracy with him. It could have encouraged him to believe that she might be open to taking him back.

She knows her husband well. Michael might have been overtly dismissive of her and her 'little' concerns, but in spite of this he had appreciated their easeful house, the calm and order she had brought to their joint lives. She probes: supposing he were to come crawling back – a distinct possibility – could she resume being married to him?

It is early days yet and she is sensible enough to know that she's in no condition to think about this, even fleetingly.

The coffee shop is not crowded but all six of its dinky tables, covered in pink gingham cloths, are occupied, mostly by medical staff. Nevertheless, unwilling just now to go back to the McMullans, Sophie goes to the counter and orders a double Espresso and a Danish pastry. Right now she feels somehow displaced, as though real life, as ephemeral as ectoplasm, is hovering outside her grasp.

Except in one respect: whereas the bonds holding Michael to Yvonne are entwined in his confused emotions about the baby and are as fragile as spider silk, Sophie is bound to that baby with steel cable. She sees her baby in her arms. Slopping food on to the floor from a high chair. Bowling along the footpath on a little trike. In uniform, waving at her from the school gates. Despite darts of apprehension about what can or might happen in the next few months, she refuses to talk herself down from those images. She will deliver that baby safely to her arms by force of will. Her husband is dealing with a different Sophie from the one he knew.

In fact, only in the light of such deadly purpose does Sophie see how vaguely she had meandered through life up to now. No wonder Michael had got irritated with her. In that, at least, he was justified.

What a waste. Well, no longer.

She pays for the coffee and Danish and turns around to seek a table. One, right by the window, is occupied by just one individual, who is tapping on a laptop. Wearing twin symbols of white coat and stethoscope, he is obviously a doctor and seems so absorbed that Sophie feels she should ask: 'Mind if I sit here?'

'Not at all. Let me make space – ' The doctor, whose name badge declares him to be a Dr Timothy Ocwieja, has a distinctively American accent. He is youngish, perhaps early thirties, sandy-haired, and would be attractive if he were not running to fat. He gives her a brief once-over and moves his laptop an inch or so, although this is unnecessary to accommodate her frugal meal. Then he resumes typing.

Sophie nibbles on her Danish. It is weird, but at this distance, even so soon – giving weight to the old cliché about *out of sight, out of mind* – Michael's adventures with Yvonne seem a little less shocking and hurtful. Especially when set against the life and death situation with which Brian and Eily are dealing. And Donny. Poor old Donny.

Her table companion breaks into her train of thought by clicking heavily on his computer keys with an air of finality. He looks up and smiles at her.

Sophie smiles back. 'I hope I haven't disturbed you?'

'I was finishing anyway.' He removes a small square disk from the side of the machine, taps again, then closes it up. 'Thank God for technology. When it works, of course. Are you visiting?'

'Yes.' She tells him about Zelda.

'That's the Irish girl who's only nineteen?' The doctor's eyes flicker. 'Are you her mom?'

'No. I'm her godmother. Why? Do you know about her case, Doctor Och—?' she makes a stab at pronouncing his name.

'Don't bother.' He smiles again. 'It's Polish. Just call me Tim. Everyone else does. Look, I'd like to talk to you. Let me grab a coffee, OK? You want another one?'

Sophie shakes her head. She watches while he fetches the coffee, half-afraid to speculate about his interest or what he wants to talk about. When he comes back, instead of speaking straight away, he stares for a moment or two over her shoulder through the window behind her head. Then, 'May I ask your name?'

Sophie tells him.

'Look,' he says, 'I don't want to start any false trails. And I'm not a haematologist, in fact I'm just a lowly physician. I'm doing locum here for a few weeks, financing a vacation, really.'

'Yes?' Sophie wishes he would get to the point.

Again, however, he hesitates. 'My best buddy is interested in myeloma,' he says slowly. 'I was planning to e-mail him tonight about your goddaughter, as it happens, because she will probably enter the literature. She's the youngest patient I've ever heard of with the condition. I don't know whether you know this, Sophie, but with a few exceptions, myeloma is usually a disease of middle age and beyond. I think my friend would be very interested. He's involved in a patient study concerning the thalidomide drug. It has already started but, as far as I know, they're still at the selection-process stage for the actual trials. I'd have to check that, of course.'

Sophie stiffens at the mention of the drug she has come across so often in Donny's printouts. He misinterprets her reaction. 'I know thalidomide has a bad name,' he says quickly, 'but that was a long time ago. We don't talk about cures, of course, but apparently the results of other studies, for instance at the University of Arkansas, are encouraging – for at least some of the participants.'

He stops. Then, 'I don't mean to go on about it, but you can't be Gill Leavitt's best friend and not get your brain fried with this. It's all he thinks about.' He looks closely at her. 'He's attached to a haematology unit at a clinic in Butte, Montana. You've probably never heard of it, it's independently funded, but it is very prestigious in medical circles and they do really valuable research, so much so that they are attracting federal and even international interest now.

'Do you think the family would be interested? How would the young lady herself react? At this stage, what does she have to lose?'

Zelda balks at the plan to go to Montana. Gently but adamantly, she insists she wants no extra drugs, certainly no experimentation.

'But it's not chemo.' Of all of them, Donny is most devastated at her refusal even to contemplate taking part in the trials. 'You said, Zel. You said it was the chemo you didn't want.' He is very close to tears.

Her mother, who is nearest to her at the time, is so white-faced she looks as though she might collapse from strain. She has never been well disposed towards drugs in any event and the word 'thalidomide' has horrible connotations for her. Bizarrely, Zelda, who has gleaned exactly how things stand with Jay Street and whose soft heart continues to bleed for the older woman's bewilderment and distress, hears herself reassuring her mother that, as she understands it, thalidomide is safe in the way it is proposed to use it in these trials. Anything to soften those lines of suffering on that face.

My God, she thinks in the next instant, *what are you saying*?

Whether it is these reflexive reassurances or the unctuous encouragement of the clinic's CEO who, now that Zelda is a medical celebrity, has descended not once but twice on her room, over the next half-hour or so she can sense her mother coming round to the idea.

As for her father, it breaks her heart to see the way he keeps leaving the room and coming back in with red eyes. At first, he had been on her side against the others. 'Leave her alone,' he had said more than once to both

Donny and her mother, whose silences are in some ways more agonising than their pleas. Then, taking her hand, 'we won't ask you to do anything you don't want, Zeldy. I promise.'

But bit by bit, his resolve to be in her corner has worn away and although he doesn't come right out and say it, she can see that he too desperately wants her to go to Montana. 'And you're happy enough that the thalidomide used this way is safe?' He glances at her mother.

'Of course it is!' As is her wont, Zelda's mother has done such a spectacular U-turn that no other option now exists for Zelda. 'They wouldn't be doing these trials in a clinic like this one if it wasn't. Isn't that right, darling?'

Zelda gazes past the circle of tense shoulders and fraught expressions through her window, where the sky is blithely blue. What is the point of going through all this? Death postponed is still death. She should have kept her mouth shut and not allowed her mother an opening. She wishes with all her heart that she could simply vanish.

Or it would be even better if she had never existed, had never been a daughter to her mother and father, nor a sister to Donny. That would be the only torment-free way for all of them.

But that, of course is not an option.

She is running out of arguments because if she is to be clear-eyed about it, who is she to turn down this gift? There are probably hundreds of other patients in her position who would kill for this one last chance. And who knows what benefits it could bring? Who is she to say?

As they all sit there in tense silence, the ginger-haired American doctor with the funny name comes in again and, with great timing, gently enquires whether or not they have made a decision.

And so, in the shadow of this impossible dream, emotionally worn out and physically exhausted, Zelda gives in.

Instantly, the atmosphere in the room changes. Donny is incandescent, short only of dancing. This is the kind of thing he had been pushing for all along. 'I told you all, I told you, but nobody would listen. Wey, hey, Zel.' He grabs her hand, too roughly, causing her to wince. 'Sorry.' He backs off and looks around wildly: 'Anyone got change for the Coke machine?'

Their mother's reaction is a teary 'thank you, darling, thank you,' but as her brother crashes out of the room in search of his Coke, their dad simply sits, sagging like a big old beanbag, with a look on his face she never wants to see again because to perceive that relief hurts even more than to watch his pain.

Even Aunt Sophie, who is normally a rock of sense, bursts into tears when she is called in to be told the news.

'Jesus.' Zelda, who wants nothing now but for them all to leave so she can sink into blessed sleep, finds one last ounce of strength to throw her gaze to the ceiling. 'I'd hate to be around to see you lot get *bad* news!'

With Zelda sleeping and her things packed and ready, her parents and Donny go for a meal in a small beach restaurant where the food on offer is fish, chicken, potatoes – roasted or chipped – and fruit. To Riba's disappointment, Sophie, pleading tiredness, has cried off. It would have been nice to have her along for this last night on the island.

For once, Riba's appetite has deserted her, and although the red snapper on her plate is well presented and very fresh, she merely picks at it. In the seat opposite, Brian, too, is chewing desultorily. The only one of the three of them who seems to be enjoying the meal is Donny, wolfing a plateful of chicken and chips. 'You might as well be in McDonald's.' Riba tries to lighten the atmosphere with gentle ribbing, but Donny doesn't get it. He stares at her, his mouth full, before shrugging and going back to concentrating on his meal. Brian hasn't even lifted his head.

The cooking smells are mingled with a perfume as musky as incense from a lush, bell-flowered creeper covering a little bluff to the east. Inhaling deeply, she turns to gaze out at the Caribbean sunset. The restaurant is literally on the beach, its tables sheltered by a canvas awning bolted against the tin shack cooking area and supported on a row of rusting poles embedded in the sand. Only yards away, the sea gleams like the satin skirts of a peach-coloured ball gown, spread to reflect the lights of the sky; it has calmed to a whisper as the island hushes and cools itself in preparation for night. For Riba, this would be perfect if it wasn't for the void in her heart.

What is ahead for them all in the long term?

She decides not to be so negative and to concentrate on the immediate future, wherein she and Donny are to go with Zelda to the States. There had been some discussion about this because Donny has already missed quite a bit of school and his Junior Cert looms in June. But both Riba and Brian had felt there was no real choice now. He deserved to go, for a while anyway. The trials are to last a month, four weeks of closely monitored medication plus an additional period of follow-up. Donny himself had dug his heels in. 'For God's sake, it's only a few weeks. I can catch up. Easily.' And so it had been decided to allow it. Accommodation for the two of them would not be a problem. Luckily Brian has friends – travel trade contacts again – in various cities around the Midwest and western states. He has already hit the phones in an effort to find a family living within reach of the institute. Brian himself, understandably, has to

go back to EconoCar, at least for the moment. He will fly out to join
them again as soon as he can, although he did permit himself a small
grumble about Montana not being the easiest of locations to reach from
Ireland.

So much for Jay's implications about the severity of Zelda's condition.
Riba slaps at a mosquito which is whining somewhere near her ear. Then
the thought occurs to her for the first time: actually, if you think about it,
the magic had worked, hadn't it? If Zelda hadn't been moved to the clinic
they wouldn't have met Dr Ocwieja and none of this excitement would
be happening. Yes, the Lord does work in mysterious ways after all . . . She
glances covertly at Brian, afraid he might be able to read her treacherous
thoughts. But he is still staring at his plate, cutting his swordfish into tiny
pieces.

A pall of fragrant smoke, from barbecue fires and flaming torches, hangs
over the compound; the music, from three separate steel bands, is raucous.
The wedding feast is in full swing.

Sophie came upon it just as the ceremony was concluding and, to much
ribald cheering from the staff, the couples were embracing within their
individual arches.

Despite the gaiety and eclecticism of the bridal parties, the most
imposing person present – if you liked that sort of thing – was Jay Street,
looking on with an indulgent smile. He had dressed all in white as usual –
white slacks, white shirt – but over this he was now sporting a full-length
cape in white silk, fastened at the throat with a showy gold clasp in the
shape of two eagles' heads joined by a chain. To Sophie's jaundiced eye, all
he needed was the curly hair and the fiddle and he could have been
impersonating Nero. Or an actor for *Star Trek*. Or even the Pope.

Yet she could not avoid being seduced by the colour, smells and activity
as the formality dissolved and the bridal couples swirled around, admiring
each other's outfits and swarming towards the huge buffet.

Street spotted her as she watched from the sidelines and, before she
could escape, bore down on her, cape billowing. 'Join us, Sophie!' He
gestured towards the piles of different meats, fish and salads.

'No, thank you. I've already eaten.' Up close, she was again, unwillingly,
struck by his charm. The guy was an enigma. How could anyone so vain
be so attractive?

He did not linger. 'If you change your mind, you'll be welcome,' he said
then moved off to join a group, leaving Sophie kicking herself for being
affected by his charisma even for a second. She watched for a few minutes
more but then was forced to succumb to the tiredness in her bones and

went into her bungalow where, without even undressing, she crawled into bed.

Forty minutes later, sleep continues to elude her, however, and not just because of the continuing ruckus only yards outside her window. Round and round the thoughts go, Brian, the baby, Michael, Brian, Eily, Donny, the baby, Brian . . .

And, of course, poor Zelda, off again on her travels. Fearing that this could be another false dawn for her goddaughter, Sophie half wishes she had not met that doctor in the coffee shop.

It is relatively cool outside, but the air inside the bungalow is clammy and she throws off the sheet. It wasn't her fault, dammit; he was interested in Zelda on his friend's behalf from the start. He had already met her. He would have made contact with Brian and Eily sooner or later.

Although they had invited her, at least Eily had, she could not have borne to eat with Brian and his family this evening. In spite of the warmth of the reunion earlier between herself and Eily, she could not have carried on with any further pretence that nothing had happened between herself and Eily's husband.

She has considered staying on for one more day because of the emotional dangers inherent in travelling home with Brian, but has decided she will have to deal with it. She didn't come here on holiday, after all, and in any event she is very anxious to get back to real life. And to be near her baby. She will attempt to sleep all the way on the plane. She will certainly need it.

What time is it in Ireland? She squints at the face of her watch: eight o'clock here, midnight at home. What are Yvonne and Michael up to?

Sophie turns on her stomach and with her pillow over her head, tries to block out the jollity outside. Within minutes, she is too hot again. She cannot wait to get home to her quiet, cool house.

It is after midnight and beside Yvonne, who is snoring heavily, Michael is still uncomfortably awake in the narrow bed. He hasn't had one decent night's sleep since he was turfed out of his home and he is tired to the marrow.

Earlier today he had caught himself daydreaming again about the kid. Must be getting seriously soft. He had thought that, after the initial panic, he wouldn't be as keen. But that hasn't turned out to be the case.

Of course it's early days.

He had been surprised to get the call from Sophie. She is obviously obsessed with this baby. Michael hopes that if he plays it cool, does everything right and keeps his bib clean he could possibly climb out of this trough he has got himself into. It's ninety/ten that himself and Yvonne won't last the course in any event. Why would he stay, when Sophie has his child?

Yvonne, who is no fool, probably knows the way the land lies. He doesn't blame her, he thinks, quite admiring her for her savvy in holding out for the money. Who wouldn't, at her age? It is a passport to freedom for her.

At the same time, they will both have to play the game, won't they? For a few more months in any case.

The odds on his getting back with Sophie are not all that great, though, he thinks gloomily, maybe thirty/seventy, although horse races have been won on higher odds. Sophie certainly needs him right now. And the more he keeps Yvonne on track so she hands over the child without a fuss, the lower the odds might get . . .

Oh God – his calf is cramping now and he can't even turn over without waking her. This is a nightmare.

Right. Enough! This is the last time he is putting up with this, they'll find a new flat tomorrow or he is moving into a hotel for a couple of nights until they do.

Or – here's a thought: could he risk going home for just one night? Unknown to Sophie, he has retained a spare key to their house. She need never find out.

Before he can change his mind, he steals out of the bed and, grateful for the easing in the cramp, tiptoes across the floor, then dresses surreptitiously at the furthest corner of the room. Maintaining watch on Yvonne, who, luckily, is a heavy sleeper and hardly ever wakes up before the alarm goes off, he writes her a note on the back of an envelope.

Had to go out really early. Will explain when I see you at work later.
Sleep well! M.

He'll think of some reason. Something he has to do at the house, maybe, arising out of the telephone call from Sophie.

No. Not that. She'd probably freak.

Something at work. Something he'd forgotten to do. After all, he is in charge now. At least for another day or so. Michael is quite sorry Brian is coming home so quickly. Being the boss has been a buzz.

Quietly, he moves the snib on the alarm clock, turning it off. He'll make sure to be back before half past seven in the morning, but just in case . . .

Then he creeps across to the door and opens it an inch at a time.

Keeping his eyes on Yvonne, he slips through and clicks it carefully behind him. If she does wake and miss him, she'll be suspicious, of course, but what the hell. A man has a right to his own bed.

Riba slips quietly through the door of the bungalow. It is almost midnight now. She has had to wait and wait until Brian was deeply snoring. She didn't worry for a moment about Donny: she could clump around in hobnailed boots without disturbing him.

The air along the beach is balmy, heavy with the chirruping of nocturnal insects. To her right, a bright quarter-moon hangs out over the sea but Riba barely glances at it because she must be quick. She has to talk to Jay before she leaves tomorrow. After what happened this week, particularly after the fracas in his house, she fears that their relationship will never be the same again, but she has to effect what repairs she can while she still has physical access. She also has to let him know that whether he was conscious of it or not – and although she didn't understand it at the time, even kicked against it – the magic still works.

She'll try the boma first. Her hunch is that he could still be there with some of the staff.

As she hurries along the row of bungalows, she sees that in the grand assembly the torches and barbecue fires have died down but the embers are still smoking. What a party that must have been! She, Brian and Donny had returned to the complex just as the procession of brides and their grooms were setting off for their wedding night in the rondavels. Preceded by Jay – magnificent in a white cloak – and three steel bands, flanked by staff showering them with blossoms and petals, they were all in high good humour, dancing along in clothes ranging from sixties flower power to high-glam *Dynasty*. Two of the brides were even wearing proper meringues, one with a heavily seed-pearled bodice. Although she had been longing to join in, Riba did not dare and had meekly followed Brian down to their own quarters.

Jay is not in the boma. No one is. Its long table is already set for breakfast. Riba realises how much she had been counting on the remains of the party being here.

What now? With the brides and grooms safely nestled in the forest, everyone else has probably moved up to Jay's house.

Riba hesitates. Should she go up there or not? It would probably take the best part of an hour or so, by the time she had walked up, found Jay – assuming she was right and he was still about – talked to him and walked back down again. It is probably foolhardy to be absent from the bungalow for that long.

On the other hand, Brian is a seriously heavy sleeper and he was very tired.

She leaves the stockade and, slowly, still debating, walks back towards the grand assembly. As soon as she comes out into the open, she sees Brian coming towards her. *Oh Christ!*

'What are you doing, Eily?' Brian is more sad than angry. When he had woken up and found that she was not in the room, he had known exactly what she was up to.

'I couldn't sleep. I'm just getting some air.' In the low light from the moon and remains of the torches, her face is pale.

'Don't treat me like an idiot.' Without another word, he turns to walk back to the bungalow.

From behind, he hears her footsteps, uneven because of the ankle injury, swishing through the sand. Her voice is urgent as she calls to him. 'Wait, Brian, wait – please! It's not what you think.'

Brian speeds up a little.

CHAPTER THIRTY-SEVEN

Michael has got away with it.

The job was Oxo. Drive to the house, key in the door, in like Flint, set the alarm clock, kip soundly for six hours, up like a lark, drive back. And now, stroll back into Yvonne's flat as if you own the joint, make no attempt this time to be quiet.

She has just woken. She is up on one elbow, cigarette packet and lighter in her hand. 'Where were you?'

'Out to get a few fags at the garage. I'm going to have a shower. Want a cup of coffee?'

'I wouldn't mind a shag—' She throws the cigarettes and lighter back on to the night table and flops back on the pillow. Then, grinning, she holds up the duvet to show him what's underneath.

Two weeks ago, Michael would not have hesitated for an instant. He must not hesitate now but in any event, he wouldn't actually mind a roll in the hay. The benefits of a good night's sleep are amazing. So is the effect of a splayed, naked young body, especially when Yvonne throws off the duvet completely and cups her breasts in her hands. He groans, dives on top of her, and they go at it, ignoring the outraged knocking on the wall beside the bed-head.

It is over within minutes and, panting, he kisses her ear. 'You're a wicked little bitch, Yvonne Leonard, do you know that? But you needn't think that your talent in the scratcher gives you licence to stay in it. I'm still the boss, you know, and there'll be hell to pay if I find you're late!'

'Feck off!' She pushes him off and whooshes herself a little higher in the bed. 'Mick, we need to talk.' Her tone is abruptly serious and Michael quails.

'Not now, surely? We have a business to run.'

'I just want to talk about the financial arrangements? I've decided that as soon as I get the money, I'm giving up work. It's all right at the moment but a pregnant woman shouldn't have to truck up to that airport every day, especially in the summer when I'm as fat as a pig – ugh!' She shudders, then draws the duvet up around her chin. 'But that money is mine. Understand? I haven't decided what I'm going to do with it yet but it's not for day-to-day expenses. I'll help out with food and stuff, but it's not for rent in the new flat or anything like that. That's your department.' She looks down at him through eyes like blue stones. 'And you'd better make sure you get me the first half quick like she promised. Before it's too late for me to get on that plane, right? I know she's not back until tomorrow, or whatever, but the clock's ticking, Mick. Any messing and the deal's off. You can tell your wife that from me.'

Looking at her determined little face, Michael knows she means every word.

He is thoroughly sorry for himself when, ten minutes later, he is shaving at the black-specked mirror in the communal bathroom. He looks with distaste at the scummy, cracked tiles of the splashback. Never has a man suffered so much for his indiscretions and never again will he take for granted his own pristine, white-tiled enclosure at home with its sliding glass walls. Even if – best case scenario – their flat-hunting produces something decent within their price range, he knows that, however clean it is at the beginning, Yvonne, who is a slattern, won't keep it that way.

All right, Dolan, stop whinging and plan. What does he actually want – say, a year from now? To give himself courage, Michael uncharacteristically tries to indulge in a daydream. He makes it just like one of those TV commercials, picturing himself and Sophie and the baby in the autumn, swishing along through drifts of fallen leaves in a Dublin park. The picture grinds to a halt because he's a practical man; this coming autumn, the baby, who would be still very young, would have to be in a buggy and you can't push buggies through leaves. Anyway, Sophie will need some time to come round to the idea of the three of them together. He will have to be really creative there. Michael buzzes his face with his electric razor. What can he do to get back in with her? She needs him at the moment to keep Yvonne sweet but he's already thought of that and that's what he's doing, plus he's making all those phone calls for her and all the rest of it. What else can he do?

And where is Yvonne in this scenario? It will have to be somewhere nice. Maybe Greece. She loves sunshine. And how many times has she watched the *Shirley Valentine* video?

Yeah. His mood lifts. It's do-able. He and Brian have a huge network of contacts. They should be able to find someone who'll help Yvonne locate somewhere really nice and sunny to live. Michael feels actually quite good now, generous. He'll even pay her air fare when the time comes so she won't have to touch her nest egg.

Yvonne's voice sounds outside the closed door, calling on him to hurry up.

He pretends he hasn't heard her and shaves near his right ear, trimming carefully. All he has to do is stay on top of the situation. He's not stupid. He will be able to manage this.

'Mick!' Yvonne's voice has risen dangerously. 'Are you going to take all day?'

'Keep your hair on,' he yells back good-humouredly. 'I'm coming. I'm coming!'

He switches off his razor and unplugs it, then smiles at his reflection while reaching into his toilet bag for his bottle of *paco rabanne pour homme*.

Unlike check-in procedures with scheduled airlines, the formalities before boarding an air ambulance are speedy, too speedy for Riba, as it happens, because she finds herself on the apron of Palm Tree Island International Airport with the misunderstanding between herself and Brian still unresolved. She is standing with him beside the open door of the ground ambulance, waiting while the crew of both ground and air ambulances confer and consult their paperwork, prior to the handover.

Although he had remained polite, he had refused to engage with her in the bungalow last night. And since early morning, whether deliberately or otherwise, he had seemed to manoeuvre it so that others were always with them: Donny, Sophie, the staffs of the complex and the clinic, taxi-drivers.

He wasn't aggressive or sulky, just remote. And busy, organising, making telephone calls, filling in forms.

Sophie was in a funny mood too and Riba is even beginning to wonder if their rapprochement the previous day had been for real. Finding herself alone with her friend at one point, she had attempted to confide in her about what had gone on between herself and Brian but Sophie had suddenly remembered she might have left something in the wardrobe of her bungalow and had rushed off. By the time she came back, Donny was on the scene.

At least one good thing has come from Brian's preoccupation: one of the travel trade buddies has come up with an Irish family who live within commuting distance of the clinic in Butte, which turns out, to Riba's surprise, to have a large population of Irish extraction. The wife, a radiologist, actually works for the hospital. It's perfect. The couple, who have three children, even have a boy who is only two years younger than Donny. (On the latter, of course, from the heights of fourteen, Donny hadn't been impressed. '*Twelve!*' But one look from his father was enough to quell any further moaning. He is excited by the novelty of travelling in a small plane in any case and went aboard the instant he was cleared to do so.)

The handover has concluded and Zelda is helped out on to the Tarmac. Thank God she doesn't have to suffer the indignity of being carried and is able to go on to the plane under her own steam. Riba follows her and the travelling medics, with Brian bringing up the rear. At one point during the discussions yesterday, just so Brian could hear it with his own ears and wouldn't accuse her of further endangering Zelda's health by 'dragging' her on to another plane, she had pointedly asked Dr Ocwieja and the clinic's director if they were sure that to travel again would be OK.

'This isn't really travelling in the sense you're familiar with, Mrs McMullan,' the clinic's director had said. 'We're talking here about a hospital plane, with specialised equipment and specialist medical staff who are highly qualified. To put your mind at ease, think of it as being considerably less traumatic for Zelda than a land ambulance, for instance.' Riba had curbed her instinctive impulse to search Brian's face for his response. Instead, she had simply nodded gravely.

'Good morning, folks!' The pilot, wearing headphones and with a clip-board in his hand, turns around briefly to greet them. The officer beside him is talking into a little microphone and acknowledges them with just a quick glance.

'Not long now, darling.' Riba smiles encouragingly as, with practised efficiency, the medics strap Zelda into her specialised stretcher-seat.

Without warning, the pilot does something to the controls and the engine starts to whine, sounding loud through the open doorway. Quickly, Riba takes her own seat, behind Donny, who, to judge by the expression on his face, thinks all his birthdays have come at once.

'I'd best be off.' Quickly, Brian stoops to talk to Zelda. 'Good luck, sunbeam. I'll be ringing every day – and I'll see you in a couple of weeks. You do understand why I have to go? I have to fix things up at home?'

'Of course, Daddy.' Zelda raises her face for a kiss.

'Be good now!'

As Brian straightens, as far as he can under the low ceiling, Riba sees that there are tears in his eyes. But she feels helpless, at sea. 'Brian—' She reaches out to catch his arm. He pats it, then kisses her firmly on the cheek and, by moving away immediately, kills any attempt she might make to hug him.

''Bye, Eily. We'll talk soon. I'll ring just as soon as we touch down in Dublin, all right?' Now he is bending to hug Donny. 'You look after your mother and sister, now. Do you hear?'

The second engine whines into life and quickly he turns to wave again at his daughter. ''Bye, darling. Good luck.'

Riba watches him stride across the Tarmac and, right up to the time he disappears through the door of the terminal, continues to hope that he will turn and wave. He does not.

She must not read too much into this. He'll calm down and get over it. He always does. He's just in a snit, that's all. Things will get back to normal.

She twists in her seat to look back at Zelda. 'How are you doing, sweetheart?'

Zelda smiles back. 'I'm fine, Mother. Don't fuss. Please!' She closes her eyes.

Startled, Riba remembers the phrase, or something similar and, *déjà vu*, is brought back to the beginning of this whole adventure when the two of them were preparing to take off from Dublin airport on that black Monday.

For goodness' sake! She chides herself as the engine note rises to a scream outside while one of the crew closes the door and locks it with a heavy lever. *Don't even think about that day*!

The aircraft begins to move, quickly gathering speed and while the medics belt themselves into their own seats, Riba looks through the window. What's Jay doing right this minute? He certainly won't hold a grudge.

She leans forward, tapping Donny on the shoulder to offer him a piece of chewing gum. 'Isn't this really exciting, honey?'

Sophie is sitting on her suitcase – and minding Brian's – inside a breeze block fence, part of the airport's boundary, overlooking the Tarmac. She chose to go outside, where there was at least the possibility of some movement of air, rather than suffer in the stifling Departures area; their flight is due to leave for New York in just over an hour and a half and the queue at the single check-in desk is already long and complaining.

Yet, although it is definitely more comfortable out here, it is still hot and her cotton T-shirt is clinging to the skin between her shoulder-blades.

She said her goodbyes to Zelda, Donny and Eily earlier but from her present, discreet vantage point has watched the transactions around the air ambulance on the apron. Zelda, thank God, had seemed to need only minimal assistance.

Although she was pretty sure he could not see her, she has watched Brian's every step as he walked back across the Tarmac towards the terminal and, despite the sunglasses he was wearing, when he came close, read his loneliness. But what help could she offer?

Swiftly, Sophie made a decision. None. She could offer him no help.

This was his private family matter and it was best left that way for all of their sakes.

Having fought it, thought she had won, then discovered she had actually lost the battle against this topsy-turvy sensation in her stomach every time she saw him, or even thought about him, Sophie had decided during the short time span of Brian's walk back to the terminal that she could no longer allow herself to be even his friend. After this journey home, she would have to organise her life so he would not be part of it. Brian and Eily, yes. Brian alone, no. No cups of coffee or casual lunches, no phone calls, nothing until this internal bonfire dies down, as it inevitably will, given time and a sensible attitude.

He reaches her just as the air ambulance makes a U-turn at the end of the runway to line up for take-off, and she stands up. 'She'll be OK,' she says quietly as he stoops a little to watch through one of the openings in the blocks.

'We'll see.' His voice is unsteady and Sophie feels she has to keep talking.

'I know it's not my place to say anything,' she says quickly. 'It's probably even heresy, but you never know what good might come out of this. This adventure might prove to have been worth it in the long run.'

He continues to stare through the aperture in the concrete so she does not persist with the reassurances. Instead, she too gazes out at the revving air ambulance.

'This is where we came in you know,' he says.

'What do you mean?' She is puzzled.

'Watching a take-off at an airport.'

The only way Brian has been able to deal with the tumble of events – *all* of the events – of the past fortnight has been to keep his emotions buried as deeply as he could manage. There have been breakthroughs, but never for long. He had seen to that.

But he is in serious difficulties now as, beside Sophie, he watches the air ambulance tremble on its little wheels, then catapult down the runway. It takes off when less than half-way along, climbs very steeply, then banks to take a course around the side of the terminal building and out of their sight. Its absence in the sky is shocking.

He has to curb the impulse to run back out into the car park at the front of the building to see it again for one last time. It had been too quick. He hadn't been ready.

He had not been ready either for the surge of renewed desire and love he had felt on coming upon Sophie sitting on her suitcases and he needs to put physical distance between them. Without asking her if she wants one, he tells her he will fetch two coffees and hurries inside, fighting his way to the tiny bar. By the time he gets back, he is again in control. He hands her the coffee. She smiles as she thanks him, although he has the distinct impression she is avoiding looking at him directly.

Both turn again to look through their individual viewing boxes at the airfield, bare now of all activity, as though it will yield some amazing secret if they will only watch long and hard enough.

The silence between them is getting to Sophie. 'Should we check in, do you think?'

He doesn't turn to her. 'Plenty of time,' he says, sipping at his cup.

His physical presence is threatening her resolve. She has to put physical distance between them, or at least be in a crowd. 'I think we should join the queue, I really do.'

'All right. Just wait until I've finished this.' Still he doesn't turn towards her and short of actually running away from him, Sophie doesn't know what to do next.

Perhaps she should simply tell him the truth?

Definitely not! She sips at the bitter coffee. 'Five minutes, and then we'll go in, OK?'

'OK.' He sips at his too.

Then, almost unbelievably, all in a rush, Sophie hears herself telling him all about the meeting with Yvonne at her house, the baby, her desperation in case anything goes wrong, the money, everything.

Throughout this sorry narrative, he watches her intently, his sunglasses glinting. He hasn't moved a muscle since she started and she is becoming very upset at his lack of reaction. The least he might do is say something. 'All right,' she says flatly in the end, 'I can see you disapprove. I know that in some people's eyes it could be seen as immoral. But—'

'Who says I disapprove?'

'Well, don't you?'

Instead of answering, he picks up his suitcase. 'We'll talk about it on the plane. Come on, we said five minutes.' His voice sounds strangled but now he is disappearing from her view through the door into the building. Sophie, feeling stupid – and the same time a sense of letdown – slowly picks up her own case and follows.

She gets inside just as a huge crowd of people surge through the entrance doors and begin, it seems, to have a party. They have even brought a steel band with them. It bangs away, cacophonous in the close confines of the tin-roofed hall, and people are clapping their hands, even dancing. 'What's going on?' Sophie, who has temporarily lost sight of Brian, asks one of the people queuing for the New York flight.

'We come here, they go there,' the man shrugs. 'I sure hope they're all not getting on our aircraft!' A uniformed official then explains that a local couple is going on honeymoon to Paris.

'Oh, I see.' Sophie retreats, abandoning, for the moment, the plan to join the queue. It appears that the newly married pair had brought to the airport, not only their joint extended families, but possibly half the population of the island, and although in normal times she would have been enchanted, she is not at present receptive to the uninhibited party mood. She is heading back out to her breeze block retreat when her arm is caught.

'Where are you going?' It is Brian.

'It's too noisy in here, I'm going to wait outside again for a while.'

'I will too.'

Brian leans against the wall, back at their station where it is considerably quieter, although they can still hear the jolly clamour from within, now augmented by incomprehensible announcements through a crackly loud-speaker.

For something to say, Sophie remarks that the bridal couple are lucky to be starting out so happily.

'Are they?'

She is brought up short by his tone. 'Do you not think so?'

'I don't know what to think any more. Look, Sophie – ' he takes off his sunglasses. 'I don't know what to think about anything. You, Mick, the baby, marriage, my family. Just tell me one thing. Are you and Mick likely to get back together?'

'No!' She is shocked at the turn this is taking.

'Are you sure? Because I know that shagger. He'll want to. It all happened very quickly, are you sure you don't want to give him another chance?'

They both turn as they hear, simultaneously, the roar of a plane. It is theirs, unheralded and unheard up to now because of the party inside. As they turned, their arms touched and neither moves to break away. Their ignoring of the connection serves to heighten it.

As they watch the jet's flawless touchdown, Sophie, whose blood is pounding, feels that, beside her, his skin is as taut as a drum. Unable to stand it, she breaks away and backs off a little. Then, just as the jet's engines slam into reverse thrust: 'Why did you ask me that, Brian?'

'What?' He bends his ear to her lips. 'I can't hear you—'

'Why. Did. You. Ask?' She raises her voice a few further decibels. Right into his ear. The jet's engines quieten.

'No need to shout—'

They look at one another. Then both of Brian's hands go around the back of Sophie's head to cradle it. He kisses her, gently, although she can feel the thumping of his heart as he fights for control. She accepts the kiss but, because she too is still battling hard, doesn't kiss him back.

He holds her away from him a little. 'We're middle-aged friends, Sophie. This kind of thing is not supposed to happen to middle-aged friends. I've fought it, God knows.'

'Me too.'

He releases her. 'Look, I'll have to stay with them at least until—'

'Of course you will.' She reaches up to touch his mouth. 'Don't even think about it, Brian.'

'And it would be on the rebound. For both of us. That's bad news, Sophie.'

'It certainly is, but rebound? Not for you, surely.'

'Eily and I may have to—' he hesitates, then, 'reconsider our position, shall we say. I'll tell you about that some day, but not now.'

'I wouldn't want to know about it. Anyway,' she adds quickly when it looks as if he might be about to pull her towards him again, 'I'm going to have enough to do, with the baby, you understand—'

'Yes, you will. And I do understand. And I will have a lot to do too.' He does kiss her again, harder this time and this time she kisses him back.

'There's something else, very important.' His breath catches in his throat as he eyeballs the tiles at his feet. 'At the moment, this clinic thing sounds as though it's at the very least going to give us a bit longer, but however long or short all this is going to go on, Donny is going to need both his parents, Sophie.'

'Of course he will.'

'Afterwards too. For quite a while.'

'Of course!'

He looks frankly at her. 'And she'll need me too, for a while. In her own daft way.'

'Yes she will.' Although Sophie wants desperately to kiss him again, she hangs back. Instead she reaches out and takes his big warm hand in her own. He squeezes tightly and she can feel his blood pumping strongly through his fingers against her own. They turn to look through the apertures cut into the breeze blocks.

The jet has completed its landing run. Now it swings around, glides on to the taxiway and, nose towards them, comes in slowly to collect them and take them home.